REINING IN TROUBLE

TYLER ANNE SNELL

COLTON'S COVERT BABY

LARA LACOMBE

MILLS & BOON

First Published in Great Britain 2019
by Mills & Boon, an imprint of HarperCollins*Publishers*
1 London Bridge Street, London, SE1 9GF

Reining in Trouble © 2019 Tyler Anne Snell
Colton's Covert Baby © 2019 Harlequin Books S.A.

Special thanks and acknowledgement are given to Lara Lacombe for her contribution to *The Coltons of Roaring Springs* series.

ISBN: 978-0-263-27422-6

0619

MIX
Paper from
responsible sources
FSC™ C007454

This book is produced from independently certified FSC™ paper to ensure responsible forest management.

For more information visit: www.harpercollins.co.uk/green

Printed and bound in Spain
by CPI, Barcelona

REINING IN TROUBLE

TYLER ANNE SNELL

This book is for Girl Group. Virginia, you continue to be fierce. Faith, you continue to be crafty. Jasmine, you continue to be true. Thanks for always being ready to lift others up when life tries to push them down. You're all absolute queens!

Chapter One

Detective Caleb Nash switched his jeans for jogging shorts and hoped to high heaven no one he knew saw him. It was a particularly pleasant day in Overlook. The humidity was down and the heat wasn't too bad. He'd have to clean the pollen off of his truck before he went to the department unless he wanted his partner, Jazz, to give him grief again. She always reminded him that they represented the sheriff's department, vehicles included. It was easy for her to say. She drove an obnoxious gray four-door that barely showed any pollen. Not to mention her husband detailed cars for a living.

Caleb drove an old dark blue pickup that showed every speck of yellow, and as for a spouse with a helpful job? His last girlfriend had split because the only real marriage he was interested in was to his job. Her words, not his. Though he couldn't deny they held some truth. She'd also never been a fan of small-town Tennessee. The last thing she'd be worried about was him driving around town with a pollen-coated junker.

Though that insignificant mark of shame would be nothing compared to what would be said if any of Overlook's residents saw one of the Nash triplets jogging in the *short* shorts he was currently sporting. Good, bad, or embarrassing, the town already had enough to talk about when

it came to the family. Adding his bare legs to the mix was something he wanted to avoid. Never mind keeping the sheriff away from the image. *That* grief would last for months longer.

But what was a man supposed to do?

The reappearance of his short shorts from track in school had been his mama's fault. Her latest drop-in had resulted in a surge of spring cleaning he hadn't asked for but couldn't stop. The casualty in the latest cleaning war had been the accidental destruction of his normal workout wear. Now he was popping in his earbuds at the mouth of Connor's Trail with more skin than he was comfortable showing, hoping that none of the people living or working on the Nash Family Ranch would find themselves up that way.

On a scale of one to five, one being a kid-friendly walk meant to enjoy the scenery and five being a laborious attempt at training for trails that went up the Rockies, Connor's Trail was a three. It began where the woods that were scattered across the back half of the hundred acres of ranchland curved, forming a crescent-moon shape that rose and dipped the farther you went inside the tree line. The uneven terrain warranted several new signs warning guests from the Wild Iris Retreat to be careful. Caleb knew for a fact that there were three in total surrounding the trail because he'd been the one to stake them in the ground. It was supposed to have been his brother, Declan, who did the deed, but work had pulled him away. There wasn't much Caleb could do about that. He could argue until he was blue in the face with his eldest brother, but he didn't dare try the same tactic with the sheriff. Even if they were one and the same.

Caleb leaned into the beat of his music as thoughts of his brother led to thoughts about work. Caleb had been a

detective with the Wildman County Sheriff's Department for five years. In that time he'd learned the importance of routine, especially when it came to exercising.

"There's never enough time to do every *single* thing you want to," his father, Michael, used to say. "But there's always time to do at least one thing. You just have to make that one thing count."

While his siblings, Madeline and Desmond, thought that was a bunch of bologna, Caleb had taken his late father's words to heart. That mantra had served the patriarch well throughout his life.

Until it hadn't.

But that hadn't been his fault.

Caleb's thoughts started to darken. The upbeat music did little to stave off that darkness. No matter how many years passed, Caleb knew there would always be moments where what had happened clawed its way to the forefront of his mind. Where it would sit. And wait.

A horrifying collection of memories from what felt like a different lifetime. The Nash triplets stuck in a loop of helplessness, fear, and pain.

His feet dug into the dirt as he made physical distance from the home behind him. It had taken years for him, Madi, or Desmond to go back into the woods. To move between the trees without fear. Without worry.

Yet, sometimes, when Caleb thought about his father he couldn't help but think about the man with the scar along his hand. Then, suddenly, Caleb was a child again. He'd hear Madi scream. Hear Desmond cry out in pain. He'd hear his own voice quaver in anger and fear.

Then Caleb would remember that, even though the memories felt so real sometimes, that's all they were. Memories. Ones that had no place on the ranch at the end of Winding Road.

"But, how can it be over if the man with the scar is still out there?" asked Caleb's inner voice. It was a question that always followed the memories, darkening them even further.

Today, though, Caleb refused to entertain them for long. He leaned into the beat of his music and focused on the comfort of routine.

The burn of exertion didn't kick in until Caleb was passing the third mile marker. Scots pines lined either side of the dirty trail, their roots gnarled and reaching every few yards. Caleb had run the trail since he was fifteen and knew when to jump over or step around the ones that threatened to take a jogger by surprise. Just as he knew the exact spot to veer off the beaten path and forge over a less-known one to his favorite place across all of the ranch. The trees clustered closer but Caleb wove around them and kept going.

He heard the stream before he saw the water.

The trees thinned out and the ground dipped. Caleb jumped off a dirt ledge and slapped the trunk of a tree that had his initials carved into it. Rocks worn by erosion lined flowing water that was clear enough to see more rocks making up the bottom in the distance. It wasn't a particularly wide waterway, neither was it that deep, but it was always cold.

Caleb was already thinking about stripping down, wading to the deepest point and dunking under for a quick refresher before he rounded the last line of trees. He stopped in his tracks. He wasn't the only one who had been thinking the same thing.

A woman was already standing in the middle of the stream. Her back was turned to him but there was no denying the top layer of her clothes was somewhere else. Her raven-black hair was twisted up and showed smooth tanned

skin, bare and reflected in the water just over her waist. Caleb couldn't tell if she had any bottoms on but thought it ungentlemanly to find out. Though he wasn't above admitting that, even from his limited view, there was an attractive curve to the woman. It brought out a feeling of curiosity that mingled with a more intimate excitement, but he wasn't about to search out that feeling. Not when the woman had no idea she was being watched.

Caleb started to backtrack but whatever cool he'd had on the trail had been lost due to the new scenery. He missed his step and grunted as he tried to catch himself from falling. A splash of water was followed quickly by a gasp. Caleb's palm bit into the smaller rocks on the shore. He managed to get his balance from them and went back to standing tall.

Now *he* was the one with an audience.

The woman had sunk down so far that the water was only an inch below her face. If that very same face hadn't been scowling at him, as red as a cherry, Caleb might have taken an extra beat to appreciate the beauty of her sharp features, dimpled cheeks and dark brown eyes. As it was, he barely had the time to defend himself.

And even that he did poorly.

"Before you get any ideas," he called, raising his hands in surrender. "I was on a run. I didn't know anyone would be here."

The woman, who he placed around late twenties, stayed red hot. Even her words had heat to them.

"Heck of a place for a run," she yelled, motioning with one hand around them. The other he assumed was fastened across her chest.

Her implication that he was lying transferred some of that heat to Caleb. He crossed his own arms over his chest.

"I was running on the trail but decided to come and

cool off," he defended himself. "This is the deepest part of the stream."

"How *convenient*," she replied with bite. Her eyes skirted to a log that had been on its side for the better part of two years a few feet away from him. Caleb saw a pile of clothes and a pair of tennis shoes on top of it. "Could you please look away now? Or does that take away part of your fun?"

Caleb rolled his eyes, once again not liking the insinuation that he had been lying about his intentions, and made a show of turning all the way around.

"Just so you know, I've been coming to this stream for almost two decades. In all of that time I've never run into another soul."

The woman's feet slapped against the rocks behind him as she ran for her clothes. When she spoke he could tell she was struggling into them as fast as she could go.

"I was out checking the trail, if you must know. I was also specifically told that no one is supposed to be out here for another week," she tried. "Especially not walking the woods."

That got the detective side of Caleb prickling. The only people who'd been given rules on the ranch were employees and he sure didn't remember meeting her. And, he was fairly certain he would have remembered.

"And who told you that?"

"The owners. I work here," she said with pride. "So I suggest you get on your way before I report you to them."

Caleb snorted.

"I wouldn't be so smug about it," she added. "One of them happens to be the sheriff. I don't think he'd look too kindly on Peeping Toms and liars."

"You're right, Declan doesn't like liars," he said, feeling that heat again. He'd never been accused of such a

crude thing. The only women he'd been interested in seeing naked he'd let them know, not stalked them off to the side. "He doesn't care for trespassers, either. The ranch might be open but it's private property."

He chanced turning around. The woman was fully dressed in an outfit that gave credence to her claim of exercising. Her eyes drifted down to his shorts before they were back staring defiantly at him.

The resolve she'd been swinging cracked with uncertainty. Still, she held her shoulders back and her chin high. She actually huffed.

"*I'm* not trespassing. I'm coordinator for the Wild Iris Retreat. I just started last week."

A snatch of conversation flitted through Caleb's memory. His mom had been asking Madeline if she would be willing to show the new girl around town a few weeks back. That had been at the height of the Keaton case. He'd barely been around the Retreat since he'd finished the job. While they all had a stake in the Retreat, his mother was the one who ran the technical details, including the hiring. Though he still was hard-pressed to believe the woman scowling at him. All of the Nash family had agreed they wanted to hire locally. It was hard to pass on a genuine experience if the Retreat was being run by an outsider.

He ran a hand across the back of his neck. It was covered in sweat. The water sure would have felt good but he doubted the woman would stand for him stripping, too, and walking into it. He settled for leveling with her.

"I don't remember the job being open for anyone who wasn't local," he said honestly.

A flicker of emotion he couldn't decipher crossed her expression. Her scowl deepened.

"Dorothy said I gave one hell of an interview," she shot back.

For a moment they just looked at each other. This time it was Caleb's certainty that wavered. He believed the woman was telling the truth.

"Well I never like to doubt my mother's decisions."

The woman's face pinballed between surprise, disbelief, embarrassment and stubbornness. Somehow she fell between all of them when she spoke.

"You're one of the triplets."

"In the flesh."

NINA DRAKE FELT like a damned idiot.

She'd spent the last two weeks practicing what she'd say when she met the family whose ranch she was now employed by, desperate to make a great first impression. Not that she thought she'd make a bad one without the practice but because she desperately wanted the job. She *needed* it. So she'd gone over enough scenarios in her head about how she'd meet Dorothy Nash and her four children that by the time Nina had met the mother she'd been cool and confident.

Dorothy had smiled with her, laughed at Nina's attempt at humor and even praised her work ethic.

Preparation had been *key*.

Meeting one of her sons while taking a topless dip and then immediately accusing him of being a creep?

That certainly wasn't the key to anything other than a world of embarrassment.

"I'm Caleb Nash," he continued while she continued to scramble for the right thing to say to make the last five minutes disappear. He was still grinning, which only made everything worse. "I'd prefer Caleb and not Tom, if you please."

The burn of embarrassment that had crawled up her neck was now a steady flame across her cheeks. Still,

Nina couldn't just stand there any longer without saying a word. On reflex she cleared her throat and pasted on a smile that felt tight.

"I'm sorry," she said, hoping she sounded at least marginally regretful. She still wasn't convinced the man hadn't been trying to enjoy the free view. Nina might have liked Dorothy but she had yet to meet her sons. One, she knew, was the sheriff. The other two were a part of the triplets. Past that she hadn't heard anything about their jobs or personal lives. Dorothy had kept close to the topic of work. "I guess it wasn't the best idea to go exploring. I thought for sure I would be alone." She strode forward and stretched out her hand. "I'm Nina. Nina Drake."

Caleb's grip was strong and warm. Not that she expected the man in front of her to offer anything less. His arms and legs were toned and muscled, both threatening to break out of the tight shirt he wore and the shorts he barely had on. Even without the show of muscles he just seemed like a man who was sturdy. Well over six feet and broad shouldered, he made Nina feel more than petite next to him.

It didn't help that she was already feeling small because of embarrassment. It *also* didn't help that Caleb had a good-looking grin that matched an extremely handsome face. When Nina had applied for a job on the ranch she'd pictured rugged men in cowboy hats roaming around the property on horses. Not the clean-shaven, dark-haired man wearing short shorts in the middle of the woods in front of her.

Not those baby blues focused solely on her.

Half of the reason she'd taken the job was to curb excitement like this.

Not that *this* was anything more than an awkward situation.

Still, she couldn't imagine being in the presence of the

triplets if they had been identical. It would, she suspected, be intimidating to say the least.

"Well, nice to meet you, Nina," he said after their hands had fallen. "I'm sorry I interrupted. I usually stop here to cool off."

Nina was already backing away in the direction she'd originally come. She shook her head and waved off the concern.

"It was my fault," she tried. "I was just trying to familiarize myself with the trails before guests started arriving. I should have stayed on the path." Caleb looked like he was going to say something but she was already retreating into the tree line. "Enjoy your dip," she called. Then she turned on her heel and hurried back to the dirt trail.

It wasn't until she had passed the one-mile marker that she slowed enough to catch her breath. Instead of seeing the humor in the situation, Nina couldn't shake the feeling that she'd almost cost herself a chance at a fresh start.

She balled her hands into fists, resolve to be the perfect employee flooding through her. Not only would she stick strictly to the rules, she decided, but she would also avoid the man who had caught her breaking them.

A branch snapped somewhere off to her side. Nina's blush surged back up her neck, heating her skin, at the thought of Caleb following her. However, as she paused to look between the trees, she saw no one.

Nina finished the trail with a little more urgency in her step, all the while reasoning that the outline of the man she thought she'd seen was just her imagination.

Simply a ghost from her former life.

Chapter Two

The Wild Iris Retreat was a new build on the Nash Family Ranch but it by no means looked out of place. Four cabins were spaced out for privacy and were placed near a network of trails that led to the best fishing on the land, the horse barn for riding lessons or trail riding and a field where, according to Dorothy, one had the best views of the stars.

The main building that housed the Retreat's operations, as well as Nina's office and apartment, was the only part of Wild Iris that had been original to the earlier generation of Nashes. After a flood had forced Dorothy's grandparents to build a new house a good five-minute drive up the road, the old family home had sat in ruins until the idea of the Retreat had been born. It was now standing tall, repurposed and very much alive. While it wasn't as cozy as the cabins near it, Nina couldn't help but favor it above the others.

It reminded her of her mother, if she was being honest. Warm, worn and beautiful.

Nina jogged around to the back door and pulled the key from the waist of her athletic shorts. She slipped her shoes off and carried them through the back hallway to the stairs that branched off what used to be the old living room. The second floor was modest, converted into a studio apart-

ment. It had been created for the manager of the Retreat. Dorothy had wanted the guests to have full access to them without the need to trek up the road to the main house or even farther to two of the Nash sons' houses.

The Nash sons…

Caleb.

Nina stepped into the shower, trying to physically move away from the embarrassment that had overtaken her again. She remembered a time when she had been great at first impressions. *Charming*, according to her father, *intriguing* as a compliment from her mother. At a young age Nina had decided she wanted to use those traits to follow in her mother's footsteps. Maybe become an inspirational speaker for nonprofits too, traveling the state to talk at schools and other organizations.

But then everything had changed.

Nina's mood darkened until nothing but the echo of sadness pinged in her heart. She finished her shower, dressed in a pair of jeans and a button-up, and walked downstairs to the front of the house. Another key unlocked the two spaces of her living quarters and the business side of the retreat and soon she was trying her best not to stew on how cruel life could be sometimes while settling in behind her desk.

The Wild Iris Retreat could be one of many things for guests. If they wanted to relax while feeling like they were in the wilderness, the retreat had beautiful scenery and peace and quiet for them to enjoy. If guests wanted to feel like they were a part of the authentic ranch life, there were horses to ride, trails to adventure on, and a small town where everyone knew everyone else to visit. It could be anything and Nina was there to create more options for it and future guests.

The retreat would be opening in two weeks. Nina

had already been there for seven days. In that time she'd worked alongside the manager of daily operations, Molly, and the cook, Roberto. Molly was married to the horse trainer and both lived just outside of the ranch. Nina only got the option to live in the old house because Molly and her husband had had no interest in the space upstairs when they had their own home already. Roberto lived in Overlook but because of the set meal schedule didn't need to be around 24/7 either. So it had been Nina's perk alone to savor. Not only did she not have to deal with the hassle of finding a place to live, her commute had been reduced to nothing.

She brought up her email and read through a few informational ones from Molly and then reached out to local stores asking about any events they might have coming up. It was her job to stay up-to-date with the small town's entertainment so she could always have options for guests who wanted to explore locally. She'd already spoken to a few business owners but at least half of the town's shops didn't have email addresses listed. Or websites, for that matter. If she was going to talk to them, she'd have to do it in person. By the time her email refreshed and a new message popped up in her inbox, Nina was still thinking about going into town and making small talk. She clicked on it, wondering how to be polite but keep her distance as she met the locals, as an image loaded on the screen.

Nina's breath caught.

It was a picture of her. And not just any picture.

She was standing in a stream, back to the camera, but obviously not wearing a top. It was from that morning. No less than a few hours ago.

Her blood went cold at the text in the body of the email.

And everyone thought you were a nice girl.

CALEB STOOD BACK and looked at his handiwork. His truck was gleaming. The pollen was seeping into the mud. He'd thought about going into town and running through the automated car wash at the gas station but had needed the water hose to cool off. He'd decided against using the stream and instead had run the rest of the trail hot. By the time he'd driven home, on the exact opposite side of the ranch, Caleb had been desperate for quick relief. He'd stripped down to nothing but his short shorts and rinsed himself off before working on the truck.

By the time he was done his skin was already dry.

The pleasant day had turned angry. If he hadn't already been tan from living his free time outside, Caleb might have burned beneath the constant shine and heat. He doused himself once more before cutting the water off. He'd use the time between now and when he was dry to finally fix the porch swing he'd been meaning to repair for the last year or so. He'd never used it much but his mother had insisted. If there was ever any one thing true about Dorothy Nash it was her love for porch swings.

Caleb went around back to the shed and grabbed his tools. He was walking across the side yard when an unfamiliar car came barreling up the road. He cursed beneath his breath at not having changed out of his obnoxious shorts as soon as he'd gotten home and hoped once again it wasn't anyone from the department.

No such luck. It was the only person he would have liked to avoid more than his brothers. Caleb dropped his tools on the wraparound porch and groaned.

"Well, howdy-do there, Mr. Nash!"

Jasmine "Jazz" Santiago came out of the car smiling for all she was worth. As a transplant from Portland, she had done a fine job of fitting into Overlook, the department and even the ranch on the occasions she'd stopped

by over the last five years. Tall, thin and with a complexion she once had called *smooth mocha*, she was one half of their mismatched detective pair. While Caleb erred on the side of contemplation and quiet, Jazz was blunt and always ready to be heard. Even now she cut the engine and bounded toward him, laughing.

"I'd always wondered what you *really* did on your off days," she continued, motioning to his bare chest and shorts, and then pointing toward the tool box. "I never would have guessed you were working on an audition for one of the Village People."

Caleb groaned again.

"First of all, that's a throwback," he said, leaning into the teasing. "If I was auditioning for anything it'd clearly be something *Magic Mike*-related." Jazz laughed as Caleb searched out his shirt. He tugged it over his head while Jazz inspected his freshly washed truck. She seemed to approve. "Now, other than coming out here to roast me, what's up?"

Jazz switched moods in a flash. Work mode crinkled her brow together. She met his stare with severity.

"I tried calling but the sheriff told me just to go ahead and come out here. I was already out test-driving Brando's new car so it worked out easier." Brando was Jazz's husband and the fact that she hadn't brought him along felt even more foreboding. Caleb felt himself go on alert. Not only that but Declan was a stickler about privacy. Even more so about privacy when his staff was off the clock. That he'd sent Jazz out wasn't a good sign. She pulled her phone out and swiped until she got to the picture she wanted. "When's the last time you went out to the Overlook Pass behind Nancy Calder's house?"

Nancy Calder had been a staple in the community for longer than Caleb had been alive. Her father opened the

local grocery store thirty years ago. Now, her son ran it. She had a farm with some acreage out near the Overlook town limits, but after turning ninety she'd moved out of state to be with her daughter. Part of her land was rented out to cattle farmers but no one lived in the house. Overlook Pass was a bridge just outside of her property line that had been given historic status. No one used it for transportation but tourists liked taking pictures of it and fishing the water beneath it. The last time Caleb had visited either place had been with his ex, well over a year ago. He said as much to Jazz.

She handed her phone over.

"Apparently no one has been out there for a while."

The picture was all wrong. Where there should have been an aged but beautiful bridge there was now bits of charred wood and nothing else.

"What the—" he started, anger threatening to become hotter than the weather. "Did…did someone *burn* it?"

Jazz nodded.

"The fire chief is heading that way now to investigate but, so far, there's no way to know if this happened recently or a while back. Which may or may not be related to this." She took back her phone and swiped to another picture. "Last night there was a house fire out on Brookewood Drive. They're still investigating if it was arson or not. It might not be connected but Declan's telling everyone in the department to keep their eyes open, just in case."

Caleb didn't blame his brother for the department-wide warning. Or the urgency with which he'd deployed the caution. Overlook had a fair amount of forest stretching around it. Arson was always a threat everyone took seriously. One match could make a devastating difference. Plus, Brookewood Drive was a five or so minute drive

from the burned bridge. He would have done the same thing in Declan's place.

Once Jazz had said her piece she hopped back into her car and raised a cloud of dust as she left on the dirt road. Caleb returned to his toolbox but he didn't feel the same ambition to attend to the broken swing as he had before.

The burning of an unused bridge was something he'd take over a home or business burning down any day. Yet he couldn't stop the stab of loss in his chest. His father had loved that bridge. He'd taken Caleb and his siblings there at least once a month to fish when it was the season. It had become a routine that Caleb had hoped at a young age they'd keep as he got older. Although that plan had changed due to circumstances no one had seen coming, Caleb still thought fondly about their time there.

Now it was just another part of his father that had been chipped away by a senseless act.

Caleb abandoned the toolbox and showered off. He returned his missed calls—Declan and his mother, the only people who ever seemed to call him nowadays—and decided to live dangerously and crack open a beer with his lunch. He was about to go out to the porch to enjoy it when another car crept up and stopped just behind his truck. This time he was ready for possible company. His short shorts had officially been retired. Now he was in his favorite pair of blue jeans and sporting a beige Stetson cowboy hat he'd bought himself for Christmas.

The driver's side door swung open just as he placed his full beer down on the porch railing. For the smallest of moments Caleb didn't recognize the woman barreling toward him. Then, as her petite frame got closer, he fully remembered seeing that very same scowl only hours beforehand.

Nina Drake most certainly looked like she had a bone to pick.

"Well, how do you—" he started, hoping to keep whatever fuse she had unlit by making a better second impression than he had the first. However, Nina wasn't having it. Her cheeks were flushed red and her chest was rising and falling much faster than was normal. She crossed her arms and interrupted him with fire in her eyes.

"And here I thought *you* were a nice *guy*," she said, voice high. "There I was feeling bad for our little misunderstanding earlier, but now? Now I should report you to the authorities!"

Caleb raised his hands in defense, of what he wasn't sure. His eyebrow slid up in question.

"Excuse me?"

Nina was close enough now that he could see the freckles across her cheeks and the bridge of her nose—barely there in the shadows of the trees but undeniable in the full force of the sun. Her nostrils were flared, her fists were balled. Caleb almost took a step back, worried she was readying for an attack.

"Not only were you *watching* me at the water, you took my picture," she said, voice dipping into nothing but ice. "And I came here to make sure you delete that picture or I will go straight to the sheriff *and* your mother."

Caleb lowered his hands. Any amusement he'd felt was long gone.

"I told you, I wasn't spying on you. I've been going to that spot on my runs since I was fifteen. I was just as surprised to see someone there as you were. And I sure as hell didn't take any pictures."

A small look of relief passed across Nina's expression. It was quickly replaced by one he'd seen in the eyes of countless people during his career in law enforcement.

Fear.

"Nina, what happened?" Caleb pressed. "What pictures are you talking about?"

She hesitated for a moment. Then met his eyes with concern crowding every bit of dark brown she had in them.

"Someone took a picture of me at the stream today. And they sent it to the Retreat's email."

Caleb's reaction was immediate. He felt every muscle in him go taut.

"What?" he asked through his teeth.

"I can show you on the computer back at the office if you want. That email isn't attached to my phone and I... I didn't want to forward it. I didn't want to look at it anymore."

Her eyes broke contact. She looked down at her hands. It was such a vulnerable action that Caleb had a hard time not venting his disbelief that someone would do such a thing and anger at the person who had right then and there. But then the lawman side of his brain started to kick in.

"Let me get my keys," he said instead. Nina nodded. She was still standing there when he came back out. This time she was staring off toward the fields behind the house. The very same piece of scenery he had been getting ready to enjoy. Tall grass waved lazily in the breeze as if waving hello. Unaware that something was wrong.

"I'll follow you back to your office," he said, breaking the spell she'd fallen under. Her expression was impassive now, yet her question was nothing but troubling.

"Caleb, if you didn't take that picture, who did?"

Chapter Three

Caleb completely forgot about Overlook Pass burning as soon as he saw the email that had been sent to Nina. Not only did the caption make his blood boil, the location from which the picture had been taken had him itching for answers.

"That was right next to where I was when I first saw you." He pointed to the left corner of the picture. Caleb pictured the woods he had grown up knowing like the back of his hand. "Whoever took this was crouched down."

Nina leaned over the back of the office chair to take another look. A few strands of hair escaped her braid. The unmistakable smell of lavender invaded his senses. It caught him off guard.

"It was obviously taken before you showed up," she said, voice calculating and focused. "And not long after I'd first gone in. I had just wanted to cool down. I probably was only in the water for two to three minutes before I heard you. Are you sure you didn't see or hear anything on your way to the stream?"

"No. Though I wasn't actively trying to catalog my surroundings," he admitted. An idea Caleb didn't like pushed into his thoughts. He had to voice it. "I left the stream the way I came and you went out through there." He pointed toward the tree line closer to the stream that led back out

to the trail's path. "There's a good chance our photographer was still there when we left."

Stress pulsed out from Nina like an electrical surge of energy. Suddenly Caleb was hyperaware of more than just her scent. The warmth of her skin radiated out to him, as if she was the flame of a candle. Licking out and taking the air around it. She tilted her chin down a fraction to run her eyes over the picture again. It brought her cheek even closer to his. In the fluorescent light her freckles took on a harsher contrast with her tanned skin. He suspected then that she had, at least in part, inherited her complexion and dark hair from a Hispanic parent. Her tan was too even, too rich, to be just from living in the sun. It made the shine of her lip gloss even more pronounced in contrast.

Caleb wondered how shiny felt before reality doused out the sudden curiosity.

"Whoever they were, they followed me."

Nina's voice had hollowed. Those shiny lips were downturned, sunken. Caleb returned his focus to the computer monitor.

She was right. Someone had either followed her to the trail or had already been on it before following her to the stream.

"There's also the possibility that they were already at the stream when you showed up and took advantage when you didn't see them," he said without much enthusiasm. "That would be one heck of a coincidence, I'll admit, but ruling out something just because it's unlikely isn't good practice either."

It sounded scripted because it was. Caleb had had the misfortune of being partnered with Neil Stewart before Jazz had moved to Overlook. He was a man who thought so squarely inside the box that, to him, even attempting to think outside of it was criminal. Caleb had told him over

and over again to look from all angles and not just one.
Neil hated the advice. To say the least, he and Caleb hadn't
had the best of partnerships. The several complaints Neil
had had filed against him for "conduct issues" had put a
definite strain on them before Neil had finally transferred
out of Overlook.

"But they sent an email to *me*," Nina said. "If they took
the picture because of opportunity then they sure committed to making it personal really quickly." She pointed
to the timestamp of the email. "I wasn't even back for an
hour when it came in."

"There is that," he conceded. It didn't *feel* like a random,
spur-of-the-moment thing. Still, that didn't mean it wasn't.

"It could have been a prank, too," he had to say. Nina
scowled and he held up his hand to stop her from attack-
ing. "I'm not saying it's a good one or one that should be
taken lightly. But, as pretty as Overlook is, it's dreadfully
boring for the younger demographic. One time Jesse Lang-
ford stole a surveyor's reel and a garden roller from the
local hardware store and made crop circles out near the
county line in Dresser's fields. Because, as he claimed,
there wasn't anything to do in town that got his blood
pumping."

Nina stood tall, leaving only the smell of her shampoo
to linger, and went around to the front of the desk. She
balled her fists on the top of her hips.

"That email reads a lot more sinister than crop circles
made by a bored teenager, don't you think?"

Caleb stood, still trying to show he wasn't trying to of-
fend her or make light of the situation.

"I just meant that we don't know what this is yet." He
grabbed his cowboy hat and held it against his chest. "But
I promise you I'll find out. Okay?" Nina considered him a
moment before nodding. "Now, I'm going to head out to

the trail and see if our photographer isn't still out there. Are you doing anything in town today or hanging out here for a while?"

"I can stay here for now," she decided quickly.

Caleb nodded and put on his hat. He asked for her phone number and immediately called it. Nina saved his number.

"Call if you get another email or anything else happens that seems out of the ordinary. I'll come back by when I'm through."

Nina thanked him but before he could clear the doorway she called his name. Her eyes bore into his with a new intensity. Caleb was caught off guard once again.

"That's my work email for the Retreat. I've only used it for, and given it out to, shop owners and a few people around the ranch. It's not even on the website yet."

She didn't say anything more. Caleb didn't respond. They both already knew what that could mean.

Nina had already met whoever had taken her picture.

THE OFFICE DOOR remained shut and locked. Not that it made much of a difference if it were unlocked or even wide open. From the two large windows that sat behind her desk, she could see if any cars approached. Still, she felt better for throwing the deadbolt as soon as Caleb had left. The mysterious photographer hadn't had a car outside of the trail that she'd seen when she'd first arrived. He hadn't needed it to do what he'd done.

To spy on her, to take advantage of what she would have sworn was a private moment.

The email stayed open on her computer but she didn't want to use it. Not until this person was caught. Instead, she spent the time between Caleb's departure and when she could see his truck kicking up dirt along the road when he returned trying to stay on task. She double-checked events

the town had going on through the next half year as well as notes for suggested events for the Retreat. They were already booked through the first month but she didn't want a slump in reservations soon after.

The need to succeed pulled at the center of her gut.

She wanted to help put the Wild Iris Retreat on the map. Even if she'd rather spend her life beneath that same radar.

Caleb parked out front and took a second to finish up the call he was on. He leaned against his truck, cowboy hat in line with the angle of his head tilt, brow drawn in and a frown darkening his expression.

He was a relative stranger to Nina. She'd caught him at the stream. He'd admitted to knowing the area and the trail by heart. Knowing where she worked and getting access to her email address would have been easy and more than plausible.

And yet…

Nina had believed him.

He wasn't the person who had taken her picture and, what's more, he'd been just as surprised at the email as she had been. Angry, too.

She bit the bottom of her lip in thought, watching his concern through the window. Caleb had certainly been a different kind of surprise, that was for sure.

He was handsome. There was no doubt about that. A cowboy who wore the title of detective well. Imagining him sitting behind a computer or sleuthing through a crime scene with a gun at his hip and a badge at his belt was as easy as picturing him out in the fields with the horses or down at the docks with a fishing pole. It was an interesting dynamic Nina hadn't thought to put together.

Though it certainly fit the attractive, strong-jawed man currently concentrating on a conversation she couldn't hear.

It was almost a pity when he finished it and headed to

the Retreat's front door, ending the small show he'd unwittingly been giving her.

"I didn't find any clues other than some footprints and broken twigs and disturbed ground near the stream." He greeted her as she opened the office door wide. Caleb had already pulled his hat off and had it tucked against the side of his leg. "Whoever they were, once they got back onto the main trail I lost them."

Nina rolled her bottom lip over her teeth. She didn't know which she preferred, no clues at all or inconclusive ones.

"Don't worry," he continued. "I'm not going to just let this go away. Do you mind if I get on your computer to look up the IP address of the email that was sent?"

Nina didn't mind in the least. She waved him toward the desk and stepped aside. Beads of sweat ran along his neck. It seemed like morning had turned into late afternoon in the blink of an eye. A hot one, too, by the looks of it.

"Could you also make a list of everyone you've given your email address to?"

"I'm not the greatest with names yet," she admitted, a bit of heat pooling in her cheeks. "But those I can't remember I'm sure I could point out."

He fell into the office chair, eyes already narrowing in on the email.

"That works out fine. I can just fill in the blanks," he said offhandedly. "Overlook is a small town. Everyone knows everyone."

Nina decided to hold her tongue about the likelihood that someone he knew had no problem spying on women and got to work. It was a tedious task trying to remember the many faces she'd smiled politely at and hands she'd shaken. If only she had been more detail oriented—or, at the very least, invested in creating more than just business

relationships—she wouldn't have had so many question marks in lieu of first names and surnames.

But she did. Something she apologized about when, after he was done with the computer, Caleb finally finished his second call outside the office.

"You do know you're in customer service, right?" he asked, eyebrow raised and a small smirk turning up the corners of his lips. "Usually that means remembering names."

Nina resisted the urge to place her hands on her hips.

"Our introductions were brief," she defended herself. "I just needed to know the basics and say hello. Then, at the grand opening party, I was going to spend more time getting to know everyone. I just didn't have the time to do that yet." It wasn't that much of a lie. Nina knew she'd have to play nice at the grand opening event Dorothy was throwing for the locals and the employees on the ranch.

Caleb snorted but didn't press. He folded the paper and put it in his pocket.

"Well, I'll look into the few names you have here and tomorrow we can try to hit up the rest in person. I have a buddy looking into where the email came from until then. He said he can give me an answer tonight or early tomorrow. Does that work for you?"

Nina nodded.

The sky outside of the window was darkening. A feeling of unease started to clench at her chest. Caleb's expression softened.

"Hey, it's been a weird day," he said, voice light. "I haven't eaten since breakfast and, well, we got off on a really strange foot. I'm going up to Mom's for dinner. Why don't you come along? That woman doesn't make a meal you can't take seconds and thirds worth of leftovers home with you, so there will be more than enough."

He smiled. It made the handsome man even more so. Even his eyes, brilliantly blue, held an easy charm.

Her feeling of unease transformed into something else. An ache that was familiar yet just as raw as it had been the day, years ago, she realized her life would never be the same again. Like a switch had been flipped, Nina felt herself shutting down.

"I haven't even been here for a week and I got caught basically skinny-dipping," she said, voice hard. "I think it's best I focus on my work, if your mother decides to keep me around after all of this. I've already lost most of the day." When she wasn't sure if he was getting the point she was trying to drive home, she added, "I'll eat here. Alone."

Caleb's smile faded, but once again, he didn't press.

"I'll see you tomorrow then."

Nina didn't watch him go. Instead, she locked the door and walked up to her room. The familiar ache became a bellow in her chest. She sat on the edge of her bed and looked out of the window. In the distance the curve of the mountains held a beauty that did nothing to dissuade the memories about to overwhelm her.

Nina watched darkness veil the field and trees.

It would come for her heart next.

Chapter Four

The Wildman County Sheriff's Department was in need of a paint job. For whatever reason, the previous sheriff had painted the once copper-and red-toned bricks light blue. Since then the weather had changed that to a worn and chipped muck gray. Forget a happy-looking place, the one-story building now looked like a depressed cloud. And that was on its good days.

Yet peeling paint couldn't squelch the pride Caleb had in the department and the work he and his brother had done during their time there. He still felt it the next morning when he began his day. His metal desk with a perpetual stack of papers in the out tray, a framed candid picture of him and his siblings and the one empty coffee cup that always rested on a coaster felt as much of a home to him as the ranch.

Even on mornings where frustration clung to him like a second skin.

"Hodge said he'd call as soon as he was done talking to his boss," Jazz reminded him from over the tops of their desks. The fronts were pushed together leaving no space between. It made working together easier than having to hunt each other down. She didn't look up from the paperwork she was filling out as she continued. "I know patience

isn't always your strong suit but that's what you're going to have to wear until he calls."

Caleb pulled out a stress ball Madeline had given him when he'd been promoted to detective. He squeezed it once, hard.

"Would *you* practice patience if some creep had sent that email to you?" He shook his head, answering for her. "You should have seen her, Jazz. It scared her and it happened on *my* land."

Jazz paused, her pen midword. She sighed.

"Just because someone sleazy did a sleazy thing on the ranch doesn't mean it's your fault," she said. "It's the fault of the sleazy person. Plus, you're trying to help catch that very same sleazy person. That counts for something."

Caleb snorted.

"You just said sleazy four times."

Jazz shrugged.

"If the shoe fits."

She went back to the paperwork. Caleb glanced at the clock above the closed door of the sheriff's office. Declan wasn't in and probably wouldn't be until they knew if there was an arsonist running through town. Caleb had decided to keep the incident with Nina under wraps for the time being. Partly because he could handle it, thanks to having no actively open cases, and partly because of Nina.

He had no doubt that his mother wouldn't have given the woman any grief over what had happened. Almost everyone at the ranch had, at one point or another, used one of the ponds or streams to cool down after a long day of work or exercise. That was nothing to be ashamed of, definitely not to be punished for. Yet the way Nina's words had hardened as she declined his offer to eat at the main house the night before had made him feel oddly protective. Not just of her physically, either. With a start, Caleb realized

he wanted to help alleviate the embarrassment and worry that had colored her cheeks rosy.

He wanted to keep her safe.

He wanted to make sure she *felt* it, too.

"What about that list of people she gave you yesterday?" Jazz continued, pen moving across her paper. "Did you finish going through it?"

Caleb put the stress ball down and eyed the list in question. There was an X next to each name.

"Yeah. I talked to everyone she could remember the names of already this morning. Everyone had a solid alibi."

"Did you tell them what was going on with Nina or did you use that Nash family charm I keep hearing about to trick them into talking?"

Caleb chuckled. Jazz was trying to keep him busy, he knew, but she'd been giving him grief about the so-called Nash family charm since she'd moved to Overlook. She never saw it, she'd said time and time again. To be honest, neither did he, but that hadn't stopped the women in town from bringing it up to each other.

"Since I view you as a brother, does that mean I'm a part of that family charm, too?" she'd asked one day.

Caleb had chuckled then, as well.

"You know how small towns work by now, Jazz," he said. "All you have to do is say 'yes ma'am' and 'no sir,' and compliment their pecan squares."

Jazz snorted but didn't disagree. Caleb had gone back to squeezing his stress ball, distracting his hand from texting Hodge again, when his phone finally went off.

"Talk to me, Hodge," Caleb greeted him.

Hodge Anderson, the king of IT in town, answered in his usual gruff tone.

"Good news, bad news," he said. "Tracked the IP address to one location in Overlook."

"Bad news?"

"It's at Claire's Café."

Caleb grumbled. Claire's Café sold coffee, pastries and a small selection of books. It also had free wi-fi. It wasn't unusual for locals and out-of-towners alike to make the trek to Arbor Street with their laptops. Fast internet wasn't always easy to find in Overlook, and at the café it came with Claire's homemade pecan squares.

"Could you track it to the computer that sent it?" he asked, hopeful. Sometimes they couldn't get an exact location but just a general area.

"That *is* the bad news," Hodge persisted. "I think it's *Claire's* computer. It seems to be stationary, the best I can guess. It hasn't left the address in over a week."

Caleb felt his eyebrow rise, confusion pulling the strings.

"Are you sure?"

Hodge sighed.

"That's where the computer is that sent the email. You'll have to figure out the rest."

Caleb thanked the man before both said their goodbyes. He'd known Hodge since they were teens. Caleb questioning him had been more out of the need to be thorough. He trusted Hodge and his skills. However, that didn't mean he thought Claire Jenkins was the culprit behind the email. She'd been friends with his mother since *they* were teens. She didn't exactly strike him as the malicious type. Still, he put his stress ball back into its drawer and put his badge around his neck. He glanced at Declan's closed office door and then was in his truck, pointed toward the heart of town.

THE AIR WAS cool and the breeze was gentle. There wasn't the smell of salt water from the sea clinging to it like her childhood home, but the freshly mowed grass and the

promise of rain was still a nice tradeoff. Nina picked her way along the manicured trail that led to the stables, trying to savor the charm of the ranch while pretending she wasn't tired to the bone. Falling asleep had been hard. Once she'd managed it, it had been restless. When Molly had shown up that morning, eager to run a fine-tooth comb over every inch of the cabins, Nina had welcomed the distraction.

Now that it was almost lunch, she decided that she didn't want to be alone just yet and took up Molly's offer to show her the horses. The manager, like most of the employees on the ranch, had soft spots for them. Because of this, Nina didn't mention that the last time she'd ridden had been when she was ten…and that she'd been terrified every minute of it.

"I hope this rain business keeps well enough away when we open," Molly said, clipboard checklist for the cabins beneath one arm. Her blond hair was braided tightly against her scalp. She'd left her cowboy hat in the office. Nina knew she'd need to get one soon. She needed to help sell the idea of a ranch getaway. She needed to look like she belonged and buying a Stetson seemed to be the easiest way.

"If it does end up raining, what do you think about taking the guests out to the barn near the trails?" Nina thought out loud. "Dorothy said it was once used for storage but is now empty, right? Maybe we could set something up in there to make them still feel like they're getting a camping or outdoorsy-type of experience without getting soaked. Maybe set it up to look like a makeshift campsite. Just a bit more comfortable."

Molly's brow scrunched in thought but her lips pulled up into a smile.

"You know, that could work," she said. "We could put in lanterns and decorate the barn like one of those old Western town attractions. I have to meet with Dorothy this af-

ternoon. I'll run it by her and see if we can't go ahead and start working on the backup plan tomorrow."

Nina felt a swell of pride.

"I'll see if I can't come up with some activities, too. Maybe I can arrange something in town with one of the bars." As soon as she said it Nina's stomach clenched.

She had spent the night going over every person she had given her email address to but still couldn't pinpoint anyone who had seemed *off*. Her gut hadn't yelled or even whispered through meeting or talking with the locals. No red flags, no strange behavior. Yet that email was still in her inbox, taunting her.

Nina had decided not to bring it up with Molly or anyone on the ranch. Not when Caleb already knew. She was sure it was only a matter of time before the news was out and she was let go for being so careless. That had been half the reason sleep had evaded her for so long the night before. Between the memories she had tried to leave behind to the very real possibility that she'd have to move back to her childhood home and live with those same memories again had almost put her in a cold sweat.

This had been her best chance at moving on. Starting over. Yet less than a month had gone by and her fresh start was being soured.

"That's a good idea," Molly responded, unaware that Nina had fallen back into a seemingly unending loop of memories and fears. "You should talk to the Nash triplets. They've spent their lives on this ranch. I bet they know how to keep entertained during every season around here."

"I can't imagine having triplets," Nina confessed, thankful for the slight distraction from her darker thoughts.

Molly laughed.

"Amen. Poor Dorothy has only been pregnant twice and yet has four children. Have you met any of them yet?"

Nina didn't want to lie as much as she didn't want to talk about the email. She nodded and went with a vague in-between response.

"I've only met Caleb, briefly."

Molly lifted up four fingers and ticked them off as she began.

"We have the eldest, Declan, who's the sheriff. He lives on the ranch in a house that used to belong to Dorothy's in-laws before they passed. He's a nice man but lets his work consume him. Which I guess you have to if you want to keep your community safe."

"Dorothy mentioned him. She said I wouldn't have to worry about any flak for throwing large scale events from local law enforcement since her son was the sheriff."

"A definite perk! Though, let me tell you, he's an intense fellow but it's just his way." Molly held up three fingers. "Then we have the triplets. Desmond, Caleb and Madeline. The only triplets born in Overlook in seventy years." Her smile disappeared. Her humor fell away. It was such an abrupt change that Nina wondered if they should stop their walk. But, just as quickly, Molly reverted to normal. "Desmond is a businessman, as best as I can describe him. He lives here on the ranch in a house built right behind the main one. He has a bit of money beneath his belt that he's made outside of the ranch. He's usually out of town on some work trip or another. Madeline lives there, too, since he's hardly ever home. She works with him, but last I heard she was trying to find something else to do. Then there's Caleb."

Obvious affection threaded around the detective's name. It prompted a flutter in Nina's stomach.

"I know you've already met him but, as a local gal, let me be the first to tell you that he spelled trouble when we

were younger. Kids are kids, sure, but Caleb was an absolute wild child. Fearless. I was better friends with Declan yet I still have several stories of Caleb being a little daredevil." That change passed across Molly again. It was like the air deflated from her words. This time the change was slower to leave. "He's a detective now, one of the best Overlook has had, if you ask me. He lives on the ranch, too, in a cabin the triplets started to build after their father died."

Nina thought of the cabin she'd seen the day before with new attention. She didn't interrupt to say she'd already seen where the man lived.

A wistful smile lifted the corner of Molly's lips. "I once thought it was a bunch of bull-hockey that twins and triplets had a different kind of bond between them than other siblings—I mean, I have a sister who's my best friend—but once you see them together you'll understand it to be true. Maybe it's just genetics or maybe it's what they went through back in the day, but either way, once you meet the Nash triplets, you don't forget them easily."

They were getting closer to the stables. Nina could make out Molly's husband, Clive, with a beautiful almost-silver white horse in a pen. He waved at them, cowboy hat in his hand. Molly returned it with a wide smile. An ache of loneliness joined the ache from last night still radiating through Nina. Still, she didn't want the conversation to end.

"What they went through back in the day?" Nina repeated.

Molly gave her a sheepish look.

"I didn't mean to bring it up," she hurried. "It's just one of those things that I assume everyone in town knows." A haunted feeling crept over Nina. It pulled at the hair on the back of her neck. "When the triplets were eight someone abducted them from a park in town." Nina felt her eyes

widen. She stifled a gasp. "That triplet connection they have saved their lives, at least that's how it was told to me by my mom when I was older. They were held for three days. Three. Can you believe that? Then, by the grace of God, they helped each other escape. Sure, they got hurt in the process, but all things considered it was a miracle. One the town still likes to talk about today, especially since the man who took them was never caught. And, believe you me, they looked for him for years." She shook her head. Her frown managed to pitch lower. "Honestly, since you're now employed by the Nash family, I'm sure someone in town will try to get more information out of you about it. Some insights they'd never heard before or, maybe, just some kind of theory they have about who was behind it. Still, it's not something the family likes to talk about so, please, keep it to yourself. The Nash family is a lot more than their tragedy."

"I won't say anything," Nina promised.

Molly gave her a polite nod. Her history lesson and rundown on the Nash siblings transitioned into talk about the stables and the horse Clive was with. It wasn't until Molly and her husband started talking about their daughter's latest homework assignment that Nina excused herself.

She walked along the side of the barn until she was at the wooden fence a hundred or so feet behind the stables. It encased a long-stretching field. A few horses were grazing in the distance, cresting along the curve of a hill. Nina watched them with admiration, and a small amount of dread. The last time she'd ridden a horse had been with her mother. She'd been terrified. Her mother had made her a promise.

"I won't let anything happen to you, Nina. Trust me."

Nina had still been terrified but nothing bad had hap-

pened. She'd been convinced her mother had worked some kind of magic. A spell.

Nina wished her mother had used that same magic on herself.

She placed her hands on the twisted wood of a fence post and took a long, deep breath. Caleb's face appeared in her mind as clearly as the green grass and gray, cloud-filled sky. She felt herself soften.

She often forgot that, just because she'd lived through something traumatic, didn't mean she was the only one who had.

Tragedy had a way of taking a person and changing their shape. Nina found herself wondering how it had affected one detective in particular but she finally came out of her thoughts enough to realize the cloud she'd been looking at in the distance wasn't a cloud at all.

It was smoke.

"Hey, Molly?" she called over her shoulder. Geography had never been Nina's strong suit in school but she was pretty sure the only building in that direction belonged to the same man she had been thinking about. Maybe they were doing a burn pile? But why there?

Nina ducked between two wooden posts and stepped out into the field. She glanced down at her watch.

Did Caleb take normal lunch breaks?

Was it her imagination or was the smoke cloud becoming larger?

Unease started to kick up in her stomach. Then Nina was running.

Chapter Five

No one was at the Retreat or the main office. Caleb thought about calling Nina since she'd given him her number the day before but decided to try the stables first. He didn't mind stretching his legs anyhow, especially since he was starting to get that mid-afternoon drag. He'd skipped eating lunch in lieu of going to Claire's Café.

Which was the reason he wanted to talk to Nina.

One of the reasons.

The other wasn't based in facts but feelings. He wanted to check on the woman, to make sure she was okay. As little contact as they'd had in the last twenty-four hours, she'd still managed to make an impression. One that passed itself on to Jazz. She'd offered to finish off the paperwork on their last case while Caleb figured out who was behind the email.

The walk to the stables was nice. It would rain soon. There was something inspiring about the charge in the air before a storm. Like everything around him was building up to something powerful. It put a little pep in his step, a little more focus in his gaze. For the first time since seeing Nina at the stream, Caleb wondered if she liked the ranch. She'd said she was from Florida, living on the coast.

He tried to remember what his mother had said after she'd interviewed and then hired Nina. She wasn't mar-

ried, he knew that. No kids either. She had a business degree, but the specifics and where she'd gotten it, he didn't know. Like Caleb's ex had pointed out, he fell down the rabbit hole of work quite often. Sometimes when he'd resurface he was faced with a world that had passed him by.

That used to bother him when he was younger but now he was used to it.

Yet he couldn't help one surprising fact. He wanted to know more about Nina.

The stables were housed in an old tried-and-true weathered red building. It held twelve box stalls plus an office that Clive kept, a small room for the farrier and vet to use when they made their rounds and an attic loft overhead. Caleb was fond of that loft. The Nash siblings had each spent their fair share of time sneaking out of the house and congregating there with their friends growing up. Admittedly, it had been a while since he'd been there, but Caleb couldn't help but smile as he padded in through the tall, open front doors.

Clive was standing on the opposite end, finishing tacking up another reason for Caleb to smile.

"Well, if that isn't the most handsome stud I ever did see," Caleb exclaimed. Clive finished adjusting his horse's girth and then gently tugged on the saddle. He gave a good-natured laugh.

"Don't let Molly hear you calling me handsome like that," he said. "She might go and get jealous."

Caleb patted his friend on the back and focused on the horse staring at him.

"Been a while hasn't it, Ax?" he whispered, running a hand up and then down the side of Ax's neck. He was a frame overo Tennessee Walker. As beautiful as they came. Like Caleb could navigate the ranch with his eyes closed, he could perfectly imagine every white patch across Ax's

dark copper hair without looking. The horse had been born on the ranch, just as Caleb had been.

"I was going to take him for some exercise," Clive said, taking down the tacking ropes. "The forecast said there was a good chance we'd be getting storms tonight and through the next few days. Thought I'd take him along the fence to make sure everything is on the up-and-up."

This wasn't anything new; once a week someone checked the fences. It was as much for keeping out predators and ill-willed humans as it was keeping the horses and livestock in and safe. Though the mightiest of fences didn't keep everyone out, especially if they were in tip-top shape. Case in point, the person who'd sent the email to Nina.

"I'm on my lunch break right now. If you don't mind the company I can tag along." Caleb patted Ax's head. The horse nudged into him.

"Sounds good to me," Clive said. "I can take out Isla—"

"*Clive!*" Molly skidded into the stables, eyes wild and cheeks flushed. She looked between them as her chest heaved up and down. "I looked for Nina after she yelled for me but—but she's running through the field. There's smoke in the distance. Caleb, I think it's your house!"

Caleb didn't waste any time. His fingers wrapped around Ax's reins.

"Time to run."

The air took on the distinct smell that came with something large burning. It only propelled Nina forward with more urgency. What could she really do if the detective's house was the reason that smoke was climbing against a darkening sky?

Nina guessed cutting across the field at her fastest run would put her there before Clive and Molly could get there in the car. Maybe in that time she could do some good?

Make sure no one was inside? Try and put it out herself until real help came?

Nina's lungs started to ache as she pushed up and over the top of the hill. The free-roaming horses had already run closer to the barn, not liking her frantic energy. She didn't blame them. As soon as she crested the hill she let out a strangled cry. She hadn't misremembered. The cabin in the distance was Caleb's. Though it was a lot farther away than she had thought, there was no denying that was what was burning.

Nina couldn't see the dirt driveway from her current angle. She couldn't tell if the truck was there or not. It renewed her drive to keep pushing. Her feet dug into dirt and grass harder, her legs took the force with a strained ache.

She couldn't stop. Flames were greedy. Lost seconds meant everything. She had found that out the hard way at the heartbreakingly high price of her mother.

A different kind of ache twisted within her so hard Nina almost stumbled.

I can't do this right now, she thought with decided concentration. *I can't think about her. Not when he could be in—*

Nina's thoughts were interrupted by the sound of hooves beating out a thunderous rhythm behind her. It wasn't until she felt them in the ground that she turned, worried the horses had been spooked even more and were about to trample her in their mad dash to escape.

What Nina saw brought her to a stumbling halt.

None other than Caleb Nash was charging toward her on horseback, detective's badge swinging on a chain around his neck and cowboy hat firmly on his head. Up until then Nina had never really gotten the appeal of cowboys, in the movies or real life, but right then she finally understood the allure. There was just something to be said about a man

blazing across the earth with power beneath him and fire in his eyes. Yeah, she understood now.

Caleb was exactly where he belonged, sitting astride one of the most beautiful horses Nina had ever seen with an ease that somehow added to his appeal. When he stopped right next to her, Nina said the first thing that came to her mind.

"I-I thought you might be inside."

Caleb leaned over and outstretched his hand.

"Get on," he replied, voice all baritone.

It was all Nina needed to hear. She took his hand, put her foot in the stirrup, and let the man and momentum do the rest. It wasn't until her backside hit the saddle and her arms were firmly around the detective's stomach that Nina thought about her fear of horses. But then it was too late. They were cutting through the rest of the field with speed. The movement was jostling—she'd definitely feel it in the morning—but Nina clutched the man at the reins, trying to focus on anything other than the fence they were coming up on way too fast.

Was he going to stop or—?

Nina tucked her head against Caleb's back and squeezed her eyes shut.

"Hold on," he yelled into the wind. Like she wasn't already doing just that.

Nina felt the cowboy readying for the jump before the horse had even lifted off the ground. She clung to Caleb, focusing on the hardness of his chest and stomach instead of the fact that for one terrifying moment they were in the air. It wasn't until they hit the ground on the other side of the fence and ran a few feet that Nina loosened her death grip a fraction.

She heard the fire before she opened her eyes to see it. Flames licked the left side of the cabin. From the porch

to the roof, red and orange and black swirled together. The fire crackled and roared as it ate up the wood. Glass shattered as the heat hit the window, just out of reach of the flames. Caleb's body hardened within her arms. He brought the horse to a stop several yards out at the road. Nina held on as he swung his foot over and jumped to the ground. Wordlessly, he reached up and brought her down.

He handed her the reins, his face impassive.

"Stay here," he ordered, already turning.

"But you can't—"

He didn't give her the chance to argue. Caleb ran up to the porch and swung around it in the opposite direction of the fire. He disappeared around the corner.

Nina realized her heart was in her throat. The fire was consuming one side of the house but it wouldn't be long before it was destroying all of it. Movement flashed in front of the window next to the front door. She clutched the reins. Why had he gone inside?

A loud crack split the air. The left side of the house shuddered. Flames spiked higher in the air as half of the roof crumbled.

"Caleb!"

Nina dropped the reins, hoping the horse wouldn't go too far if he got spooked, and ran around to the house. The back door was wide open. Smoke had already filled the inside.

"Caleb." She tried again, taking an uncertain step forward. She couldn't hear anything else over the fire burrowing into the structure. No one moved.

Terror clawed at Nina's heart. Then she thought about her mom.

Only one person had been able to help when Marion Drake had been trapped. He had felt the heat, choked on

the smoke, but decided not to move. He had watched instead, dooming her mother to a fate she hadn't deserved.

Nina didn't know Caleb. Not in any conventional sense, at least. They weren't friends or lovers. She hadn't grown up in town. She didn't know his middle name and he didn't know that she was allergic to scented fabric softener. She had no idea if he was single; he had no idea that she had broken up with her last boyfriend because he'd wanted to marry her. He wore a cowboy hat and a badge; she hid behind a wall of fallout left over from the trial of her mother's killer.

Yet it didn't matter.

Bolstered by thoughts of her mother and two of the bluest eyes she'd seen, Nina covered her mouth and nose with her arm and ran into the cabin.

CALEB DIDN'T MAKE it into his bedroom before the ceiling over it collapsed. He *did*, however, make it into the hallway that led there. The house seemed to moan and exhale all at once, unable to fight the pain that the fire was causing. He didn't have the time to watch through the open door as most of his belongings were crushed by weakened and burned wood. Instead he had to ensure he wasn't the one crushed next.

He retreated to the next open door. He didn't use it often but the office was still a room he hoped not to lose. At this rate though, he wasn't sure it stood a chance. All he could do was get out of the house and hope the fire department was speeding in their direction after Clive called. Caleb didn't have the time to puzzle out what could have started the fire but he wasn't an idiot. He knew they were past the point of using the water hose or an extinguisher.

Now the house was on borrowed time.

Just like him.

Caleb spun on his heel as he cleared the office door. He unintentionally sucked in a breath as the small hallway filled with debris. His lungs filled with smoke. It nearly doubled him over as a coughing fit took hold. The house shuddered again.

He moved to the middle of the room, trying to recover.

The only reason he'd come into the cabin in the first place was to make sure his mother wasn't inside. Like the pop-up surprise of spring cleaning, it wasn't unheard of for her to walk from the main house to his or Declan's and let herself in. She called it loving visits from the woman who'd raised them. Caleb called it her ninja training since she was always so sneaky about them.

Which was why he'd been terrified she had somehow started, and then become trapped by, the fire ravaging his home. He'd run into the house yelling for her, relief only partially coming through when no one has responded and he'd seen each room was empty.

Now that he knew she wasn't inside, his focus needed to shift to escape.

The window looked out to the wraparound porch and the field just beyond. He hurried over to it. He kept it open almost every time he used the office, preferring the smell of grass and daylight over the stuffiness of being confined, and it had a perfect track record for easily flipping open. Caleb pushed up on the glass. This time it wasn't easy. The window didn't budge.

Caleb coughed into his arm before he could zero in on what was making the window stick. His eyes were watering something fierce. It took him longer than it should have to figure out what he was looking at.

The windowsill was nailed to the frame.

From the outside.

The reflex to swear was only tamped down by another

wave of coughing. The smoke had already been thick when Caleb had run in, now with the structure failing, it was undeniably worse. Never mind the coughing, it was getting hard to breathe.

Caleb backtracked to the armchair in front of his desk. It was what his sister had called a decorative chair, made to be pretty and not so much to be used. He'd thought that was silly but had obliged her. Now he was going to use the unnecessarily heavy piece of furniture to save his life.

He bent over to get purchase on the chair, hoping to use it like a battering ram, when he realized it wouldn't be that simple. He'd breathed in too much smoke. Now he couldn't breathe at all. Coughs racked his body. The house moaned again. Glass shattered. Something shifted.

He slumped against the side of the chair, trying to fight through the lightheadedness that bowled him over. All he had to do was pick the chair up and he'd—

"Caleb!"

The voice was competing with the fire but it was undeniably there. Caleb turned around. Through watering eyes he saw two things back-to-back.

There was broken glass on his desk.

Nina was standing on the other side of the window, brandishing a shovel.

"Stand back," she yelled.

On reflex he turned his head. More glass shattered.

The urge to breathe twisted in his gut. Ached in his chest. Burned in his lungs. His head swam.

A hand grabbed his.

Even through the smoke Caleb was pulled into the dark brown eyes of Nina Drake. She'd not only broken away all of the glass, she'd come in after him too.

It was the shot of adrenaline he needed.

Caleb led her to the window but she pushed him through

first. He climbed out onto the porch and took a stuttering breath, trying not to pass out. He waited until she was at his side, tucked Nina under his arm and together they ran straight into the field.

There Caleb's body decided it had been through enough. His knees buckled and they both went down. Nina did her best to catch them but only managed to put herself beneath him so she was on her backside with him on top. He tried to roll off onto the grass but she held him fast with one arm across his chest.

"You're—you're okay," she said, pushing up so that they were doing the best approximation of sitting they could manage. It took him a moment to realize she was propping him up, her chest against his back, her legs on either side of him. Something hard dug into his back but Caleb couldn't find the focus to wonder what it was.

Instead he let Nina hold him and together they watched as his home burned.

Chapter Six

The rain came next.

At first Nina didn't notice it. They just sat there, both trying to breathe again. The heat from the house traveled with ease. It didn't even seem possible that she'd ever feel the cold again. But then the darkness around them became hard to ignore. The smell of rain became the water that soaked into their clothes.

It wasn't until Clive and Molly came running around the house yelling that Nina even thought to move. Still, Clive was the one who got the ball rolling. He pulled Caleb to his feet and Molly helped Nina up. The four of them went back to Caleb's horse and then backtracked farther away from the house. Sirens came quickly after that. The sheriff was the first to arrive, beating them by a few minutes.

Declan Nash jumped out of his truck with his badge shining and his expression hard. He was a tall, solidly built man with a wholly intimidating disposition. When he saw his brother, however, every bit of him sagged with obvious relief. The rain rolled down both of their backs as they shared a heartfelt embrace. Nina kept her spot at Caleb's shoulder, silent.

They broke the brotherly hug with somber smiles. Both fizzled out quickly. Declan's voice was laced with disapproval.

"Were you inside? I thought you were with the horses when it happened."

The sheriff looked his little brother up and down, then glanced at Nina. She tried to remain impassive, not wanting to get any more grief thrown Caleb's way. Though she *was* curious about why he'd run inside. Then she felt the weight of what she'd taken from his office before leaving the house hidden beneath her shirt. No one had noticed the slight bulge. She'd wanted to give it to Caleb but until the sheriff had come flying down the road, the detective had been in fervent conversation with Clive and Molly. That conversation had concluded with both leaving, Clive on the horse named Ax and Molly in their car. Nina had decided to wait until she could have a moment alone with the man.

Caleb's voice had a rasp when he answered. The coughing fits had finally stopped but there was no denying he had been affected. Black smears from the smoke and ashes streaked across their clothes. The rain had washed most of it from their skin.

"I wanted to make sure Mom wasn't inside. You know how she wanders around here."

Declan's face softened. So did Nina. Caleb ran a hand through his hair, shucking off excess water. He'd lost his cowboy hat somewhere along the way.

"I got trapped in there," he continued. "Nina had to bust out the office window with a shovel and come get me."

Nina flushed with surprise at the sudden attention. Declan raised an eyebrow. She shrugged.

"Anyone else would have done the same in my place," she said modestly. Declan flashed a quick smile.

One thing was for certain, the Nash sons sure knew how to own the simple gesture.

"Don't sell yourself short," he said. "It sounds like you saved the day."

Nina returned the smile. Then it was down to business.

"Declan, we need to talk about the fire," Caleb said.

There was a line of tension in him that seemed to tighten. He looked over his brother's shoulder. The fire had destroyed the office. The rain wasn't coming down hard enough to do any good. They'd been out there for over fifteen minutes and were just now hearing the sirens getting closer. "I don't think it was an accident," he continued. "The window in the office was nailed shut."

Declan reacted immediately. Rage burned behind his eyes. His fists balled.

Nina couldn't help the twist in her stomach. When she'd realized Caleb was trapped she'd run outside, hoping he had made it into the office before the hallway fell. That relief had been short-lived when she'd seen the nails embedded in the wood...and Caleb hunched over. Grabbing the shovel from the porch and using it to make an exit for him had been a blur.

"I was afraid of that." The sheriff swore. "I sent Jazz to Mom's and told them both not to leave until we showed up."

"We need to make sure every place on this ranch is safe," Caleb said, determination warring with his rasp. "Molly and Clive have gone back to the stables to keep an eye on the horses."

"What about the Retreat?" Nina spoke up. It wasn't just a job, it was her new home.

"I'll make sure everything is okay," Declan told them both.

The fire department finally showed up, followed closely by an ambulance. Declan grabbed his brother's shoulder and looked him in the eye.

"This sucks," he said, simply. "But it's nothing we can't handle."

Caleb didn't nod but he didn't disagree, either.

The firefighters focused their attention on the fire while the EMT focused her attention on Caleb. She gave him oxygen and Nina a place to escape the rain. She sat on the bench along the wall in the back of the ambulance, watching with a feeling of detachment as the men and women tried to stop the flames. Not that it would matter much. Whatever wasn't touched by the fire was probably destroyed by smoke and water damage.

Caleb had undoubtedly lost his home.

Nina chanced a glance at the man. Sitting up on the gurney, he had an oxygen mask in one hand and a look of frustration on his face. The EMT shared that frustration. She spoke to him like a mother would a child.

"You need to come to the hospital," she tried. "Smoke inhalation can be serious, Caleb."

There was a familiarity in her words. Like most of Overlook, Nina bet she knew the Nash family personally.

"I'm fine, Linda," he said, still sounding hoarse. "I wasn't in there that long."

Linda shook her head.

"It doesn't matter. By the sound of it you took enough to almost pass out."

Caleb gave her a look that clearly said he was going to argue until he was blue in the face. Yet all Nina could see was the man in a room filled with smoke. She could still smell it on him. On herself. In the air, mingling with the rain.

She'd only ever seen the aftermath of what a fire like that could do.

If she hadn't come around to look for him, would he have made it out? Or would he have died like—

"Linda, listen," he started, his voice taking on the charming edge of a man who was used to getting his way with women.

Nina didn't know if it would work on Linda or not.

And she would never find out.

Something inside Nina shifted. She said exactly what was on her mind.

"My mom died from smoke inhalation. We should go to the hospital."

Caleb's blue, blue eyes widened. Nina felt a flush of embarrassment at being so blunt, not to mention personal, but stood her ground. "It's better to be safe than sorry."

Linda turned back to her patient expectantly. Caleb continued to look at Nina.

The rain picked up. It pounded against the roof in an unforgiving rhythm. The firefighters continued to yell back and forth in the distance, calling out orders as they became drenched. The fire was a constant, menacing roar.

Nina kept one arm over the small bulge in her shirt. Not that Caleb was looking anywhere other than her eyes. His stare was mesmerizing in its own right. She couldn't have looked away even if she'd wanted to.

Which she didn't.

She needed him to see what she was feeling. She needed him to understand the grief and anguish that still clung to her heart after all of these years. She needed him to take the trip that her mother had never gotten the chance to take.

She needed him to be okay.

And maybe he saw that in her. After a moment he nodded.

"Alright," he said. "Let's go."

OVERLOOK HAD A small but well-kept medical center on the south side of town. Nina had been surprised it had one but was grateful. The commute was short and the center wasn't crowded. They were led through a lobby that contained a handful of people before being sent back to a big

room split into sections by faded green plastic curtains. Since she'd also been in the house, she was offered one of the sections while Caleb was given the one next to it.

Like most people, Nina wasn't a fan of hospitals. She eyed the bed and its paper covering with determination to not sit on either. The nurse promised she'd be right back before repeating the message to Caleb. She also seemed to know him. It made Nina feel like an outsider.

Which was good because that's what she had wanted.

To be seen and heard only when necessary.

To do her job with a smile and then go home, alone.

To live under the radar.

Not to get close to anyone.

A quiet life was better than the loud one she'd been forced into when she was younger.

The curtain next to her slid to the side. Caleb, still dripping wet, motioned to the space between their beds.

"Do you mind if we keep this open?" he asked. "I hate hospitals but I hate feeling cooped up in them even more."

Nina nodded, surprised that she instantly liked the idea despite just reminding herself that her desired lifestyle was keeping her head down. That was easier said than done, she was finding, especially when Caleb was the one looking at her. Like he wanted to say something more but the words seemed caught somewhere between his mind and his mouth.

"Yeah, sure. That's fine." She gave him a smile that echoed the sentiment. "I actually meant to give this to you outside of the house but, well, it was raining and I didn't want it to get messed up. Then the ambulance showed and, honestly, I got used to holding it and then forgot I was at all."

Nina pulled the picture frame from beneath her shirt. It was small and thin with chestnut-colored wood and a

golden back. That's what had caught her eye in the first place. It was beautiful and compact, easy to carry. Though it was the picture encased inside that had made Nina decide to take it.

"I know it's not much in the grand scheme of things," she continued, holding the frame out. "But I know some things are a lot harder to replace than others."

Caleb took the frame but didn't speak right away. Nina worried she'd somehow misjudged the picture's importance to him, but then a smile pulled up the corners of his lips ever so slightly. He let out a small breath. The tension in his shoulders eased enough to show he was, at the very least, relieved.

"I was so focused on making sure Mom wasn't inside that I didn't even think to grab anything." He ran his thumb over the glass with affection. "This picture is one of a kind."

Warmth spread in Nina's chest at the admission. Caleb took a step closer and angled the frame so she could see the picture.

"This was taken when I was eight." He pointed at the eight-year-old version of himself. He was all smiles and blue eyes. On either side of him were a boy and girl who shared those blue eyes. "These are Madeline and Desmond," he explained before moving his finger along to a taller boy. "That's an almost-teenaged Declan, thinking he's hot stuff because he lucked out and got to kiss Corina Hoover during Spin the Bottle. Believe me, I know, because he wouldn't shut up about it for *weeks*."

Nina stifled a laugh. His finger moved over to a younger Dorothy. Her hair was dark and long, her smile warm and inviting. "You've met Mom." Then Caleb pressed his finger against the image of the man holding Dorothy's hand.

He looked so much like Caleb did now that Nina had no doubt it was his father. Still, she waited for him to say it.

"And this is my dad, Michael."

The smile that should have grown, faltered. Nina knew it well. No matter how many years went by, no matter how much she thought she'd moved on from her mother's death, there would always be those moments when the happy memories she had collided with the emptiness her loss left behind. Whether it was a smell of something familiar, a sound that stirred some forgotten story or simply a picture. It could make and break a child all at the same time.

Nina stepped closer and touched his shoulder.

"It's a beautiful picture."

Caleb nodded.

"It is."

Metal rings scraped along the curtain rod behind them. A woman Caleb seemed to recognize came in. She saw to Nina first. Caleb went back to his gurney.

He looked at the picture until it was his turn.

IT HAD TAKEN Caleb an hour's worth of phone conversation to convince Desmond and Madeline not to hop on the next plane out of Texas and come back to the ranch. He knew they were in the middle of securing a new investor that would mean a lot to their work. To leave would hurt their cause while showing up in Overlook wouldn't help solve the mystery. Caleb had had to use every excuse in the book as to why their flocking to him would only make things harder. The main reason being the simplest one.

He had a job to do.

While the fire investigator hadn't yet finished combing the aftermath of Caleb's house, he already knew what he'd say.

There was an arsonist in Overlook.

Caleb hated just thinking it, but the nails in the window were fairly damning evidence that the fire wasn't some freak accident. Someone had put them there before the fire.

Not only did he have a job to do in catching the culprit, he also had a ranch to protect.

And everyone who lived on it.

Caleb looked across the front porch of the Retreat's office at Nina. The rain was still falling but had lost its ferocity. Now it was a sound in the darkness of the night. A rhythmic backdrop to a day that had gone from relatively normal to hell.

After being cleared from the hospital, Caleb and Nina had been driven back to the ranch by one of the sheriff's deputies. Instead of going to the Retreat or the site of the fire, they were taxied to the main house. There waiting, sat his truck, his partner and his mother.

"Oh, Caleb," his mother had cried, pulling him into an embrace. She repeated the sentiment with a partially contained sob.

"I'm okay, Mom," he'd consoled her. "It's just a house."

It was what his mother had needed to hear. She'd nodded then turned her attention to Nina. Word had already spread about her help and his mother had made sure the ranch's newest addition knew just how much she appreciated what Nina had done. They'd disappeared into the house together while Caleb had rendezvoused with Jazz outside.

She'd hugged him, offered up any and all help from herself and her husband, and then gotten down to business.

"Declan has a deputy at all of the properties not being watched by ranch employees tonight," she'd said. "Plus patrols around town. I don't know what he'll do tomorrow about it all, but at least tonight everyone here can hopefully sleep a little easier." She'd given him a pointed look at that.

"Don't worry," he'd said, picking up on the thought she wasn't voicing. "I'm not going to do anything crazy tonight."

It was true but only because there was nothing he really *could* do.

But he wasn't about to tell her that.

"Good. You need to get some rest. We can start figuring this out tomorrow," she'd promised.

They'd all convened in the kitchen for dinner. His mother was what his father used to call a nervous chef. When things went sideways, the cook-and bakeware came out. Together they'd eaten a late and extensive dinner. Jazz had helped his mother make a list of everything he might need while Caleb had fielded another call from each of his siblings. Nina had used the landline to make a call but had, for the most part, remained quiet.

Caleb hadn't forgotten what she'd said in the ambulance. Her mother had died from smoke inhalation. Which meant there had been a fire. The pain that had swept across her face as she said it hadn't been fresh. No. It had been old. Worn and felt over and over again until it had become the fabric of who she was. Caleb didn't need to know the specifics of what had happened to know the feeling.

And to guess how hard it must have been to go into the burning cabin.

Yet, she had.

He wanted to press, to understand how she was feeling, but decided to keep his distance. When and if she wanted to open up, he'd listen, but he wasn't about to push. He also knew how it felt to be prodded. To be watched. People waiting for him to break. He wasn't about to put that on the woman who had risked her life to save his.

Now, a few feet from where he stood wearing a borrowed pair of sweatpants two sizes too big and a jacket

he'd found in a box in Madeline's old room, Nina held his stare with a sympathetic smile.

"I'm really sorry about your house," she said. "It *is* just a house but that doesn't mean it can't still hurt. Let me know if there's anything I can do."

"Helping me out of the burning building was more than enough," he replied. "But thank you."

He waited for her to unlock the Retreat's door and walked her to the office. Her purse and phone were still on the desk. Caleb checked the window to make sure it wasn't nailed shut while she went through her phone.

A feeling of shame washed across Caleb. With everything that had happened he had forgotten what he'd gone to the stables that morning to do in the first place.

"We tracked down the IP address from the email you received today. It led to Claire's Café in town," he recounted. "Have you been there before? It wasn't on the list you gave me."

Nina's eyes widened in recognition.

"I haven't been there yet but Molly and I ran into the manager at the grocery store." She gave him a sheepish look. "I couldn't remember her name. She talked mostly to Molly. Wait, *she* sent the email?"

Caleb shook his head.

"It traced back to the café, to Claire's office computer. She had no idea what I was talking about so we looked at the security footage and saw Daniel Covington pick the office's lock and sneak in there yesterday."

Nina's brow furrowed. By the looks of it she didn't seem to recognize the name. Which wasn't surprising.

"Daniel is a nineteen-year-old pain in the ass, to be blunt. We've had trouble with him in the past for taking pranks too far," Caleb continued. "He hasn't done something like *this* but he's sure going to answer for it.

A uniform took him into custody just after lunch. Claire is pressing charges for the invasion of her privacy, plus breaking and entering. I assume you might want to, as well, considering the invasion of yours."

"I do," she agreed. "If only to make him think twice before trying this again."

Caleb nodded at that sentiment. The motion somehow felt exhausting all of a sudden. He ran a hand through his hair. His cowboy hat had fallen off when he was in the house. Just another piece of his life gone.

"Hey, Caleb?"

Nina's expression had gone impassive. Caleb could no more read her now than he could back at dinner. He took a step forward, though. There was something magnetic about the raven-haired woman.

"What happens now?"

It was such a simple question.

It only made sense to give it a simple answer.

He straightened his back and answered in a low yet clear voice.

"Now I'm going to catch whoever did this and stop them from doing it again."

Chapter Seven

The fire was ruled arson. Not even a particularly clever one, at that.

Residue from fireworks was found beneath what used to be Caleb's bed and all the windows had been nailed shut. They couldn't decide if that was meant to trap someone or to keep them out, considering the doors had not been tampered with. As for leads on the arsonist, Caleb and Jazz only had the fireworks to go on. There was a big chain store that sold them two cities away but there were also roadside stands that popped up on occasion. Even if there had only been one store, that didn't mean too much. They couldn't track down everyone who had purchased fireworks.

So Caleb had tossed around the idea that he was targeted because of his job—maybe someone he'd closed a case on or their kin was angry?—and had been working through that long list for alibis. He had also worked with the fire chief by getting information on all fires in Overlook in the last five years.

He wanted to be thorough.

Whoever the arsonist was had made it personal, which only drove Caleb's heels harder into the dirt. The news had had varying effects on the other Nash family members.

Dorothy Nash was a force to be reckoned with. Her

worry for her family and the ranch focused on Caleb. Convincing her that he was alright during the next week was almost as hard as skirting Jazz's and Declan's concerns. At least Desmond's and Madeline's calls and texts were more manageable. The only person who gave him any space to breathe was Nina.

Although he had holed up in Desmond's house since they would be in Texas for at least another week if not two, Caleb had made a deal with her the day after the fire. Since Declan couldn't keep deputies stationed outside every building on the ranch, Caleb had offered to keep an eye on the Retreat at night. Losing his home had hurt him, but losing the Retreat would hurt the family.

And then there was Nina.

She'd risked her life to help him. He'd do no less for her.

For the next week they fell into a routine. He would spend the night camped out on the office's couch and get up in the morning and head to Desmond's to shower and get ready for work. Then he'd be back by dinner and they'd repeat the routine. During that time Nina had been friendly and polite. They took turns handling dinner and breakfast, her inviting him up for something she'd made or his bringing something from the main house, and they'd even played a game of Scrabble one night. Sometimes Molly showed up for a few minutes and sometimes they didn't even speak.

It was comfortable. Nice, even.

Yet the longer their time together went on, the more Caleb started to realize Nina wasn't keeping to herself for his benefit.

No. It was for hers.

That's when he noticed the walls.

When she seemed to want to say something but would stop herself. The smiles she cut off before they grew too

big. The way she quieted when he got too far out of the range of small talk.

Nina Drake was a guarded woman.

And it only made her more intriguing to him.

When Friday morning rolled around Caleb's curiosity finally bonded with this frustration over the case. He finished his coffee and set it down on the picnic table with purpose. Nina looked up from her half-filled cup and laptop. They were at the communal area between the Retreat's office and the first cabin, enjoying the sunshine that had been hit or miss the last few days. Caleb hadn't missed how it made Nina's hair shine, or how every freckle seemed to be highlighted beneath the light.

"Would you like a tour of the town?" he asked without any preamble. Nina's eyebrow arched high. "Well, less like a tour and more like being a fresh pair of eyes to places that previously burned to the ground."

If possible her eyebrow went higher.

"Sadly not the weirdest proposition I've gotten." She laughed. "Care to elaborate?"

Caleb tapped the printout he'd been looking over since he'd woken up.

"I'm trying to figure out a pattern to the fires that were ruled arson in the last few years, but I think I'm too close to them. Every place on this list I've been to, not only as an adult, but a kid. Maybe you can see something I'm missing."

Nina glanced toward the office. While it had been a pain, they had all decided that if the arsonist wasn't caught by Monday it would be best to cancel the reservations set for the following week. Never mind the grand opening party. Sure, it wouldn't be good for business, but having someone set fire to the guest cabins during their stay would be, without a doubt, worse.

"If I can help, I'm definitely in," she told him. "When do you want to leave?"

"I need to head up to Desmond's and then I'll be ready. Does that work for you?"

She nodded and took a long drink of her coffee. "I just need to let Molly know. There's not much else I can do here if we can't open the Retreat."

Caleb helped her clean up and then they went off in separate directions. It wasn't until he was out of the shower and putting on his boots that he realized the new excitement dancing around his gut wasn't just about potentially finding a lead.

NINA DIDN'T KNOW what one wore to an old crime scene so she opted for a black undershirt with an open, flannel button-up and a pair of Levi's she was proud to say had fit her for the last three years. She pulled her long hair back into a ponytail. Then she put on lip gloss.

That move surprised her. She almost took it off before the cream-and-brown striped truck she was getting used to seeing came to a stop just outside. Nina waved goodbye to Molly and tried to tamp down the sudden uptick in the speed of her heartbeat. She'd spent the last week with the man, more or less, and had been fine. Changing locations shouldn't make a difference.

The inside of the truck cab smelled of men's cologne and the woods, both wrapped into one surprisingly intoxicating scent. It made Nina's heart beat a little bit faster against her chest. She gave Caleb a polite smile, hoping to cover up the new feeling.

"So, these are the places in the last five years that have had fires that did a good amount of structural damage," he told her. Nina took the paper from him as they

started out to the road that led out of the ranch. There were five addresses.

"Were all of these arson?"

Overlook was small. Five acts of arson in the last five years was shocking.

"No. Only two were ruled arson," he explained. "The other three were caused by human error. Accidents. The first on the list is the earliest one."

They drove out to a large middle school, two minutes from Overlook's main thoroughfare. It was one of the few stretches of land outside of the ranch that wasn't surrounded by fields of grass or trees. Instead it was boxed in by houses. Caleb drove to a house on the other side of the fenced-in schoolyard. He parked and pointed through the windshield to the two-story house. There was a wooden For Rent sign staked in the yard.

"The fire started in the bedroom and destroyed the entire house. The owner, Angelica DeMarko, fell asleep watching TV and woke up to flames. She said she had no idea how it started, but an investigation showed she fell asleep with a lit cigarette in her hand, dropped it and it caught the curtain next to the bed on fire. From there it made it to the closet where she kept some camping supplies, including kerosene. The fire became much more violent before the fire department could even get there. She was lucky to wake up when she did and get her and her kid out." They got out of the truck and walked up to the house.

"Is this any of the old house?" she asked, admiring the wood and stone porch columns. Nina had always been a fan of the rustic style.

"No, the original had to be demolished. DeMarko didn't have insurance so the land ended up going to the bank and the bank sold it to a man who rebuilt and made it a rental property. Only one family has rented it since but

then moved. I think because of a new job opportunity for the mother."

Nina walked around the house before coming to a stop at Caleb's side. He was staring at the school playground. A wistful, almost vulnerable smile graced his lips. Nina felt like she was intruding on a memory. She started with an apology.

"I'm sorry but I don't know exactly what I'm looking out for," she admitted. "If there's a connection to the fire on the ranch, I'm not seeing one here."

Caleb nodded, not at all nonplussed.

"I thought the same when I came out here earlier this week. But I'm glad for an outsider's point of view to back it up."

Nina felt a small sting at him calling her an outsider, even if it was exactly what she had wanted when coming to Overlook in the first place. Caleb let out a long exhale but kept his gaze on the playground.

"I went to Overlook Middle," he started. "All the Nash kids did. You see the monkey bars over there? For as long as I live I'll never forget when Madi punched Nico Meyers right where the sun don't shine when he was trying to swing across." He chuckled. It pushed his smile wider.

"Did Nico deserve it?" Nina ventured, curious despite herself.

Caleb shrugged.

"I wouldn't say that should be the penalty for doing a dead leg but that's exactly what he paid."

"A dead leg?"

Caleb gave her an incredulous look.

"You don't know what a dead leg is?" When she shook her head Caleb only became more amused. It was nice to see him smile so much, she decided. For good reason he'd been trapped in a constant state of seriousness. Their brief

conversations over the last week had gotten a few smiles but none that reached his eyes.

And Nina should know, she'd spent more time than she should have staring at those beautiful blues.

"It'll be easier to show you instead of tell you. Do you mind?"

"I don't mind."

Caleb told her to stay still and moved behind her. Nina felt heat starting to crawl up her neck in anticipation. She tensed.

"I won't let you fall," he said. "Just trust me."

Before she could respond Caleb put his knee into the back of hers. The sudden pressure and surprise made her buckle. Two hands wrapped around her upper arms. They were warm and strong and stopped her descent with ease. The blush that had been stretching from her stomach to her cheeks finally reached its destination.

"*That's* a dead leg," Caleb concluded. He let go but the warmth of his hands still lingered. Nina turned to face him while also adding an extra step back for more distance. "Nico did that to Madi in the cafeteria in front of the entire sixth grade class, but more importantly her crush. She *and* her food tray hit the ground hard."

Nina tried to cover the sudden heat within her by laughing.

"Then I might have given Nico the same treatment," she decided.

"Mrs. McGinty wasn't as understanding." He moved back to her side and, together, they looked at the playground again. "She grabbed Madi's hand and marched her across the yard, yapping about her actions being unladylike." He snorted. "Madi told her it was unladylike to *not* stand up for herself."

"I like the sound of little kid Madi," Nina admitted.

"You'll have to tell her that when she gets back with Des." Caleb's smile burned bright once more. Then it fizzled out. "I can only convince them to stay away for so long."

A small silence settled between them. Nina didn't know what to do. Caleb was strolling down a more intimate conversational path than he had in the last week. Which meant it was only a matter of time before he tried for more personal details about her.

No sooner had she had the cringe-worthy thought than the question came from his mouth.

"Do you have any brothers or sisters?"

Caleb gave her an expectant look. Nina shook her head.

"I was what my father affectionately liked to call a 'happy surprise.' They had me when they were just twenty. At the time they barely could take care of me so they decided to wait before trying again." Nina traced the playground's slide with her eyes, careful not to give anything away. "My mom passed away before they could get there."

"I'm sorry, Nina."

She shrugged.

"It's okay. It happened a long time ago."

"Just because it happened a long time ago doesn't mean it's okay." Nina wanted to go back to the truck without another word but stilled her feet. The man's words had been too sincere to walk away from, especially since they rang true.

"I know," she agreed.

They went back to looking at the school in the distance. A new guilt emerged in the pit of Nina's stomach. Caleb and his siblings had been abducted and held for three days.

Had they hollowed him out?

Were his smiles and bright, blue eyes a show?

Or had he moved on?

Nina found a question forming on the tip of her tongue, wondering aloud how he managed to stay in a town filled with terrible memories, but then she thought of her mother and decided to give the man an answer to an unasked question.

"She was trapped inside of a burning car. My mother, that is," she said, perhaps with a little more bluntness than she intended. "I was told the smoke is what actually…" The words trailed off. They never came easy when on the topic of what happened.

Even when Nina wasn't telling the whole story.

Caleb waited for her to gather her thoughts. She did after a moment.

"Tragedy. That's what everyone in town called what happened, and then, in another breath it seemed they'd tell me that I would move past it one day. I would wake up knowing what had happened had and yet find the ache had lessened."

Nina chanced a sad smile at the man next to her. She pressed her hand to her chest.

"It's still there. After all these years, it's still there."

Caleb's face filled with an emotion Nina couldn't describe. He let out a small breath. His shoulders sagged slightly.

"Tragedy. Death. Trauma. I don't think it's supposed to go away," he said. "I think it only moves. Some days it's right next to you, staring you in the face. Others? It's all the way at the edge of your memory like a whisper. Like a bad dream." That unaccounted for emotion was replaced by the face of a man who had lived through his words. It made Nina want to dive into Caleb's past right then and there. Yet, again, she stilled herself from the impulse.

She knew the headline about the Nash triplets. She

wasn't going to expect intimate information about his past that she wasn't willing to part with either.

"At the end of the day I think it just comes down to how fast we can wake up," he added.

It pulled out an unexpected smile from Nina. Caleb matched it before she'd explained its presence.

"That sounded wonderfully poetic," she admitted.

Caleb chuckled.

"Don't let the brains and brawn fool you," he said, jokingly. "I can also make pretty words."

And just like that the moment was over.

Nina went to the truck and Caleb followed.

Chapter Eight

The second fire had been caused by an unattended grill in the back of an at-the-time new restaurant on the main strip. Instead of stopping and walking around the building like they'd done with the last, Caleb pointed out the still-standing restaurant while stopped at a pedestrian crossing.

"They were quick on their feet and used an extinguisher to put the fire out," he said. "They lost a grill in the process but had no problem replacing it. The cook didn't even lose his job."

He took a left off Main Street. The road twisted and turned and then they were driving up an incline to two rows of houses. This time they stopped at the curb. Caleb pointed to a house with a bright yellow door. It reminded Nina of the beach houses she'd grown up around.

"This fire wasn't a fun one, not that any are," he started. "Gloria, the owner, left some candles burning while she went to the store. When she came back the living room was engulfed. Gloria's two dogs were still inside. She fought off her neighbors to go back in after them but passed out before she could get back out. Firefighters managed to rescue her but she had to spend a few weeks in recovery."

Something in Nina's memory sparked. "Is this the same Gloria who runs the nonprofit animal shelter?"

"The one and only." There was pride in his voice. "Glo-

ria has been volunteering, and helping people and animals alike for as long as I can remember. Her and her ex-husband started a no-kill shelter in the next city over. She puts a lot of her own money into saving as many animals as she can. We even have a few from her organization out on the ranch."

"I remember reading about her when I was looking through old news stories in my search for local events. When did the fire happen?" Nina was trying to recall the date on the article but she'd looked through so many pieces since accepting the Retreat job that they all had blurred together.

"Two years ago," he answered, putting the truck in Drive again. "The town came together to help in any way we could. She was able to get repairs and still lives there. *With* her two dogs."

Nina couldn't help but smile at that.

They drove to the opposite side of town. Caleb rolled his window down. Nina did, too. The wind smelled like sunshine and sweetness. It tangled her hair but she didn't mind. Caleb turned the radio up and started to sing along with a song she didn't recognize. Nina was surprised at first, worried talk of fires would only plunge him back into a distant mood, but then she realized what must have been the key to Caleb Nash's happiness.

Sunshine.

It was such a warming thought that when he turned her way Nina gave him a genuine smile. There was something beautiful about a man who took delight in such simple pleasures. The same man who had admitted that the pain of trauma never really went away, it was just a matter of distance. It amazed Nina that Caleb could still seem whole after everything, even after the recent loss of everything he owned. His good mood was contagious and as they drove

down a dirt road that cut through a field of green and grain, Nina felt the weight of worry lift from her shoulders. For a little bit they were just two people enjoying the country air, hair in the wind and the radio on.

But then that dirt road led to several BEWARE and DO NOT ENTER signs. The truck stopped. The windows went up. The radio cut off. Caleb's easy smile shut down. He didn't offer any preamble as he got out. Nina followed, her stomach knotting slightly.

The signs, plus traffic cones and a barrier, were standing sentry across the road, stopping any drivers from plowing straight over a drop-off and into dark blue water. On the other side of the water was the same collection of signs and warnings. Declan had already arranged for the debris to be cleared during the last week but there was still some that had sunk into the water.

"This is Overlook Pass. Locals usually come here for fishing since it's one of the deeper parts of the river." Caleb stopped just before the edge and motioned from one set of signs and then to the other. "The bridge that *used* to be here was given historic landmark status a few years back. Last week one of the sheriff's deputies realized it burned down."

There was a tightness to Caleb's voice. An anger igniting below the surface. His hand balled at his side. Nina felt the sudden urge to reach out to him. To let him know whatever was wrong would be okay. Yet she stilled herself and let him continue.

"It was ruled arson. They think kerosene was the accelerant but apparently the unknown timeline has thrown them for a small loop. No one knows when it actually happened yet since this spot isn't as popular this time of year. Plus it's far enough out of town that if the wind was blowing in the other direction, no one in town would have seen it."

Nina took one small step forward and looked down at the water. It wasn't the ocean but it still was pretty. When she turned back she saw a house in the distance.

"They didn't see when it happened? The people who live there?"

"No one has lived there since the owner moved out of state to live with her daughter." Another memory sparked in her mind but Nina couldn't catch it this time. "The last fire on the list is at a house a few minutes from here. It happened the day we met."

The house on Brookewood Drive landed a more impactful punch. It was one thing to look at the restored buildings and an empty space where the bridge had once been, it was another to see a beautiful home burned to its core. Caleb's tension was palpable as he stood at the curb.

Nina hadn't stepped away from the Retreat since the fire on the ranch. Molly hadn't either. Together they'd wordlessly been protecting it while Clive had done the same with the horses at the barn. Caleb had moved between his brother's house, his mother's house, the Retreat and work. Nina felt like an idiot for just realizing that circuit would, of course, have included at least once the remains of his own house.

Did it look like this? Was it recognizable or just a pile of debris and ashes?

Nina didn't think she could ask, though guilt welled up inside of her. She should have already talked to him about it.

"Kelso and Maria Gentry's neighbors called it in while the couple was in town," Caleb started. Nina came to a stop at his side. She couldn't help but stand close to him. The sight of the husk of a home was almost painful to look at. Part of the house had survived the flames but she doubted anything else had. "The investigator and lab found traces

of kerosene. That plus the couple's new fancy furniture that had polyurethane foam padding, and everything burned fast. It was a miracle the fire department made it here when they did or everything would be gone."

"So, no fireworks then."

Caleb shook his head. Standing as close as she was Nina caught a wonderful, spicy smell that must have been lingering from his shampoo. It was, in one word, intoxicating. In another, inappropriate. She tried to refocus.

"This fire was started in the study." He pointed to the debris to the left of the still-standing portion. "Unlike my house, it was a room more in the heart of the house instead of outside. There's also no nails in the windows."

"Okay, so, other than them both being fires, they don't have anything else in common?"

"Not that I can tell."

"But surely two cases of arson in the same town within two days of each other, not to mention the bridge, aren't coincidences. Especially with traces of kerosene at two," she pointed out. "Right?"

In profile, Caleb's jaw hardened.

"Right."

They looked at the house for another minute or two before they were back in the truck and headed toward the ranch. Six fires in the last five years. Three accidental, three arson. Two different methods for those arsons. Kerosene and fireworks.

Were they all connected?

Or *were* they just a series of coincidences?

Was there an arsonist in Overlook setting random fires? Or had Caleb been targeted?

Nina sighed. The distant curve of a mountain made her feel impossibly small. Just like she had the night her mother died.

"I'M SORRY."

Caleb put the truck in Park and gave Nina a look that revealed his confusion. The raven-haired beauty continued, eyes dropping away from his.

"If there are any connections or clues that could give you a lead, I'm still not seeing them."

Caleb shook his head.

"I wasn't expecting to show you these places and you have a magic answer to solve everything," he admitted. "I just wanted to make sure what you saw was in line with what I had."

He tightened one hand on the steering wheel and pulled his gaze away from the windshield ahead of him. Molly was outside one of the Retreat cabins, her laptop in hand. She kept her attention on it, giving them privacy.

"See, I love Overlook," Caleb continued. "I was born here, grew up here, and even though I left for school, I came back here. I know every road, every incline, every trail like the back of my hand. That almost goes the same for the people. That kid Madi punched on the playground? He's in the running to be the mayor. His sister, Bekah? She works at the library, though she didn't always. After her and her husband, Kevin, split because he was getting too friendly with Marla over at the flower nursery, she decided she wanted to get back to her roots of what she was passionate about. She loves to read, just like the other librarian, Lamar. His father wasn't happy he didn't join the military like his brother did, but they've since buried that old fight. Now you can find Lamar and his dad eating lunch together almost every day in town." Caleb glanced over at Nina. Her eyebrow was arched up in question. Why had he just babbled on about town gossip, he guessed she was wondering. He held up his index finger.

"That's just one, long connected thread that makes up

this town. You give me a name and I bet dollars to donuts I can follow it through every person and home in Overlook. *That's* how well I know this place." He paused, trying to keep the flash of anger he felt from showing. "Which is why an arsonist showing up and doing what they did has thrown me off my game. Sure, there's people here who don't respect the law—we have our fair share of misconduct and violence like any town or city—but usually I can understand it and why the person did what they did. But this? Destroying the Gentry's home? Nailing windows shut so my place could burn without interruption? I can't even guess who it is. That's rarely happened to me before in this job and it's gnawing at my gut. Which is exactly what happened to Dad."

Saying it was like a jolt to his system. Caleb hadn't meant to say exactly what he was feeling. Not out loud, not to Nina. Yet there was something about her that made him feel comfortable. Or maybe it was his curiosity that had prompted the admission. How could he hope to know more about her if he never opened up about himself?

"He was a detective too," he explained. "A great one, but there was one case that ate him up. He didn't understand the why of it and he certainly never got any answers. The stress, well, it killed him."

Caleb wondered then if Nina knew about the abduction. He was so used to everyone already knowing about it that the possibility that she hadn't been told hadn't crossed his mind. It had been years since any of the Nash family had told the story themselves. It seemed to circulate just fine without them, making its way through the locals even all these years later.

But Nina wasn't local.

If she didn't know, now would be the perfect time to tell her. To open up to her even more.

However, an old resentment flared to life just beneath his skin. The child in him, the teenager, the young adult... They'd been questioned off and on throughout the years about those three days held captive. He'd been asked to tell the story more times than he could count, bombarded by curiosity that had no business being so curious.

He wanted to open up to Nina—after risking her life to save his, especially—but that resentment at sharing the single worst experience the Nash family had gone through kept the story buried. The weight of pain that pressed into his chest when he spoke again was only for his father.

"He thought he knew this town, these people, and yet he died with nothing but questions."

Caleb let out a long breath. He was back to the fires. Just like his father, he had so many questions. The most urgent ones being who and why.

Nina's hand pressed against his shoulder, surprising him. A small smile graced her lips. Her shining pink lips.

"Hoping that we know that our neighbors don't have bad intentions is like hoping no one ever acts on those bad intentions. If I've learned anything in my life, it's that people are people. They're complex, confusing, wonderful and terrifying. You can't beat yourself up because you don't understand why someone would do something bad. The best any of us can do is continue to struggle to understand. It just shows that we would never do the same things." She squeezed his arm. "The people who take from us shouldn't be allowed to keep taking from us. Don't beat yourself up because someone else finally showed their true colors. Okay?"

Caleb nodded, stunned.

"And I'm sorry about your father," she added, voice as soft as a feather.

"Thanks." He meant it.

Nina smiled a bit brighter and then dropped her hand.

"Will you be eating dinner here tonight?" she asked, opening the truck door.

"If that's okay with you."

"That works for me. Molly brought in some leftover stew today. There's plenty for the two of us." Her eyes turned sharp. Her smile faded. "You'll figure this out, Caleb. And I'll do my best to try and help you."

Caleb didn't get a chance to say thank you again. He watched as she walked away. The tightness in his chest lessened.

He drove back to Desmond's house and nodded to Roberto, the Retreat's cook, who was sitting on Dorothy's back porch on the phone. He'd been a lifelong friend of the Nashes and had offered to do his planning work at the main house to keep the Nash matriarch company. Caleb had no illusions that Declan hadn't helped with the arrangement. The department was being stretched thin at the moment. They needed to grab peace of mind where they could.

Desmond's house was a two-story farm house, with white shiplap, exposed wood and a tin roof that made the rain sound like a song that put Caleb to sleep every single time. It was a nice, solid house, but it wasn't Caleb's no matter how much he tried to ignore the reason he was there in the first place.

He bounded up the stairs and into the guest bedroom across from Madi's room. He'd gone through the ashes of his home, looking to salvage what was left. All that could be saved fit into a plastic container his mother had gotten from Walmart. It was shut and pushed into the corner. Caleb could still smell the smoke.

He fell down onto the edge of the bed. He needed to figure out who the arsonist was and fast. Yet the more he sat there, Caleb realized, the more his thoughts pulled away

from him. As the afternoon darkened into night and every phone call and theory hit wall after wall, he finally looked at the only piece of his home that had escaped the fire and smoke unscathed. Thanks to Nina.

Caleb gently picked the framed picture up.

It had been a warm and happy spring. Dorothy and Michael Nash had been happy. So had their children. None of them had had any idea in the world what was going to happen next. The weight of worry, the burden of tragedy. The decline of a detective who couldn't solve the case that nearly cost him his family. No. Not yet. Instead they were frozen forever in a pure moment of happiness.

And Nina Drake had saved that just for him.

THE STEW WAS delicious and the night was beautiful. Nina enjoyed both alone. The cowboy detective apologized when he came in late to the Retreat before answering one of several calls that kept him at a distance. It bothered her, if Nina was being honest. She was starting to find that wanting to be alone wasn't as easy as she'd been pretending it was.

Though maybe that had more to do with the man with steel-blue eyes and an arresting jawline. Not to mention a quiet sweetness she hadn't expected after their first awkward meeting. She suspected that finding the person who had destroyed his home wasn't an act of vengeance but of concern. Concern for his family, the ranch that served as their livelihood, the town that was their community and her. Whether that was wishful thinking or not, Nina couldn't shake the feeling that something was changing between them.

She had meant what she'd said in the truck. When he had revealed how his father had passed away, she had seen the stress and pain pulling him down. Nina was also

presumptuous in thinking she saw a struggle there too. A hesitation. The case that Caleb's father had tried to solve had to have been about the triplets' abduction.

Molly had said the man behind it was never caught. She could imagine how that might tear apart not only a detective, but a father, as well.

The realization that the abduction had eventually cost Caleb his father too had pulled Nina's personal experience with her mother's death to the forefront.

The car accident hadn't been an accident, yet she kept that detail to herself.

And she made sure to extend the same courtesy to the man who had been vigilant about keeping her safe.

Nina knew it was easier to keep quiet than relive your worst experience over again. She owed him that.

So, she waved goodnight to the detective and put all thoughts of him out of her mind as she showered and got ready for bed. She finally called her father, Trevor, and they spent almost an hour talking about his newest adventure with his wife, Denise. They'd been married for a little under a year but had been dating for three. Nina had grown to love Denise. It had been easy after seeing how happy she'd made her father. Now they were spending time in Montana with her son and his family. Apparently Nina's dad had finally found the secret to fishing that had long escaped him on the Florida coast.

"And how are you, *mija*?" he asked, somehow sounding just as her mom had when she'd used the term of endearment. "How's the ranch? Make any friends yet?"

"I really like it here, actually," she answered honestly. "Molly, the Retreat manager, acts like we've known each other for years. Her husband is nice, too. I also finally met two of the Nash sons." Nina was glad she didn't have to hide the blush that heated her cheeks.

"Oh, really? What are they like?"

"Well, one is the sheriff and the other is a detective, so I feel like you'd really approve of that."

Her dad let out a whooping laugh. Denise must have asked what he was on about.

"My baby girl is living on a ranch with the top dogs in law enforcement," he exclaimed. "Talk about a way to make me worry less."

Nina chuckled and they spent the rest of the conversation talking about his time in Montana. Guilt started to spread through her as the minutes went on. She hadn't told her father about Daniel Covington and the email and she definitely hadn't told him about the fire. She should have told him but Nina knew she wouldn't. Not until the perpetrator was caught. Not until she could ease his mind seconds after she caused it to worry.

They ended their conversation with *I love yous* and *goodnights* before Nina finally crawled into bed.

A breeze blew in from the crack left open in the window above her. The ranch at night was starting to become one of her favorite collections of sounds. Sometimes she could hear the horses, other times she heard owls. Always she heard insects. Their chirps reminded her of home. It usually carried her to sleep.

Tonight?

Thinking of home only made her think of her father and the guilt in her stomach. Which led her to her mother and, as it always went, eventually to the trial. Another detail she'd kept to herself. Nina rolled over. She threw the covers over her head, trying to put distance between memories and the present.

But there she was at the trial. Afraid, sad and wishing more than anything she could become invisible. The press

had made that almost impossible. She'd been on the front page of the local newspaper almost every day.

Nina tossed the covers off and sat up, mind racing. "They're all connected!"

Chapter Nine

A string of surprises had dictated the last week of Caleb's life. He knew those surprises would continue to change his life from normal to a life he hadn't plan. Then, eventually, he'd reach a new normal. It was just how life went.

If it was derailed you could either adapt or crash with it.

That simple.

At least, that's what Caleb was trying to convince himself of as he settled onto the couch that night in the lobby. When that pep talk didn't work, he went to the makeshift break room in the office portion of the house. The bottle of water he chugged was refreshing. The sound of a door in the main area swinging open and footsteps rushing in was not.

Caleb balled his fists and hurried to meet whoever was flying through the next room. He couldn't tell which door they'd come in through, whether it was the front door or the one that led to Nina's apartment. His gun and badge were next to the couch, along with his shirt and pants. If it wasn't Nina then Caleb had one heck of a fight coming.

Luckily it wasn't their arsonist deciding to ambush the Retreat. Nina held up her hands in surrender as they met next to the couch. "Whoa there, cowboy!"

Nina's eyes were wide. She looked him up and down before a red tint came across her face. Caleb might have

been only in his boxers but it was Nina who was the distracting one.

Her hair was down and loose, spilling over her shoulders and partially covering her breasts. Caleb was used to seeing her in blouses and jeans—and had no complaints when she wore either—but now she was wearing anything but. Instead, a soft pink silk camisole stole the show, matching a shiny pair of sleep shorts that stopped midthigh. Both gave Caleb a vastly uninhibited view of her smooth, tan skin. It was an arresting image. One he hadn't expected to see. Not even the thin robe that was loosely held around her shoulders could hide the truth.

Nina wasn't just beautiful, she was sexy as hell, too.

Just as her gaze had swept over his body, she took a moment to look down at herself. Her face went from a light red to blazing cherry.

"Oh, my gosh, sorry!" she squeaked out, grabbing the robe and pulling it tight to cover herself. "I—uh—I might have been a little too excited and forgotten I was in my pjs."

"We can say you're just trying to match me."

Caleb chuckled and motioned to his bare chest. Nina's eyes once again traveled down his body before snapping back up. Caleb couldn't help but grin. He moved to the couch and grabbed his jeans. Nina hugged the robe around her and looked anywhere but at him.

"So, what's going on?" he asked, trying to land on the reason why she was excited. It felt like it had been a long while since they'd had a reason to be excited. Though, with what Nina had beneath that robe, Caleb could feel the start of some other kind of excitement.

"I found a connection," Nina exclaimed, demeanor changing so swiftly any lustful thoughts about the woman went to the back burner. "Well, at least I think." She hurried closer. Her dark eyes were ablaze with enthusiasm.

"You mean the fires?"

A small dose of adrenaline shot through him as she nodded emphatically.

"Three sites for the fires we visited today sounded familiar, but I couldn't figure out why. That's when I realized I'd seen them...on the front page of the local newspaper."

Caleb felt his brows knit together as he tried to recall any of the stories. While he was tapped into the community much more than most because of the ranch and his job, he'd never been that much of a reader when it came to their newspaper. It was a small press that had been owned and operated by the wealthy, and mostly absent, Collins family. The patriarch, Arlo, owned several more papers across the south. His setting up a press in small-town Overlook had been an interesting business choice that always perplexed Caleb's father. Either way, Caleb hadn't actively read a story from its pages since the top story was Declan Nash being reelected for sheriff.

"Which three?" he asked, giving up on trying to recall anything of note. Nina held up three fingers.

"The woman who runs the nonprofit animal shelter. There was a spotlight on her because she was throwing a fundraiser."

"Gloria," he supplied. "I remember that fundraiser. She threw that before she opened her no-kill shelter." She nodded and ticked one finger off.

"The Overlook Pass was in one issue I found. The mayor was there for some reason. I can't remember what but I do remember the picture. It took up almost everything above the fold."

Caleb couldn't recall that article. Nina ticked off another finger.

"And most recently, an article ran about a couple trying to bring more nightlife activities for the younger residents

to Overlook." She waved him along with her to the office. She went to the recycling trashcan in the corner and rummaged through the papers and empty water bottles until she found what she was looking for. She held the newspaper up, its top story and accompanying picture clear.

"Say hello to Mr. and Mrs. Gentry." Caleb took the paper from her. Nina continued with her spiel. "When I took this job I wanted to learn as much as I could about what goes on around here while *also* looking for opportunities for events and good press. I've only done a cursory look over issues from the last few years and definitely haven't read them all but..." She shrugged. "I know that's a thin connection, especially for a small town but I thought it might at least be interesting. Three of five places that have experienced fires in the last five years have been showcased as top headline stories in the newspaper. Maybe that's something that can lead somewhere else. Or am I just reaching?"

A spike of adrenaline followed closely on the heels of a memory. Caleb tightened his grip on the paper, staring down at a smiling Kelso and Maria Gentry.

"Four," he answered.

Nina took a step closer. She smelled like flowers. Lavender? Either way it was noteworthy.

"Four?" she repeated. "What? Four places?"

He met her dark gaze. Her eyes really did look like dark honey in the right light.

"The restaurant. Its moving onto the main strip was a big deal. It was an above-the-fold story. I remember Mom reading it."

"So, four out of the five."

"Five out of six, actually," he corrected, anger and excitement starting to mix together. "I didn't have a huge

picture or anything, but a case I closed before you got here made it into the paper. Above the fold."

Caleb gave her the paper back and ran a hand over his chin in thought. On one hand, like she said, Overlook was a small town. The weekly newspaper had done stories on almost every aspect of town since it was first published when Caleb was a kid. It could have been a coincidence, plain and simple.

But what if it wasn't?

"It's more than we've had to go on so far, but we definitely need more information," he decided.

Nina went to the computer and turned it on. She must have been too caught up to be self-conscious about her outfit anymore. Her robe opened but she didn't bother to close it. Her smooth, tan skin and curves in all the right places created a ripple effect that reached out to an urge he was having a hard time denying.

Caleb cleared his throat.

There was no time for any of that. If there had been one clear thing about the last week for him, it was that Nina Drake was a woman who stayed behind walls.

And, despite his small attempts to open up to her, Caleb wasn't on the same side.

THE *OVERLOOK* EXPLORER'S website only kept current editions posted and, of those, you had to pay a fee to read more than two stories. Various other internet and social media searches were no help, either. The only story they could track down that coincided with the fires was a blog post written on Gloria's animal shelter blog. It referenced the newspaper article, along with a small, slightly pixelated picture of Gloria and the same two dogs she would later risk her life to save.

When midnight rolled around, Nina and Caleb had nothing more than potentially, well, nothing.

"I guess it's a little too late to go to the *Overlook Explorer* office, huh?" she asked when they'd officially given up on searching. She rolled her shoulders back, trying to free the kink in them. Caleb, in a chair much too low for him, cracked his neck and sighed.

"Usually I'd consider it but I know Lydia, the current editor, takes her sleep seriously. She'd tan my hide *and* probably not help out of spite until the morning anyways. Plus, she'd ask a million questions about why it's so urgent. I don't want any hunch we have on an open investigation to be front page news." He scrubbed a hand down his face. "We'll have to wait until the morning. There's not much we can do right now."

Nina tried to hide her disappointment. Morning seemed like such a long time away. She was too high-strung now to go back to sleep.

Plus, if she was being honest with herself, she enjoyed his company and it was easier to be together with something else to focus on than the things she was still keeping from him about her past.

For a moment Nina worried that that thought somehow showed on her face.

Caleb gave her a quizzical look.

"*Or* we can break the rules and get some answers before then." A wry grin spread across his lips. "That is, if you don't mind slightly breaking and entering. Twice."

A bubble of excitement had already expanded within her. Before Nina had met Caleb she would have asked a lot of questions and, most likely, turned the weird proposition down. Yet, Nina surprised herself by nodding.

"I'm in."

THE OVERLOOK LIBRARY was a stone's throw away from Town Hall. Nina had visited neither. Now she was wearing her dark exercise wear and sneaking through the library's shadows, looking between both buildings with an almost giddy kind of nervous. Her partner in crime was back in his day clothes minus his button-up. His simple black shirt and dark jeans helped him blend in.

Not to mention they looked good as all get-out on him.

Caleb stopped at a side door, the detective's badge on his belt glinting in the flashlight's beam as he swept it up to the lock. He slid the key in and turned. It was like the movement was attached to Nina's stomach. She had to suppress a nervous giggle.

The door opened to a series of beeps. Caleb was inside and running toward the front where the key panel was. Thankfully, he'd already warned her of the alarm. Still, Nina stood just inside of the door in the darkness, a knot of concern. Caleb had the badge, not her.

It took what felt like an impossibly long minute before the beeping cut off. A flashlight beam found its way back to her before the glow showed a purely mischievous face in the tight space.

"I feel like I'm in high school again," Caleb chuckled. He locked the door behind her and then led the way toward the archives.

"You've done this before?"

Even though she couldn't see his face, Nina heard the smile in his voice.

"Since Overlook isn't the most exciting place for a bunch of teenagers, we had to find ways to *make* it exciting. Which includes the one day of the year when the high school seniors try to take the riskiest picture they can to impress their peers."

They turned down a hallway and into the main room. The smell of old and new books filled Nina's senses. She couldn't help but inhale deeply before asking for an explanation.

"Basically, all the seniors trespass on local businesses and buildings and take pictures of themselves once inside," he continued. "The pictures of everyone who didn't get caught are judged at the big end-of-the-year graduation party. There's even a king and queen title if you win." He shrugged. "Sure, it's not the smartest thing to do, and definitely illegal, but it's one of those quirky town traditions. Honestly, I don't think we could stop it if we wanted. Mostly because all the adults *now* definitely did it *then*. It also helps that, so far, no one has gotten hurt or done anything royally stupid." Caleb stopped walking. Nina ran into his back. It surprised a laugh out of her.

"Sorry," he said through his own laughter. "I'm trying to remember which switches turn on the lights in the back room and which turn on the lights in the main room."

Nina gave him some space.

"So you broke in here to take your rebellious senior picture then, I'm guessing?"

"Not only did I sneak myself in here, I decorated this entire place and brought in Missy Calder for a date."

Caleb decided on a switch to flip. Luckily it was the right one. A small hallway next to them led into a room now filled with light. He turned and winked.

"I even hired a violinist from the college the city over to come in. I included her in the picture. Needless to say, you're looking at one of the kings."

Nina smirked.

"And here I thought I was special."

Caleb let out a booming laugh and together they went to the back room. It was a small space meant to do research

or study. Two tables sat along one wall with a communal computer between them while most of the room was filled with wooden cabinets, each drawer labeled with a date.

"Since Overlook is as small as it is, if we were going for much older issues we would have to worry about microfilm," Caleb said, sliding right into work mode. "But since we're working within the last five years…"

He scanned the dates on the cabinets closest to the tables until he found the ones he wanted. Carefully he opened the first one and pulled a newspaper out. Nina was gentle, too, as she took it.

A stern-looking Caleb wearing a suit and shaking the hand of the mayor stared up at her.

"The above the fold article of the most recent fire victim. Me." He spelled the information out for her. "Now let's see if we can't find the others, arson or not. Might as well cover all of our bases."

Nina started to follow him but he stopped again. This time she was able to keep from running into him. Still that didn't keep him from turning and giving her another wink.

"And just to set the record straight, I *do* think you're pretty damn special, Miss Drake."

Heat exploded in Nina's cheeks. Luckily she didn't have to worry about hiding the blush. Caleb was already back to work, moving through the cabinets with purpose.

For the first time since she'd met the man Nina felt a sudden rush of worry. Once the arsonist was caught and everything calmed down, would Caleb still be around if he didn't have to be?

And, more importantly, did she want him to be?

Chapter Ten

Caleb spent the next half hour hunting down the issues featuring the Gentrys, Overlook Pass, Gloria and her fundraiser, the restaurant and any mention of Angelica De-Marko, the first fire. After he found each, Nina combed through the articles looking for similarities or anything that could link them.

She was coming up short and said as much.

"I'm not seeing any connection other than they've all been featured as headline news," she said, defeated. A slightly grainy picture of Main Street and the then-new restaurant sat beneath her hand. Caleb's head was bent over a paper in front of one of the cabinets. Nina traced his body with her eyes, appreciating the sight, before her senses came back to her. A sigh dragged her shoulders down, like she was melting into the chair. "I might have been grasping at straws a little too enthusiastically."

"You won't find me upset that we came here. That we tried." Caleb brought his paper to the table and sat down, still looking at the print. Stubble was growing along his jaw. Nina felt the urge to touch it but batted that down. "Part of my job is following leads, no matter how big or small. Plus, there's still some facts that I'm not ready to rule out as pure coincidence just yet." He slid the paper over. The top story featured a picture of a woman and

boy facing a house in flames while firefighters worked around them. "Here's the story about Angelica DeMarko's house fire."

He reached over and tapped the edition number and date on the masthead.

"This story obviously ran after the fire," he continued. "But the other stories ran one week before each fire."

Nina felt her eyes widen. To prove his point Caleb fanned out each newspaper until they were side by side. Then he handed her a slightly crumpled piece of paper she hadn't realized he'd been holding. It was a list of the addresses of the fires and their dates.

"The restaurant is a top story," Nina reiterated. Caleb touched the coinciding newspaper and its date. "A week later the fire happens." He moved to the next paper while she read the date on the list in her hand. "Gloria graces the above the fold—"

"She nearly dies saving her dogs a week later."

"And then the Gentrys talk about reviving the Overlook nightlife—"

Caleb slid his finger to the date on the paper and finished her thought.

"And a week later lose half of their house."

"What about Overlook Pass?" she asked. "No one knows for sure when that happened, right?"

"True, but if this pattern *is* a pattern, it more than could have held. That means it would have burned down a week before you got into town. Almost a month ago. It's plausible that no one would make the trip out there in the time between, especially given the time of year."

Nina looked at the date on the article about Caleb.

"Your story for closing the Keaton case ran a week before the fire at your house," she said, simply. He nodded.

"If you're grasping, then so am I."

Nina chewed on her lips as she looked over each newspaper again. Could there really be something there? Or was it a series of small-town coincidences parading as a hopeful lead?

"They're all written by Delores Dearborn," she said after a moment. "I can't imagine there's that many staff writers for the local paper so that might not mean much," she admitted.

Caleb grinned.

"We won't know until we ask her."

THE NASH FAMILY RANCH buzzed with a restless, quiet energy the next morning. A week's worth of standing guard at their respective posts without any sign of the arsonist being caught was grating on already grated nerves. Molly came in early complaining about a fight she'd had with Clive over "something silly" while Roberto had shown up just long enough to grumble at Nina about the kitchen. She hadn't used his kitchen at the Retreat, and she told him so, but there was no budging his mood.

Then, right before Caleb took off to his brother's house, the eldest one came in hot. Fear gripped Nina, worried there had been another fire, but Declan was venting about lawyers and criminals. After that Caleb and he walked off, surveying the cabins as they spoke. Nina assumed Caleb was telling him about their flimsy, maybe-there lead. Both men stopped near the last cabin, heads bent in concentration.

She couldn't help but feel a bit guilty at how tired Caleb looked.

When they'd gotten back from the library it had been three in the morning. She'd had trouble falling asleep and she'd have bet Caleb had barely scratched the surface himself.

Nina was giving the two privacy by returning to her notebook when the sound of tires made her turn. Dorothy Nash jumped out of her car and greeted Nina with a wide, genuine smile.

"Beautiful day, isn't it?" she sang as she made her way over.

"It sure beats the rain."

Nina could have been working inside but the sunlight had been calling her name. She'd even traded in her blouse and jeans for a breezy dress. An outfit choice that made her a little self-conscious now that she seemed to have lost track of her sandals.

"You got that right, honey!" Smoothing the gray braid hanging over her shoulder, Dorothy stopped next to Nina. "A few years back we had nearly two weeks straight of rain. I'm talking torrential, too. It washed out roads, trees were uprooted and everything was just so dreary. It also put everyone in a mood. Irritable and grumpy. A lot of little fights that were as draining as the dreary skies. When the sun finally came back out for more than a day it was like the spell was broken. Now I can't help but appreciate every single moment it's out."

She sighed and glanced toward her sons. Declan answered his phone. Caleb was looking at them. On reflex, Nina smiled.

"But I'm not here to just talk about the weather," Dorothy continued. The lines at either side of her eyes deepened as her own smile grew. "You know, I was sitting out on my porch, too, this morning, enjoying the view, when I realized we never did throw you a welcome party, now, did we?"

Nina was surprised at that.

"A welcome party?" she repeated. "No, but that's defi-

nitely not necessary, especially with everything going on right now."

Dorothy waved her off.

"For every employee who has worked on this ranch, the Nashes have made it a point to throw a little get-to-gether to celebrate." Nina heard "Nashes" but assumed that meant Dorothy was the mastermind. "Nothing too big or fancy. Just some food, dancing and general merri-ment out at the barn."

"The barn?"

"Molly told me about your idea to turn it into a just-in-case attraction if we ever get swamped by rain. I thought we could decorate it a little for the party while also getting an idea about how we could really tie it in to the Retreat."

Talking to Molly about the barn felt like ages ago to Nina. Since Caleb's house fire happened so soon after their original conversation on the topic, neither woman had revisited it.

"I would love to look at it with you but I'm just not sure a party for me is what anyone needs."

"No one ever *needs* a party, honey," Dorothy laughed. "That doesn't mean we shouldn't have one."

Nina wanted to continue to argue her point—How could they celebrate *her* when one of their own just lost every-thing?—but Caleb and Declan had made their way over and cut the conversation off.

"Hey, Ma, did you need something?" Caleb asked, his tone softening despite the hardened expression that was reflected on Declan's face. Something had happened. Both men were tense, even more than they had been when De-clan first arrived.

"I came by to tell you all about the little party we're throwing out at the barn tonight." Dorothy's eyes narrowed as they swept across her boys. Her eyebrow raised but she

kept on. "I was also going to see if Nina would accompany me to town to get some supplies."

"You want to have a party," Declan said, deadpan. "Right now?" He looked like he was going to say more but Caleb touched his shoulder. His smile seemed forced but not unpleasant.

"That sounds like fun, Ma," he said. "Just let us know what time to be there and we will. Right now, though, we have to leave."

Nina felt a pang of disappointment. Caleb had been waiting to call the *Overlook Explorer*'s editor so they could all meet up later that day to talk about the articles and Delores Dearborn. He'd included Nina in that plan just as he had said they both needed to follow the lead from the night before.

But just as quickly as she'd felt disappointment, Nina felt silly.

She wasn't a detective, Caleb was. It was one thing to have her along to look for information when no one else was around. Why would he need or want her when he was actually on the clock?

"Is everything okay?"

Dorothy looked between her sons.

Declan tensed even more.

"Yeah, everything is fine," Caleb answered. "We just need to get rolling." He bent over and laid a kiss on his mother's cheek before pausing in front of Nina. "I'll call you later."

They each left in their own truck, kicking up dirt as they hauled toward the main road. For a moment Nina and Dorothy didn't say anything; they just gazed after the two cowboy lawmen.

The stress both men shouldered was only growing.

It was a feeling that pulled at Nina's gut and pressed

worry into her chest. One look at Dorothy and she knew the older woman felt it, too.

"The party sounds like it could be fun," Nina found herself saying. "I'm ready to leave when you are."

Dorothy smiled again. This time it didn't reach her eyes.

DELORES DEARBORN LIVED in one of two apartment complexes within the town limits. It was a nice, clean place with good landscaping and enough parking that Caleb cut his engine no more than a few feet from her front door. Declan had gone to the department to deal with some sheriff-related issue he'd only mumbled about before getting into his truck and leaving the ranch. Caleb was solely focused on Delores at the moment. The idea that she was a link to the fires was probably nothing more than a small-town reporter covering what she was told, bound to write several headline stories over her career.

It could mean nothing.

Caleb was ready to find out.

He knocked, and a young woman with blond curls and a pleasant smile answered the door. Her eyes went to his badge first. They widened when she recognized him. He'd almost forgotten she'd been the one who had interviewed him for the article that ran about the end of the Keaton case.

"Sorry to bother you on a Saturday morning," he said, moving past pleasantries. "Do you mind if I ask you a few questions? It could help with a case I'm working on and I'm kind of on a tight timeline here."

"Not at all." Delores beamed, waving him inside. "Please excuse the mess. I had a late night working on a story." She cleared two empty coffee mugs off the small dining room table and motioned to one of the chairs. "Would you like some coffee? I can make a pot really quickly."

Caleb waved her off.

"No, but thank you. I've already had more than a few cups this morning."

Delores perched on the edge of her seat and slid into a familiar look. Eyes sharp, brows furrowed, jaw hard. She had gone from a slightly flustered, tired woman to a reporter paying rapt attention.

"Alright. So, what can I help you with, Detective?"

"How long have you been writing for the *Overlook Explorer*?"

She thought about it for a moment.

"Almost six years. Though I moved back home to Alabama for a year during that time. I came back eight months or so ago." Caleb made a mental note of that. He kept his detective's pad in the car. If there was one thing he'd learned over his career it was how to keep reporters friendly. In his experience they weren't fans of role reversal, just like he wasn't a fan of being questioned as a detective.

"In that time how many stories do you think you've covered for the paper?"

"Oh, wow," she said around a laugh. "A lot. Um, let's see. The first year or so I actually did more copyediting than writing but since then I've written in almost every edition. Minus the year I was gone. So, once a week for around five years. I'll let you do the math on that one."

Caleb didn't have to do it. No matter what the math added up to, it still showed the same conclusion. She had written a lot of articles because she was one of the few staff writers who worked at the paper. It had to be a coincidence. Still, Caleb wanted to finish asking his questions.

"How many times would you say that your stories have been features on the front page, above the fold?"

Delores had to think about that one too. Her eyes unfocused as she tried to remember.

"Since I'm not a senior staffer and also still do split my time between writing and copyediting, I typically don't cover the stories that land there but I've had maybe about twenty or so while at the *Explorer*. More if you count beneath the fold."

Caleb could see the curiosity in her pushing to the forefront. Soon she'd be the one asking questions so he hurried to his next point.

"I'm going to list out six of your stories that made it above the fold and then ask you a few questions about those, then I'll explain. That sound fair?"

Delores nodded. As far as Caleb could tell, no suspicion had crossed the woman's features. She was no more guarded or worried than he was. It was a breath of fresh air compared to when he had to question obviously guilty parties as a part of his job. There was just something to be said about not worrying that the person you were talking to was trying to figure out if they should fight or flee.

Caleb listed her articles about the fire at Angelica DeMarko's house, the new restaurant opening on Main Street, Gloria's fundraiser, the Overlook Pass, the Gentrys trying to revitalize Overlook's nightlife and the article about his closing the Keaton case. Again, Delores hung on his every word, brows pulled together in thought.

"Okay. I remember all of those," she said after a moment. "Why do you bring them up?"

"Is there anything about those stories that seemed weird? Something that maybe stood out to you or maybe connected them all?"

Delores looked down at her hands folded on the table's top. Caleb gave her time to think it through. If she didn't

flag anything then he was going to count this as a dead end. Then he'd go back to the drawing board and hope the arsonist didn't strike again before he found a different trail.

"I'm sorry," Delores finally answered. "I can't think of anything that really jumps out at me other than those were the last six articles I wrote."

"What do you mean? The last six that made it above the fold or in general?"

"In general." She held up her index finger and went into the next room. She came back a minute later with what looked like a planner. "Let me make sure." Caleb saw every day was filled with writing as she flipped through the previous months. She stopped at one in particular and then turned the book so he could see it easier. "The story about Gloria's fundraiser for strays was my last story in the paper before I went to Alabama. Before that, the fire and the restaurant." She flipped forward and stopped again. "And this is when I came back. Marla went on maternity leave so I took over the bulk of copyediting with some website work thrown in. That's why I've only written three articles since I've been back. It just so happened to be three that landed the front page."

Caleb chewed that over for a moment. He wondered if his father would have thought that was enough to be a connection. And *that* caught Caleb by surprise. It had been a long while since he'd tried to puzzle out what his father would have said about a case.

"What's special about these last few stories?" Delores asked. Caleb decided to answer truthfully. Thinking of his father, no matter how briefly, reminded him of one of his father's rules in law enforcement.

Give the truth to get the truth.

So Caleb told her about the five fires that had each hap-

pened one week after her stories ran on the front page. When he got to his house fire, he even gave her privileged information that fireworks had been the cause.

"All of this is off the record," he pointed out, after her eyes widened when he was done. "This is still an ongoing investigation. I just wanted to see if there might be a connection or if you had any information I'm missing."

Delores's gaze was unfocused again in thought. Caleb pulled out his card. She apologized and stood with him after taking it.

"It's okay," he assured her. "I knew it was a stretch. Just let me know if you think of anything else that might be helpful."

"I will."

Delores walked him back outside but hung in the doorway as he opened his truck door. For a moment it looked like she didn't know what to say. Then she called out to him.

"The fire at your house... Was anyone hurt? I mean, I assume not because you didn't mention it, but I just wanted to be sure."

Caleb meant to smile, to be polite, but he couldn't stomach it. He shook his head.

"All I lost was everything I owned."

Delores didn't respond. Instead she closed her door with a sinking frown.

Caleb's mood had fallen, too. He pulled out of the parking lot and, for a moment, found himself wishing there was a raven-haired woman sitting there with him. Hours later, sitting frustrated at his desk, that feeling surfaced again.

It left just as quickly as before, though not of his volition.

Jazz's ID scrolled across his phone's screen. As soon as he answered she was talking.

"Caleb, something's happened and it's *not* good."

Chapter Eleven

Caleb met Jazz in the hospital's lobby. Declan arrived separately but timed it just right, walking up to them before she could start to talk. She had her detective's badge around her neck and a scowl across her face. There was blood on her blouse. Caleb already knew it wasn't hers but the sight made him angry. Outside of his siblings, Jazz was his best friend.

"How is he?" Declan asked, phone pressed against his ear but attention fully on the detective.

"Tough to look at." She motioned to the blood on herself. "I barely touched him when I was helping the EMTs get him out of his house and still had this happen." She shook her head. "There's a strong chance he won't survive the night. It's a miracle he's even breathing now. My personal and professional opinion? Whoever did that to him didn't intend for him to live. I think they just got spooked by the girlfriend showing up and bolted before the job was done."

"What do we know? Any idea who did this?" Caleb asked. "Did the girlfriend know?"

"No. She came over after her shift started when she found him. She heard a car drive off but was too hysterical to look for it. She said that everyone loves him and can't imagine who would do such a thing but, honestly, I think

that's just shock talking. We had two people in the last week or so press charges against him." Jazz gave Caleb a wary look. He decided to get out in front of the accusation, whether or not she would make it.

"I called Claire on the way over here and, like every Saturday afternoon, she was at the shop. And Nina has been with Mom and Molly all day. There's no way either could have attacked him."

Jazz held up her hands in surrender.

"All I was saying is that Daniel Covington doesn't have this great track record his girlfriend thinks he does. To be honest, I don't even think she knows about the email he sent Nina."

Caleb pushed down his anger. Even if he didn't like Daniel, what he disliked more was the timing of the attack. The creep who had taken Nina's picture at the stream and then taunted her with it was now clinging to life in the hospital. It didn't feel right.

"I need to talk to his girlfriend," Declan declared. "Where is she?"

"Down there and to the left. They're prepping Daniel for surgery, so Brando is waiting in the hallway with her." Jazz pointed behind them to her husband, who sat with a girl Caleb didn't recognize. "He was already here at the hospital visiting his sister, so that was a stroke of good fortune on our part. He had to use his magic soothing voice to calm her down." She stopped Declan before he could leave. "She's not a fan of the cops, which is another reason why I left Brando with her. Tread lightly with this one. I have a feeling she's close to shutting down on helping us soon."

Declan nodded and was off. Jazz redirected to Caleb. She was frowning.

"Daniel may be annoying but we've never had him pop up on our radar like this before," she said. "The last of-

fense that caught our attention was when he taped that freshman boy to that tree when he was seventeen. Now we have a decent amount of creepiness, harassment and trespassing? And then he gets beaten nearly to death in his own home? Why? What do you think we're looking at here? Another coincidence?"

"I've been throwing that word around a lot lately and I don't like it," Caleb admitted. "Do you know if whoever did this broke into Daniel's place or did Daniel let him in?"

"As best as I could tell he was let in. There were no busted windows or locks. Either the door was unlocked or Daniel let them in. I'm about to go back there now and take a better look. We have two deputies sitting on the place so no one disturbs it." Jazz looked at him with a considerable amount of concern. "Daniel camps out in the woods, takes a picture of Nina, breaks into Claire's office, uses her personal computer to send that picture and then gets caught. He gets arrested for breaking into Claire's and then bailed out. Then he gets attacked and almost killed a few days later. And during all of this, someone burns down Overlook Pass, the Gentrys' house and yours." She took a small step closer and lowered her voice. "We went from a relatively sleepy town to whatever *this* is in the stretch of two weeks? Caleb, what's going on?"

Caleb wished he had a concrete answer.

He didn't.

THE NIGHT WAS cool and beautiful.

The town was far enough away that the lights from Main Street didn't reach the ranch. Nina stood in front of the Retreat, staring up and marveling at the stars. They were scattered across the sky like electric sand. Dazzling. Worth more than just a second of her time.

Yet there was somewhere she had to be.

Smoothing down the pale blue dress she'd bought from a boutique that morning, Nina tried to quell the nerves that had taken over since she'd gotten back from the barn. Dorothy, Molly and she had spent the entire day shopping, cleaning and decorating the old red barn a few minutes from where Nina now stood. It was supposed to give them an idea for future ways to entertain Retreat guests but had had a more immediate effect.

Molly's mood had gone from annoyed to cheerful.

The weight pulling down Dorothy's shoulders, despite her winning smile, had turned into a fierce determination.

And Nina? Well, she'd forgotten for a while that her plan to stay beneath the radar and out of trouble had failed. That the only chance she had at a new life was hanging on a Retreat that may or may not ever open. That, even though she was two states away from Florida and the tragedy of her mother's untimely death, smoke and fire had found their way back to her.

Putting together the party had lifted all of their spirits.

Nina inhaled the cool night air before releasing one long, body-dragging exhale. The tension in her shoulders lessened. Her weight shifted the heels of her sandals into the dirt. Somewhere in the distance the melody of insects started up, much closer was the sound of a man clearing his throat.

Her cheeks flushed with heat as she turned. Caleb was wearing what she had come to think of as his trademark grin.

"I didn't mean to interrupt," he said. "But if I didn't, my growling stomach would have."

Nina tried not to look the man up and down—*really* tried—but with the soft glow of the office's porch light behind him, she couldn't help but take him in. All the pieces of his work and day-to-day attire were there. His classic

button-up shirt, crisp and fitted, his blue jeans, dark, fit him in all the right places and his boots made up the ensemble she was used to seeing.

Yet it was like they had been repurposed somehow. His shirtsleeves were rolled up and the neck of his shirt was unbuttoned to just beneath his collarbone, showing off some of his bare chest. It was still tucked into his jeans and there was a casual swagger to the way they hung on his hips. Like the artist Michelangelo had painted them on the cowboy.

Or maybe Nina was just full of it.

She'd already noticed, several times in fact, that Caleb always looked good. Smile or not, she couldn't deny he stirred something in her just by being near.

Her eyes slid down and then up his body before landing on that grin. From there they traveled to those baby blues. There she stayed.

"Did you walk here?" she asked, trying to still the nerves that had just sprung alive in her stomach. Her car was the only one in the parking area that she could see.

Caleb nodded.

"After everything that's happened, I was itching for a nice night." His grin grew. "And just like that, I got one. I thought I'd take advantage of it." He sidled up beside her and held out his elbow. "How do you feel about taking a stroll to a barn that Desmond once told me was haunted by the ghost of the Roaming Mountain Lady?"

Nina surprised herself by hooking her arm through his and laughed.

"The Roaming Mountain Lady?"

"A faceless woman with bangles that clatter up and down her arms, and several skirts and scarves made for suffocating little kids who have the deep misfortune of hearing her moaning in the rafters." Caleb laughed at Ni-

na's questioning look. "Desmond had a flair for the dramatic when we were younger. I think that's why he's so good at his job as a businessman. He's good at helping people see his vision and ideas. He's always been able to spin a story, truth or otherwise, in a pinch. Still, I'm not above admitting that, to this day, the barn gives me the heebie-jeebies. You might have to save my life again if she makes an appearance. I don't think my gun would work on a ghost."

Nina patted his forearm with her free hand.

"I'll do my best, detective. I won't let the mountain lady get you."

They followed the dirt path that led through the Retreat before branching off and cutting through a stretch of nothing but grass. Nina told him about their tentative plans to turn the barn into an indoor–outdoor camping ground in bad weather plus a few other ideas the three women had thrown together as they decorated. The soft sound of music in the distance became louder, pulling them in. Caleb thought their ideas were great but the closer they came to the music and the barn, the more his steps slowed. Nina glanced over and saw his eyes weren't entirely focused on the world in front of him.

"Is everything okay?" she asked timidly. Since he hadn't come right out and told her any news about the arsonist, Nina assumed he'd found nothing but dead ends. She'd decided not to push it, waiting for him to open up instead, something of a pattern when it came to how she interacted with the man. However, this time, her patience ended. Caleb's thoughts were being drowned by something. "Did you get a chance to talk to Delores today?"

"Yeah, I did, but it wasn't as enlightening as we'd hoped." He recapped what he'd learned, ending with a sigh. "I even talked to Arlo, the owner of the paper, on the

phone today and poked around a bit. He confirmed what Delores said and even gave her alibis for three of the fires due to work. I wasn't accusing her of anything but Arlo is a good guy and wanted to make sure we knew she was on the up-and-up. I also think he wants her to marry his son, but *that* is just a piece of gossip I heard from Mom."

Nina smiled into the night. The way Caleb talked about his mother, no matter how small the detail, rang clearly with love. It was touching, even if the end of their lead was not.

"So, back to the drawing board, then?"

Caleb slowed to a stop. The back of the barn was visible in the distance. The outdoor lights made the once derelict building glow with joy. Yet Caleb had turned his entire focus on her.

"Nina, there's something I need to tell you." He angled his head down to look into her eyes. She kept her arm around his, breath catching as their innocent contact suddenly felt charged. Caleb wasn't just close, he was holding her.

"Yes?" Even her voice was affected by the change in mood. The one syllable came out as little more than a whisper.

Baby blues swept across her face, two pools of wonder visible in the moonlight. They were just as dazzling as the stars.

Caleb opened his mouth. Then closed it. His lips pulled up into a barely there smile. Nina had a sneaking suspicion he had decided against saying something to her. Something important. When he did speak there was a lightness to it.

"I'd like to have a dance with you tonight, if you don't mind. I'm not going to win any contest with my moves or anything, but I don't have two left feet either. Could be fun?"

The charge she'd sensed heated at the question. Nina felt the rising temperature in her cheeks. It was unexpected.

It was exciting.

"I guess it could be," she answered with a matching smile. "Though you can't get mad if I step on your feet. I haven't danced with anyone since my junior prom." Just like that, a coldness expanded in Nina's stomach.

It was the truth, told in a bout of humor, but no sooner had she said it than another truth replaced it.

Her life in Florida, the one filled with heartache that still managed to touch her years later, was one she didn't want anymore. She'd left it and its memories behind to start over. To live every second on her own terms, not anyone else's.

As Nina swam in the steel-blue waters looking down at her, she knew that to live the life she wanted was to live a life she could control.

However, if there was one thing she was starting to realize, it was that around Caleb, that's exactly what she lacked.

Chapter Twelve

There were no scary ladies, ghost or otherwise, lurking around the barn. Instead, what had once been an eyesore of a structure was now a thing of beauty, filled with people who were trying to forget their stressful week and enjoy one another. Music played through speakers set up in the corners. Wooden tables that had been in the main house's storage had been cleaned and covered in delicious dishes.

Roberto wasn't the only one who had contributed, either. Caleb spotted his mother's homemade apple pie, Clive's homemade-but-legal moonshine and Brando had a good portion of the table's real estate sectioned off for his famous buffalo and cheese dip. Walking in and being hit by the wall of great and familiar smells surprised a feeling of comfort out of Caleb. Most of the employees of the ranch, plus Jazz and her husband, had come at his mother's behest. Like Caleb, they marveled at the world she had set out to create.

"Yeah, it looks nice and smells good but we shouldn't be letting our guard down." Declan came up to Caleb's side with a beer in his hand and a scowl on his face. Caleb chuckled.

"For not having a triplet link with me you sure have a weird way of knowing what I'm thinking," he said. "Sometimes you give even Madi and Des a run for their money."

Declan rolled his eyes.

"I don't need your voodoo triplet telepathy to know what you're thinking, kiddo." He pointed to the table on the other side of the makeshift dance floor. "You keep looking at that table." He pointed up. "The lights and—" He lowered his hand but his eyes skipped to the sitting area that had been staged like a campsite at the front half to the barn. Nina was perched on a tree stump and in the middle of a conversation with Jazz and Molly. "Right at her." Caleb averted his eyes and took a pull from his beer. Declan snorted. "Not hard to put together what you're thinking about."

"Can you blame me?" Caleb asked, lowering his voice so Brando and Jensen, one of the ranch hands who helped with the horses, wouldn't overhear them. "The last two weeks have been insane and yet look at this place. Look at everyone, Declan. They're smiling, dancing and eating some damn good food together. It's a good idea for them *and* us to be here."

Declan didn't look convinced. Caleb sighed.

Out in the field he had been about to tell Nina that Daniel Covington was in the hospital, beaten nearly to death. That the department was digging in to try and figure out who had done it and why. That she had been a suspect, just as he had been, though both of them had been cleared. Caleb had wanted to tell her because in the short time she'd been at the ranch and in Overlook her path had been tied to Daniel's and, maybe the most poignant reason, Caleb wanted to be honest with her.

But then he'd looked into her dark eyes and felt something shift. Standing there in a blue dress with her hair free and flowing, Nina had become someone he wanted to protect. In every way. The whole point of the night was to distance themselves from worry and pain. Did he want to burden her with more?

No, he wanted her happiness.

"If you like her so much, just ask her to dance," Declan said after a moment. There was a smile in his voice. "I'm sure she'd say yes. She ran into a burning building after you, for goodness' sake. Awkwardly swaying to the beat while our mother and friends look on should be a piece of cake for you two."

"I already asked her to dance, thank you very much."

Declan quirked up an eyebrow. "And she turned you down?"

"Actually, no." Caleb hesitated, wondering if he should confide in his brother. Then he caved. "She said yes, but right after that it was like she shut down. Like she'd hit some kind of panic button at the bank. You know, the ones that shoot up those metal walls to protect the teller? Her eyes glazed over and the tension in her body made *me* uncomfortable."

"What did she say? Did you ask her about the change?"

Caleb took another drink of his beer. The bottle was cold in his hand. He shook his head.

"She got quiet after. I mean, we kept up a conversation but it was like we were two strangers battling through small talk. It's not the first time she's done it but I didn't want to push the issue."

"It could be all in your head, you know," Declan pointed out. "Or maybe she's just shy."

Caleb had wondered about both options after they'd come into the barn and gone their separate ways. It was like Nina was avoiding him. She still was. He hadn't spoken to her in well over an hour.

"I thought about that but neither sat right with my gut. I think it's something else. Something I keep accidentally triggering." Caleb paused, glancing at his mother at the food table. She was laughing. "Do you remember

how Mom was after what happened *happened*? You know, when we were kids?"

His brother stiffened. "I remember Dad a bit more, to be honest. But I remember she was always smiling to keep our spirits up."

"Even though you could tell she was close to breaking." Caleb hadn't said this to his brother before, not even to the Madi and Des, but now the observation he'd made as a child made him feel it was necessary. "One moment she'd be telling us it would be alright, all smiles and comfort, but then I'd catch her staring off in the distance when she was alone. It was like she'd taken a mask off, the one she wore for her family, and all the fear and worry would be there, in plain sight." He sighed. "That's what happens with Nina but in reverse. Most of the time she's quiet, contemplative, and I swear she does this thing with her eyes that makes me feel like she's a million miles away. But then I'll catch her staring up at the stars or looking at the lights across the rafters, and for a moment she just—" Caleb tried to find the right word but came up short. So he said the first thing that came to mind. "Is."

"She just is," Declan repeated.

Caleb grinned at his brother, letting him know that *he* knew what he was saying sounded crazy.

"I know. I'm starting to sound like Madi when she went through her poetry phase, but I swear Declan, this woman walks like the weight of the world is crushing her with almost every step. And I, well I just want to help." Declan's eyebrow rose again in question. "She *did* save my life, after all," Caleb added. "I just want to repay the favor."

Declan was, and always had been, a straight shooter. He told it like it was, never mind if you were a stranger or family. He just didn't lie and it was as simple as that. It was one of the reasons he'd been elected sheriff in the

first place. It was also one of the reasons Caleb respected him as much as he did. While Madi and even Desmond would dance around a hard truth to try and save his feelings, Declan always gave his opinion with a refreshing kind of brashness.

Now he fingered the label on his bottle before meeting Caleb's stare. When he spoke it was with even yet not totally detached emotion.

"Just because someone saves your life doesn't mean you know them. And just because someone saves you doesn't mean they did it because they know you. The best part of this job is when we see ordinary people doing extraordinary things for strangers and that's what we saw with Nina. Not everyone would have gone into that house after you but she did and you two seem to have formed a quiet kind of partnership since. But, Caleb, what do you know about her? About her past? And, honestly, what does she know about yours? Outside of the Retreat business and the fires, have you ever even told her about what happened at Bluerock Park?" Caleb didn't have to answer. His expression must have given away the fact that he hadn't. Declan put his hand on Caleb's shoulder and gave it an affectionate squeeze. "You can't expect someone else to let down their walls and open up if you're holding out, too."

"Someone needs to make the first move." Caleb spelled it out. Declan nodded.

"That's how I see it, at least."

He patted Caleb's shoulder one more time and excused himself. Caleb finished off his beer and surveyed the group and the party around them. His eyes were drawn to the rafters. Strings of lights cobwebbed between them. Out of all of the decorations, Nina seemed to enjoy those the most. Just as he'd seen her staring at the stars in awe in front of

the Retreat earlier, he'd caught her glancing up on more than one occasion since they'd arrived.

A small smile would brush across her lips and that invisible weight would seem to disappear. If only for a moment.

Now, across the room, that weight was back. Nina might have been smiling and talking to Jazz and Molly but the way she held herself reminded him of someone standing on the outskirts. Close enough that she looked engaged, far enough that she could disappear at any time.

And Caleb didn't want that.

He put his bottle down, straightened his belt and walked across the room with purpose. Nina watched the walk, her eyes looking more golden than dark in the light, and received him with the same polite smile she'd been wearing since they arrived. Caleb wanted to see the real one so badly he decided exactly what he was going to do.

"Sorry to interrupt but I was wondering if you wanted to join me for that not-winning-any-contests bad dancing I offered earlier?" He held out his hand. For the briefest moment he worried she'd turn him down. Instead, she turned that polite smile to Jazz and Molly and excused herself. Then the warmth of her hand was cradled within his. Caleb couldn't help but reflect the feeling as he pulled her along to the middle of the barn and its makeshift dance floor.

"Now, get ready to have your mind blown by how amazingly fifth grade this is about to get."

Nina laughed and it was just as quiet as her smile.

A new song started just as his boots hit the designated dance area. It moved along a slower tempo than the previous song. Which was a relief. Trying to show Nina she could trust him while trying to keep a bump-and-grind rhythm wouldn't have been ideal.

Caleb slid his hands around Nina's waist and matched

the slow pace. She put her hands firmly on his shoulders. There was an undeniable rigidness to them. Her cheeks were tinted red. The thought that he was the reason behind her uneasiness was a new kind of pain in Caleb's chest.

"You know, I have to say, this place looks great," he said to start the conversation. "I was a bit skeptical when Mom told me about fixing it up but, really, I guess it wasn't as bad off as I thought. You did a great job here."

"Thanks," she said, that red tint burning darker. "It was definitely a team effort, though. I've never met someone as driven to throw a party as your mother. I would have given up the moment we ran into this spider in the corner that was as big as my hand." She shuddered. "I voted to leave and never come back but Dorothy rallied on. She is definitely a spirited woman."

Caleb chuckled.

"She definitely is that." They swayed to the beat, holding each other. Caleb traced the woman's face, taking in the freckles along her cheeks as he had the first day he met her. "Mom *is* spirited but that's not the whole reason why she did this. Why she threw this party now, in the middle of everything going on." He took a small breath and then dove in. "You've been in Overlook for about a month?"

She nodded.

"In that time, has anyone told you about what happened to our family? Or, really, what happened to the Nash triplets?"

Nina averted her eyes for a split second. She nodded again.

"I've heard a little about it," she admitted. "I know you three were abducted but later escaped. And the person behind it was never caught."

A slow wave of anger and resentment washed over him.

It always happened when he thought about that day. It probably always would.

"We were eight and being stupid," he said. Even years later he could remember the smells of summer that had clung to them, and the humidity and heat that made them sweat but not enough to deter them from playing outside. He could hear their laughter clear as day, just as he could hear their screams. "Bluerock Park wasn't much to look at back then. No playground equipment or well-kept trails. Just dirt that, if you got lucky, led to a picnic area. Nothing fancy, just some tables and an old rusted grill. But to us? It was anything we wanted it to be." The song grew into a crescendo. They moved along with it. Nina's eyes stayed with his through every movement. "That day we were playing hide-and-seek. I was It so I stayed at the campsite to count while Madi and Desmond hid."

Caleb felt himself draw in. Nina moved her hands around his neck, bringing her closer. He continued. "I'd never heard Madi scream like that before. It was like it came from the trees themselves. It was everywhere. I didn't even know which direction to go in until I saw Desmond running." Caleb hated the next part. Still, he wanted her to know. "The man was waiting for us with a gun already pointed. He told us that we were coming with him and if we didn't that he'd hurt Madi." Nina's eyes widened. She stifled a gasp. A new song poured out of the speakers around the barn. It was slower than the last.

"There was too much distance between us and them, so all Des and I could do was promise we wouldn't do anything. But the man hadn't counted on Madi. See, Dad had been in law enforcement for years, just as his dad had been. He used to tell us that if anyone tried to put us in a car to go somewhere that we were to fight like hell, no matter if they had a gun or weapon, because our chances

for survival were more than cut in half once we got into a vehicle. Madi took that lesson to heart. She punched—and I mean *punched*—this fully grown man in the throat. We hadn't even hit our growth spurts yet and there she was, putting force into his windpipe." Nina shook her head in wonder at the young girl's courage. He couldn't help but share it for a moment before getting back to beginning of his nightmare. "It surprised him enough to stagger but not drop his gun. He used it to hit Madi. It knocked her out and enraged Des and me. We rushed him and, for a little bit, the two of us had the upper hand, but then he shot the gun."

"Oh, God," Nina whispered. He tried to give her a reassuring smile. While it had been terrible, they had survived it. A point that he still made to himself when his thoughts turned back to that day and the two that followed.

"I don't know if he meant to miss or was just a poor shot but the bullet grazed my arm." He tilted his head to his left. The scar was still there on his left biceps. It was a reminder. Not that he needed one. "But, man, it bled. Freaked out Des, too. He jumped on the guy's back and just started whaling on him but, you know, we were eight. The man had height and weight on us. He slung Des off on the ground and then—" Nina's eyes widened. Caleb realized his grip had tightened. She didn't complain. He loosened his hold and took a small breath. "He stomped on Desmond's leg and broke it."

"That's horrible," Nina said. "You were children."

"A fact that didn't stop him from threatening to kill Madi if we didn't follow him. He carried her to the car while I pulled Desmond along with me." He omitted the part where Desmond had cried in anguish at his broken leg but still had refused to stop, knowing it endangered their sister. "Then he got us into the car, blindfolded us, and told us to get down so we wouldn't be seen. Normally we

wouldn't have listened but, Madi was unconscious and Des couldn't walk by himself. I was the only one who could have gotten out and run but I wasn't going to do that. I wasn't going to leave them."

To this day Caleb felt that absolute resolution that had rung in his chest then. If he'd had a chance for a redo he would have made the same choice over and over again.

"When he finally took the blindfolds off we were in a basement. No furniture but three beds. A bathroom. No windows. That was it. We were there for three days total."

Nina shook her head, disgust clearly written on her face.

"But why?" she asked.

It was a simple yet profound question. One that had haunted him and his family for years.

"I don't know. The only time he spoke to us after we got there was to threaten us with harming the others if we disobeyed him. That only happened when he came down with food, trying to make sure we didn't attempt to escape. After Madi regained consciousness he focused on threatening Desmond. He was in so much pain every single second we were in that godawful place. We didn't want to make his pain any worse... But then we realized the risk was the only way we had to save him from that same pain."

Caleb didn't like any of his story, but this was another part that hurt more than the rest. Nina kept rapt attention on him as he hurried through it.

"We pretended Des had stopped breathing," he continued. "Screamed for the man, cried our eyes out, yelled until our voices broke. For a second I think even I forgot that it was an act. Our captor was absolutely fooled. He dropped his guard when he went to check for a pulse. That's when the three of us attacked."

Nina's eyes widened. It was a look that had been reflected back at him when he told the story to his father and

mother after they were rescued. That memory, that feeling of shock and fear and relief at being safe, inspired a truth no one outside the family had been told.

"For all the times I have thought about what happened then, I can't seem to remember how exactly we did it," he said. "We just somehow synced up and became this unstoppable force. Even Desmond with his leg, the three of us overpowered him, managed to buy enough time for us to get to the door, and lock him in. Then we just left. Went into the trees and kept going until a Good Samaritan found us and took us to the department."

"The man was gone when you led law enforcement back?" Nina asked.

He nodded.

"We had been held in an abandoned house just outside of the town limits and deep inside the forest. By the time we could lead them back nothing and no one was there. But that didn't stop everyone from trying to solve the who and why of it all."

He looked around the barn. The music had picked up but he hadn't noticed. They were swaying to their own beat. One that was just the two of them. "My dad was a detective then, and even though we eventually learned to cope with what happened and move on in our own ways, it beat down on Dad. For years after, he continued to work the case. Late nights, early mornings, weekends and holidays. It just…it got under his skin and stuck and there wasn't anything any of us could do about it. He wouldn't listen. Not only had it happened in *his* town, it had happened to *his* kids." Caleb looked over Nina's shoulder. His mother was laughing at something Declan said. Even the sheriff was smiling. It helped loosen the ache that had formed at thoughts of the past. "The reason why my mom felt like she had to throw this party was because she saw firsthand

what stress could do to someone. That case, that tragedy, as many people in town call it, sent him to an early grave. He couldn't find any peace and his heart just gave out. So this—" he looked around the barn once more. "This is my mom's way of making sure we see the light in the darkness. See that, even though something bad happened, that something hurt us, doesn't mean that everything is hopeless."

Caleb searched Nina's face. Her focus had never wavered once as he had spoken, empathizing where most people would have in the story, yet now her expression was changing. Into one he couldn't recognize.

After a moment she slid her hand down to his chest. Caleb felt its warmth through the fabric of his shirt.

"Thank you for telling me. I know how hard it can be to carry something like that. Even harder to let it go." She averted her eyes and took a breath so deep her chest nearly touched his. Somewhere during his story and their dance, they'd gotten close. Closer than he'd meant to…or maybe exactly where he wanted to be.

Had she wanted that, too?

Nina exhaled. Her eyes climbed up to his.

"And *I* know this because of the real reason my mother died."

Chapter Thirteen

The mesmerizing glow of the lights twinkling overhead had been doused by an overwhelming darkness. The music cut off so quickly there wasn't even a whimper. The partygoers all quieted for one lost and lonely moment. Fear exploded in Nina's chest. Her breath caught. She clung to Caleb's shirt.

There she had been, for the first time, sharing a moment with someone and having the desire to share back. Nina had seen the pain and sorrow in Caleb's eyes as he recalled what Molly had referred to as the famous Nash triplet abduction. She believed he was genuine in what he said. Nina didn't understand why he was sharing but found herself entranced by the vulnerability behind his blue, blue eyes. It was like she was being pulled deeper into them. Closer to the man until she felt the heat of his body against hers.

He had cast a spell on her with his honesty.

And Nina was going to return the favor.

That's when the power cut off.

"It's probably the breaker," someone called into the darkness. "This place hasn't been used in years."

"I'm closest to the door. I can go check on it." Nina felt the rumble of Caleb's words through her hands against his chest. A small flash of shame went through her at how

tightly her fingers had burrowed into his shirt. He pressed his hands over hers. When he spoke again it was directed to the partygoers. "If you have cell phones, pull them out and use the flashlights."

Caleb pulled her hands away but kept one in his own. "Let's go," he said, voice low so she knew he was addressing her.

"Thank you for not leaving me," she whispered, meaning it with all of her being. Shame or no shame, she was terrified of the dark.

They moved slowly as the partygoers started to talk. Small beams of light sprang up on either side of them. Nina wished she had her phone. She'd left it back at the Retreat, trying to embrace the party and its social side with more enthusiasm. She wondered if Caleb had left his phone behind, too. It wasn't like he'd miss a work-related piece of information. The sheriff had been eating pie in the same room last she'd seen him. Not to mention his partner was a few feet away.

Caleb directed them off the makeshift dance floor and past the few chairs that they'd set up earlier that day. Nina's foot caught something. She stumbled. Her hand slipped out of his as she tried to steady herself.

"You okay?"

"Yeah, I just tripped over something." She swung her hand back out until it connected with his. His grip was tighter. She doubted that would help if her clumsy feet decided to take her out again.

They moved around whatever had blocked her way. She could feel his impatience. Not that she blamed him. The darkness was impossibly thick. The only things she could see were the slightly illuminated faces of those who had their phones out. They were far enough away that their light did very little to help guide them.

But they had to be close to the side door now.

"Nina? Where are you?"

The hand around hers tensed. Nina's blood turned to ice in her veins.

Caleb's voice wasn't in front of her, leading. It was behind her.

Which meant the hand she was holding—

"*Caleb!*"

The hand yanked her forward. It caught her off guard. She yelled out again, this time terror garbling her words.

"Nina," Caleb shouted. His voice was closer but felt impossibly far. "Someone bring me a light!"

The barn behind her exploded in noise and movement. The grip on her hand tightened to the point of pain. She dug her heels into the floor and pulled back.

"Let go!"

And just like that, the person did.

The unexpected release sent Nina cartwheeling backward. Before she hit the ground, she bumped into something solid. Two arms encircled her. Nina tried to fight out of fear.

"It's me," Caleb said at her ear. Relief flooded through her but dried up quickly.

"Someone was dragging me!"

Caleb didn't hesitate. He pushed her around and behind him before she could completely right herself.

"I need a light," he yelled again.

"Here," Declan said behind her shoulder.

The light from his cell phone was the answer to a prayer. It moved across her, pausing to make sure she was okay, before going to his brother. But Caleb wasn't there anymore.

"Someone was dragging me," she repeated to the sheriff.

"Stay here." Declan's voice was hard. Nina didn't argue.

The beam of light went ahead of him as he swept the area in front of the door. "Jazz, check the rest of the room. No one leaves."

Jazz said she understood. Declan and his light went after his brother.

A few moments later another small light found Nina. It was Brando. She had only talked to the man briefly but now she reached out and took the arm he offered her. Wordlessly, he led her back to the dance floor. The rest of the partygoers had converged there. Some with lights, some without. They waited in silence. Whether it was out of fear or that they were simply trying to listen to any clues that could tell them what was going on outside, Nina didn't know. She watched in muted fear as Jazz took her light and went across the barn.

"It's just us," Jazz confirmed. She came back to the dance floor. Her husband's light showed the detective had a gun in her hand.

Did Caleb have his service weapon?

Nina ran her thumb over her wrist.

Would he need it?

The sound of metal scraping against something outside tore Nina's attention to the wall behind them.

"The breaker box," Clive said from beside her. Molly's eyes were glowing orbs of concern in the dark at her husband's side. He had one arm around her and another placed on Dorothy's, a steadying grip that was easy to see despite the poor lighting. In fact, everyone around her was holding on to each other. Like the survivors of a sunken ship, huddled in a lifeboat lost at sea. Even she was threaded into that group by Brando's arm.

Nina would have stopped to think about how that made her feel, to be included by relative strangers in such a scary situation, but then the power went back on.

The twinkling stars that dotted the spaces between the rafters came to life while the slight thrumming of power vibrated the speakers. Slowly the members of the group disengaged from one another.

Nina was the first among them.

Her gaze caught and stuck on the floor between where they stood and the side door.

"Oh, my God."

Her hand went to her mouth, already trembling.

When Jazz had swept the room for someone hiding in the shadows, she hadn't focused on the floor. Neither had Nina as she walked with Brando to the middle of the room. Why would they?

But now, beneath the lights she'd once thought beautiful, there was no denying someone had been focused on her in the dark.

And way before the lights went out.

"What the hell?" Jazz breathed, following Nina to the first pile.

Caleb hurried through the side door. Nina felt the relief in her chest but couldn't bring herself to express it. Instead she dragged her gaze back to the floor.

Scattered on the weathered wood were printed-out pictures and not just a few. She guessed there were at least fifty between where she stood and the door. Which would have been odd all its own.

Yet the subject of every picture was her.

THE DEPUTIES OF the Wildman County Sheriff's Department spread across the ranch with a vengeance. Nina stood next to one of its best detectives in the barn, trying to detach from the situation as much as she could. The pictures hadn't been touched, at Caleb's insistence. Ap-

parently more people were coming to try and see if they couldn't lift prints from them.

Not that Nina particularly wanted to pick the pictures up. Nearly all of them were visible as they were. Plus the theme was obvious.

"Some of these were taken before we met. Before the stream and the email," she said to Caleb. Since talking to Declan and Jazz he had been circling the area covered by the pictures. Like a creature stalking its prey, even though neither he nor Declan had seen whoever had been in the barn. A point of deep frustration for both men. "I mean, that one over there, the one where I'm laughing and wearing the striped shirt, that's a few days after I came to town. And that one—" she pointed to a slightly out of focus picture taken of her profile as she stood in front of one of the cabins at the Retreat "—I'm pretty sure that was my first day of work. I'm holding my clipboard with my first week's checklist."

"And some of these are after we met," he stated, voice tight. He was right. Nina wasn't the only person in all of the pictures, just the common denominator. Caleb could be seen at her side, just as Dorothy, Molly, Roberto and Clive were in others. However, whether it was because she had spent more time with Caleb than the others in the past week or not, the detective was in the majority of those featuring Nina and someone else. Several were from them around the Retreat. The two closest to her were of them at Overlook Pass. One had been taken at his house the first day she'd met him. When she'd blamed him for the picture and email.

It scared her.

It made her angry.

"I know Daniel Covington said that he just happened to be at the stream when I showed up and decided it would be

funny to freak out the outsider with the email but this—"
she waved her arms out over the closest pile "—this isn't
funny."

Caleb let out another frustrated breath. He placed his
hands on his hips, showing his badge now prominently
positioned on his belt, and faced her.

"This isn't Daniel Covington's handiwork." Nina was
about to point out Daniel had already admitted to sending
the email but Caleb gave her a look akin to guilt. She held
her tongue. "I was going to tell you before the party but
decided to wait until later. I didn't think it was connected
at the time, but now?" He shook his head and rubbed a
hand across his jaw. There was still a smattering of dark
stubble across it. "Daniel Covington was attacked in his
house late this afternoon. We don't know who did it yet
and his girlfriend had no clue, either."

"You think he was too hurt to do this?" She refused to
let Daniel off of the hook. He'd already proven how much
of a creep he could be.

Caleb shook his head again. "He's in the hospital."

Nina put her hand on her stomach, worry further knotting inside.

"Oh."

"Yeah." Caleb's eyes flitted down. Slowly he took her
other hand. Nina's heartbeat leaped at the contact. Caleb,
however, looked the opposite of pleased. His thumb ran
over her wrist. There was still a red mark where their mystery person had grabbed her and squeezed. "Coming in
here to scatter the photos and to do this was…"

"Nightmare inducing?" she offered, partially trying to
lighten the mood with a teasing tone while also meaning it.

Caleb ran his thumb over the spot once more. When
his eyes were on her again there was an icy chill to them.

"It was incredibly brave *and* stupid. A bad combina-

tion," he spelled out. "Whoever did this wants us to know they're still out there."

Nina barely resisted a gulp of fear.

"They want us to know they're—what?—stalking me?"

"Why else go to all of this trouble? And that's what it is. Trouble. This took time to keep up. Again, not to mention, they chanced this big reveal at a party. One the sheriff and other law enforcement officers were attending. They just basically flashed a sign saying, 'hey there,' as though they're taunting us."

Nina couldn't fight that point. The pictures of her were more than damning evidence that whoever was behind this was no longer remaining under the radar.

"If Daniel Covington didn't do this and it's not a prank, then that means that there's someone *else* out there who's following me." Her nerves froze over. She felt her eyes widen as she realized something that had been floating on the edge of her thoughts. "Caleb, what if *I'm* the reason your house was targeted? What if I'm the reason everything you own is gone?"

Caleb's expression hardened. He took his hand out of hers and ran it along the side of her cheek. Nina's body pulsed at his touch but her mind stayed focused on his words.

"You listen to me, Nina Drake, and you listen to me good," he said. "The only person at fault is the person who physically set my house on fire. Whether that's the same person or not, you have my word that we *will* catch everyone who's guilty. And that isn't you. Not in the slightest. Okay?"

Nina breathed in and out slowly to steady herself. She nodded.

"Okay," she murmured.

The detective smiled.

Then it was back to work again.

SAMANTHA NOVAK WAS smiling down at Nina, her braces looking particularly gruesome in the weird light around them.

"You're so stupid," Samantha said, full of glee. "I swear, I don't know how you function."

Nina knew Samantha was fourteen. Just like Nina knew she was also fourteen. They were out on the private beach near their school. Nina was lying on a quilt, the sand around it so white it was blinding. Samantha was hovering over her, still grinning.

"You're going to be late, idiot."

Nina looked around, confused. The ocean was dark and rolled toward them. A horse neighed somewhere in the distance.

"Late for what?"

Nina stood. She tried to brush the sand off herself but it wasn't sand anymore. It was chunkier. Darker.

Samantha's smile turned menacing. It always did when she was bullying Nina.

"Who do you think I am? Your mom? Figure it out, idiot."

Nina blinked and Samantha was gone. The sand was darker, the waves angrier. The quilt was covered in the weird sand. Nina walked away from it, still brushing it from her clothes.

The beach went on forever. Nina was late for something. She just knew it. But what? Where was she supposed to go? It was somewhere close, right? And she was late. So very late.

The urgency pushed her legs faster across the sand and made her heart race. She gripped the keys in her hand. They made the palms of her hands bleed.

She was still late.

Wind whipped her hair around and finally cleared the

ash off her clothes. All of the sand around her was swept away with it. Then she was standing on the road.

She knew where she was but that urgency in her still raged on. Being there wasn't enough.

She was *still* late.

"Hey." A man waved to her from the dirt shoulder a few feet away. He was sitting on a patio chair. There was a mug in his hand and a newspaper on his lap. He tipped his cowboy hat to her. "Got it?" he asked.

Nina couldn't see his face but felt such a warmth in her heart that she nodded.

"Got it."

He nodded and opened his paper, sipping on his drink.

Nina wanted to join him, pull up a chair and live in that moment with him forever, but a voice inside of her was yelling a warning.

She was still late.

And something bad had happened.

Metal scraping against metal pierced the air like a gunshot. Halfway down the road Nina noticed a car flipped on its side. Smoke rose from it at an alarming pace. Then Nina saw the man and the boy in front of it in the middle of the road. The boy was staring at her.

Nina dropped her book bag and ran toward the car. Her bare feet tore as they raced across the asphalt. She screamed but nothing came out. She cried but it didn't help.

The boy was running now, too, but not toward the car.

Nina was still trying to scream by the time he was upon her.

"You can't," he yelled, throwing his arms around her.

Nina tried to get past him but he was too tall, too strong.

She heard the *whomp* as something within the car ignited. Flames twisted together with the smoke. They were so close she could feel the heat.

Nina screamed in anguish as the car disappeared. All that was left was smoke and flames.

And the man.

He stood in the middle of the road, smiling.

Nina's body didn't have room for rage yet. She could barely hold on to the pieces of her heart that had just shattered.

She had been too late.

"You can't," the boy repeated.

Ashes from the beach started to fall around them. The last thing Nina saw were three faceless children. One had blood running down his arm.

Then the smoke came and all she could do was try and scream.

Chapter Fourteen

Nina's heart was nearly beating out of her chest. She sat up in bed, struggling to breathe.

No. She'd been too late to save her.

Adrenaline coursed through Nina's veins. She ran a hand across her face. It was wet. The darkness around her only added to the terrified confusion.

Then she heard the insects. A soft melody that wound its way through the woods and fields. The ranch. She was in her apartment at the Retreat.

Nina fell back on the bed, trying to catch her breath, relieved she wasn't back on that road. At that car. Held by arms she couldn't escape, just as her mother hadn't been able to escape.

Nina placed a hand over her sweat-soaked shirt and felt the weight of heart-wrenching memories through it.

She hadn't had one of those dreams in years.

Then again, with the discovery of the pictures of her, and the mystery person trying to drag her out of the barn, she hadn't been this scared in years, either. Try as she might not to, she must have associated that new fear with the old terror.

She let out a long, trembling breath and searched for her phone. It was beneath the pillow next to her. She had no missed calls or texts. Of course, she'd only gone to bed

at ten. Now it was just before midnight. The only person she could imagine wanting to get hold of her with new information was downstairs in the lobby.

A distance that made her uncomfortable now.

Caleb.

He'd been the man in the cowboy hat in her dream; even without seeing his face she knew it by how he had affected her. How he made her feel warm. Safe. That's what Caleb made her feel like in the waking world.

Nina blushed despite being alone.

She'd even managed to bring him as a child into her own personal nightmare. The three children had been the triplets, she was sure.

How had one man consumed her thoughts like this in less than two weeks?

Nina threw the covers off and went to the bathroom. She showered off the sweat and exhaustion as much as she could. There was no way she was going back to sleep. Not when that particular nightmare could be waiting in the depths of her unconscious mind.

Being tired was the much preferred option.

Nina slipped into a camisole and jeans and made her way down the stairs. The Retreat side of the house was open between them, as per Caleb's insistence. If she called for him from her apartment, the sound would carry into the main room where he stayed. Even though the only difference was that one door was left open, it made her feel a little bit better.

A ring of light was just inside of that same door, showing that Caleb was still up. For a moment he didn't see her standing in the doorway. She used that moment to take another long look at the man.

He was tired.

He was frustrated.

That showed in how he sat on the couch with shoulders hunched, hovering over a box on the coffee table. It was also reflected in the set of his eyes and brow. A line crinkled above both. His jaw and the dark stubble across it only added to the image of a man who was ready to put their troubles to bed. Even his lips were thinned.

"Knock, knock," Nina said, softly.

Maybe the detective had known she was there. He didn't look at all surprised to see her. Though he did smile.

"Going somewhere?" he asked, gaze running down her outfit.

"It's more of where I'm not going." She walked along the wooden floor, feeling the coolness against her feet. The same feet that had once been bloodied by running across an uneven and pocked road. Caleb raised an eyebrow in question. Nina took the armchair next to the couch. "To be honest, I had a nightmare. An old recurring one I thought was gone." She shook her head but tried to keep her body loose. Not that she thought much got past the detective. "I'm not going back to sleep anytime soon. What's going on here? Any new information?"

He tilted the box so she could see inside. It was the pictures from the barn.

"They were processed but no prints whatsoever. Whoever handled them was probably wearing gloves." Nina had already tried to remember if the hand she was holding had been gloved but couldn't be sure. She had been afraid of the dark and worried. She definitely hadn't been expecting the hand holding hers not to belong to Caleb. "Declan just brought them by. I don't expect him to sleep tonight, either."

"Can I help you look through them? I think feeling useful would help with my mood."

Caleb slid the box to her. She took a handful of the pic-

tures, moved away from the coffee table and sat on the floor. There she started to arrange the pictures in a line on the hardwood. Caleb followed her example so they were seated on the floor next to each other.

"Maybe if we put them in order of time they were taken? At least, from what I remember?" she offered, eyeing the closest one.

"That could help us narrow down who could have taken them."

For the next fifteen minutes or so Nina arranged the pictures in chronological order. At least, as much as possible. There were a few that were just close-ups of her face. Others she simply couldn't remember. Not enough to be helpful, anyway.

When they had done the best they could, they'd moved the chair and the coffee table to make more room. The sheer number of pictures made a shiver run down Nina's spine.

"Eighty-four," Caleb said, voice clipped. "That's how many there are."

"Eighty-four," she repeated. "And here I thought I was doing a good job of staying out of the public eye." She bent over the row closest to them and sighed.

"All of these were taken from hidden vantage points, the best I can tell." He pointed to a few different pictures and cited examples. "The field of tall grass near my house. The trees close to the Retreat and the horse barn. Even a few spots in town have an angle that makes me think the photographer was in between shops. It really makes me wish more kept security cameras outside but, well, we don't have enough crime here for the shop owners to pony up that kind of money. Even though it's been suggested, especially around tourist season."

"They could have been standing in the middle of the

sidewalk in front of me, pretending to take a selfie and I wouldn't have known the difference. I still only know a handful of people in Overlook and they all live or work on the ranch." A chilling thought went through Nina. Caleb seemed to pick up on it.

"No one from the ranch is behind this or the fires," he said, confidence clear in his voice. "Trust me. If anything, no one here would be stupid enough to pull this kind of crap with the sheriff and a detective on scene. If anyone on the ranch was going to turn into a criminal, I have full confidence they'd be more subtle."

Nina didn't push the subject. Partly because she believed he was right. What she knew of the people she'd met in the last month didn't quite fit the profile. Then again, people were nothing if not surprising.

"At least whoever the photographer is they managed to get my good side," she noted. "I'm smiling in almost every one."

Caleb's back straightened so quickly Nina's focus shifted.

"There's no almost to it."

"What is it?" she asked.

The detective was scanning the pictures, eyes moving side to side until he focused on the ones near their feet.

"You're smiling in every one of these."

It was Nina's turn to re-scan them.

Caleb was right.

"Eighty-four smiles," he kept on. "That's hard to get naturally on camera that often unless you're waiting for it."

"So, not only are they stalking me but they're stalking my smiles?"

Nina couldn't handle how ridiculous that sounded. They were slipping closer and closer to some kind of Edgar Allen Poe story come to life. One where Nina ended up being

trapped inside of a wall at the end. She tamped down another shiver threatening to move across her skin.

"They don't just want to capture you, they want to capture you at your happiest," he added.

It didn't help the creepy factor from rising even higher.

Nina made a sound that fell between a grunt of frustration and a cry of defeat. She fell back onto the couch and buried her head in her hands. The nightmare's fresh wound pulsed new life into the realization of just how little control she had of the situation.

"Do you know why I came here? To Overlook?" Her voice was muffled from her hands across her mouth. She didn't move them.

The cushion beneath her dipped to the side as Caleb's weight pressed against it.

"No, I don't."

The memory of her mother's death tricked her into smelling salt water. The last time she'd sat on the beach and looked out into the ocean without a care in the world.

She should tell Caleb, she thought. Tell him about that day, about her mother's death, about Rylan Bowling. That's what she'd been about to do before the power was cut in the barn. He'd opened up to her. Why couldn't she do it, too?

Because you haven't moved on, she thought sourly. *You just ran away from it and you're ashamed to admit it.*

"Nina?" Caleb's voice had softened. She imagined the blue of his eyes would match the ocean from her dream. Before it turned into a nightmare.

It coaxed her away from her hands.

She was right. His eyes had transformed yet again. Blue waves, lapping over her, making her sink deeper into the sand.

"One day I woke up and realized that if I started over, went somewhere new, I'd have a chance to live a quiet

life. And, God, how good that idea sounded. After how loud my old one was. Just the thought of being able to live under the radar. I can't tell you how badly I needed just the thought of the possibility."

She motioned to the pictures on the floor and realized how heartbreaking it was to see them.

"Now I'm back on repeat, just stuck in a different song." She put her head back in her hands, afraid that looking into the detective's eyes any longer would pull out more truth than she wanted to share. "I know how selfish that sounds, especially after what you lost, but I can't help it," she admitted, voice once again muffled. Like she was some kind of child. "It just—it's too much for me. I can't handle it."

The cushion beneath her shifted. Warmth brushed against her hand before Caleb gently pulled it. For a moment she didn't let him move her. But she was starting to see that resisting Caleb wasn't her strong suit. She relented.

"I don't pretend to understand what happened to you, to know what you went through, but I can tell you something I do know." He placed their hands on the couch in the space between them and then brought his other to her chin. Slowly he angled her face up so she couldn't go back to hiding. "It's easier to be alone. There's no real pain there, none that can stick because you can go on ignoring it all day and all night without anyone to call you out on it. After my dad died I pushed everyone away, telling them that I was fine and everything was okay. I had moved on, made sense of what I had once thought was a senseless death, and was just dandy."

A whisper of a smile crossed his lips. There was nothing but sadness there. "But in all of that time, what I really wanted—what I really needed—was someone to ignore me. Because having the burden of pain and no one to share it with isn't doing anyone any good. It's not honoring mem-

ories or the fast track to finding closure. It's just a wound that never heals." His smile disappeared. He leaned forward, driving his point home by getting so close she could smell the lingering scent of cologne along his neck.

"And I don't want that for you, Nina." His voice had become deeper. Almost raspy. Something inside of Nina woke to the change. Her breath caught, hanging on to every syllable he uttered next. "You don't have to hide here. Not from me. Got it? You can tell me anything. You can share the pain. I'm here for it. I'm here for you."

Nina closed the space between them, pressing her lips to his in an instant. The kiss was soft and quick. She didn't linger, even if her body wanted nothing but to stay. The flush of desire was burning across her skin, her heartbeat was galloping, her chest was heaving in staggering breaths.

She wanted Caleb.

Did he want her?

"I'm sorry." She sounded breathy but couldn't help it. His words and touch had broken the dam between her desire to be alone and the desire to feel him.

For a moment Nina worried she'd crossed a line. Caleb's face was impassive, his eyes hooded, but then he moved his hand to cradle the side of her face.

And then his lips were covering hers with a hunger that spread through every inch of her body.

Chapter Fifteen

Good heavens, if kissing Nina wasn't exactly what Caleb wanted to continue doing. He could have sworn he tasted a sweetness on her lips. Though he didn't know its origin. Or maybe that was just Nina. Either way, Caleb was drawn in hook, line and sinker.

At least, he was until the less carnal part of his mind spoke up.

For the first time since he'd known the woman she was openly vulnerable. What kind of man was he to take advantage of that?

Did he want to kiss Nina Drake?

Absolutely.

Did he want to do it solely because she was afraid for her life?

Not particularly.

Gently Caleb pulled away. Nina's eyes were hooded, her long lashes dark against her cheeks as she tried to blink away the haze they'd both fallen into. Then it was those dark brown beauties that were searching his expression for an answer to why he'd been one heck of a fool to end what they both had started.

"I–I'm sorry." She stumbled through the words, trying to create some distance between them by scooting back to the arm of the couch.

Caleb sighed. He dragged his hand down his face and hoped he looked like the respectable lawman he was and not a teenager whose excited body wasn't syncing up with his mind.

"No, don't go doing that," he said. "Believe me, there's nothing more I'd rather be doing than exactly what we were just doing, but I don't want you getting the wrong idea about why it is I'm doing it."

Nina's eyebrow rose in question. He couldn't help but note her lips were a bit swollen.

"I want you to know I kissed you because I'm attracted to you and not because of what's happening *to* you," he decided to say. That didn't seem to help with the confusion so he continued. "See, my ex used to accuse me of finding my job more exciting than I found her. That I got too wrapped up in cases. While I don't think that's what I did, at least not to the extent she suggested, I want to make sure you know that I didn't kiss you back because of the excitement of what's been going on. I kissed you back because I wanted to. Truly."

He felt himself soften, giving her a grin he hoped conveyed the trio of feelings he was stomping through—hope, guilt and a little shame, considering his body was still ready to go and ravage hers despite his well-intentioned grandstanding. "Believe you me, I want to pick this back up again but maybe we should hold off until everything has calmed down."

Nina's eyebrow lowered but there was a tightness to how she held her jaw.

"Oh, yeah," she said. "No, you're right. This definitely isn't the time. Not with everything that's going on."

She was off the couch in a second flat. Caleb felt like even more of a dunce. He grabbed after her but she was

fast, already weaving her way through the pictures, eyes down and on anything but him.

Most people called him charming, but when it came to Nina Drake he'd had more foot-in-mouth moments than he cared to admit.

"Caleb?"

He was off the couch just as fast as she had been. He wanted to explain himself better, if he could, but Nina didn't seem to want anything he was selling. She'd gone stiff as a board. It wasn't until he was at her side that he realized all of her attention was on the picture at her feet.

"What is it?"

Nina lowered herself slowly. Caleb followed suit. She picked the picture up. Caleb angled himself so he could get a better look. It was one of the few close-up shots. Not much else could be seen other than her profile and smile. The small stretch of background was out of focus and red. Almost all of the close-ups made it hard to figure out location and time.

"I wasn't sure where this picture was taken at first. I mean, where do I even go that has red around me?" Her voice was strained. "But I just thought of something."

She took the picture and walked out of the room to the back stairs. Caleb followed, his gut keyed up and in tune with the fear that seemed to have crept into Nina's movements. They went up to her apartment without any explanation. There she led them to a door along the wall to the right of her bed. She handed him the picture. Her hand hovered for an uncertain moment over the handle. Then she opened it to reveal a closet.

"How does this look?" she asked.

At first Caleb didn't understand.

Then he saw the red dress hanging on a hook on the inside of the door. Nina stood next to it, staring into the

closet. Caleb looked down at the picture. If she had been smiling it would have been an exact match.

"They were in here with me," she said, not bothering to wait for his input. Not that he had any assurances to give. He turned and followed the sightline to the only object in its path big enough to hide someone. The only area that offered any cover was the kitchen. It was small and tucked into the corner of the room as soon as you walked in, but had two rows of cabinets.

Caleb moved around the barstools next to the first row and stood in front of the refrigerator.

"If you were ducked down right there, I wouldn't see you," she confirmed. Her voice fell flat. "And if you were already there when I came in, there's a chance I wouldn't notice you. Though it would be easier to come in while I was in the bathroom."

The feelings their kiss had created were burned away by an anger so intense, Caleb couldn't help the unflattering words streaming from his mouth.

Taking pictures of Nina—stalking her—while she was out in the open was bad enough. But taking pictures of her while in her apartment?

"Caleb?" Nina's expression had gone blank again. He couldn't rightly blame her. "Could you stay up here tonight?"

He didn't even have to think about it.

"I sure can."

The truth was, even if she hadn't asked, he would have stayed.

CALEB DIDN'T FIT on the love seat in the apartment. When Nina offered him to share the bed with her, an offer that would have surprised her a week ago, he turned it down with a little too much vigor. That smarted but then there

were bigger fish to fry than the distance the detective kept putting between them.

Like the fact that someone had been in the apartment with her. She should have seen them. She should have heard them. Yet how often do you worry that people are in your living space, playing a one-sided game of hide-and-seek while taking secret pictures of you?

Not to mention she always locked the door. A point she made to Caleb after he got off the phone with his brother. According to him the only people who had a key to the living portion of the house were Nina and his mother. She kept a spare in a safe at the main house. Nina didn't want to wake Dorothy up so he promised to check on that key in the morning.

Now Nina lay awake in bed, staring at the ceiling and trying not to feel so violated. Up until now the apartment had been her safe space, a place where she'd always felt comfortable. But now it was tainted.

She sighed.

She heard Caleb shift on the too-small furniture. It was mostly dark in the apartment but, given the new information, Nina couldn't bring herself to turn off all the lights. Instead, the bathroom light was on, shielded slightly by the door. It cast enough of a glow that when she angled her head just right she could make out Caleb's legs, hanging over the edge of the love seat.

It had been a good half hour since they'd said anything to each other. At first that had been fine by her but now it made her skin itch. She hadn't been lying when she'd first gone downstairs—she didn't want to fall back asleep. Not after the nightmare. Caleb was supposed to have been her distraction. Yet she'd also wanted his company.

Not because of her needing a distraction. No, it was more than that. In the last week she'd grown accustomed

to him being around mornings and nights. Grown used to the charming smiles he offered every time they talked, the way he chuckled when he was reminded of something from growing up in Overlook and the way he had fallen in sync with her despite her always holding back.

He'd never pushed her to talk more than she wanted. In fact, he never pestered her at all. The only thing he'd done was listen to her concerns and theories about the fires and whoever was fascinated with her smile.

She'd never met a man who had treated her with such cool-headed respect.

Suddenly Nina felt like an idiot.

She'd bet stopping their kiss before it grew to more was his way of keeping to his good manners. The very same ones that had endeared him to her in the first place. That's what he'd been trying to say on the couch.

They just didn't make them like Caleb Nash anymore.

And there she had been, keeping the man at arm's length at every turn.

Sure, she had been about to open up to him in the barn, but after the commotion she'd been slightly relieved for the interruption.

What was she so afraid of?

Was sharing such a key moment in her life what really scared her or was it being vulnerable?

Nina sat up in bed.

"Caleb?" she whispered, hoping she wouldn't wake the man if he had fallen asleep. Judging by how quickly he answered, she hadn't.

"Yeah?"

Nina took a deep breath. The darkness was oddly emboldening.

"I was fourteen when my mom died," she started without a segue. She just needed to finally get it out. "We were

supposed to go shopping in town but I'd followed some friends to the beach after school. This awful girl named Samantha Novak had shown up with her cronies and we all started doing that high school thing where you just kind of insult each other before the winner eventually leaves. I realized too late that I'd lost track of time and had to run home. There was this street that was a shortcut between our house and the private beach. No one really used it. There were potholes everywhere, it was uneven, and it had trees and construction on either side of it. Not something most people took when they could stay on the main streets and have an ocean view."

The image of the street from her dream rose to the front of her mind as well as Caleb sitting off to the side of it with his coffee and paper. "Mom knew I was at the beach and, since she'd shown me the shortcut when I was little, knew I'd take it home. Dad had said she'd told him on the phone that she'd had a bad day at work and was impatient to get out and stretch her legs." Nina paused, smiling slightly at that detail. Only her mother counted walking around the outlet mall and eating snow cones or giant pretzels as "stretching her legs."

That smile didn't last, and neither did the affection there. Now she was diving into the worst day of her life.

"Her car was already on its side when I got there. Another car had hit her and pushed her off the road. It took me longer than it should have to realize she wasn't the one standing in the middle of the road. It was a man. He was just looking at the car. That's when I saw the smoke and flames. Then I realized she was still inside."

Pain lit up Nina's chest. She pushed past it. "I ran as fast as I could, but a boy met me before I could get there. He was the son of the other driver. He'd run to a nearby house to call the cops, and when he saw me running to-

ward the fire had decided it was too dangerous. He held me there as the car became engulfed in flames. Held me there while I screamed and cried. Stayed until my dad showed up…which is why he didn't see that his father watched my mom's car burn with a smile on his face. I'll never forget it for as long as I live. He just smiled."

Nina took another steadying breath. This part of the story brought in a deep, dark anger. She became lost in it. Caleb's voice sounded far off, like an echo in a dream.

"I'm so sorry, Nina. I can't imagine going through that."

Nina snapped back to her senses. She still wasn't through with her story but she'd already come this far in sharing it with him. She might as well end it.

"I'd like to say all the horrible ended with that day, and every day after was just us trying to grieve and move on, but then the trial happened. Apparently my mom's bad day had to do with a man she worked with named Rylan Bowling. She'd had to fire him that afternoon for harassing another female employee. He hadn't taken it well. Threatened her. And, well, you can guess how it played out from there. He saw her on the road, followed her, rammed into her when no one was around and didn't help her when he could have. You would think this was an open-and-shut case, but he got some fancy lawyer from up north. Said it was an accident. It made everyone nervous that he'd get away with it. So I offered to be a witness."

Another detail Nina wouldn't forget was how her palms got sweaty, her stomach turned and how truly terrified she was during the trial. But she'd wanted nothing more than to have that man pay for what he'd done. "I told them about the smile and then his son, Jeremy, told them he couldn't confirm or deny it since he'd been too focused on keeping me safe. Along with everything else, the jury was convinced. Rylan Bowling went to prison, and Jeremy and I

made all of the papers. The daughter who was saved by the son sends his father to prison for killing her mother. The media really loved the poetry of it. They even ran anniversary stories once or twice." She snorted. It held no amusement. "Jeremy left town to live with some relative and I stayed. After everything that had happened, I guess I started hating the spotlight. Then that kind of turned into shying away from any normal attention, too. It became who I was. Then, one day, I realized that, even though the spotlight had faded, the memories of it never would."

"So you came here, hoping to stay beneath the radar. And instead got caught up in whatever the hell it is that's going on."

Nina nodded in the dark.

"I used to not believe in bad luck, but I tell you what, I'm starting to lean toward believing it," she half-joked. "Either way, I wanted you to know."

Caleb was quiet a moment. Then his voice was a whisper in the dark.

"Thank you," he said simply.

It was enough to make a difference. The weight of her memories somehow felt lighter now that she'd shared them. Maybe there *was* something to talking about things.

Nina settled back into the sheets.

Caleb continued to move around, undeniably uncomfortable on the small furniture.

"And Caleb?" she called.

"Yeah?"

"Let me sleep on that ridiculously small couch or come to bed. Those are your options."

The detective played it smart.

He came to bed.

Chapter Sixteen

It started out innocently enough.

Caleb stayed, fully dressed, above the covers; Nina didn't think it nice to force him beneath them. She kept as much distance between them as she could in the full-sized bed. They said goodnight and then quieted.

But then Caleb got a call and that put them on a downward slope that only really had one outcome.

"Sorry," Caleb apologized for the third time before he reached for and answered his phone.

Nina didn't mind. A phone call this late had to be important. She just hoped it was good news and not worse news.

"Caleb Nash here," he answered, voice flipping straight to business.

Nina wanted to inch closer to hear the person on the other end of line but thought better of it. Caleb had been nothing but forthcoming about everything so far. If he thought she should know what was going on then he'd tell her.

Though that didn't stop her from straining to listen.

Whoever was on the other end must have been soft-spoken. She couldn't hear anything.

"Okay, yeah," Caleb rattled off at intervals through-

out his conversation before ending with, "Thanks. I'll see you tomorrow."

The bed shifted under his weight as he put his phone back on the nightstand. Nina tried not to seem overeager. And immediately failed. "Everything okay?"

The bathroom light outlined the detective. He had moved onto his side and was facing her now. It made Nina's body react more than she cared to admit.

"That was a friend of mine at the hospital. I asked her to let me know of any significant changes with Daniel Covington."

Nina wasn't a fan of Daniel's, by any means, but for a moment she worried he'd passed away. Sure, being a creep wasn't the greatest, but he definitely hadn't deserved the beating Caleb described. "Apparently the kid made a turn for the better. He might even be able to talk to us tomorrow."

She wondered if she was a part of the "us" but decided not to ask.

"Hopefully he can tell us what happened and who almost killed him," Caleb added.

Nina heard him sigh. She couldn't help but reach out. She fanned her fingers across his chest, hoping to offer some kind of comfort.

"You'll figure it all out and everyone will get what's coming to them," she said, confident. "If there's one thing I've learned in my limited time with you all it's—you don't give up."

She couldn't see his smile but imagined it there as she felt his touch when he placed his hand over hers. Nina worried that she'd overstepped until he ran his thumb across her knuckles. It was a slow, tantalizing motion.

That's when Nina knew they were doomed to fall prey to the inevitable. Their kiss earlier had pushed over the

first domino in a series of pieces leading to a conclusion they could no longer avoid. At least, Nina didn't want to. Not after being this close to the man she should have realized sooner made her feel absolutely safe. A feeling she hadn't had in a long, long time.

"Caleb—" she started, unsure of what she was going to say. Thankfully, she didn't have to figure it out. His touch transferred from her hand to her wrist. From there his fingers skimmed along her bare skin up her arm. Nina barely contained a shiver of pleasure at the contact. When his hand trailed over to the side of her neck, Nina knew whatever resistance she might have had in reserve was gone.

The space between them disappeared.

Nina angled her lips up, easier to be found in the dark.

Not that Caleb had any problems.

His lips were warm and diligent. They pressed against hers with insistence. Nina had to dig her fingers into the fabric of his shirt just to steady herself from the onslaught of excitement running rampant through her. He deepened the kiss at her display. Nina moaned against him, unable to hide how much she wanted this.

Caleb seemed to agree.

He let go of the side of her neck and grabbed her hip through the blanket. On reflex Nina tried to push closer. Frustration broke through her haze long enough to break their embrace. Caleb was on the same page. She didn't have to complain about the layers separating them. He was already sliding beneath the same sheets.

They collided again. This time there was more urgency there. One of his hands wound into her hair while the other grabbed her hip again, pulling her flush with him. Nina moved against him, feeling his excitement, before she decided she needed to be closer. She slid her hands up his shirt, marveling at the firmness beneath, until he was

forced to pause so he could rid them of the annoyance. Nina took that time to mimic the action. She threw her own shirt away from their island of sheets and darkness.

A gasp escaped her lips as Caleb appreciated her now-bare chest. He kissed down the slope of her breast before directing his tongue to her nipple. It beaded instantly. Nina moaned again.

Another instantaneous reaction.

Caleb crashed back into her lips, his hands hungry against her body. Nina reached out, just as ready. She pulled at his jeans and before she knew it they were gone in the darkness, too.

Then Caleb was above her, straddling her.

He was gentle as he lowered himself to her lips. His kiss was a whisper.

"You're one hell of a woman, Nina Drake."

Nina couldn't help but grin.

She had spent so long trying to live a quiet life that she'd forgotten that not all excitement was worth missing.

"You're not so bad yourself, detective."

CALEB WOKE WITH the sun on his back and a beautiful woman in his arms. Not what he had planned but he definitely wasn't complaining. Nina was fast asleep, her bare back against his chest and her hair splayed out on the pillow they shared. When Caleb had first gotten into her bed he had noted its small size. Now he appreciated how it worked perfectly when he held her.

Nina stirred against him. Caleb enjoyed the sensation. He wouldn't have minded exploring it further when she woke up, but along with the sunlight, the duties he needed to perform for his job started to filter through. As carefully as he could, he pulled his arm from beneath the pillows and lifted the one around Nina's waist. The raven-haired

beauty shifted onto her stomach but didn't wake. Caleb checked his phone.

He'd always been an early riser—one of the perks of being raised on a ranch—and was glad to see it hadn't failed him despite his active night. It was six-thirty. Plenty of time to get ready, eat and head out to the hospital. He slipped out of bed, felt the chill of the air conditioner against his naked body and strode off to the bathroom. When he came out, dressed, Nina was awake and sitting up in bed.

She smiled a little uncertainly. The sheets were up around her chest. There was a blush on her cheeks.

"Good mornin'," he drawled in his most Southern accent. Over the last week he'd noticed how Nina would smile when his Southern twang slipped out.

"Good morning," she repeated, her smile growing. She motioned to the bed. "Sorry if I was a bed hog."

Caleb went over and kissed her full on the lips.

"I have no complaints here," he assured her.

Nina nodded.

"Good," she said. Her expression went from open and sweet to determined. She eyed his phone. "So, what's going on? Are you going to go see Daniel Covington?"

"I am, but not until after breakfast." He patted his stomach dramatically. "I seem to have worked up an appetite after last night."

Instead of falling back into her quiet, slightly detached ways, Nina surprised him. She laughed and sent him a wink.

"Now that's a workout I can get used to."

A deep-chested chuckle escaped Caleb before he gave her one more kiss and then got to work. He excused himself and called Declan to update him about Daniel Covington before calling Jazz. She sounded much less enthused.

"I hope he can tell us who the heck attacked him because I haven't been able to track down anyone who can," she said, irritated.

"I want to know who else had an interest in Nina," he said. They had already talked about the possibility of Daniel knowing the person who had cut the power at the barn. The picture he had taken of Nina and sent in the email was framed differently than the ones left across the barn floors, but that was too much of a coincidence to pass off as unrelated. "I bet my bottom dollar he knows who that sonofabitch is."

Jazz agreed with an added huff.

"We need a win somewhere," he said. "Between this and the fires I think some people around here are losing morale. Roberto was even talking about heading to his parents' place until all of this chaos was controlled. His words, not mine."

Caleb didn't blame Roberto for what he'd said, though it grated that someone from the ranch would consider leaving it because they felt unsafe.

They ended the call by agreeing to meet up after he went to check on Daniel. Then Caleb turned his attention to Nina. She had dressed in an open flannel shirt with a black skinny-strapped thing beneath it and pair of jeans that acutely reminded him of how long and smooth her legs were, despite her petite frame. She even had on a pair of boots that went over her jeans at the ankle. Her freshly washed hair was pulled back in a wet braid.

"If you don't look like a bona fide cowgirl," he said, admiring her. "All you need is the hat and you're cooking with gas."

She laughed.

"Never thought I'd be called that, but I'm not going to lie, I'm not against it." She sidled up to him and that

concern came back. Caleb had never met a woman who went from lighthearted to down-to-business so quickly. He wondered if his changes between the two were just as abrupt. "I don't think I should go with you to the hospital," she said, sure in her words. "Not that you asked me to go or anything, it's just that I wanted you to know that I prefer not to."

Caleb had been on the fence about inviting her along. He was glad she'd brought it up first.

"I don't want to see Daniel in bad shape any more than I want to see him in good shape," she continued. "I think my emotions might get the better of me. I might say something I'd regret later."

Caleb nodded. He'd been there before as a rookie. There were some instances where it had been a struggle for him to keep his cool talking to men and women who had done things he definitely hadn't approved of.

"Do you mind hanging out at the main house while I'm gone? Mom offered to make breakfast for us last night before we left the barn." He gave her a soft smile. "She's worried about us worrying. Plus, I'd also worry less with you not being alone."

There was a softness to his words. A touching concern that Nina appreciated.

"That sounds wonderful."

They made their way five minutes up the road to the main house. Declan's truck was in the driveway. When they went inside he was asleep on the couch. Caleb's mom descended the stairs with her index finger pressed against her lips. She waved them to follow her out to the back porch. Caleb should have been surprised that there were covered plates of eggs, bacon, biscuits and gravy but he wasn't.

When Dorothy Nash was trying to keep her own stress

levels low, she cooked. It was therapeutic for her. It threatened the rest of their waistlines.

"Your brother was up until dawn," she said once the back door was closed behind them. She motioned to the benches on either side of the table. "That man will avoid sleep at any and all costs if I don't holler at him about it."

Nina took the spot next to his mother and the three of them immediately went to eating. To his mother's credit she didn't talk about what had happened at the barn and instead kept talking about the Retreat. It seemed to be exactly what Nina needed. Work talk energized her, and before long the two of them had commandeered a notebook where they wrote out their ideas for future events for the ranch. The decision to open on schedule or postpone wouldn't be made until the next day. Neither woman let that worry them. Caleb believed that to be in partial thanks to his mother. She let Nina know right then and there that, even if they delayed opening, Nina's job was still secure. That, plus his mother refused to let someone take away her dream of the Retreat without fighting for it. So, until she said otherwise, they would continue to plan for every eventuality they could think of, which included events from the grand opening party to months away. One in particular caught Caleb's fancy.

"A good old-fashioned dance out under the stars," he repeated. "We could invite the town to that. You know Jazz's husband, Brando, is in that band. I heard them at the bar once and they were pretty great. I'm sure they'd loved to play it." He smiled at Nina. "Though I suppose I might need to figure out that dancing thing beforehand."

Nina returned his grin.

"I think you managed just fine before."

His mother looked between them. Then she was beaming. Caleb was sure the next time they were in private

their main topic at hand would be the dark-eyed beauty from Florida.

Caleb had to say goodbye once his food was finished. Both women adopted looks of concern but neither voiced them, which he appreciated. He already felt guilty about leaving them, but he had to do his job. Despite his mother's objections he woke Declan up on his way out and made sure he'd keep an eye on both women. Declan promised and then Caleb was in his truck, staring at the house in the rearview.

He couldn't help but wish he'd grabbed a kiss for the road.

THE HOSPITAL WAS QUIET. Caleb met his friend Katie in the hallway outside of Daniel Covington's room. She got right down to business.

"That kid is a freaking miracle." She greeted him, pulling a peppermint from her scrubs pocket. She worked third shift and would be leaving soon. Caleb had grown up around Katie due to her close friendship with Madi. She had occasionally helped the sheriff's department, namely him and Declan, with her expertise and connections to the hospital and her colleagues' insights. "He shouldn't even be awake, let alone able to talk." She shrugged with a sigh. "But, you know, youth and all of that. If that had been me I think my body would have already called for the check."

"So I can talk to him now?"

She nodded.

"I'll warn you, though. He's still medicated. He might be able to form words but I don't know how much of those words you should trust." Caleb thanked her and started for the door. She held out her hand to stop him. "I have to ask, does he need a lawyer here? I mean, I love you Nashes,

but I've got two kids at home who need their mama to not get sued if this all goes sideways."

Caleb smirked. Katie had always been clever. Even when they were kids she'd been fierce.

"He was the victim this time. I'm just here to see if I can figure out who did that to him and see if he has any connections to another case I'm currently pursuing."

Katie smiled and waved him past.

Daniel's room was small but private. The rhythmic beeping of a heart monitor indicated the young man lying on the bed, propped up and looking like hell, wasn't out of the woods yet. Caleb was glad Nina wasn't here to see him. With or without a connection with the kid, it was hard to see at how bad off he looked.

"Hey, Daniel," Caleb greeted the boy, catching his eye. He moved slowly to the other side of the bed and pulled up one of the two chairs next to the window. "Do you remember me?"

It took a few seconds but then there was a small nod.

"Good. Well, I'm here to ask you a few questions," Caleb continued, using a soothing voice he adopted for sensitive situations. "I was wondering if you remember who did this to you. Who attacked you yesterday morning?"

Daniel's eyes widened but no sound came out. Instead, he looked around the room, moving his head slowly to gauge it in its entirety.

"Can you talk, Daniel? Do you understand me?"

He moved his head back. His gaze slid slowly up to Caleb's. He opened his mouth a few times before any words formed.

"You alone?"

Caleb leaned forward.

"Am I alone? Yes, I am. I wanted to talk to you as soon as possible so I could figure out who did this to you."

Daniel seemed okay with this answer. He licked his lips and blinked slowly before speaking again.

"—paid me but—but I didn't know..."

Caleb tried to keep his mounting frustration tamped down. Katie was right. It was a miracle Daniel had even survived, let alone could talk.

"Someone paid you," he tried instead. "Who paid you? And to do what? Get beaten up?"

Daniel inhaled loudly and let it out with a wince. Caleb wasn't the only one frustrated by the situation.

"He said—it—was for camping." Daniel paused, confusion changing his expression before he seemingly regained his train of thought. His brows pulled in together, disapproval cascading over his bruised and scabbed face. "...didn't believe him. Then she called—and—" Daniel's hand made the smallest of waves.

"Then you were attacked," Caleb guessed.

A small, barely there nod confirmed it.

Caleb took a steadying breath. He didn't want to push the boy but he wanted answers. Needed them.

"Daniel, who attacked you?" Daniel's eyelids were drooping. "Daniel? Who attacked you?"

Caleb believed Daniel was really trying to be cooperative but the miracle man was already low on steam and losing it fast. Only one answer came out of his lips before he slipped back to sleep, pulled under by exhaustion and pain medication, but Caleb still heard it clear as day.

"Kerosene."

Chapter Seventeen

The sky looked like it had been flipped upside down. One moment it was sunny and blue, the next it was as dark and menacing as the bruises across Daniel's body. The darkness cast ominous shadows inside of the sheriff's department. They reached out and made the whiteboard set up between his and Jazz's desks even more daunting.

"Daniel, the fires and the incident at the barn," Jazz said, reading out the three headlines along the three time-lines they'd reconstructed. She tapped the spot beneath Daniel's line. "He said he was paid to do something and all we know that he's done is take the picture of Nina at the stream and then send it from Claire's. He also dramatically said 'kerosene.' And then you were kicked out before he could corroborate anything at all."

Caleb nodded.

"It wouldn't have mattered if I'd stayed. That boy is going to be out for a while. Katie was right. It was a miracle he was able to say what he did. She said her husband would give one of us a call if anything changed. He's working day shift on the same floor as a nurse."

Jazz shrugged, attention back on the whiteboard. She moved to perch next to him on the edge of the desk facing it. "So, what's your gut telling you, cowboy? Because mine is saying we're missing something."

Caleb was quiet a moment. He'd already gone over what they knew three times since they'd started. It made him angry every time he spoke of the parts that included Nina, knowing how scared and violated they had made her feel. He rubbed his chin and started back at the beginning.

"Daniel took the picture and sent the email. No denying that. But there's no way he was at the barn. Honestly, my gut is saying he had nothing to do with it. The pictures at the barn were all similar. Nina's face was always visible and she was smiling. The one Daniel took was of her back. He also left a message about everyone thinking she was a good girl." Caleb's jaw clenched in fresh anger. He pushed past it. "There was no message at the barn."

"But they tried to grab her at the barn," Jazz pointed out.

"Daniel could have easily grabbed her from Connor's Trail. Either before I showed up or after she left the stream. If the goal was to get Nina, then he had the perfect opportunity."

"*And* Daniel wasn't at the barn," she said.

"No. He wasn't. But if he was working with the person who was, they're not on the same page about what they want."

"Which seems to be Nina."

"Which seems to be Nina," he repeated.

"Okay, so Daniel is paid by—who? Nina's stalker? Statistically stalkers are loners. Not to mention, what's the point of using Daniel at all to send the email? Especially if they're going to do something as daring as what happened at the barn while Daniel had one heck of an alibi."

"It makes no sense," he agreed.

"And we're not even touching on the fires yet."

A thought occurred to Caleb, stirred by a memory. Then it was like the flood gates had opened.

"Daniel was a distraction." As soon as he heard it out

loud, Caleb believed it to be true. He went to the white-board and touched Daniel's name. "He's paid to take Nina's picture and send her the email. We arrest him and suddenly he has a lawyer who gets him out." He touched the note about Daniel being attacked. "But then he has a change of heart because he's told something he didn't know and investigates. He finds—" Caleb touched the one word that he'd have preferred to be the name of whoever was behind the barn incident. "Kerosene. He said it was for camping."

Adrenaline shot through Caleb at the rush of seeing something he'd missed. He jabbed the spots on the white-board beneath the Gentry's house fire and the one at Overlook Pass.

"Kerosene was used as an accelerant at both. Did you hear what the fire chief said about kerosene?"

Jazz nodded, standing. The look of excitement he recognized from leads panning out crossed her expression.

"Yeah, that it's not a popular tool for arson because of the smell and how careful you have to be to use it. There are much easier and less deadly ways to start a fire."

"But what if there's a reason you use kerosene?"

He picked up the dry erase marker and wrote down *Angelica DeMarko* at the beginning of the timeline for the fires.

"This is the only fire to not be related somehow to a front-page story in the paper that ran a week before it took place. This fire spread so quickly because it hit camping supplies, namely kerosene."

He tossed the marker to Jazz, who caught it, and then went to his computer. He started a search, emboldened by a potential connection.

"So, what? You're thinking Angelica is our arsonist? Kerosene was only at two of the four other fires," Jazz pointed out. "Not to mention yours was started by fire-

works. Once arsonists find their grooves, pathologically they usually have to stick to that method, like a serial killer might. Breaking that pattern would be nearly impossible for them. And how does that tie in with Daniel?"

Caleb didn't respond. Not yet. He was working through a hunch, one that he knew was a long shot. A hefty, long-wing-spanned stretch.

Then he found what he was looking for and felt another wave of excitement.

"I don't think Angelica had anything to do with the fires. She hasn't been back since she left town for a better job out of state." Caleb looked at Jazz. "But her son, Jay, was cited for drunk and disorderly in town a month before the Gentry's house fire."

"That's a stretch, Caleb," she warned.

"Oh, I know," he said, breezing past it. "But what if, after Jay watched his house burn, he realized he liked it? It triggered something in him."

Jazz continued to look skeptical. She opened her mouth to argue but then closed it fast. Her eyes widened.

"Caleb, he was the grill cook."

"What?"

This time she went to her computer and did a search. Caleb hurried around his desk to look at her screen. She pulled up a picture of the newspaper article about the fire at the restaurant that he'd taken at the library. She pointed to one of the last paragraphs. It was a quote.

From Jay DeMarko.

"He said he looked away for a few seconds before the fire started," she paraphrased. "He was the grill cook."

"This might be a stretch but it's more than we've had in a while," Caleb said, grabbing the keys off his desk before going back to his computer. He wrote down the ad-

dress on his screen. "I say it's time we go have a talk with Jay DeMarko."

"You think he's trying to make us think he's a stalker when really he's our arsonist? But how does Daniel fit into this?"

"I don't know. This could be nothing, just me trying to find a win," Caleb admitted. "Or we could have just found our missing piece."

THE RAIN HELD off as Caleb and Jazz drove to Jay's apartment. Instead the air was filled with that same electric charge that he'd felt the day his house had burned down. It was foreboding. Caleb hoped it wasn't a sign of bad things to come.

He parked his truck outside a set of stairs that led to the second floor unit that was listed on Jay's citation. His brows knitted together.

"Delores Dearborn lives right there," he said, pointing to the apartment on the ground floor.

"Eerie coincidence?" Jazz asked, checking her service weapon discretely below the dashboard. Caleb followed suit.

"I'll let you know."

They had both donned their blazers, a tactic they adopted when they had to deal with potential suspects. It hid their guns and badges until they were ready for either to be seen. Hiding the badge especially kept perps from running before they ever got a chance to talk to them. Caleb straightened his to make sure the badge on his hip wasn't peeking out and went up the stairs. He knocked on the door. The force pushed it open.

Caleb and Jazz shared a silent look. Both pulled out their guns and held them low.

"Hello?" Caleb called, cautiously. From his vantage point the living room was empty.

No one responded.

"This is the Wildman County Sheriff's Department," he tried again. "We're here to talk to Jay DeMarko."

Again, no one replied.

Caleb and Jazz nodded to each other before they entered the apartment.

It was the same layout as Delores's downstairs unit. Caleb led the way as they cleared the living room, kitchen and bathroom. There were two doors left. The first was open. It was a bedroom. Sparse, no sentimental items or decorations. Caleb opened the closet. Also sparse. Only a few shirts were on hangers. There was a closed suitcase on the floor. Caleb decided to come back to that after they checked that the last room was clear.

This time Jazz led the way. He threw open the next door as she rushed in, gun drawn. She was met with no resistance but Caleb heard her gasp clear as day.

"Holy—" she started before letting the thought trail off.

Caleb wholeheartedly agreed.

On the wall next to the bed there were cut-out newspaper articles taped across it. Caleb silently scanned them while Jazz went to look in the open closet.

"Delores wrote all of these," Caleb said, voice low. "Not just above-the-fold stories, either."

"If this Jay guy has a thing for Delores, I'm guessing he also has a thing for kerosene."

Caleb looked away from the collage. Jazz pointed to the floor of the closet. Caleb went to her side.

"I know I'm no camping enthusiast but I feel like that's more than what you need for camping," she added.

Caleb crouched down and eyed several containers of kerosene. He cussed.

"You definitely don't need fifteen canisters of it."

Jazz got out her cell phone and started to take pictures. They didn't have a warrant and the excuse they had come inside to make sure no one was in distress would only get them so far. Caleb was careful not to touch anything as he leaned into the closet to make sure he hadn't missed a clue.

The bad feeling he'd had since they walked into the apartment was only growing.

"Let's say Jay DeMarko is our arsonist, triggered by the fire that destroyed his home," Caleb started, rolling forward to the balls of his feet. "He pays Daniel to be a distraction with Nina so he can split our focus. Then, when Daniel comes and sees the kerosene and doesn't believe when Jay says it's for camping supplies, Daniel decides he doesn't want any part of it."

"Then Jay goes and beats the crap out of Daniel to try and shut him up, but Daniel's girlfriend scares him off." Jazz added to the theory. Caleb stood and looked back at the wall and the newspaper articles. Jazz voiced his next question. "But how does Delores fit into this?"

Adrenaline threaded back into Caleb's system.

"She covered his house fire," he said. "She interviewed Angelica and Jay. It was the only article that she wrote about a fire that came *after* one actually happened. It started with her when she wrote that story." He slapped his thigh as more puzzle pieces fit with each other. "And that's why there's a gap in the middle of them all. Delores left town for a year. She didn't write anymore stories. The fires didn't start until she came back and started again."

"Do you think she's in on it, then?"

Caleb shook his head. His gut and her alibis said no. Still, the bad feeling that was growing was reaching an all-time high.

"But I think we need to talk to her. Now."

They rushed out of the apartment and down the stairs to Delores's front door. Caleb didn't have time to curse when they found it was slightly open. He shouldered in and immediately tensed.

The neat living room was trashed. The couch was overturned, a lamp was shattered and the coffee table was cracked. There was blood on the wall closest to one of the bedroom doors.

Wordlessly Caleb opened the first one. It was a stark contrast to Jay's rooms upstairs. The walls were covered in framed pictures and accolades, knickknacks lined the top of a massive dresser and books were stacked on the nightstand. The closet was open and only held hanging clothes.

They went to the next bedroom. It was set up as an office and had nothing of note. It also didn't have a Delores. Caleb finally spoke.

"Call this in while I call Declan. Something bad happ—"

"Detective Nash?"

The voice was far off but he recognized it.

"Delores?"

"I'm in here!"

They rushed back into the first bedroom. One of the large wardrobe doors opened up. Delores Dearborn spilled out. There was a moment when Caleb and Jazz stared in stunned silence. He knew that fear could give people the power to do things they normally couldn't but Delores stuffing herself into the cabinet was a bit startling. She winced as she rubbed her neck and then elbows. It shook the two detectives out of their temporary awe.

"What happened?" Jazz asked, crouching down to help the woman sit up.

A cursory look showed no outward signs of physical

distress, other than being stiff from her position in a confined space.

"I figured no one would think to look in there so I hid. Thank God for ten years of gymnastics."

"Why?" Caleb asked as Jazz helped the woman to her feet. "Did Jay attack you?"

Delores's eyes widened.

"Jay saved me from him."

Caleb and Jazz shared a look.

"From who?"

A look of acute alarm crossed Delores's expression. That's when Caleb realized why nothing had been completely adding up. Why the pieces they had weren't forming a puzzle that made sense.

There was a third man.

Chapter Eighteen

Nina was in the kitchen at the main house when she heard a car speed up the road and then slam on its brakes. She didn't recognize the man behind the wheel but it didn't matter.

She saw the gun in his hand when he stepped out.

The glass she was holding clattered into the sink. Nina ran into the hallway between the kitchen and living room. She hurried to the front door and threw the deadbolt just as a shadow appeared on the other side. She didn't wait around to see if he saw her and hurried through to the living room.

The sheriff had been riding on two days with no rest. The glass breaking in the sink hadn't woken him.

But Nina was going to have to.

There were two large windows in the front of the room. Thankfully the couch Declan was on was facing the opposite direction. Nina hit the floor next to it and hesitated.

She hoped Declan wasn't one of those people who woke up swinging.

The front door knob shook. Then the sound of footsteps moved across the wraparound porch. Another shadow appeared. This time on the hardwood on the other side of the couch.

Nina placed her arms over Declan's chest and stomach.

Then she whispered his name next to his ear. The tension was almost instant. His eyes flew open, his nostrils flared and he tried to push her off. Nina fastened her grip across him like two seat belts.

"Shh, Declan it's me," she whispered quickly. "It's Nina."

His eyes swiveled to her, his breathing already fast. Nina bet adrenaline was rocking through him, blasting away the haze of sleep and confusion. He gave her a small nod. She pulled her arms back to her sides.

"There's a man at the window with a gun," she said, voice so low she worried he might not have heard her.

Apparently he had. His eyes roved the floor next to her. She assumed he saw the shadow. His eyes widened.

"Hand me my gun," he said, matching her volume.

Nina did as she was told, gently moving the holstered weapon between the coffee table and the sheriff. She moved back so he had room to crawl to the floor next to her, careful to keep the couch as cover.

"Where's Mom?"

Nina pointed up.

"The attic."

Nina was supposed to be with her but had taken a detour to get more water.

Declan checked his gun. The shadow moved, footfalls going in the opposite direction. She guessed he was headed to the next large window. It belonged to the study.

"Use the stairs, grab Mom and hide," Declan urged her.

Nerves knotted Nina's stomach but she nodded. They moved at the same time but she lost track of what Declan was doing; her mind had zeroed in on one task and one task only. Keep Dorothy safe.

She took the stairs two at a time and hurried across the second floor landing to the small set of stairs at the op-

posite end that led to the attic. Somehow she managed to stay quiet, at least, enough that when she ran into the room Dorothy looked none the wiser.

The older woman had braided her hair back and donned a worn apron. In one hand she held a duster, in the other a thick binder. When she turned to Nina her expression was nothing but exasperated.

Then it quickly turned to worry.

"There's a man outside with a gun." Nina bowled through. "Declan told me to get you and then hide."

Bless her, Dorothy didn't hesitate.

She put down what she was holding and motioned for Nina to follow her.

"I've got a gun in my bedroom," she said as she passed.

Nina felt a small amount of relief at that. At least they wouldn't be defenseless if anything happened to—

A gunshot and glass shattering imploded the silent urgency around them. Dorothy stumbled backward on the landing. For one terrifying moment Nina thought she'd been the one shot. She wrapped her arms around the woman to steady her.

The second, third and fourth shots went off next. Each one made them both jump where they stood. A loud bang followed, shaking the floor slightly. Nina guessed someone had thrown open the front door. She tried to push Dorothy into moving but was met with surprising resistance.

That's when she realized what had the woman grounded.

Her son might be hurt. Or worse.

The fact that the shooting had stopped and Declan wasn't calling for them was more than gut wrenching.

But Nina had to keep Dorothy safe. They couldn't help Declan any more than they could help themselves if they were targeted next.

"We need your gun," Nina reminded the woman, whispering next to her ear.

Instead of pushing Dorothy, Nina moved around her and pulled her along, heading for the room she assumed belonged to the matriarch. It wasn't an easy task but Dorothy seemed to limber up once they had crossed the threshold into a room that Nina would have admired in any other situation.

"It's in my nightstand."

Dorothy pointed to the one she meant and turned to face the door. Nina hustled, every second without any sounds from downstairs grating against her skin. The gun was there, like Dorothy said. Nina didn't know much about them but knew just because it was small and fit easily in her palm didn't mean it wouldn't do a good amount of damage.

Nina went and grabbed Dorothy's hand. She pulled the older woman to the closet. It was a large walk-in. Stacks of luggage along one of the walls made the perfect place to hide. She started to say as much when a man shouting met their ears.

And it wasn't Declan.

"Nina Drake, if you don't come down here right now I'll kill the sheriff."

Nina froze.

Dorothy didn't.

She started forward, not even bothering to ask for the gun.

"Wait," Nina insisted.

"He's got my baby!"

Dorothy had such a fierce look in her eyes, Nina knew then there was nothing she could say to stop the woman. No matter that he'd asked for Nina and not her. No matter that they didn't even know if Declan was still alive.

No matter that the angry man might just kill anyone who walked down the stairs.

No, Dorothy was going to go save her son no matter what.

So Nina made a decision right then and there.

Her mother had been killed by senseless anger. She wasn't going to let Caleb's mother suffer the same fate.

"Let me go first," she said, fear releasing its hold long enough for her to form a plan. "He asked for me. Here, you can take the gun and watch my back."

Dorothy's maternal rage saw sense in that. She took the handgun and let Nina leave the closet first. A choice she was about to regret.

Nina whirled around and shut the closet door in Dorothy's face. She pushed her hip against the wood while reaching for the nightstand next to it. The piece of furniture was heavy, not cheap. Nina barely managed to pull it close enough to wedge it against the door.

"Nina," Dorothy warned through it.

"I'll save Declan," she said right back. "I need you to be safe."

Nina didn't wait around to discuss it any further. She left the room and made it to the stairs.

"You better not be doing anything dumb," the voice warned from the first floor, close enough that Nina knew he was near the foot of the stairs. From this angle she couldn't see his face. Or Declan's. "That includes having a weapon. If I see anything, I'm going to kill both of you and then go hunting for the Nash mother. Got it?"

"I'm unarmed," she promised. "I'm coming down now."

Her legs shook but Nina slowly descended, arms raised to prove she wasn't holding anything. It wasn't until her shoes hit the hardwood floor that the reasons she hadn't wanted Dorothy to come down really sank in.

A man she didn't recognize stepped into view from the living room. Tall, lanky, young. His hair was pulled back in a low ponytail and his dark eyes were blazing with defiance. He had a gun pointed at her.

"Glad to finally meet the infamous Nina Drake," he said, sounding not at all glad. "I've heard so much about you, but I'm afraid we're going to have skip the talking and leave. You first."

He motioned to the front door. It was off its hinges, the glass portion now scattered along the floor. Nina took a breath and walked across it to the front porch.

"Who are you and where's—" she started but then gasped. "Declan!"

On the porch, outside of what had once been the living room window, was the sheriff. He was lying on his side, eyes closed, blood collecting across his shirt.

"He's not dead, just shot," the man said at her back. "But I'll make sure he's dead right now if you don't help me get him into the car. We're kind of on a timeline right now."

Nina didn't question him, especially after she confirmed Declan was, in fact, still breathing. He'd been shot in the shoulder and stirred as they struggled to lift and then drag him to the car. A feat in itself, given how large the man was. Nina slid into the back seat with him, refusing to leave his side. The gunman got into the front and started the engine.

"Put pressure on it," he commanded, voice tight. Nina raised her eyebrow. He saw it in the rearview. "Put pressure on the wound to help stop the bleeding."

Nina was about to question why the man had given her the advice when he'd been the one who created the wound in the first place, but their attention flew to a second car racing their way. The man cussed something awful and tried to peel out. The other car didn't want that.

It slammed into them.

Nina didn't have time to yell. She tried her best to keep Declan from flying out of his seat. A warm wetness pressed against her face as she wedged her body between the sheriff and the front seats. Their captor strung together several not-so-great words again. He stopped the car, flung open his door and then opened the one behind her. Nina couldn't scramble away from his grip. He grabbed the back of her shirt and pulled.

"Let go," he ground out when Nina refused to move. "Let go or I'll shoot him in the head."

Nina didn't want to but she believed the man. She let go and was yanked right out of the car. The man kept his grip on the back of her shirt. He didn't move them, though. Instead, his attention was on the driver of the car that had just hit them.

"You did this to yourself," he yelled out. "You went after mine so I went after yours!"

The car door opened but before the newcomer stepped out he had a word of warning.

"If you hurt her, I'll kill you."

The voice was low yet booming.

And familiar.

"You need me," her captor replied with vehemence. He shook his grip. Nina winced at the movement, her nerves more than shot at this point. "So let us leave."

The man behind the wheel of the other car slowly got out.

He was grinning.

The man at her back readjusted his grip on her shirt to around her neck. It forced her head to tilt back, but she still could see the man across from them.

Every part of Nina split in two.

Half was in the present.

The air had cooled because of the impending storm. She smelled the promise of rain on the breeze and the sweet smell of Dorothy's blooming flowers from her garden just beneath it. She could see the ranch and its green grass, bountiful trees and beautiful fields stretching out all around them. She could feel the dirt displacing beneath her shoe as the man behind her forced her to change her stance to keep steady.

The other half of her was in a much different place.

The asphalt burned her bare feet, her flip-flops long abandoned. The smell of the sea mixed with the wind that gently blew across the trees next to her. An acrid smell of burning metal was cloying.

A boy had his arms around her, a weight that kept her tethered to a world that was burning in front of her.

And there was that smile.

His father, staring at the wreckage, like he didn't have a care in the world.

Then, all at once, the past and the present collided.

Thanks to that same smile.

This time, it was worn by the son.

Jeremy Bowling met her gaze without any surprise whatsoever. He even gave her a small nod of hello.

"Nina, why don't you come over here?" he said, patting his hand against his leg like she was a dog. The man who had a grip on her neck didn't want her to comply to the new command.

"If you even think about it I'll kill the sheriff," he seethed. Jeremy heard the threat. He tilted his head to the side, looking into the back of their car.

"You're using the eldest Nash to control her," he stated analytically. His eyes roamed back to hers. "I'm surprised it works, to be honest."

With a speed that didn't seem possible, Jeremy pulled

his gun up and shot. Nina didn't have time to scream. She didn't have time to even move. The hand around her neck loosened and then the pressure was gone. Shaking like a leaf, Nina chanced a look behind her.

The man fell to the ground. His eyes were wide. He looked down at the bullet wound in his chest.

Footsteps crunched across the dirt, coming closer. Nina cursed herself for not scooping up the gun when she had the chance. Jeremy appeared at her shoulder, so close she could smell the spice of aftershave.

"Maybe you are a good girl, after all."

Nina opened her mouth but, like the shot, Jeremy was once again painfully fast.

The blow against her head knocked Nina out cold.

Chapter Nineteen

The throbbing of pain let Nina know she was alive. That was her first thought. It wasn't as comforting as it should have been.

Pain pulsed along every blink as she clawed her way out of unconsciousness. A gray room materialized through the fog, filled with odd, dingy white shapes. It took longer than it should have to realize they were pieces of furniture covered in sheets.

Nina was tied to a chair among them.

She turned her head to try and see behind her. The moan that escaped happened before she could stop it. Pain stabbed at her so quickly, the wave of nausea that followed nearly overwhelmed her. She closed her eyes tight and took long breaths. Waking up in a room she didn't recognize, alone and bound to a chair, wasn't a good situation. She didn't want to add getting sick all over herself to that list.

The urge to vomit lessened. The pain didn't. Nina took the small win and, this time, slowly turned her head. A window was set at the back of the room. She only saw dark skies.

"Not helpful," she grumbled.

Next she tested her restraints. Rope dug into her wrists behind the chair. There was no leeway. No give. Jeremy had done more than a great job at that.

Jeremy.

Nina didn't say the name out loud, but after she thought it a shiver ran through her.

His last words before he knocked her unconscious had rooted themselves in her memory. They echoed the email Daniel Covington had sent.

And everyone thought you were a nice girl.

Maybe you are a nice girl, after all.

Jeremy had been behind the email, she was sure of it, but why? And who was the man who had shot Declan? And where was the sheriff?

Fear was an emotion she was becoming desensitized to at this point, confusion and frustration not so much.

Why was Jeremy in Overlook?

What did he want from her?

A pang of longing nearly brought that fear to a new level, one where she could feel it again. Just last night she'd let her guard down and gotten close with Caleb. Sharing the burdens of their pasts had done more for her heart than she ever thought it would. Sharing that burden with Caleb had done even more.

Yet she'd never thought her burden, her past, would put him and his family in danger.

Nina moved her feet around, testing the restraints at her ankles. Surprisingly they weren't as tight as the rope around her wrists. She pushed out her feet in opposite directions. The knot on top seemed to loosen.

A flash of hope burned through her.

She did the same thing again but moved each foot to a different spot before pushing out. The rope became more slack. She continued, rotating where she pushed out on the rope each time until it finally came untied.

Riding another jolt of adrenaline, Nina rocked forward and stood, thankful the chair was of the dining variety and

not something clunky like a lounger. It was an awkward move but after a few moments she managed to steady herself, despite being hunched over.

Then she had to look around the room.

If she had to guess she was in an attic of some sort, much like the one at the ranch's main house. There were no closets, only one light that hung in the middle of the room, and in between the pieces of furniture were several boxes labeled with names like Christmas, Halloween and Rider's Graduation. Nina went to the Christmas box and set her chair down. With her feet she tried to finagle the box open.

It didn't work.

She gave up and went to the closest sheet, sat down and pulled it off. Beneath it was a wide and narrow bookcase Short, too. The edge of it was just the right height.

Nina stood and turned around again. She stifled a yelp as she lost her balance and collided with the floor. Unable to stop herself, her face took the brunt of the fall. She almost got sick again as a new source of pain exploded along her right brow. Warmth immediately slid across her skin.

Nina didn't have time to writhe in her mistake.

Wherever Jeremy was, if he was in the house he would have heard that.

She struggled back up to her feet and moved as close as she could to get the rope at her wrists near the edge of the piece of furniture. It looked like it was handmade, the top piece one long plank of stained wood. Its edge was what Nina was placing all of her hope on. It looked sharp, despite the rest of it seeming worn.

Whatever Jeremy had planned for her, it was nothing good.

A few minutes went by but no one came to the door. Nina was counting that blessing as she sawed. At first she

felt like a fool, doubting she was doing anything at all, but then the tension in the ropes lessened. It encouraged a more ferocious approach. Her legs burned and trembled as she supported the weight of the chair while hunching over so the ropes would meet the edge. Still, she didn't stop. When the rope was finally slack enough to give her confidence, Nina sat back down. She took a steadying breath and then pulled as hard as she could.

Feeling that rope break was better than sex. Or, at least, a close second.

She brought her hands in front of her and shed the rest of her bindings. Then she moved to the one around her waist. It was tied on the side but not impossible to unknot. She hurried through it, ignoring the stinging in her eye that was only getting worse. Once she was completely untethered from the dining chair she wiped the blood from her brow and crept to the window.

Finally Nina knew something.

Looking down and into the distance she spotted the familiar river where there used to be a bridge.

Overlook Pass, she thought with more excitement than it probably warranted to finally know at least one part of the situation. Which meant she was in the house that was just behind it. The owner had moved to be with her daughter, according to Caleb.

She scanned the room again with new attention. Nothing just screamed out weapon. She ended up going through most of the boxes, hoping the owner had labeled them incorrectly. Nina imagined a box full of guns that could help her defend herself hidden in a box that said University Things.

Nina decided to not waste any more time. She didn't even take a deep breath before she was opening the door as slowly as if a sleeping baby were right next to it. The

motion was easy but a low squeak sounded. Nina bit her lip and opened it far enough that she could slide through.

Like she'd suspected, she was in an attic much like Dorothy's. It opened into a slightly different layout but the important aspect was the same. She was on the second floor and the stairs were right in front of her. Theoretically she was closer to freedom than she had been. Two doors were on either side of the landing. Both were closed.

Declan.

What if Jeremy had taken him and he was tied to a chair in one of the other rooms?

Nina thought of Caleb and his obvious love for his family. It put the fire of courage in her belly, calming her quaking limbs. She hadn't even realized she'd been shaking.

The first room was much like the attic. Things were boxed up, furniture was covered by drop cloths. There was no Declan. The second room was a bit trickier. The door was locked.

Nina froze for a moment, worried she'd alert Jeremy if he was on the other side. When nothing happened she pressed her ear against the door, hoping to hear the sheriff.

She was both relieved and disappointed. It was nice not to hear a man tied up and in pain but there was no guarantee he would be making any noise. The last time she saw him he'd been unconscious.

Which brought her to the top of the stairs.

Nina bit her lip again.

Her head was throbbing. Her face was bleeding. The closer she came to escaping, the more she realized Jeremy could be waiting for her downstairs. What did he want?

This time anger came to the forefront of the emotional gauntlet she seemed to have been running for the last two days. It cut through her nerves and worries and she hurried down the stairs, trying her best to be quiet while also ready to turn her walk into an all-out run for her life if necessary.

Once she was off the last step she took that energy and spun around to look down the hallway. It seemed to run through the middle of the house, ending at the back door. The urge to run burned across the soles of her feet but she refused to leave Declan. If something happened to him, she would never forgive herself.

She crept along the hallway, pausing to listen every few steps. It felt like just an empty old house. Had Jeremy left her there? What was the plan?

The kitchen, former dining room and living room were empty. No boxes, no furniture with sheets. No signs of anyone else. Did that mean Declan could be upstairs?

If Jeremy wasn't in the house then surely she could go back and try to open the locked room without being caught, right?

Nina was about to turn around when a crack of thunder made her gasp. Like a scene from a horror movie, the back door opened. The man in its frame was for the briefest of seconds draped in shadows, blackened skies his backdrop.

Jeremy's eyes widened a moment then he smiled.

"I was about to come get you but this saves me a trip up the stairs."

Nina backpedaled so hard she almost toppled over. However, she refused to be the woman in most of those same horror movies who fell when she was being chased by the bad guy.

Yet Jeremy didn't make one move.

He didn't have to.

"You run, I kill Declan," he said simply.

Nina froze, eyes now on the front door. On freedom.

"I won't chase you," he added, voice nothing but conversational.

"What do you want, Jeremy?" she asked, her voice low and angry. "What could you possibly want?"

Nina turned back to face him. His smile was gone. Somehow that was more unsettling.

"I want to talk and then I want you to make a decision."

CALEB WAS SPITTING MAD. Hell, he was more than spitting. There was blood on the ground outside of the main house and not just in one spot. It started on the front porch, across the shattered living room window glass, and continued into the dirt. Then it disappeared, along with whatever car had been hit by the one he and Jazz had seen when they drove up.

Though that detail hadn't filtered in as fast since his mama was hanging over Jay DeMarko's prone body, cell phone on the dirt next to her, gun clearly sticking out of her apron pocket and hands covered in blood as she applied pressure to Jay's gunshot wound.

"I called the department because your phone was busy," his mother yelled as soon as he was out of the truck. Jazz was right behind him, pulling up in Delores's SUV. They hadn't wanted to leave her alone but hadn't had the time to wait for a deputy or to take her to the department themselves.

"I was calling you," he yelled, adrenaline making him lose control of his volume. Neither Nina nor Declan had answered so his mother had been his next call. Her phone had been busy. Now he knew why.

"After I broke down my own closet door I called an ambulance and Chief Deputy Murdock," she kept on, eyes wild.

Caleb came to her side but didn't remove his hand from his gun. Now he had more information. Jay wasn't the only man he had to worry about. Yet his mother let him know with one look that the threat was gone.

And the woman threatened with him.

What he didn't know was another kick to the gut.

"Caleb, a man took Nina and Declan." The look that accompanied that bad news was darker than the sky ever would be. "And I think Declan was shot." Caleb felt himself shift into work mode, detaching from the emotions broiling in his chest.

There was hell to pay and he couldn't afford to make any mistakes.

Chapter Twenty

"I met Jeremy when he moved upstairs." Delores stood at the head of the dining room table, chin up and voice strong. "We hit it off immediately and I even became friends with Jay. He seemed normal enough and Jeremy, well, he seemed perfect. I suppose that might have been on purpose now. He just had an answer for everything... until he didn't."

She directed her gaze at Caleb. Jazz stood at his side. His mother had gone to the hospital with a deputy and Jay at Caleb's insistence. Chief Deputy Murdock was leading the charge across the county to try and find Nina, Declan and Jeremy. Since every second counted, Caleb had been authorized to do a more pointed search, running down whatever leads Delores might be able to give them.

Not that he'd asked permission.

"When you showed up asking about the articles I wrote and the fires, I genuinely had no idea if or how they were important. Until you mentioned your house fire had been started by fireworks," she continued. "See, Jeremy and I never hung out at his apartment. He said he liked mine better since he hadn't had a chance to decorate his yet. But the week before you showed up I tried to bring him some dinner. The door was unlocked because he'd gone down to the mailboxes. I went into his room to see if he

was there but found a bag of fireworks instead. I thought it might have been a romantic surprise but when I asked him about it he gave me the oddest answer. He said it was a means to an end and none of my business."

Her jaw set.

"No one condescends to me without a fight. So I started digging. I looked past his Facebook and called a friend and finally found a news story about him. And Nina. I knew it couldn't be a coincidence that, after all these years, both of them wound up in small-town Overlook, Tennessee. Then I remembered what I'd heard about Claire and the new girl in town teaming up to take down Daniel Covington. I know his girlfriend so I called and she said he'd been released from jail. So then I called him and said if he was connected to Jeremy or Jay and knew anything about the fires or Nina he better come clean. Daniel may be full of himself half of the time, but he genuinely seemed to have no idea what I was talking about."

She managed to look sheepish. "Honestly, I was feeling so silly about it then, thinking I'd jumped to conclusions. So I was going to wait and call you in the morning—this morning—but then Jay woke me up."

There was no denying the fear that skated across Delores's expression at the memory.

"I never really talked to him but when he told me that I needed to hide because Jeremy was coming, I believed him with all of my heart. I ran into the bedroom, thanked God my Grandma Tildy gave me her larger-than-life wardrobe and stuffed myself into one of its cabinets. No sooner had I shut the door than they started fighting in the living room. I couldn't make out what they were saying in the scuffle but they both cut out of there quick. You showed up shortly after. And that's all I know."

"You're who Daniel was talking about," Caleb said

thoughtfully. "When he said, 'but then she called.' I think you're right. I don't think he had a clue about the fires. I think he went and confronted Jay and Jeremy and found the kerosene. Decided he didn't want any part of it. Jeremy or Jay found out and one of them tried to end him but his girlfriend spooked them before they could finish the job." Caleb refrained from adding *then Jeremy went to try and end you*, but by the look in her eyes, Delores had already put that together.

"We can get into the specifics later," Jazz intervened. "We know Jay doesn't have Declan and Nina, Jeremy does. We know, based on what you told us, Caleb, that Jeremy probably wants some kind of revenge for her testimony against his father, but where would he do it? And how? I hate to say it, but if he'd wanted both of them dead he could have done it easily right here."

Caleb didn't like that thought, though he knew it was true.

"Why did he go through all of whatever it is he did when it would have been much simpler and less risky to just grab her? Or, well, kill her."

"He has to make it dramatic."

Caleb was sure of it the moment it came out.

Realization lit up Jazz's expression.

"Because the trial was."

Caleb nodded. "Not only was his father facing prison and then sentenced, but it was turned into a spectacle. Some of the media even called the outcome poetic." He balled his fists in anger. "The pictures taken of Nina here were all of her smiling. A smile was what doomed his father. The smile she saw but he didn't. It's not just enough for Jeremy to win, he has to do it in style for it to count."

"That theory makes sense," Delores said. "Almost like an eye for an eye."

"How do the fires figure into this? He's trying to rec-reate the actual event?" Jazz paused before she said the next part. "Trapping her in a car and setting it on fire?"

They all quieted as they thought. Caleb pushed past his rage again. He didn't need the distraction right—

"Distractions," he said, more to himself. The one word sent a series of thoughts tumbling. "Jeremy has been in town for months, masterminding some kind of finale. We might have messed that up but he's not just going to scrap everything. Now, why would a man that dedicated and clever team up with someone like Jay DeMarko? An arsonist. Starting a fire isn't hard." He knew he must have looked crazed when he spoke next but his gut was finally syncing up with his head. "What are fires, Jazz?" Her eyebrow quirked up. He answered before she could. "They're dangerous, hard-to-miss, distracting."

"So you think he only used Jay to keep our attention on Jay."

"And Daniel Covington," Caleb reminded her. "We didn't even know there was a third guy and might not have if it wasn't for Delores."

Delores didn't comment on the compliment. Instead she voiced her own question.

"If he's not going to mirror what happened to Nina's mother then maybe he doesn't have a set pathology. Maybe he doesn't need to be that dramatic."

"You don't go through this much trouble just to smear the details at the end," Caleb said, sure in his words. He rubbed his jaw. Another uncomfortable thought pushed its way through. "Nina said that smoke inhalation was what killed her mother. But that's not true." Both women raised their eyebrows in question. "She was trapped. That's what

really killed her. That's what sealed her fate. And Jeremy's father didn't try to save her."

"But where would Jeremy try to trap her?" Delores asked.

Caleb's mind was racing.

"If he was using an arsonist as a distraction, then maybe he'd get his revenge in the last place we would think to look for one."

NINA LOOKED FROM the car down to the river. Her wrists were now tied behind her back and she was terrified.

"I thought you wanted to talk," she reminded Jeremy. He had walked her at gunpoint from the abandoned house's back door to where the Overlook Pass bridge had once been. Together they now stood at the river, Nina so close to the edge the temptation to leap in swayed through her while Jeremy kept his distance. The car she'd originally been forced into was parked a few feet from them, facing the water. Nina's heart squeezed as she saw Declan hunched over in the back seat.

Jeremy didn't make any assurances that talking was the only topic on the agenda. Instead, he jumped into a story that hardened his gaze and felt more than rehearsed.

"I see the way you look at me," he started. "You're trying to figure out if I've always been crazy or if it's a more recent development. Why am I in Overlook? Why did I abduct you? Why, why, why. The truth is, I'm not crazy, which honestly is worse, I think. I'm smart, hardworking and no stranger to sacrifice. I'm a trifecta, Nina. One this little town never stood a chance against." He smirked. "But why, the little girl thought?" he added, adopting an almost whimsical tone. Nina found it more frightening than if he had been yelling.

His smirk was wiped clean by practiced indifference.

"You know, I didn't think about you for a few years. I actually did quite well for myself. I'd always had an interest in the medical field but figured out that the mind is a much more challenging beast to tame. So I became a psychiatrist. I went to college on an academic scholarship, graduated with an MD, completed a quite grueling residency and then joined a psychiatry practice where everyone called me Doctor Bowling. It reminded me of all the things I'd gained. And then my father died in prison."

Nina was speechless on more than one account. Jeremy was right. She had assumed he was crazy, imaging a young boy warping into a disturbed man. But a psychiatrist?

And his father had died?

How had she missed that information? The local media had proven to be sharks when it came to the trial. Surely they would have used his death to rehash it.

"Not many people know," he said, picking up on her thoughts. "His suicide wasn't tantalizing enough. The money I spread around to keep it quiet helped, too, I'm sure."

"I'm sorry." Nina meant it, even if she would never forgive the eldest Bowling. Still, losing a parent was heartbreaking, especially when they didn't die naturally.

Jeremy gave her a critical eye, then nodded.

"Do you know he was one of the only two living relatives I had? After the trial I was shipped off to his mother's. I don't think I'll ever meet someone as horrible as her. She didn't care for my father and she only cared to yell at me. When she died the world became a brighter place. I was finally free of all the bad." There was a fire in his eyes. Nina wondered how his grandmother died but didn't want to interrupt his speech. Every moment they kept talking was another moment given to Caleb and the department

to try and find them. Nina didn't know how long she'd been unconscious. She wanted to make sure she stalled as long as she could.

Plus, Jeremy had an intriguing air about him. He was oddly captivating when he spoke. Nina assumed that was thanks to his profession.

"But when Dad died, I realized freedom and escape were illusions I'd made to cope with my grief. That there was a truth I'd been avoiding for years." He lowered the gun. Somehow it made him appear far more menacing. "You, Nina Drake. You lied. My father never smiled."

Nina broke through her decision to keep quiet.

"He was smiling, Jeremy," she said, voice low but strong. "I saw him. He was standing there and—"

"He said it was an accident," Jeremy roared.

Nina flinched but refused to cower.

"He hit the car on the purpose," she shot back. "The investigation showed that he didn't once hit the brakes! You were in the car! Did it seem like an accident?"

Jeremy's face reddened in anger.

"I never saw him smile!"

"But he did!"

Jeremy brought the gun up and shook it. He took a step closer. This time Nina did move backward.

"Shut up," he seethed. "You lied! I saved you and how do you repay me?" Nina couldn't step back any farther without falling off of the ledge and into the water. She had nowhere to go as Jeremy moved so close to her that she felt his breath against her face as he yelled. "You lie! You lied to the cops, you lied on the stand, and worst of all, to everyone you became the hero!"

He pushed the gun to her chest and used his other hand to point to himself.

"I was the hero!"

Nina feared that this was it. That she had run out of time. Whatever poise Jeremy had possessed was clearly gone.

What did they say about reasoning with a madman? Don't.

Nina kept quiet, her heart hammering in her chest.

Finally the heat behind Jeremy's eyes seemed to cool. He lowered the gun and actually laughed.

"Now it's time to go."

He stepped back and motioned to the car.

"What?"

He continued to point.

"Go to the car now and get into the driver's seat or I'll go kill the sheriff."

The space between the riverbank and the car seemed dreadfully long. And it felt too much like a dead man's march.

"So you're going to kill us?" She chanced the question as she reached the door. He still had his gun trained on her. "As punishment for what you believe?"

He cracked a smile that in every way was opposite of the ones Caleb had given her. The detective's were warm, kind and compassionate. Jeremy's were twisted and menacing, and promised pain.

"I'm going to give my father justice by showing you the truly bad intentions you made others believe he had that day." He glanced at the water. "This is the deepest part of the river for miles and miles. I convinced Jay to hone his arson's method on the bridge that used to be here so there would be enough room." His twisted smile stretched. "You're going to drive this car right into it, where you'll then sink to the bottom and become trapped."

Nina's blood froze.

"Why would I do that?" she asked, unable to stop the

waver that broke through. "Why wouldn't I just let you shoot me now?"

Jeremy pointed to the backseat.

"Because of him," he said of Declan. "If you drive the two of you into the water there's a high chance you'll both drown. But if you don't there's a one hundred percent chance he will receive a bullet to the head and then I'll simply throw you in the car myself to get the job done. Now, get in the car or—" he moved so his aim was on Declan's unconscious form "—the sheriff never wakes up again."

Nina nodded that she understood. Jeremy opened the car door and let her maneuver into the driver's seat. He put the car in Drive.

"Not only am I smart, Nina, I'm an excellent shot, even with moving targets," he said. "All you will do is floor it, and gravity and inertia will do the rest. Anything else and you'll just drown with a corpse."

Nina felt sick to her stomach.

"This won't change anything," she said. "This won't bring either of our parents back."

Jeremy shook his head.

"What you don't understand Nina, is that I know people. I know what they're thinking. In hindsight you would have died, too, that day, trying to save your mother. You're only here now because I saved you. Now I'm correcting the mistake. *We're* correcting a mistake."

Jeremy started to shut the door but paused. He had one last dramatic parting shot.

"And then, while you're drowning down there, do you know what I'll do, daughter of the victim?"

She didn't respond.

She already knew the answer.

"I'll. Just. Smile."

Chapter Twenty-One

Nina thought they would be okay. At least, she had hope still as they started to sink. She guessed the water was around twelve-feet deep, maybe more. The drop to meet it she hadn't been nearly as far. All the windows were up which meant they would hopefully just go to the bottom and sit there, giving Caleb and company more time to find them. At least she hoped that was what might happen. In truth she had no idea what to do. She also hoped the man who attacked them at the main house, who she guessed was their arsonist, had survived and told Caleb everything. Including where this plan had ended. Though, as the water rose above the door handles just outside, Nina made another guess.

Their arsonist hadn't been in the loop.

Which meant there might not be any bread crumbs to follow to save her and Declan.

Those weren't happy thoughts to have but, again, she still had hope as the windows were covered by a brilliant, cool blue.

But then the water started coming in.

Declan groaned, bringing Nina fresh relief, until she saw what had stirred him.

The window behind his head was cracked open and water was coming in fast. On reflex Nina tried to angle

her hands to the power window controls but nothing happened. She let out an anguished cry. Now their hope of sitting at the bottom of the river was gone. Now they had until the water filled the car.

"Declan?"

The sheriff's eyes opened slowly, water spilling down his shoulder. Nina did an awkward scurry over through the middle of the seats until she was falling against the man.

"What's going on?" he managed, catching her.

Nina could have sung for joy in an instant.

"Untie my hands," she yelled.

Bless him, the sheriff immediately went into action. The power in the car cut out. The light outside was fading as the water poured in.

Her bonds loosened and fell away. Nina immediately turned and helped Declan move as far away from the water as the back seat allowed. The movement came along with a string of moans from the man. When he spoke again his voice was dangerously weak.

"When—when the water gets to your chin you—you might be to open the door. If not, wait. It'll pressurize when it's—when it's full" He started to fall over. Nina used her position against the door to wrap her arms around him, letting her chest hold up his back.

"Then we'll swim out," she said defiantly.

He was barely able to shake his head.

"Leave me."

"I'm not leaving you, Declan. Do you hear me? I am not letting you die down here."

Nina waited for his retort. Instead his body went limp against her. The added weight was surprising. It pinned her against the door.

Declan remained silent.

The darkness was a terrifying companion to the rising

water. Nina should have been scared, and yet her body was calm.

And she had Caleb Nash to thank for that.

She hadn't known the man for long but knew one thing was certain. He would fight to his very last breath to save the ones he loved.

Which was exactly what she was going to do for him.

She pressed one hand against Declan's gunshot wound and waited. If she couldn't get out when it got to their heads then she'd have to get them out as fast as possible when the inside was completely flooded.

There were no other options.

The cold from the river wrapped itself around her, crawling higher and higher.

"Easy peasy."

CALEB HAULED ASS to the Overlook Pass. He didn't even slow down as he rounded the house that stood sentry across from it. He didn't even reduce speed when Jeremy Bowling raised his gun and started shooting.

In fact, what Caleb felt was an overwhelming amount of relief. He had been operating under a theory, a hunch. One that could have been devastatingly off. Yet, there Jeremy was, standing by the river.

That relief fell as fast as Caleb's stomach did.

The river.

Caleb took a sharp turn and hit the brakes. He jumped out shooting, using his car as cover. Jazz and Delores were right behind. There was nowhere for Jeremy to run and hide now.

He took three bullets to the middle before he dropped his gun. Caleb was running to the riverbank before Jeremy's body hit the ground.

"In the water," he yelled back as soon as he saw the

distorted darkness at the bottom of the water and bubbles coming to the surface.

Caleb dropped his gun and took a running jump. He dove in headfirst, Jazz yelling behind him.

The water was cold. It would have been a shock to his system had his blood not been coursing with full-blown adrenaline. He pumped his legs and arms and descended into the darkness. It wasn't until he was a few feet from the car that he saw the terrifying sight.

The back door was open. One body was floating outside of it. Caleb didn't have time to sort through the terrible thoughts before movement caught his eye. The body outside of the car was Declan's, the one moving next to him was Nina. Her eyes widened as he reached them. She didn't waste any time. She pointed to Declan and then up to the surface. She even gave him a push.

Caleb realized then Declan's eyes were closed. It tore at his heart. Nina pointed again. Caleb looped his arm around his brother and used the car's hood to push off. They soared through the water. Two splashes displaced the area next to them as they broke the surface. Jazz was already reaching for Declan, Delores at his side.

"Help me get him to the bank over there," Jazz yelled. Delores followed directions. They pulled Declan from his arms.

"Where's Nina?"

Caleb turned, expecting to see her break the surface next to him and smile.

But she didn't.

Caleb dove back under, heart two seconds from breaking loose and going to get her itself, and swam the fastest he ever had back to the car. Nina was still moving but she wasn't going anywhere. Her foot was caught on something in the car.

Caleb reached down to her ankle. The seat belt had tangled around her. He reached for the knife in his pocket, thankful his dad had passed on the tradition to him. Nina's hand gripped his shoulder.

Then that grip loosened altogether.

He sawed through the belt with added ferocity. When it gave he grabbed her and pushed off the top of the car for the second time. Again, he soared through the water.

Again, the person he was holding wasn't moving.

Stay with me, Nina.

Please.

RAIN.

Nina heard it before she saw it.

"Oh! You're waking up!"

Nina's eyelids felt woefully heavy. They fought her and gravity as she tried to open them. By the time she did the voice was much closer—one she didn't recognize but was, at the same time, familiar.

"Hi there," said the woman. She wore a floral-patterned dress with a blazer and had a braid running over her shoulder. Her hair was an exact match for Caleb's, just as her smile was. A small but noticeable scar ran across her left cheekbone.

"You're Madi," Nina guessed. The woman nodded.

"The best of the siblings, in my opinion," she joked. "But I can talk more about that later. Right now I bet my last dollar that you have some questions. First, though, how are you feeling? What's the last thing you remember?"

Nina blinked a few times as if the movement could pull out her memories. They came slowly.

"I was in the car at the bottom of the river," she started. "Declan told me to wait until the water got to our chins or flooded the inside to try and open the door and leave him,

but I told him no." Madi's expression softened. "I got the door open and was going to push him out with me." Nina remembered the seat belt then. She glanced down at her ankle. All she saw were white sheets. She realized with a start that she was in the hospital. "When I was trying to get Declan out I got caught in the seat belt. It—it startled me and I lost some of the breath I was holding. Then I saw Caleb." Madi's pleasant smile took on an unmistakable mask of pride. "I told him to take Declan up. Then I remember he came back. Then I couldn't breathe."

Madi reached out and patted Nina's hand with reassurance.

"From what I've been told, Caleb pulled you out and gave you CPR on the riverbank after you surfaced. You coughed up water and started breathing again but had a hard time waking up." Madi motioned around the room. "The doctor said it was exhaustion. From what I was told, you had quite an intense past few days."

Nina nodded. Adrenaline and stress had been hard enough. Add in drowning and she could see how her body decided to take a sabbatical.

"How's Declan?" Nina asked, guilt pooling in her stomach. She should have asked about him first.

Madi's smile broke a little but she answered without pause.

"It was very touch-and-go at the beginning but he's hanging in there," she said. "He might not be a part of our triplet bond but I can feel it in my bones that he'll come through this. If there was one thing he got from our father it's an unwavering stubbornness."

Nina felt a weight lift in relief. Then she was looking around the room for his brother. Madi seemed to pick up on it. Her smile was whole again.

"It was hard to get Caleb to leave your side," she of-

fered. "But he knew your father would have questions so he and Des went to go get him from the airport."

Nina almost sat all the way up.

"My dad?"

Madi nodded.

"Let this be the first lesson you learn about life on the ranch—when one of us gets hurt, we all get hurt. We're all family. Nothing stops us from making sure we're all okay. That includes calling in dads when their only child gets targeted by a madman."

Days ago Nina would have argued, would have groaned at the idea, but now she found she didn't have the heart to do it. In fact, she realized a visit from her dad, even with the stress of what had happened attached, might do her heart some good. She'd been living so long with it locked up, it sure needed some fresh air. Though mention of a madman brought her to the next series of questions.

"What happened to Jeremy?"

This time Madi hesitated.

"I'll give you the bare bones of what I know but the rest you should get from Caleb. I think he's still putting it together. But what I *do* know is that Jeremy was killed in the firefight next to the river. Caleb and Jazz defended themselves and then immediately went into the water."

Nina didn't know how to feel about Jeremy's death. Relief wasn't the right word; sadness wasn't either. It was something she would, no doubt, think about for a long time to come.

"Now that we got that out of the way, I have to ask you a personal question," Madi continued. "If that's alright with you."

Nina found herself nodding. She liked Madi already.

"So, Mom told me in the hallway before Caleb left that *she* thinks you two have kissed and I am trying my hard-

est not to be nosy but—" Madi stopped mid-thought and busted out laughing. Nina's cheeks were warm and she was smiling like a schoolgirl. "Just a word of advice— when this all settles down and Mom comes at you with relationship questions, you might want to work on your poker face."

Nina couldn't help it. She laughed.

Chapter Twenty-Two

Nina found him at the fence line closest to where his house used to be. His horse, Ax, was roaming next to him while the man sat on the posts, gaze sweeping over the debris that used to be his home. Nina felt her heart squeeze. Part of it was sympathy for the man, most of it was just because of the man in general.

"Hey there," she called. Caleb looked over his shoulder and graced her with one of his famous smiles. He started to get down but Nina shook her head. "I'll join you."

She set the big bag she'd been carrying against the wooden fence as he helped her up and over the top. For a moment they were quiet. Nina took in a deep, cleansing breath and let it out. Caleb was still smiling. She still marveled over how their silence was always companionable.

"I just came back from dropping Dad off at the airport," she said after a while. "He wanted me to thank you again for all the hospitality you've shown him the last week. And for the whole saving my life thing again."

Caleb chuckled.

"I was just paying off a life-saving debt I owed you," he teased. "It's what any good cowboy would do."

Nina laughed as he looped his arm around her shoulders and pulled her closer.

It had been a week since Nina had woken up in the hos-

pital. In that time she'd seen less of Caleb than she had the week they had basically lived together. Between Declan's condition, dealing with the investigation and Nina's father wanting to spend every second with her, they'd only managed to snag a few minutes here and there to talk. Now things were starting to settle again, slowly but surely. Caleb had called her that morning, telling her he'd be at his house around lunch to finally talk about what had happened.

She couldn't deny the idea had been daunting, but now, in the sunshine and the embrace of a charming man, it felt easier.

Caleb must have sensed that, too. He dove in.

"We finally talked to Jay yesterday. The doctor said he'd recover, which seemed to have made him decide he needs to cooperate with us since he's not going anywhere anytime soon and neither are we. Turns out Jeremy approached him in a bar in town where they became fast friends and roommates. Jeremy saw the anger in Jay and exploited it."

"About the house fire when he was younger?"

Caleb nodded.

"That fire was an accident, but when they couldn't afford to rebuild and then had to move, Jay blamed the town for it. The only person he claimed showed them any kindness was Delores when she wrote the article. After that he became obsessed with her. He said he believed that when her stories were above-the-fold it was her way of showing him what was most important to the town. That way he knew what to take from it to make everyone here hurt like he and his mother had. The fire at the restaurant and Gloria's were his way of trying to find a method he enjoyed using to start the fires. But then Delores moved away and he became depressed. He found a friend in Jeremy and even found an apartment near Delores when she came

back. Eventually Jay realized that kerosene was his preferred method when he tested it out on the Overlook Pass."

"But what about the fire at your house?" Nina asked. "Fireworks started it."

Caleb ran a hand through his hair.

"This is where it starts to get bananas. Jeremy set the fire at the Gentrys' and the fire at my house while he tasked Jay with following you and taking pictures. Jay said Jeremy told him it would give both of them airtight alibis if the cops ever came looking. Jeremy apparently wasn't that great at using kerosene, though, and burned his arm pretty badly. That's why he switched it up to fireworks on my place. They were easier."

"How does Daniel Covington fit into this, then? What was his role?"

Caleb sighed.

"I think Jeremy was using him as a patsy." He shrugged. "It could have worked, I suppose, had Delores not spooked Daniel into going to confront Jay. He found the kerosene. He already knew about the fireworks and realized that Jeremy was actually targeting you and not just doing some elaborate, petty prank. Daniel went home to pack a bag, worried about retribution, and was ambushed by Jeremy. Jeremy figured out it was Delores who had gotten Daniel to question things and went after her. To Jay that was basically sacrilegious. He was okay with Jeremy dating Delores as a way of keeping her close, but hurting her? Jay wasn't having any of that."

"So that's why he came to get me that day." She realized the truth. Caleb nodded.

"He said he just needed to hide you and use you as leverage so Jeremy would leave Delores alone."

"So who tried to grab me in the barn? Who took all the pictures?"

Caleb's jaw clenched.

"Jeremy took the pictures and Jay was the one who grabbed you. But, according to Jay, it was only meant to scare you. The plan wasn't to actually take you then. Jeremy didn't want to be the one to do it on the off chance you saw him. He would have had a hard time denying it was him behind everything, given your past. The same with the picture taken inside your apartment. Jay freely admitted he picked the lock after Jeremy taught him how."

"Jeremy put so much effort into everything he did," she said. "I wished he would have used that same drive for putting good out into the world instead."

Nina leaned into Caleb's side and shook her head.

"This whole thing *is* bananas."

Caleb chuckled. It rumbled through his body and against hers.

"It is definitely not what *normally* what happens here at the end of Winding Road, never mind Overlook as a whole."

They fell into another small but comfortable silence. The smell of his cologne tickled her senses. It also made her wish they were somewhere more private. She still hadn't properly thanked him for saving her life. Maybe later she could swing it. Despite loving the main house, he'd already complained about living under the same roof as he had growing up while his house was being rebuilt. Now that Nina's father was out of the Retreat, she had a feeling that Caleb might be spending more time there.

Not that she minded at all.

"So, are you going to tell me what's in that big bag you got next to your boots or am I going to have to grab it and run?"

Nina gave a genuine laugh. She'd forgotten she even

had it. Leaving his embrace she jumped off the fence and handed it over.

"Desmond and Declan couldn't agree on one color so I decided to veto both of their choices. I thought this just screamed Detective Cowboy."

Caleb pulled out the ivory cowboy hat with a look of surprise that made Nina proud. She'd asked his brothers to keep it a secret when visiting Declan in the hospital. The eldest Nash sibling looked rough but was improving. He had enough sass in him to argue with Desmond as they suggested which hat to get Caleb. In the end she'd had to excuse herself while the two of them launched into one of their silly sibling squabbles, as Madi had affectionately called them.

Caleb ran his hand across the brim of the hat. His smile grew. He put it on.

"I love it," he said simply.

"It definitely works for you."

Caleb laughed and was off the fence in a second flat. He picked Nina up and spun her around. It felt undeniably cheesy and yet unimaginably perfect.

"I can wear it to the Retreat's grand opening party," he exclaimed, all giddy like a child. The party was the next day. After the news had gotten hold of what had forced the Nash family to keep the Wild Iris Retreat closed a little longer, guests had called left and right to rebook. None were angry, which meant Nina still had a job. Not that she wanted it for the same reason she'd had when she accepted it in the first place. "I've even been practicing my dance moves a little bit. I have to admit, you might be more than a little impressed by this fancy-hat-wearing date of yours."

Nina laughed as he twirled her with enthusiasm. Then she was back in his arms. Those true-blue eyes searched her face. He must have liked what he found.

Caleb pulled Nina in for a kiss that she felt throughout her entire body and soul.

Right then and there Nina knew she'd never want that life under the radar again. Not as long as Caleb was by her side.

He helped her back over the fence and across to his horse. Nina didn't even think to worry when he extended his hand out to her once he was in the saddle.

Instead she took it with a smile, put her foot in the stirrup and let the cowboy and momentum do the rest.

* * * * *

Chapter One

I'm not going to make it.

Molly Gilford walked quickly through the main floor of The Lodge, headed for the gondola dock at the back of the massive structure. As the only five-star resort located on Pine Peak, The Lodge catered to guests who enjoyed winter sports. Skiing, snowboarding, hiking, even camping—the outdoor activities were designed for every skill level, from beginner to expert. And when the guests were done playing in the snow, they came inside to enjoy all the luxuries The Lodge had to offer.

As director of guest services, Molly couldn't help but view the space with a critical eye, even as she dashed past. There was snow packed into the weave of the mat by the main entrance, tracked in by guests and staff alike. A few discarded coffee cups sat on a table in one of the many conversation nooks arranged throughout the room. One of the curtains was askew, and was that a…nose print on the window? Molly squinted, pausing in her journey. Yes, it looked like the glass bore a smudge from what was likely a dog's nose, given its location on the window and the extent of the smear. She shook her head and set off again, her low heels sounding out a rapid tattoo on the pale gray marble tiles. Overall, not a bad state of affairs, but not up to the lofty standards of The Lodge, either.

She took her phone out of her purse as she stepped into the gondola carriage, typing out her observations in a message to the head of housekeeping. Nadia Carrington was Molly's right-hand woman, and she knew the older lady would ensure that the small issues Molly had noticed would be addressed within minutes.

That task done, she checked the time. Two fifty-seven. Three minutes until departure. She'd meant to take the ride down the mountain an hour ago, but time had gotten away from her. There was nothing to do about it now. Her doctor's appointment was at three thirty. It took fifteen minutes to ride down, giving her the same amount of time to find her car and make the drive into town. She was going to be late for certain, but hopefully the same could be said for Dr. Allen, who offered Sunday appointments once a month as a courtesy to her patients.

With nothing to do but wait, Molly glanced around the interior of the gondola carriage. It was a large space, big enough to hold twenty people at a time. A few small tables and chairs were arranged along the curve of the glass wall at the front of the carriage, which maximized the view for guests as they glided down the mountain. The soft gray carpet and matching drapes ensured that the interior of the gondola did nothing to distract from the scenery—if you stood at the front of the carriage, with the sky above you and the snowy slopes below, it was easy to imagine you were floating down the mountain.

Molly had the carriage to herself, which wasn't too surprising. At this time of day, most guests were either enjoying the outdoors or staying inside to pamper themselves at the spa. Traffic would pick up again in the evening as guests from The Lodge made their way to The Chateau or the town beyond for dinner.

There was a small refrigerator next to the gondola en-

trance. Molly retrieved a bottle of water and sank onto the seat of a chair. It felt good to get off her feet, if only for the short ride.

She rubbed her hand absently over her belly, anticipation building in her chest as her thoughts turned to her upcoming appointment. It was time for the twenty-week sonogram, when the doctor would do a thorough exam of the baby to make sure everything looked as it should. She'd been excited about this date for months, imagining what her baby might look like. She couldn't wait to see the little hands and feet, hear the steady *thump* of the heartbeat. And perhaps most exciting of all, today she would learn if she was having a girl or a boy.

Molly smiled to herself, warmth blooming inside her as she considered each possibility. Of course, a healthy baby was her top priority, but she had to admit, she was kind of hoping for a girl. Boys grew up and left their mothers behind, whereas girls were better at staying connected to family. Her own situation was a perfect example—if not for her reminders, Molly's brother, Mason, would never remember to call their mother on her birthday or send their dad a Father's Day card. She and her younger sister, Sabrina, were the ones who kept in regular contact with their parents.

"I hope you'll do the same," she said softly to her baby. She couldn't bear the thought of her child growing up and forgetting about her.

Especially since she was probably the only parent her offspring would have.

Molly hadn't planned to wind up a single mother. Some days, she still couldn't believe she was pregnant. She hadn't told anyone about the baby yet.

Not even the father.

Guilt speared through her at the thought of Max. He

deserved to know about the pregnancy, and she had every intention of telling him.

Just as soon as she figured out how.

Their relationship had been more of a fling than anything else, a series of intensely passionate encounters during his quarterly visits to The Lodge. Molly knew he wasn't looking for anything serious, and she'd convinced herself that was fine.

Except the past few times she'd seen him, her emotions had grown stronger and stronger, demanding acknowledgment. Six months ago, she'd decided that during his next visit, she would break things off. She wanted more, but Max was totally devoted to the charity he had founded and ran.

She'd figured out what she was going to say, considered every possible reaction he might have. Then she'd steeled herself to see him again.

But he hadn't shown up.

Max had missed his regularly scheduled visit. Not a big deal, but then she'd started having symptoms, and after putting two and two together, she'd realized she was pregnant. She knew she needed to tell him, but the whole "hey, you're going to be a father" conversation was one best had in person rather than over the phone. So she was going to have to wait for his next visit to share the news.

Provided he ever came back to The Lodge. If history was any indication, he should be arriving within the next two weeks. But Molly checked the reservations regularly and his name was nowhere to be seen.

Maybe this was his way of breaking things off? If so, he was definitely not going to be happy when he heard her news. Like it or not, a baby was going to tie them together for the rest of their lives. It was a bit ironic that their casual connection had produced such a permanent bond, but life was sometimes funny that way.

The carriage shuddered a bit as someone stepped on board. Molly didn't turn around—she wanted one more moment to herself before she had to slip back into work mode.

She took a sip of water as the gondola began its journey down the mountain. Casting aside thoughts of Max, she let her gaze track across the pine trees and mountain rock, all still dusted with snow thanks to the high altitude. It was like a Christmas card come to life, a sight she didn't think she would ever grow tired of seeing.

With a small sigh, she stood. Time to greet her company on the ride down. She wasn't in her office, but she still had a duty to ensure that all guests of The Lodge were satisfied, no matter what part of the property they were using.

Molly turned, smiling as she moved. She opened her mouth to speak but as she caught sight of the other passenger, the muscles of her throat seized, trapping her words. Her eyes widened, taking in the man before her.

Tall. Broad shoulders that tapered to a slim waist. Red hair. Light green eyes. A hint of stubble, softening the lean lines of his face. And even though he was dressed for warmth, she knew that underneath his sweater and jeans he was all hard muscle and warm skin.

Heat suffused her limbs as her body responded to his presence. *Finally!* her libido seemed to say. But then her brain kicked into gear, asserting control over her raw physical reaction.

Maxwell Hollick was back.

And she was going to have to find a way to tell him she was carrying his child.

Damn. She looks good.

Max stared at Molly, his heart pounding hard as he drank in the sight of her. Six months between visits was

way too long, but a small crisis at work had kept him occupied. Now that things were resolved, he was ready to kick back and have a little fun.

And Molly was just the woman he wanted to spend time with.

She'd changed a bit since he'd last seen her. She still had a blond bob and bright blue eyes, and her skin was as smooth and clear as he'd remembered. But she had a luminous glow about her now, and her curvaceous body seemed even more voluptuous, the swell of her hips a bit more pronounced. It was a good look for her. His fingers itched to lift the hem of her sweater and trace a line across her belly, inching higher until he could fill his hand with the soft, warm weight of her breast.

"Molly." His voice came out as a rasp, so he cleared his throat and tried again. "It's good to see you."

She blinked, her pleasant, impersonal smile slipping into a look of bewilderment as she stared at him. For a second, Max thought he saw fear flash in her eyes. But before he could wonder about it, she spoke.

"Max." Confusion and disbelief were clear in her tone, as if she didn't quite believe he was real. "I...uh, I wasn't expecting you," she stammered.

"It was a spur-of-the-moment thing." He'd been itching to get back to The Lodge for months, to see her again. But his schedule hadn't cooperated. So he'd simply decided to force the issue—he'd had his secretary clear his schedule for a week and he'd jumped on the first plane out here. He'd arrived without a reservation, but because he was a regular guest he hadn't had any trouble scoring one of the private cabins dotting the mountaintop.

Molly nodded, but the gesture was stiff. "Well..." She trailed off, clearly searching for something to say. "I'm glad you're here."

Her expression didn't match her words, and Max had the distinct impression she was less than thrilled by his sudden appearance.

He frowned slightly, taken aback by her reaction. They hadn't parted on bad terms at the end of his last visit. Heat danced along his skin as he recalled exactly *how* they'd said goodbye. He'd left her wearing a sleepy, satisfied smile and a promise to return. So why wasn't she pleased to see him now?

Maybe she was upset because he'd been gone so long. Normally, he made it a point to stay at The Lodge every three months. But thanks to an issue with work, he'd had to skip what should have been his last visit.

"I know it's been a while," he said gruffly. "I'm sorry about that. Things got crazy at work—a big grant opportunity came up, so it was all hands on deck as we put together our application."

Max was the founder and managing director of K-9 Cadets, a charity organization that worked to provide service dogs for veterans suffering physical and psychological wounds. As a former Special Forces operative himself, Max knew all too well how the horrors of war changed a person. To make matters worse, not all casualties occurred on the battlefield—there was a depressingly large epidemic of suicide among veterans. He had decided his mission was to help his fellow veterans cope with their new normal, and in his opinion, the best way to do that was through dogs. They were the perfect companions—loyal, nonjudgmental, wonderful listeners. Not only did dogs assist with physical tasks, the emotional support they provided was sometimes the only thing standing between a veteran and the abyss.

He loved his work. More importantly, he knew how vital it was. Matching the right dog with the right vet was life-

changing for everyone—quite often, it was life-*saving*, as well. That simple fact was the reason why he frequently put his personal life on hold. Therefore, as much as he enjoyed spending time with Molly here at The Lodge, he couldn't pass up the opportunity to advocate for his charity and hopefully secure more funds to expand their work.

Some of the tension left her shoulders. "Did you get the money?" Molly asked. She knew how important K-9 Cadets was to him—they'd talked about it often.

Max shrugged. "I don't know yet. It'll be a few months before we find out." He was trying not to obsess about it. He'd thought a change of scenery might help.

And hopefully Molly could distract him, as well.

He took a step forward, wanting to touch her. He'd missed her more than he cared to admit. If he had his way, he'd press her up against the one-way glass wall of the gondola so they could both enjoy the ride in a more... unorthodox way. But he didn't think she'd appreciate the idea, and he wanted to spend more than fifteen minutes getting reacquainted.

Molly didn't resist when he drew her in for a hug, but she didn't fully relax against his chest, either. She was soft and supple in his arms, but her stomach was surprisingly firm against him.

He dropped his nose to her hair, inhaling deeply. Molly's citrus and floral scent filled his lungs, triggering an avalanche of memories of their time together. It was the same movie reel he'd played in his head a thousand times over the last few months, but now it was even more vivid thanks to the woman in his arms.

"I missed you," he said softly.

"I missed you, too." Her voice was barely above a whisper, as if she was confessing something that troubled her.

He stroked her back, his fingers grazing lightly along the valley of her spine. Gradually, she melted against him.

"I know it's been a while," he said. "But have dinner with me tonight?"

She tensed slightly. "No."

A wave of doubt washed over him. She'd never refused his invitation before. Was there someone else?

Well, what did you expect? he thought bitterly. *It's been six months.* It was only natural Molly had moved on. She was a beautiful woman, and he'd seen the way men looked at her.

He was so caught up in his thoughts he almost missed her next words. "I can't tonight."

"Tomorrow?" he asked, sounding a little desperate even to his own ears. *Or the next night? Or the one after?* He was only in town for a week, but if he had to wait until the end of his visit to connect with her again, he would do it without complaint.

She hesitated, then nodded against his chest. "Tomorrow is fine. I've been wanting to talk to you."

"I should have called," he said. "I meant to let you know I was going to miss my last visit. But I never got around to it."

"It's—" Her words were cut off by a deep rumble Max felt in his bones. He glanced over, expecting to see thunderclouds hovering over the town of Roaring Springs. But the sky was a clear, bright blue.

The rumble grew louder, turning into a loud roar. He shifted his gaze back to The Lodge, and the sight that greeted him turned his guts to water.

A massive wall of snow was racing down the mountain, gaining speed as it moved. The tsunami of white rose up, seeming to dwarf the gondola as it hung precariously above the chaos below.

"Oh, my God." Molly gripped him so tightly her nails dug into his skin even through the fabric of his sweater.

The slight stinging pain snapped Max out of his shock. "It's okay," he said automatically.

"How can you say that?" Molly's voice trembled.

Because he wanted to protect her. He wanted to stand between her and the wall of snow and ice threatening to bury them.

But he was powerless against the forces of nature. And they both knew it.

They held each other, watching in silent horror as the avalanche barreled toward them. It passed underneath the carriage, seemingly with only inches to spare. Molly let out a deep breath, but Max knew they weren't out of the woods just yet.

The gondola cables were secured by a series of posts at the bottom of the mountain. If the avalanche destroyed them, well...

As though his thought had triggered it, the carriage suddenly dropped. It jerked to a hard stop, sending them both to the floor. The force of the impact wrenched Molly from his arms.

Max landed hard on his shoulder, sending a bolt of pain through the joint. There was a *thump* from somewhere to his left, and Molly let out a faint cry.

The sound sent his heart into his throat. "Molly?" He pushed onto his knees, searching for her amid the tangle of chairs and tables strewn across the floor.

The carriage swung back and forth on its tether in a sickening lurch. "Molly?" he practically yelled her name this time.

"I'm okay," she said, though she sounded anything but. He saw movement on the other side of the carriage and began to crawl toward her.

He found her on her hands and knees, trying to stand. "Stay down," he commanded, reaching for her. He eased her into a sitting position, ignoring the protests of his shoulder every time he moved.

Molly touched her head with a grimace. When she lowered her hand, Max saw an angry red mark on her forehead. The area had already begun to swell.

"You're not okay," he said, moving to sit next to her. "Something knocked you on the head."

She grabbed his arm, her knuckles going white against the brown of his sweater. "I don't want to die here, Max."

"We won't."

Molly searched his face, her gaze pleading. "You can't say that for certain."

She was right, but he was feeling better about their chances with every second that passed. "We don't know if the main cable is down, but even if it is, the emergency cable will catch us." The backup line should be tethered to another set of poles, to maximize the chances it would still continue to function if the main line was compromised. So even if the avalanche had taken out one set of supports, hopefully the other set would remain standing. The fact that they continued to hang in the air made him think the system was working as it should.

"I hope you're right," she said.

So do I, he thought wryly.

The rocking motion gradually slowed and Max let out a sigh of relief. It was hard to think when the world was constantly moving. Once the carriage was still, he slowly got to his feet.

Visibility outside the gondola was bad. The air was filled with a fine powder from all the snow—it was like they were in the middle of a cloud. Gradually, though, some structures could be seen through the haze.

"The Lodge is still there," Molly said, her relief plain.

Max squeezed her hand as he looked down the mountain. "And I can see The Chateau," he added, referring to the French-inspired luxury hotel at the bottom of the mountain. "The path of the avalanche seems to have angled just enough that the place was spared." Which hopefully meant the gondola cable supports were safe, as well.

But just as he began to relax, a sharp *crack* filled the air. The carriage dropped again, only to jerk to a sudden stop once more. Molly's cry sounded like a sob, and Max reached for her as the gondola began another stomach-lurching parabola.

"It's okay. We're okay," he muttered, repeating the words in the hopes of convincing himself as much as Molly.

"Max, there's something I need to tell you."

The cables groaned under the weight of the carriage as it swung back and forth. Fear gripped Max's heart in a cold fist, and he fought the urge to panic. He took a deep breath, drawing on his Special Forces training to remain calm.

Even though there was nothing he could do.

Or was there? He glanced up, wondering if there was some way they could climb out the top of the carriage. Maybe they could hold on to the cables until rescuers arrived? *No, not likely*, he thought, dismissing the possibility as he turned his gaze down. Just how far of a drop was it? It looked like soft snow underneath—could they try to jump for it? What were the odds of a safe landing?

"Max." Molly's voice was insistent. He looked back at her, surprised to find her blue eyes full of determination.

"What is it?" His thoughts continued to whirl. How long until the rescuers would arrive? How much damage had been done by the avalanche, and would the rescuers even be able to reach them soon?

"I'm pregnant."

It took several seconds for her words to sink in. But when he finally registered what she was saying, his heart skipped a beat.

"What?"

She smiled nervously. "I'm pregnant," she repeated. "And it's yours."

Chapter Two

It took at least twenty minutes for the gondola to stop its violent rocking. The carriage was never fully still—it moved a bit in response to gusts of wind, but at least the roller-coaster ride seemed to have ended.

Things appeared stable, at least for now. But Molly couldn't relax. Her heart was racing and her mouth was dry. She focused her gaze on the bottle of water she'd retrieved before the ride had even started—had it really only been half an hour since then? A mere thirty minutes ago, her life had been normal. Now she was stranded in a gondola carriage suspended high above a mountain with the father of her child her only company. Under any other circumstances, Max's presence should have been a comfort.

But thanks to her panicked confession, there was nothing but tension between them.

Not that he was talking to her. He'd been on the phone, calling everyone he knew in an attempt to get information about the search and rescue effort. He'd finally managed to connect with someone from the fire department. Molly wasn't able to hear what Blaine was saying, but if Max's reactions were anything to go by, they shouldn't be stuck here much longer.

She reached inside her purse and ran her finger along the edge of her own cell phone. She should call her parents

and siblings, let them know she was okay. But she wasn't in the mood to talk to anyone, especially not in front of Max. So she typed out a quick text, reassuring her family she was fine. No one knew she was in the gondola, and that was fine by her. Later, when she was back on terra firma, she'd fill them in on all the details.

Molly slipped the phone back into her purse. Max had ended his call while she'd been texting, and she realized he was looking at her now, watching her with a hint of suspicion.

She met his gaze, lifting one eyebrow in a silent question.

"Everything okay?" he asked. His tone was heavy with meaning, but Molly didn't have the energy or the inclination to puzzle out what he was leaving unsaid.

"Yes." She considered telling him who she had contacted, then decided against it. She didn't owe him any explanations. "What did the fire department have to say?"

Max sighed and ran a hand through his hair. "The rescue effort is still getting organized. Right now, they're trying to triage the response. But they know we're up here, and we're a high priority. Hopefully, it won't take long for them to reach us."

"Maybe we'll get lucky," she murmured. Though given the way her day had gone so far, the odds were not in their favor.

They were silent for a few moments, staring out opposite windows as though they could pretend to be alone. Finally, Max cleared his throat.

"So…" he began. "You're really pregnant?"

Molly's first instinct was to fire off a sarcastic response, but she marshaled her self-control. "Yes," she said simply.

"And you're sure the baby is mine?" He winced slightly as he asked the question, as though he knew it was insensitive.

Molly narrowed her eyes. "I'm certain. Though it's good to know what you really think of me."

"I'm sorry, okay?" Max held up his hands, palms out. "But you can't blame me for asking. You're a beautiful woman, Molly. I didn't expect you to wait for me."

If she'd had any doubts about the casual nature of their relationship, his words confirmed it. He thought she had moved on. Was that because he'd done the same? The thought of him with another woman made her heart sink, but she buried the hurt. This conversation was about the baby, nothing more.

When she didn't respond, he spoke again. "How far along are you?"

"About five months."

He nodded, digesting this information. After a moment, he asked, "Why didn't you tell me?"

Anger bubbled up inside her. "I tried," she said, her voice razor-sharp. "I was going to tell you during your next visit, but you never showed up. So I called your office, wanting to know when you'd be coming back. I left several messages with your secretary, and she assured me you had received them."

Max went pale as guilt flashed across his face. "I did get them," he said quietly. "And I meant to call you back. Truly, I did. But things just got—"

"I get it," Molly said with forced lightness. "You were busy with your work, and your girlfriend and your dog." Furbert was Max's rescue dog and near-constant companion. For a brief second, her mind flashed back to the smudged print on the window of The Lodge, and in that instant she knew exactly where it had come from.

"It's not an excuse," he said. "If I had known it was urgent…" He shook his head. "Well, it doesn't matter now."

Molly noticed he hadn't refuted the comment about a

girlfriend. She hugged herself and shuddered, trying not to let her imagination run wild.

"Cold?" Max asked, misinterpreting the gesture.

She shrugged. In point of fact, she *was* getting cold. The gondola carriage had lost power, and with it, the heater. There was a definite chill in the air, which was only going to get worse as time wore on.

Max grabbed the hem of his sweater and pulled it over his head, revealing a tight-fitting cream thermal shirt underneath. Molly tried not to notice the way the waffle-weave fabric hugged his muscles, but it was a wasted effort.

He tried to hand her his sweater. "Put this on," he instructed.

Molly shot him a look. "Really? Do you think all of this—" she gestured to her breasts and stomach and hips "—is going to fit in your sweater?"

Max blushed. "I, uh… Sure."

She smiled, amused by his discomfort. "I appreciate the gesture," she said sincerely. "But I'm fine. You're better off wearing it."

Max studied her for a moment, searching her face for signs of deception. At her nod, he donned his sweater once more. The movement made him wince, though he tried to hide it.

"Are you hurt?"

He shrugged, then grunted softly. "I landed wrong on my shoulder. Nothing some ibuprofen and ice won't fix."

"Hmm." Molly wasn't convinced his assessment was correct, but she didn't bother to argue.

"We should at least sit next to each other to keep warm," he said. He settled on the floor, then reached for her hand.

It took a little effort, but Molly managed to lower herself to the floor. She felt about as graceful as an elephant

attempting ballet and briefly wondered if things were this bad now, how would she feel at nine months pregnant?

Once she was on the floor, Max scooted closer until he was sitting next to her with their sides touching. Molly hated to admit it, but she began to feel toastier right away.

"Is it a boy or a girl?" he asked softly.

"I don't know yet," she said just as quietly. "I was going to find out today. That's where I was headed—I was supposed to have a scan this afternoon."

Max took a deep breath. "I really am sorry. I should have returned your calls."

"It's fine." She waved away his apology. "You know now. That's all that matters."

He didn't reply. The temperature continued to drop in the carriage; Molly could see the fog of their breath now.

"There's no girlfriend."

He spoke so softly, Molly wasn't sure he'd said anything at all. "What?"

"There's no girlfriend," he repeated, a little louder this time. When she didn't reply, he continued. "Earlier, you said I must have been busy with work and my dog and a girlfriend. I just wanted you to know, there's no one waiting for me back home."

She turned her head away and smiled, relief warming her from the inside out. It was silly for her to care so much about his relationship status when they had never made any promises to each other. But it was nice to know she hadn't been replaced quickly.

Hormones, she thought, mentally shaking her head. Pregnancy had certainly done a number on her emotions.

She knew his words were an olive branch, so she responded in kind. "It's the same for me," she confided. "I haven't been with anyone else. Just you."

Max didn't reply. He lifted one arm and slowly put it around her, giving her time to reject his touch.

Molly leaned against him, partly for warmth, partly to enjoy the solid feel of him. She'd spent countless nights lying in bed, staring up at the ceiling as she remembered the time they'd spent together. Their relationship had started out as purely physical, nothing more than a fling. But somewhere along the way, she'd started to fall for the quiet ex-soldier.

And now she was pregnant with his child.

Her heart ached with the knowledge they would never be a traditional family. He lived in Washington, DC, and she lived in Roaring Springs. But even if they didn't have a geography problem, there was the small fact that he didn't love her. Still, Max was a good man, and she knew he would love his baby and do his best to be a devoted father to the little one.

And as for her? It seemed that Molly would just have to get used to being left out in the cold.

"How did this happen?" There was no blame in his voice, only curiosity.

"The usual way," she replied flatly.

She felt his eyes on her. "You know what I mean. We were always responsible."

"I know." She sighed. "But you know what they say about life and making plans…"

It was his turn to sigh. "I wasn't ready for this."

And you think I was? Anger flared at his words. If she didn't need his body heat, Molly would have pulled away from him then. It wasn't as though she'd planned on getting pregnant. This baby wasn't exactly part of her five-year plan, either.

But even as she silently raged against him, her anger began to fizzle. She'd had five months to process the shock

from seeing those two pink lines on a stick. Max had only known he was going to be a father for thirty minutes. Maybe she could cut him a little slack.

"Me, either," she finally said. It was a hell of a thing, to find out your life was irrevocably changing. One minute, things were carrying on as normal. The next, you were a totally different person. A parent. For Molly, it had been like the flip of a switch—she wasn't pregnant, then suddenly she was. Max at least had a little time to ease into the idea of his new role before dealing with the reality of a baby.

"They'll be here soon," he said. "We'll get out of this gondola and figure out what to do."

Molly wished she shared his confidence. She wanted to believe that once they were back on the ground, everything would magically be okay. But she knew that even if the rescuers found them quickly, their issues were a long way from being resolved.

She glanced at him out of the corner of her eye. The red of his hair was evident even in the gray light streaming weakly through the glass. He was staring ahead, those soft green eyes of his unseeing as the wheels turned in his head.

He was so handsome. She'd thought so the first time she'd seen him, and time and familiarity had done nothing to erase that impression. Not for the first time, she wondered if she had been able to see into the future, would she still have gotten involved with Max? Was all this stress and worry and uncertainty worth the whirlwind fling?

As if in answer, she felt a fluttering deep inside as the baby moved. For an instant, she was filled with a sense of wonder as their unborn child kicked and stretched, exploring its world. *Yes*, she thought, as peace washed over her. She definitely hadn't planned this, and she wasn't sure what the future would hold. But now that her heart

knew this little soul, she recognized that it could never be another way.

"Eight times," Max muttered next to her. He shook his head with a soft chuckle. "I just realized, we've only seen each other eight times. Feels like I've known you for longer."

"I know what you mean," Molly replied softly. They'd packed a lot of experiences into each visit. Their time together had always been intense, their connection strong. Even from the very beginning they had clicked, like two puzzle pieces fitting together.

And now they were adding a third.

It was enough to make her head throb. Of course, the fall was likely the main reason for the dull pain currently vying for her attention. The sudden motions of the gondola had tossed her around like a rag doll, and something had smacked her forehead, right along her hairline.

"How's your shoulder?" she asked, wanting a distraction.

"Eh." It wasn't much of a response, but she could tell he was uncomfortable.

"How's your head?"

"It hurts," she admitted.

Max reached for his phone. "Let me call the fire department again and see if I can get an update. You shouldn't be sitting in the cold in your condition."

Molly reached for him, grabbing his knee. He glanced at her in surprise.

"Please don't tell them I'm pregnant. No one knows."

Max's eyebrows shot up. "No one? Not even your family?"

"You're the first person I've told."

Warmth flashed in his eyes. "I suppose I should be honored."

"It's only fair." She gave him a small smile. "After all, this is your baby, too."

He pressed his lips together and nodded. Then turned his attention to his phone, tapping on the screen to dial.

Molly glanced out the window, her eyes tracking the flight of a bird as it glided by. Max began to speak, but she tuned out the sound of his voice, letting her mind wander.

My life was simple once, she mused. *Will it ever be that way again?*

Chapter Three

Two years earlier...

"Max Hollick." Molly repeated the name to herself as she walked up the trail to the private cabin he'd rented for the week.

"We were in Special Forces together," her cousin Blaine Colton had told her earlier in the day. "He's a good buddy of mine. Good man, too. Runs a charity for vets."

"Wow," she'd said, impressed. For him to offer such praise meant Max must really be something.

"Yeah. He doesn't really take much time for himself, so this vacation is well deserved. Can you stop by and make sure he's got everything he needs to relax?"

"No problem," she'd replied. It was important to her that all guests of The Lodge were accommodated. But knowing Max was Blaine's personal friend made her want to do everything in her power to ensure he enjoyed his stay. "Is there anything in particular he likes to drink? I can drop off a bottle when he checks in."

Blaine had smiled at her. "That would be really cool of you. I know he likes brandy." He rattled off a brand, which Molly jotted into her ever-present notebook. "But he's not a huge drinker, so maybe just a small bottle?"

"I can do that," she'd promised.

Which was how she found herself standing on the door-step of the cabin, alcohol in hand. She rapped on the door, waited for him to answer. After several minutes passed with no response, she used her master key to let herself in. She could leave the brandy on a counter with a note welcoming him to The Lodge.

Molly glanced around as she moved through the living room of the cabin. Everything looked in order, without so much as a throw pillow out of place. The back wall of the cabin was mostly windows, designed to maximize the view for the guests. The glass was spotless, the afternoon sunlight streaming through to cast the room in shades of gold. It all looked wonderful, and she made a mental note to compliment the housekeeping staff on a job well done.

The living room flowed into the kitchen, the two spaces separated by a breakfast bar. Molly set the bottle of brandy on the counter, then withdrew a card and pen from her jacket pocket and began to write a short note.

Just as she put the pen to paper, the door to the bedroom opened. She turned reflexively to see a tall man with red hair and mesmerizing green eyes standing in the doorway of the bedroom. He hadn't shaved in a few days, and the red-gold stubble on his cheeks and chin gave him a pirat-ical air. He was handsome, the kind of man she'd take a second look at if she passed him on the street.

And he was wearing nothing but a towel around his waist.

"Whoa." He drew up short but continued to rub his hair with a towel. "Um, can I help you?"

His voice was deep and smooth, the kind that belonged on the radio. Molly swallowed hard, trying to find the words to explain her presence.

But her brain failed her. "I knocked," she blurted lamely. Against her better judgment, her eyes fixed on a droplet

of water as it ran from his collarbone down his chest and over the hard, flat planes of his stomach to disappear into the cotton at his waist. He was muscled, but not overly so. It was exactly the type of body she found most attractive—fit, but not in an intimidating way.

One side of his mouth drew up in a lopsided grin. "I believe you."

A dog trotted out of the bedroom, tail held high and tongue hanging out. He looked a bit like a yellow Labrador, but his ears and nose were black, and the fur along his back was dark. He came over to her and nosed her hand in a friendly manner, then plopped down at her feet and stared up at her curiously.

"Uh…" Molly inched back, feeling decidedly out of her element.

"That's Furbert," he said, nodding at the dog. "And I'm Max. Hold on a second."

He disappeared back into the bedroom, leaving her alone with his pet. "My name is Molly Gilford," she said loudly, hoping her voice carried into the other room. "I'm the director of guest services here at The Lodge, and I was checking in to deliver a welcome gift and to make sure you have everything you need for your stay."

"Nice to meet you," he called back, sounding a little muffled. "Sorry about before. I wasn't expecting anyone."

Molly eyed Furbert, but he didn't seem worried by her presence. She began to step toward the door, needing to leave the cabin before she expired from embarrassment.

"No, that's my fault," she called out, her face growing warm. "Blaine Colton asked me to stop by. He mentioned you two were friends." And once Max related this little anecdote to Blaine, Molly was sure she'd never hear the end of it.

"Blaine's one of the best." His voice grew louder as he

stepped back into the room, tugging a sweatshirt over his head. He caught sight of her as soon as the fabric cleared his face, and he lifted one eyebrow. "Leaving so soon?"

His question left her feeling even more flustered. "Well, yes. I mean, I have to get back to work. And everything seems to be in order here." She made a show of glancing around, then nodded. "It was nice to meet you."

Max leaned against the doorjamb with his legs crossed at the ankles and his arms folded across his chest, regarding her with an amused smile as she backed toward the door. Furbert stayed where he was, but cocked his head to the side as if she were some kind of puzzle he was trying to solve.

Almost there, she thought as she moved. Just a few more feet, and she could escape back to her office and pretend she hadn't walked in on a nearly naked guest who just happened to be a friend of one of her cousins-turned-co-workers.

Though she had to admit, the view had been nice while it lasted.

"There is one thing you can do for me," Max called out just before she reached the door.

Molly froze, feeling a jolt of alarm. But she pasted on a smile and pretended this situation was normal. "Of course. How can I help you?" she asked politely.

"Have dinner with me."

Molly's jaw dropped open. She felt as though the bottom had disappeared from beneath her feet, leaving her hanging in midair like that cartoon coyote. Any second now, she would begin to fall.

"I…" She swallowed hard, trying to moisten her dry mouth. "I hardly think that's an appropriate question."

He pushed away from the wall and walked toward her. *No*, she thought. *Stalked* was a better description. She stood

in place, watching him as he approached. She felt like a bird, hypnotized by the green gaze of a cat as he drew near.

He stopped a few feet away. "You're right," he said. "It's not. So let me try again." He tilted his head to the side, offering her a smile that was charmingly boyish. "Will you please join me for dinner tonight?"

Molly smiled despite herself. His gaze was full of warmth, his eyes regarding her with such blatant interest it triggered a flock of butterflies in her stomach. "I can't," she said, disappointment casting a net over her nerves. Although there was no explicit company policy preventing employee-guest fraternization, she knew it was frowned upon.

He nodded in understanding. "I get it. Short notice. What about tomorrow night?"

Molly laughed at his deliberate obtuseness. "I'm the director of guest services," she said.

He nodded. "So you mentioned."

She shifted, feeling put on the spot. "You're a guest." At his blank look, she sighed. "It's not advisable…"

Max waved away the excuse. He leaned forward, lowering his voice to a conspiratorial whisper. "What's life without a little risk?"

He had a point. And it had been a long time since she'd been on a date. The Lodge was booked year-round, making it difficult for Molly to carve time out of her schedule for a personal life. Since she hadn't met a man she wanted to get to know better, it was all too easy for her to focus on work.

"Don't think of it as a date," he advised.

"Then how should I think of it?" She was enjoying this flirty back-and-forth, maybe a little too much.

"A work function."

"Ah, but I don't usually have dinner with guests as part of my job."

This logical statement did nothing to deter him. "So you're saying I'm the first?"

She laughed. "I haven't agreed yet."

Amusement flashed in his green eyes. "Yet. That means you will."

Molly's resistance was fading in the face of his interest. In truth, she would like to have dinner with him. She just wasn't sure it was a good idea.

"I'll be a gentleman," he promised, holding his hands up as if to demonstrate his innocence. "No funny business."

Damn, she thought, shocking herself. It really had been too long since she'd received any male attention if she was disappointed by his promise of good behavior. *I've got to get a life.*

She bit her bottom lip. His gaze zeroed in on the gesture, heat flashing in his eyes.

Why wait?

"All right," she said, deciding to throw caution to the wind. "Where would you like to meet? And what time?"

He smiled. "How does seven sound? And we can stay right here. That way you don't have to worry about anyone seeing you with me outside of working hours."

He was teasing her, but she did appreciate his discretion. Roaring Springs might be a tourist destination, but it was a small town at heart. Molly knew that as a grown adult, she had a right to a social life. But she also knew the town regulars, and her extended family, would waste no time commenting on her choices. She simply didn't have the patience to deal with the gossip right now.

"Seven works for me," she said. "What can I bring?"

Max tilted his head to the side. "A bottle of wine? If you're comfortable with that."

Molly nodded. "Red or white?"

He considered the question for a moment. "Red, I think."

"Are you actually going to cook?" The thought made her smile. Max looked like the kind of man who could run a grill, but she had a hard time picturing him in the kitchen.

He threw his shoulders back and puffed out his chest. "Do you doubt my abilities?" He sounded serious, but there was a twinkle in his eyes. Furbert woofed softly, as if to vouch for his master's culinary skills.

Molly shook her head. "I would never question your talents," she said with mock seriousness. "I'm sure whatever you prepare will be wonderful."

Max nodded solemnly. "I'm glad one of us thinks so." He winked at her, then stepped in close.

Molly gasped at his sudden nearness. For a split second, she thought he was going in for a kiss. Then he reached past her, his hand landing on the doorknob.

He opened the door in one fluid motion. "I'll see you tonight," he said simply.

Molly nodded, relief and disappointment flooding her system in equal measure. "Later," she replied softly. She took a deep breath, inhaling detergent, soap and warm male skin as she moved past him.

She set off down the path, feeling his eyes on her as she walked.

But she didn't look back.

Four hours later...

Max dumped the last of the food from the take-out containers into serving dishes, then stuck them into the oven to keep warm. Furbert watched him as he wadded up the trash, stuffing it down into the can.

"What?" he asked the dog. "I can't serve her out of the foil trays. That would be tacky."

Furbert cocked his head to the side and barked in reply. It sounded accusatory to Max's ears.

"No, I'm not going to tell her I cooked," he said defensively. "But it's not my fault if she assumes I did."

The dog barked again, clearly unimpressed.

"Oh, whatever," Max muttered. "You wouldn't understand."

Furbert jumped onto the couch and flopped down on the cushions with a sigh.

"We talked about this," Max said. "Get down."

Furbert flicked his tail once in acknowledgment of Max's words, then closed his eyes.

"Brat." But there was no heat in his voice. Max couldn't bring himself to chastise the dog. Furbert was his constant companion, his best friend since he'd returned home from his last tour of duty.

Max had loved his life as a Green Beret. The men he'd worked with had been the best in the business, their training second to none. Every single one of them had been smart, professional and passionate about their work.

But Special Forces wasn't just a job. It was a calling, an all-consuming lifestyle that required commitment and discipline. In return, the team had been his family. Max wouldn't have hesitated to lay down his life to save any one of his brothers-in-arms, and he knew the feeling was mutual. The bonds forged among them all were unbreakable and thicker than any blood connection.

Or marriage vows.

Most of the guys weren't married. The few old-timers who were had managed to snag women who were former military brats. They knew the life, understood the sacrifices. There had been a few divorces during his tenure as an operative, but some of the guys actually made the whole marriage and family thing work.

Max had thought he was one of them. His wife, Beth, had seemed happy. In the beginning, she'd been determined to be the perfect military wife. She'd joined several social organizations for spouses, written him regularly when he was on tour and welcomed him home with gusto when he returned.

But at some point, things started to change. Max couldn't quite put his finger on when things shifted between them, but gradually the stream of letters slowed to a trickle, and her welcome-home smile started to look a little strained.

Then the fights started. Arguments over stupid stuff, like not loading the dishwasher correctly. Beth nitpicked everything he touched, to the point Max felt like he couldn't do anything right. And while part of him understood the spats were really a symptom of larger issues, the rest of him was simply relieved to go overseas again. He'd take people shooting at him over an unhappy wife any day.

He'd done a lot of thinking during that last tour. About the state of his life and where he wanted to end up twenty years from then. Being an operative was incredibly fulfilling, but it was a young man's game. One day he'd wake up and discover he was too old to keep up with the physical demands of the job. His knees already ached in the morning, and he'd twisted his ankle more times than he could count. At some point, his physical limitations were going to be a liability to the team.

And what then? He wasn't the type to sit behind a desk for the rest of his working life. Nor did he want to join the ranks of the military brass. Max knew he wanted to stay connected to the military, but he didn't want to continue to wear the uniform.

The issue dogged his thoughts for the first several

weeks of his tour. Until one day, the solution came trotting up on four legs.

His team had been on patrol—standard stuff, nothing unusual. But when they'd stopped for a break, they'd been joined by a scrawny yellow puppy with big black eyes and an inquisitive personality.

"Hey there, buddy," he'd said as the dog nosed his leg. "What are you doing out here?"

"Probably searching for food," one of his teammates said. "Look at how skinny he is."

"Poor guy," said another.

Taking pity on the friendly puppy, the men had dug through their pockets and come up with offerings of beef jerky and a peanut butter granola bar. Max wasn't sure if it was safe for dogs to eat peanut butter, but the stray scarfed it down before he could finish asking the question.

Max had offered him some water, and after his snack, the dog curled up at his feet and fell asleep with a contented sigh.

"He's really sweet," Max remarked.

"Yeah," his buddy Joseph said. "But don't go getting any ideas. You know you can't bring him back to base."

Max nodded in acknowledgment. The team rose to get back to it, and Max felt a pang in his heart as he looked at the sleeping dog. He was in for a rough life. *Just like everybody else in this desert.* He knew he couldn't save everyone, but there was something especially frustrating about the fact that he couldn't help a dog who had such simple needs compared with his human neighbors.

"Shake it off, Hollick," Brad, the team leader, said. "You can't fit a dog in your duffel anyway."

"Yeah, I know," Max replied, turning his thoughts to the mission at hand.

But damned if he didn't look behind him an hour later

to find the dog trotting after them, tail wagging despite the desert heat.

"Your friend is back," Joseph observed. They were headed to base now, having wrapped up their patrol for the day.

"Looks like," Max concurred. He tried to quash the spurt of excitement bubbling up in his chest. Even though the puppy had followed the team, there was no home for him on the base.

The group stopped again for a short break, giving the dog time to catch up. "Somebody's got a crush on you, Max," Joseph teased.

"Ha ha," Max said. He wandered a few feet away, searching for a modicum of privacy so he could relieve his bladder. But as he stepped off the path, the dog barked. He turned around to find the animal staring intently at him, as if he was trying to tell him something.

"Stay there," he told the dog. "I'll be right back."

He turned around only to hear another bark, but he ignored this one. He took two steps when Joseph let out a surprised yelp. A blast of yellow zoomed past him, and Max suddenly found himself faced with a snarling bundle of yellow fur and bones.

"Easy, boy," he said, taking a step back. What was going on with this dog? One minute, he was friendly and sweet and the next he was acting possessed. Maybe it wasn't such a bad thing that he was going to have to stay in the desert…

Brad and Joseph and some of the other men came up behind him. The puppy increased his snarling, punctuating it with loud barks for added effect.

"What's the deal?" Brad asked. "Do we need to put him down?"

Max watched the dog carefully. If someone took a step forward, he became more aggressive, going so far as to

lunge forward with a snap. But when the men took a step back, he relaxed.

He heard the creak of a strap as someone shifted their rifle. "No," he said, holding up his hand. "I think he's trying to tell us something."

Max glanced at the ground behind the dog. It was strewn with rocks and a few pieces of fabric and paper, faded from their time spent baking in the sun. Nothing looked unusual or out of place.

Except…there was one pile of rocks that looked a little *too* neat. Max pulled out his binoculars and trained them on the spot. As he focused on the ground, his blood ran cold.

There was definitely something under those rocks. He couldn't make out all the details, but he did see the curve of a wire protruding from the pile.

"There's an IED out there," he reported grimly, lowering the binoculars.

"Where?" Brad's voice was intense, urgent. A frisson of energy crackled through the rest of the men. They began to study the ground with new interest, searching for additional threats.

Max pointed out the device to the men. "I'll be damned," Brad muttered. "Let's call it in."

They were still a few miles away from base, but this was a popular trail used for foot patrols. The area was routinely swept for explosives. Either this one had been missed, or it was a recent plant.

The radio dispatcher called up the explosive ordnance team, which sent out a group right away.

"Back on the trail," Brad ordered. "No one goes off, not even to take a piss."

The men retreated to the relative safety of the marked path. As they moved away, the puppy visibly relaxed. Once

everyone was on the trail again, he morphed back into the friendly animal they had encountered before—tail up, tongue lolling out, a big doggy smile on his face.

He walked over to Max and licked his hand, then sat in the dirt and stared up at him with his head cocked to the side. Max knew dogs couldn't talk, but he swore the pup was giving him an "Are we cool?" look.

"Oh, yeah." Max knelt in the dirt next to the dog, pulling him close for a hug. "You saved our lives." He tried to ignore the way his stomach twisted as his body caught up to the realization that he'd narrowly missed being blown to bits.

The rest of the team wandered over as they waited for the ordnance guys. Everyone had a pat and a kind word for the animal. Even Brad softened toward the dog.

"Looks like we have a new member of the team," he remarked.

"Really?" Max couldn't keep the hope out of his voice. There was no way he was going to leave this dog in the desert now, but if the rest of his team was on board, it would be a lot easier to sneak him on base and take care of him.

Brad knelt to pat the dog. He slid a glance at Max, then returned his eyes to the dog. "Sometimes it's better to ask for forgiveness than permission," he said, appearing to talk to no one at all.

Max turned his head so the other man wouldn't see his smile. "Understood, sir," he said.

And that was that. The team had helped him bring the dog on base, christening him Furbert. It wasn't Max's first choice for a name, but one of the guys on the team said it was an old French term having to do with armor. "He protected us," his friend had said. "We have to give him his due."

From that point on, Furbert became the unofficial mas-

cot of the team. The other people on base turned a blind eye to the sight of the dog loping next to Max, and for his part, he made sure Furbert was cared for and well-fed. He even convinced one of the doctors on base to examine his friend to make sure he was healthy. After a few doses of deworming medication, Furbert began to put on weight until he no longer resembled a skeleton with fur, but rather a happy, spoiled young dog.

Max would have loved Furbert regardless, but it was his actions one afternoon that sealed his place in the hearts of everyone on base.

Medevac arrived with a chopper full of injured men. The medical team began working on them right away. About an hour later, the rest of the patrol staggered into base. By this time, a small crowd had developed outside the field hospital as people milled about waiting for news. Max was there, along with his fellow operatives. Furbert sat at his feet, as usual.

A few men pushed through the crowd to the front, intent on going inside. A third man trailed after them, catching them before they could enter the hospital. "Stay here," he said. His insignia showed him to be the officer in charge of the unit. "I'll go check for an update."

The two men stopped, though it was clear they didn't like it. They were kitted out for patrol, their faces grimy with sweat and dust. Both of them sported dull red patches on their knees.

Blood, Max thought grimly. It was the telltale stain of someone who had knelt by an injured colleague in a desperate battle to help them.

The officer went inside, leaving the two men oblivious to the crowd surrounding them. Max could tell by the looks on their faces they were focused on their friends in-

side the hospital, silently bargaining with the universe for the survival of their injured comrades.

After several minutes of silence, the officer returned. One look at his face, and everyone knew.

"Baker?" one of the men choked out.

The officer nodded. "And Jeffries."

One man sank to the ground while the other stood frozen in place, unwilling or unable to believe the bad news.

The officer began to comfort his men. Max and the rest of the crowd stirred, knowing it was time to leave. This was a private moment, one that didn't warrant public scrutiny.

He motioned for Furbert to follow, but the dog refused to budge. "Come on, boy," he said sternly. "Let's go."

To his horror, the dog walked over to the grieving soldiers. He nudged the man who was on his knees, as if to say, "I'm here."

Max took a step forward with the intent of retrieving the animal. But the soldier didn't seem to mind. In fact, he appeared to welcome the dog's presence. Without saying a word, he opened his arms and embraced Furbert, dropping his head against the young dog's side.

For his part, Furbert was content to sit still and let the soldier's tears soak into his fur. Max watched the pair of them from several feet away, marveling at the way the dog's mere presence brought obvious comfort to a man who was having one of the worst days of his life. *This is it*, he realized with dawning wonder. *This is what I can do.*

He was going to retire after this tour and devote his time to pairing dogs with veterans. If anyone could use comfort, it was the men and women who had seen the horrors of war. And there was nothing like the nonjudgmental presence of a dog to make it seem like things were going to be okay.

It was perfect. And best of all, Beth would be glad to have him home again.

It had taken months and a virtual forest's worth of paperwork. But Furbert had eventually made it back to the States. Max had never been so happy to see anyone before in his life.

Beth, on the other hand, had been less than impressed.

She'd initially been excited after he retired from the service. She'd even expressed support for his idea of starting a charity—K-9 Cadets, he'd decided to call it. But as he'd settled in to start the work, she'd grown more and more distant.

One night, he confronted her. "I thought you wanted this," he said. He gestured to himself as they stood in the kitchen. "You used to beg me to retire, to get out of Special Forces and find a normal job."

"I know." Her voice was dull, as though she couldn't muster the energy for this discussion.

"So what's changed? Why do you seem so unhappy now that I'm home?"

She turned to hang up the dish towel, shoulders heaving with a sigh. "I can't do this anymore."

A chill skittered down Max's spine. "What are you saying?"

Beth whirled to face him, her expression thunderous. "I'm saying I'm done! I want out of this marriage!"

Max stared at her, emotions swirling in his chest. His first reaction was disbelief—surely she wasn't serious? Except he could tell by the look in her eyes she wasn't joking.

Anger burned away his confusion. What the hell was wrong with her? He'd turned his life upside down to please her, retiring earlier than he had originally planned all so they could spend more time together and work on their

marriage. And now, after he'd made so many sacrifices, she'd decided his efforts weren't good enough?

He looked at her, studying her face as though he'd never seen her before. There had been a time when he'd known her every expression, could even predict her thoughts. Now she was a stranger. Max searched for any signs of the woman he'd fallen in love with, but she wasn't there.

Perhaps she hadn't been there for a while.

"Don't try to tell me you're happy," she said. Her voice was softer now, almost pleading.

"I'm not," he admitted. "But I wasn't ready to give up on our marriage."

She glanced away. "You were never here."

"I'm here now." He thought about reaching for her, decided against it. Some part of him sensed there would be no reconciliation, though hope still glimmered at the edges of his thoughts.

"Not really. You're so wrapped up in your charity and that damn dog."

He couldn't deny it. But that didn't mean he was going to accept all the blame.

"This isn't only my fault, Beth. Yes, I was gone a lot. But you knew what you were signing up for when you married me. And even when I was home between tours, you didn't seem to want to reconnect."

"You weren't the same person I married," she shot back.

"I could say the same about you," he said.

Beth sighed, shook her head. "Why are we arguing about this? Neither one of us is happy. Let's just call it a wash and walk away."

She had a point. Why prolong the inevitable? If she wanted to leave, he wasn't going to stop her. Max had his pride—he wouldn't beg her to stay.

Her phone buzzed on the counter. She glanced at it, and in that instant, Max saw longing in her eyes.

Suddenly, he knew.

"Who is he?" His voice was cold. He waited for the jolt of surprise, but it never came. Deep down, he'd known this day was coming.

Her cheeks flushed, and she shot him a guilty look. "No one you know."

Max merely nodded. Then he turned and walked out of the room.

Lesson learned, he thought bitterly as he packed his things. He'd left the house and never looked back.

It had been three years since that conversation in the kitchen. Now he stood in a different kitchen, with anticipation instead of dread thrumming through his veins.

He wasn't sure what had made him ask Molly to join him for dinner. He certainly wasn't looking for a relationship—his charity work took up all his time, and he was okay with that.

But there was something about her that called to him. It wasn't just her appearance, though there was no denying she was attractive. Blond hair that looked like spun gold, big blue eyes, voluptuous curves in all the right places; Molly Gilford was an incredibly beautiful woman. Beyond that, though, there was a sweetness in her eyes, a lightness of spirit that called to him.

She hadn't played coy when he'd walked out half-naked, hadn't tried to flirt with him. No, she'd been genuinely embarrassed.

It was a refreshing, unexpected reaction. It made him want to spend more time with her.

And unless he missed his guess, she wanted to see him, too.

Her initial refusal had seemed like a knee-jerk reac-

tion, something she'd said because she thought she had to. Even as the words had left her mouth, he could tell by the look on her face she was considering the possibility. It was her mixed signals that had made him ask again. He wasn't a fan of harassing women, and he definitely knew how to take no for an answer. But Molly's response had been conflicted enough to warrant another try.

He was glad she had decided to give him a chance.

"We need to be on our best behavior tonight," he said to Furbert. "Don't jump on her when she walks through the door."

Furbert's tail thumped against the cushion, though he didn't bother to open his eyes.

"Right," Max muttered to himself. "Same goes for me."

Tonight was just about dinner. But hopefully the next time could be about something more…

Chapter Four

Molly stood on the welcome mat of Max's cabin for the second time that day, holding another bottle of alcohol.

"It's not a real date," she muttered. In the hours since she'd accepted his dinner invitation, Molly had tried to convince herself she was merely fulfilling her responsibilities as director of guest services. This was a chance for her to do a more thorough inspection of the private cabins, to ensure they were equipped to meet every guest's needs. Furthermore, she had promised Blaine she would make sure Max was well taken care of. Tonight's dinner was an opportunity to get a better idea of what he would need to make his stay as restful and enjoyable as possible.

"This is business. Nothing personal."

But it certainly *felt* personal.

She knocked on the cabin door, anticipation fluttering like butterflies in her stomach as she waited for Max to answer. Their first meeting had been…memorable, to say the least. Part of her still felt a little embarrassed about catching him fresh from the shower. But that hadn't stopped her from reliving the experience all afternoon. The sight of him all shirtless and damp and warm had been running through her mind on an endless loop.

If she'd been more daring, she would have touched him. Just reached out and trailed her finger along the

water droplets running down his torso. He would have sucked in a breath, and her touch would have given him goose bumps. She would have smiled at him, one of those smiles that says more than words ever could. He would have smiled back, then pulled her in close for a hot kiss...

Her fantasy was interrupted by the man himself opening the door. Molly jumped but tried to cover it with a smile.

"Welcome back." Max grinned at her and pulled the door wide so she could step inside.

Her cheeks warmed as she moved past him. Did he have any idea she'd just been daydreaming about him? Hopefully her thoughts weren't that transparent.

He reached for the bottle of wine, his hand brushing hers as he took it from her. "Thanks for this," he said, not even bothering to glance at the label before setting it on a nearby table. Then he moved back, his hands on her shoulders as he helped her shrug out of her coat. He never touched her skin, but a shiver ran through her nonetheless.

Get it together, she told herself. *He hasn't really touched you.*

Not yet, anyway, said a traitorous voice in her head.

She turned back to Max, thanking him for taking her coat.

"My pleasure," he said. He picked up the bottle of wine and gestured for her to move forward. "I'll get this opened so it can breathe."

Molly followed him a few steps but paused when she caught sight of the dog on the couch. "He looks comfortable."

The dog cocked an ear, his eyes still closed. Apparently deciding she wasn't worth the effort, he relaxed again with a soft doggy sigh.

Max glanced back, holding the wine bottle and opener. He looked at the dog, an indulgent smile on his face. "I

can't tell you how many times I've told him to stay off the furniture."

"So you're saying he's a good listener."

Max laughed. The sound was deep and joyful and it rolled into her chest and warmed her from the inside out. He returned to the kitchen and she followed, suddenly wanting to give him a reason to laugh again.

It smelled wonderful, the aromas of something hot and Italian heavy in the air. Her stomach growled loudly; she pressed a hand over it and glanced up to see if Max had noticed.

He had.

"I'm hungry, too," he said with a smile. "Let's talk while we eat."

Molly offered to help, but Max shooed her away. "You're my guest," he said.

She appreciated his manners, especially as it gave her an opportunity to watch him move around the kitchen. He wore jeans and a dark green button-down shirt that enhanced his eyes. The sleeves were rolled up, a casual look that she found sexy. His forearms were dusted with fine red-gold hairs; the lamplight in the dining area made his skin look gilded.

In a matter of minutes, he had the table set and the food in place. He poured her a glass of wine, gesturing for her to sit across from him.

Molly hid a smile as he plated the food. The lasagna looked amazing, and also quite familiar. Che Bello was the best Italian place in Roaring Springs—apparently, it hadn't taken Max long to find it.

But would he take credit for the food? Molly decided to test him, curious to see how he would react. Would he tell her the truth? Or would he pretend to have cooked everything himself, soaking up praise for a job he hadn't done?

Either way, his reaction would tell her something about who he was as a man.

Let's see if you're as good a guy as Blaine says, she thought wryly.

"This is delicious," she remarked, careful to keep any hint of suspicion out of her voice.

He smiled. "I'm glad you like it."

"Where did you learn to cook like this?"

Max took a sip of wine. "Oh, it's just something I picked up along the way."

Molly considered his response as she took another bite. Technically, he *was* telling the truth. She decided to push a little harder.

"Let me guess—you have an Italian grandmother who taught you everything she knows?"

"Ah, not exactly." He shifted a bit in his seat, the tips of his ears turning pink.

His embarrassment made her feel a little better about their encounter this afternoon. He'd been so cool and collected the whole time, as if it was no big deal she'd walked in on him in a towel. It was kind of nice to have the shoe on the other foot.

"You know," she said, deciding to put him out of his misery, "there's a place in town that makes lasagna almost as good as yours. It's called Che Bello. Maybe you saw it on the drive in?"

Max choked a bit on his wine, his eyes flying up to meet her gaze. He dabbed at his mouth with a napkin, a sheepish smile forming on his lips.

"You got me," he said. "But in my defense, I never said I actually made it."

Molly laughed softly. "No, you didn't."

He studied her from across the table, his eyes bright with curiosity. "You're not like most women, are you?"

The question surprised her, and she took a sip of wine to stall. "I'm not sure," she finally said. "In what way?"

He lifted one shoulder in a shrug. "A lot of the women I know wouldn't have teased me about the food. And they definitely wouldn't have been bothered by catching me just out of the shower."

"Oh, no?"

He shook his head. "Most of them would have seen it as an invitation."

She tsked at him. "You poor thing. I'm sure you have to beat the ladies off with a stick." It was a scenario she didn't care to imagine, and frankly she found this line of conversation tiring. If Max was going to spend the evening emphasizing his conquests, she was going to fake a headache and leave soon. She didn't get a lot of time off, and she wasn't interested in spending it with a man who wanted to talk about his various friends-with-benefits arrangements.

He laughed, another full-throated rumble that wrapped around her like a blanket. "Oh, hardly," he said. "I haven't dated anyone in over a year. But I spend a lot of time trying to raise money for my foundation, and I meet a lot of unhappily married women." He shook his head. "Some of them have offered large donations in exchange for a bit of adventure."

Molly's annoyance faded in the face of his candid explanation. "That must make things awkward." It had to be difficult, trying to let the wives down easy so their husbands would donate to his charity.

"Yeah. It's a tough needle to thread sometimes." He took another bite of lasagna, then nodded at her. "But enough about me. I want to know more about you."

"There's not much to tell," she said, scooping more food onto her fork. Molly had never felt comfortable talking

about herself, a fact that wasn't about to change now. Still, she appreciated his interest and wanted to keep the conversation flowing. "I grew up in the area, started working at The Lodge during my summer breaks as a teenager. I went to college in Denver, then came back here."

"How long have you known Blaine?"

"Oh, for a while," she said with a smile. "Seeing as how he's my cousin."

"Ah, so you joined the family business."

She shrugged. "In a manner of speaking, yes."

Max took another sip of wine. "Well, for what it's worth, between you and Blaine it's clear you got the looks."

It was an obvious attempt at flattery, but it made Molly's stomach flutter nonetheless. "Better not tell him," she said. "You'll break his heart."

Max shot her a conspiratorial grin. "That's a risk I'm willing to take."

Molly took another drink, surprised to see the bottom of her glass. She had a pleasant buzz going, despite the fact that Max hadn't poured her a large glass.

He reached for the bottle, brows lifted in question. Molly shook her head. "Not right now."

"Already feeling the effects?" he teased.

She nodded. "What can I say? I'm a cheap date."

"I'll keep that in mind for the next time," he murmured.

Molly felt her face flush. "Tell me about your charity." Blaine had mentioned it once or twice, but she was curious to know more.

Max dabbed at his mouth with a napkin. "It's called K-9 Cadets. Basically, we work to pair military veterans with service dogs."

"Oh, wow." That sounded impressive. "How does that work?"

"It starts when a veteran contacts us. We meet with

them to determine what kind of support they need, then we begin the process of matching them with a dog."

"How do you find the dogs? I don't imagine you can pick them up at the local shelter."

"You'd be surprised," Max commented. "We do scan the shelters regularly to identify animals that look promising. If we find one, we'll adopt the dog and start training."

It sounded fascinating, and so far removed from Molly's daily activities. "You train the dogs, too?"

He shook his head. "We partner with several organizations who go through the nuts and bolts of training. But we're involved with it, and we look at how the animal behaves during training to help pair them with a veteran."

"What do the dogs do?" Molly's experience with canines was limited to her friends' pets. She was more of a cat person, though she liked dogs as a rule.

"That depends," Max said. "For veterans who have physical limitations, we pair them with a dog who has been trained to assist in daily tasks. Other veterans need emotional support, so in those cases, we pair them with an animal whose training reflects that."

Molly reached for the wine bottle, fascinated. "Was Furbert your first match?"

"In a manner of speaking." He told her how the dog had found him during a patrol in the desert. Molly glanced at the couch while he spoke. It was hard to imagine the happy, healthy-looking dog as a bony puppy. But she recalled the intelligence in his eyes when he'd met her a few hours ago, and could easily picture him warning Max and his men about the bomb.

Tears pricked her eyes as he described the way Furbert had comforted the mourning soldiers.

"That's when I knew," Max said. "Every veteran de-

serves that kind of support. So I made it my mission to help them."

Molly sniffed. "That's very noble."

"I don't know about that." He passed her a napkin, and she swiped her eyes dry. "Don't go thinking I'm a hero," he said. "I came back whole. Not everyone does."

"True, but you were willing to sacrifice yourself. Not everyone signs up for that risk. That's pretty heroic if you ask me."

Max looked down, took a sip of his wine. It was clear he wasn't comfortable with her praise. But Molly knew it was the truth.

Something cold nudged her elbow. She looked down to find Furbert sitting by her chair, staring up at her.

She smiled down at him. "I'm okay, buddy." She glanced at Max, saw him watching them with a smile. "Can I pet him?"

"Sure, but just know that once you do, you've made a friend for life."

She stroked his head, tentatively at first, then with gradually increasing pressure. Furbert's fur was soft, his ears like warm velvet. He sighed with pleasure and rested his head in her lap as she ran her hand along his head and down his back. There was something deeply soothing about petting a dog, especially one who apparently enjoyed it so much. The stress of her day melted away as she scratched Furbert's ears, and for the first time, she understood why her friends thought their dogs were worth the effort it took to take care of them.

"Would you like to move to the den?"

"That sounds nice." Molly picked up her glass and followed Max to the sofa with Furbert trotting at her heels.

Max sat on one end of the couch and she sat on the other. Furbert took the middle cushion, resting his head

in Molly's lap and wagging his tail in Max's. "He's so sweet," she said.

"He really is," Max agreed. "He's very sensitive to moods, and if he thinks someone is upset, he doesn't hesitate to try to comfort them."

"I'm glad you found him." It broke her heart to think of him wandering alone out in the desert, trying to survive under the unforgiving sun.

"I think it was the other way around," Max said with a smile. "But I agree with your sentiment."

They fell into an easy conversation, talking about everything and nothing. Max was so easy to talk to, Molly found herself confessing her irrational fear of birds. She bit her lip, expecting him to laugh at her the way most people did. But he merely looked at her with kind eyes.

"That must be hard," he said. "Especially living here, with all the wildlife."

"It's rough sometimes," she admitted. "I'm not paralyzed by fear to the point I can't go outside. But there are definitely some tough moments."

"I'm afraid of spiders," he said.

Molly eyed him, trying to decide if he was being serious or just hoping to make her feel better.

Apparently, her expression gave away her thoughts. "It's true," he insisted. "I hate them."

"They're not my favorite, either," she said.

"Too many eyes, too many legs." He shuddered. "They creep me out. The small ones I can handle, but you should have seen some of the spiders that live in the desert."

Molly wrinkled her nose. "No, thank you."

He laughed. "There was one time we were out on patrol, and we stopped for a short break. I sat on a big rock and started dumping the sand out of my boots. My buddies started laughing, but they wouldn't tell me why. My friend

Joseph waited until I had my boots back on, then pointed behind me. I turned around and found a camel spider sitting in my shadow." He shook his head at the memory. "I jumped straight up into the air with a scream that nearly ruptured my team's eardrums."

"Oh, man." Molly laughed. "If I had a bird that close to me, I'd die of a heart attack."

"I nearly did," he said. "Logically, I know they're not dangerous to humans. He was just trying to get some relief from the sun. But in the moment, all I could think about was getting far, far away."

"Was Furbert with you then?"

"I'd left him on base. And I'm not ashamed to admit I gave him a big hug when I got back."

The dog's tail thumped against the cushion, as if he knew they were talking about him.

"It's a good thing you had him," Molly said, stroking his fur.

"No kidding," Max replied. "Especially since I wasn't getting any sympathy from the rest of the guys on my team."

Molly laughed and glanced out the window. Night had fallen while they'd talked, turning the pine trees from green to black. Soft lights illuminated the path from the cabin's back door to a hiking trail, and in their yellow glow, she saw fat snowflakes dropping silently to the ground. It would be cold outside, a marked contrast to the cozy warmth of the cabin.

She glanced back to the sofa. Furbert's head was a welcome weight in her lap. The wine, the food and the dog had left her feeling content in a way she hadn't experienced in a long time. The evening had evolved in an unexpected direction, thanks mostly to the man sitting nearby.

Molly had found Max attractive from the start, but he

was even more appealing to her now. She hadn't thought they would be so compatible; in truth, she had expected him to be focused so completely on his job he wouldn't want to talk about much else.

Nothing had been further from the truth.

This is what dating is supposed to feel like, she told herself. It had been so long since she'd made an effort to connect with a man, she'd almost forgotten how nice it could be.

Too bad she'd rediscovered this feeling with a guest who would be leaving soon.

Molly met his eyes. She needed to leave now, before she got too comfortable here. This had been a pleasant evening, but it was not going to lead to anything more. Max and his dog would return to their normal lives, and she would remain here.

"You're going to leave, aren't you?"

Molly blinked at his question, which eerily echoed her own thoughts. Max sounded equal parts disappointed and understanding, matching her mood perfectly.

"It is getting late," she said. Reluctantly, she shifted on the seat, disturbing Furbert. He lifted his head, clearly confused as to why she would choose to interrupt their comfortable arrangement. "Sorry, buddy," she said to him.

The dog emitted a long-suffering sigh and jumped to the floor. Max stood, holding out his hand. Molly slid her hand into his, palm against palm.

She stood, the sudden change in position making her head spin. Or maybe that was her proximity to Max? He hadn't stepped back to give her room, so now only inches separated them.

He smelled even better than she remembered. This close, she could see the flutter of his pulse in his neck.

She leaned forward a bit, smiling to herself as she watched the beat speed up in response to her movement.

She lifted her gaze to meet his eyes. "Thank you for dinner," she said softly. "I had a nice time."

"So did I," he replied. His voice was quiet, hardly more than a low rumble that made her think of thunder from a distant storm.

Molly knew she should turn around and walk out the door. But her feet felt rooted in place, unable or perhaps unwilling to move.

"Let me get your coat," Max offered. Except he didn't move, either. They stood there next to the couch, locked in each other's gravitational pull. Who would be the first to break away?

The air between them crackled with awareness. Alcohol and anticipation were a potent combination in Molly's system, making her feel simultaneously languid and hyperalert to any subtle changes in Max's body.

Slowly, cautiously, he dipped his head. Molly recognized the invitation, and rose up on her toes. They met in the middle, lips brushing hesitantly before fully committing to the kiss.

Max's mouth was hot and tasted of wine. Molly placed her hands on his shoulders, needing to anchor herself in place so she could fully embrace the sensations running through her. Sparks of desire zinged through her limbs and settled into her core, making her feel as though she were holding a live wire.

He trailed the tip of his tongue along her bottom lip. Molly opened her mouth with a moan, her body practically melting against his. He was warm and solid and he wrapped his arms around her, filling her senses with his taste, his scent, his touch.

She tightened her grip on Max's shoulders, her fingers

digging into the fabric of his shirt. It wasn't enough. She needed more—more contact, more access. More of him.

Molly slid her hands down the flat expanse of his chest. She knew from their initial meeting he was leanly muscled, and she felt the solid strength of him under her fingertips. But before she could settle into an exploration of his body, he distracted her by skimming one hand down the side of her torso. Goose bumps sprang up in the wake of his touch, despite the fact that he hadn't actually made contact with her skin.

His hand rose up again, brushing the side of her breast. Her breath caught in her throat as he fit his palm around her curve. She stilled, deliciously shocked by the sensation of a man's hands on her body.

But Max immediately dropped his arm and pulled away, breaking the kiss. "I'm sorry," he said, touching his mouth with the back of his hand. "I shouldn't have done that."

Molly shook her head, her mind still trying to process what was transpiring between them. "I'm fine. It's fine," she stammered.

"I didn't mean to make you uncomfortable," he said, as if he hadn't heard her. "My brain just went out the window when we started kissing."

She laughed softly, happy to hear she wasn't the only one who'd been so affected. "I know the feeling."

Max ran a hand though his hair and smiled down at her. She saw a mix of emotions in his eyes: arousal, relief and amusement. His apparent feelings mirrored her own, which was another point in his favor.

But now that she was no longer distracted by the feel of his mouth on hers, Molly started to remember all the reasons why her attraction to him was a bad idea. Whatever this was between them couldn't go anywhere. And while

it might be fun to try a no-strings-attached fling, was her heart really capable of staying on the sidelines?

It was a big risk, one Molly wasn't sure she should take.

"Let me get your coat," Max said gruffly.

He stepped away, leaving her with an odd sense of disappointment. Truly, she'd never felt such immediate chemistry with anyone before. A small part of Molly acknowledged that if he hadn't misinterpreted her reaction, they would probably be in bed right now.

It's better this way, she told herself as Max helped her don her coat and they parted ways.

But as she trudged along the snow-dusted trail to the main building, she couldn't help but wonder if that was the truth.

IT WAS A beautiful day. So why wasn't he enjoying it more?

Max reached the bottom of the ski run and moved to the side, wanting to get out of the way of the people sliding to a stop behind him. He pulled off his goggles and turned back, squinting up the path he'd just traversed. Even from this distance, The Lodge was a huge complex snugged up against the steep rock face of the mountain. But despite its size, the building didn't look out of place. Whoever had designed the hotel had taken pains to make the exterior blend in well with its surroundings. The whole complex looked like a natural extension of the wilderness, as if it was trying not to disturb the area.

Somewhere up there was Molly's office. Was she sitting at her desk, typing away on her computer? Or was she standing by a window, lost in thought as she gazed down the mountain?

He smiled at the thought that maybe, just maybe, they were looking at each other right now.

Max hadn't managed to fall asleep until the stars had

begun to fade from the sky. He'd spent most of the night tossing and turning, his mind playing an endless loop of last evening's events. Dinner had been quite enjoyable, almost surprisingly so. He'd invited Molly over because he'd been attracted to her after their first meeting, but he hadn't expected to have such chemistry with her. She was so easy to talk to; she was one of those rare people who actually *listened*, rather than simply waiting for her turn to speak. It was a refreshing change from the conversations he was used to having with potential donors. He hadn't had to feign interest in subjects that he found boring, hadn't had to laugh at lame jokes. They'd been able to move beyond superficial niceties and actually start to get to know each other.

And then he'd messed it all up by pawing at her like a hormonal teenage boy.

He hadn't meant to make her uncomfortable. Hadn't intended to overstep her boundaries. He'd simply misread the signs. The kiss had short-circuited his brain, fogging up his normal clear-sightedness when it came to reading people.

He'd never forget the way Molly had stiffened under his hand. Embarrassment filled him at the memory, and his stomach churned. Max prided himself on being a man who made sure the women he was with enjoyed themselves with no regrets. But last night he had come across as a creep.

Molly had been gracious about accepting his apology. Still, it had been a disappointing way to end their evening.

But the worst part of all? How much he'd enjoyed kissing and touching her. He felt like a starving man who'd been given a taste of a scrumptious feast, only to have it jerked away after the first bite. A year was a long time to go without even a casual relationship, but between K-9 Cadets and his other responsibilities, the dearth of female companionship in his life hadn't really bothered him.

Now, though? He felt the void acutely. Last night's dinner and subsequent kiss had been like a wake-up call, a heady reminder of what it felt like to really connect with a woman. And while he understood there was no real future for him and Molly thanks to the geographical distance between them, he still wanted to make sure he didn't leave her with a bad impression.

He glanced at his watch. He was due to meet Blaine for a late lunch in an hour. Maybe he could ask his old friend about Molly? After all, the two of them were cousins. Blaine had to know something about her.

Max dismissed the thought almost immediately. Molly had been very clear yesterday that she didn't mix business and pleasure. That meant she would probably not appreciate Max talking about their dinner with Blaine. The two of them might be related, but they also worked together. The last thing Max wanted was for Molly to get any grief over seeing a guest on a social basis.

Still, there were other ways he could reach out to Molly without making her feel like she had to respond to his overture.

He walked over to the ski lift, pulled out his phone and took a seat on the moving chair. A few clicks later, he'd found exactly what he was looking for...

Chapter Five

In what was staring to become a habit, Molly once again found herself knocking on the door to Max's cabin.

This is crazy, she told herself. But she needed to see him.

The flowers had arrived at her office a few hours ago. She'd been working on a project when a knock at the door had interrupted her concentration. She'd looked up to see a veritable wall of flowers filling her doorway. From somewhere out in the hall, a voice had called out, "Molly Gilford?"

The arrangement was gorgeous, a garden's worth of red roses, pink hydrangeas, white daffodils and sprays of yellow freesia. It took up all the space on the small side table in her office, and made the room smell like a perfumer's workshop. She'd never seen such an extravagant arrangement before, much less been the recipient of anything like it.

It had taken some searching to find the card, tucked away amid the blooms. Given the scope of the flowers, Molly figured they had to be from one of her corporate clients; she'd facilitated a retreat for a major airline last week, so this was probably a thank-you gift for her efforts.

She couldn't have been more wrong.

The typed message inside the card had been simple and sweet:

Thanks for putting up with me last night.—Mike.

Molly frowned at the unexpected signature. Was Max trying to be funny?

She pulled up his reservation information, curious to find if Mike was perhaps his middle name. But he'd registered as Maxwell Hollick; there was no middle initial.

Her gaze drifted over the flowers as she pondered this small mystery. Her cheeks heated as she sniffed one of the roses. Red roses meant passion; she knew that. A quick internet search helped her decode the meaning of the other blooms: romance, new beginnings and friendship.

Pleasure blossomed in her chest as she savored this new information. Did Max know the meanings of the flowers he'd chosen? Or had he simply told the florist to create a display?

Her thoughts returned to their conversation last night. Max was a smart man who seemed to know exactly what he wanted and how to go about getting it. This wasn't a typical arrangement—she'd never seen this combination of flowers before. Given what she knew about Max, it was likely he'd been very specific with the florist.

Which meant this subtle message wasn't a coincidence.

Molly leaned back in her chair, trying to decide how she felt about that.

There was no point in denying she found him attractive. If these flowers were any indication, Max felt the same way. But should she act on her desire?

It's not smart, whispered a small voice in her head. There were a myriad of reasons why exploring her attraction to Max was a bad idea.

Still, as she tallied up the risks, she couldn't help but

wonder if she should throw caution to the wind and dive in anyway.

Her gaze drifted over the framed pictures on her desk. There was one of her with her siblings, and a formal portrait her parents had taken on their fortieth wedding anniversary. Seeing the photo reminded her of some advice her dad had given her several years ago.

"Molly," he'd said, "five years from now, what are you going to regret more? Doing this, or not doing it?"

He'd been right then, and he was right now. His words were the perfect litmus test for the major decisions in her life, including this one.

The answer came as soon as she considered the question. Despite all the risks, all of the reasons it was a bad idea, she knew she'd regret passing up the opportunity to know Max better.

One question remained, though; with all the thought Max had put into this delivery, why was the card signed Mike?

Maybe he was trying to be discreet? He had to know such a fancy display of flowers in her office would attract attention. Perhaps he'd used the name so that anyone who saw the card wouldn't connect him with the gift. She had made a big deal about not dating guests, so this could be his way of keeping their date last night a secret.

She'd reached for the phone, intending to call his cabin and thank him. Then she'd thought better of the idea. This was a grand gesture. It deserved more than a phone call.

So as soon as she'd finished work, she'd grabbed the card and hiked up the trail to Max's cabin, hoping to solve the "Mike" mystery once and for all.

She knocked, stomping her feet on the mat to help ward off the chill. *Is he even here?* She hadn't bothered to call

before setting out. Now, as the cold settled over her, she began to wonder if she'd made a mistake.

Another knock, but still no answer. Disappointment roiled in her stomach as she turned to leave. Now that Molly had made up her mind to embrace the chemistry she felt with Max, she didn't want to waste any of the time he had left at The Lodge. But it seemed she would have to wait to thank him another time.

She was about ten feet down the trail when a furry form shot past her and skidded to a stop on the path ahead. Molly froze, a burst of adrenaline making her heart pound as she squinted in the fading light. Bears and mountain lions were generally shy creatures, but they were more active at dusk. Every once in a while, there was a sighting on the trails that connected the cabins to the main building. Was this the latest incident?

Molly slowly took a step back, her brain whirling as she desperately tried to recall the safety training every employee was required to complete. Was she supposed to drop to the ground and play dead? Charge forward screaming? Or move away as calmly as possible?

The creature took a step forward. Molly's throat tightened as she suppressed a scream. Just as she took another step back, a voice cut through the air.

"Furbert? Dammit, dog, where are you?"

Molly saw the animal start to wag its tail. She took a deep breath, her panic fading as the dog trotted over and she got a good look at him.

He stopped at her feet and plopped his butt on the ground, staring up at her expectantly.

"Furbert?" Max called out again.

"He's here," she said. She knew from experience Max probably couldn't see them in the gloaming, and she didn't want him to worry about his dog.

Max was quiet for a second. Molly imagined he was frowning, trying to place her voice. Then he spoke again. "Molly?"

She smiled at his tone, a mix of pleasure and surprise. "The one and only."

Molly heard the crunch of shoes on the gravelly trail. Then Max stood next to her, looking down with a grin. "This is a nice surprise," he said.

Her heart started to pound again, though not from fear. She stared up at him, thrilled to be close to him once more.

He was wearing glasses, a simple pair of black frames that should have made him look nerdy. On him, though, they were sexy. "Hello," she stammered, feeling suddenly self-conscious. Why hadn't she brushed her hair or put on lipstick before coming out here?

"What's going on?" Before she could reply, he shivered and hugged himself. He wasn't wearing a coat, only jeans and a sweatshirt. The sun had all but disappeared, and cold came early on the mountain. "Actually, scratch that. Do you mind if we talk inside? I'm not used to this weather."

Molly nodded, all too happy to get out of the growing darkness. Even though the blurry shape had turned out to be Furbert, there was a primitive part of her brain that was still reeling from the scare. Shelter was a good choice, at least until her body relaxed again.

They started walking toward the cabin. Max snapped his fingers, which was apparently the only signal Furbert needed to follow his master. He held the door open for her, and Molly walked past him and into the soothing warmth of the living room.

"So what are you doing out here?" Max asked as he shut the door. "Not that I'm not happy to see you. But I wasn't expecting you."

Molly moved to stand in front of the fire blazing at the

hearth in the corner of the living room. "I should have called first. I came by to say thank you, but it didn't seem like you were here."

Max plucked at the cord of the earbuds dangling around his neck. "I was listening to music while I got some work done. I didn't hear you knock, but Furbert did. He kept scratching at the door. When I went to let him out, he took off like a shot."

"I'm glad he didn't run into the woods," Molly said. "Believe it or not, we have bears and mountain lions up here. I'd hate for him to get hurt."

"Oh, he's not the type to roam," Max reassured her. "He just wanted to get to you."

As if to prove his master's point, Furbert walked over to the fireplace and sat at Molly's feet. She reached down to scratch behind his ears, earning a contented sigh for her efforts.

"But enough about him," Max said. "Have a seat." He gestured to the sofa. "Can I get you something to drink?"

Molly shook her head as she walked over to the couch. She settled onto the cushion, in the same spot she had occupied last night. Max sat next to her, angling his body toward hers.

"Like I said, I came by to thank you."

Warmth glowed in his eyes. "Did you like the flowers?"

"Oh, yes." She got out her phone, showed him a few of the pictures she'd taken of the arrangement. "They're gorgeous. I've never seen anything like them."

Max glanced at her photos, then back to her. "Looks like the florist did a nice job."

"They did," she agreed. "But it does seem like someone else is trying to take credit for your work." She reached into her bag, pulled out the card. "Who exactly is Mike?"

Max read the message with a frown. "Unbelievable,"

he muttered. He shook his head, chuckling softly. "When I dictated the message for the card, I wanted it to be signed as just *M.* I didn't want to put my name, in case someone saw it. So to make it clear, I said '*M* as in Mike,' which is the military designation for the letter." He handed the card back to her, clearly amused. "I guess the person on the other end of the line just heard 'Mike.'"

"Well, that clears things up," Molly said. "But I must say, I was rather hoping you were a secret agent or something."

Max threw back his head, laughter pouring out of him. The sound wrapped around her like a velvet rope, making her want to get closer to him.

"I'm afraid I'm not that interesting," he said. "Sorry to disappoint you."

"I'll get over it," she retorted, unable to keep from smiling.

Max settled back against the arm of the sofa, watching her face. "I'm glad you liked the flowers. It was the least I could do."

Molly tilted her head to the side. "What do you mean by that?" Why did it seem like he was trying to apologize?

Max glanced down. "Last night." He sounded almost shy. "I made you uncomfortable when I kissed you."

What was he talking about? Molly racked her brain, trying to figure out what she'd done to give him that impression.

Then it hit her. "Oh," she said slowly. She'd stiffened when he'd touched her, and now that she thought about it, that had been the moment he had stopped kissing her. He'd also apologized before going to get her coat. "I told you last night, I'm not upset with you."

He glanced up at her, interest sharpening his gaze. "You aren't?"

Molly shook her head. "Hardly."

"But…you tensed up."

"I was surprised, that's all." She debated if she should say more, then decided to forge ahead. "I haven't dated anyone in a while," she confessed, reaching out to pet Furbert, who had relocated to sit at her feet once more. "I'd forgotten how nice it feels to be touched that way."

He didn't reply. As the silence stretched between them, Molly realized she shouldn't have said anything. Max probably felt sorry for her, which was the last thing she wanted.

Well done, she thought sarcastically. With only a few words, she'd managed to throw a wet blanket over the chemistry smoldering between them.

Time to go. She glanced down, wondering how she was going to stand up with the dog practically sitting on her feet. He looked quite comfortable, but he was just going to have to move.

She planted one hand on the couch to push off the cushion. But before she could shift her weight, Max covered her hand with his own.

Molly looked over, surprised by the gesture.

He had leaned in when she wasn't looking, closing some of the distance between them. His soft green eyes looked almost golden as they reflected the light from the fire. Molly felt hypnotized by his gaze, unable to move, unable to look away.

He lifted her hand, turning it over to fit in the cradle of his palm. Using the tip of his index finger, he began to softly trace the lines of her palm. His touch was featherlight, hardly more than a brush of skin against skin. But it sent electric currents of sensation shooting up her arm with every stroke.

"Do you know what I missed the most while I was on deployment?"

The question came out of left field, but his voice was

so quiet it didn't break the mood building between them. Molly swallowed, her mind growing hazy even as her body stood at attention.

"No," she said softly. "What?"

"Touching someone. Being touched in return." He looked down at her hand, continuing to trace imaginary patterns on her skin. "Not always in a sexual way, either. There's just something about physical contact that soothes the soul, don't you think?"

Molly nodded, falling completely under his spell. "It does." She'd never tried to articulate it before, but Max's words perfectly described her feelings.

"I'm glad I didn't upset you last night," he said gruffly. "I worried about it all day."

"You did?" She was surprised by his admission. Max seemed so confident and sure of himself—not the type to fret about a small misstep. His concern warmed her just as much as the fire a few feet away.

He nodded. "But since I didn't overstep my bounds, does that mean I can kiss you again?"

The question sent a thrill through her, kicking her heart rate up a notch. "I take it you want to kiss me?" Yes, she was teasing him. But the anticipation was so enjoyable, Molly wanted to make it last just a little bit longer…

"Oh, yes." His eyes dipped to her mouth, then back up again. "If you don't mind too much." The corner of his mouth quirked up in a smile, letting her know he was in on the game, as well.

She leaned over, getting closer to him. "That might be nice," she whispered. "I just need to check my calendar."

Max angled his head, putting them only a breath apart. "Busy, are you?"

Molly smiled. "Mmm. But I think I can pencil you in."

She closed the distance between them, fitting her mouth

over his. Just as it had last night, the contact sent sparks of sensation shooting through her system.

Max wasted no time pulling her closer. Her curves pressed against the flat planes of his body, a delicious pressure that sharpened her need for more.

They explored each other's mouths, tongues and lips communicating more than words ever could. Molly gave herself over to the sheer pleasure of the kiss, the voice of doubt that constantly whispered in her brain silenced for the time being.

After a moment, Max pulled back, though he didn't go far. He pressed his forehead to hers, breathing hard. "That was…" He trailed off.

"Intense," Molly finished.

"Yeah." He huffed out a laugh, his hand gently stroking her cheek.

"Don't stop on my account," she said, only half-joking.

"Really?" He drew back farther, his eyes scanning her face as if searching for signs of uncertainty.

She smiled and nodded. "Really," she assured him. As soon as she said the word, the rest of her doubts faded away. They might not have a future together, but she didn't want to pass up the chance to fully explore the chemistry between them. At least once in her life, Molly wanted to know what real passion felt like.

Max returned her smile. "Stay right there," he said. Then he rose from the sofa and walked into the bedroom, leaving her alone.

Well, not entirely alone. Furbert took notice of Max's departure and hopped up onto the cushion next to her. He curled up at her side, placing his head in her lap, then looked up at her with a pitiful expression. It was a masterful performance; if Molly didn't know better, she'd swear he was starved for affection.

"All right," she said, stifling a laugh. She scratched behind his ears, and he sighed blissfully again.

She was glad Furbert was here. Petting him was a nice distraction while she awaited Max's return. If she'd been left alone with her thoughts, her nerves might have gotten the better of her.

It didn't take long for Max to come back into the living room. He had ditched the glasses, and the earbuds no longer dangled around his neck. His hair was slightly mussed, making her think he'd run his hand through it. "Oh, I see how it is," he joked. "I'm gone for five minutes and you've already moved on to the next man."

Molly shrugged. "I told you my calendar was full."

He ran his hand down Furbert's back. "Mind if I steal her away, boy?"

Furbert's tail thumped against the cushion, but he didn't move.

"Come on," Max said affectionately. "Go lie down by the fire."

The dog let out a dramatic sigh as he got to his feet and jumped down. Molly couldn't help but laugh at his antics. "Does he always complain this much?"

"Pretty much," Max said. "He's like an old man." He held out his hand. Molly took it, experiencing a second of déjà vu as he helped her to her feet.

"Would you like some wine?" he offered.

Molly shook her head. "Not right now." She wanted to be clearheaded for what came next. That way, when she thought back to this encounter, she'd remember everything in detail.

He drew her into the bedroom, and she immediately saw why he'd left her on the couch.

The bedroom was large, with a king-size bed on the far wall. The entrance to the bathroom was on the left, and

the wall of windows on the right ended in a corner fireplace with a small sitting area arranged to take advantage of the view.

Max had lit the fire, casting the room in a golden glow. The chairs and small table were pushed to the side, and Max had pulled the quilts off the bed and placed them in front of the fire. Pillows were arranged on the makeshift pallet, creating a cozy little nest.

"Is this okay?" He sounded a bit unsure as he studied her face. "I thought it might be nice to lie by the fire, but if you'd rather not be on the floor I can put everything back on the bed."

"No, this is perfect," Molly said. She'd never made love by a fire before. It was one of those romantic scenes she'd always wanted to experience but figured she never would. The men she'd been with in the past had been nice, but not especially interested in setting the mood. Max's thoughtfulness made her feel special, as if she were the only woman in the world.

He pulled her close. "I'm glad you think so." He pressed a soft kiss to her lips, then her nose. "This isn't something I want to rush." He kissed one cheek, then the other. "I plan on enjoying our time together." His lips met her forehead. "I want you to, as well." He placed his index finger under her chin and tipped her head back to expose her neck. His lips were hot against the sensitive skin along her jaw.

Molly shivered with pleasure. "I will," she managed to choke out. Her body already ached for his, though he'd hardly touched her.

He slanted his lips over hers, cupping her face with his hands as he explored her mouth. Molly found the hem of his sweatshirt. She tugged blindly at it, seeking access to his skin.

Max jumped when she touched him. "Sorry," he muttered with a laugh. "I'm a little ticklish."

His admission delighted her. A Green Beret who was afraid of spiders and ticklish to boot? It was an unlikely combination.

"That's going to make things...interesting." How was she going to touch him without torturing him?

"It's just along my sides," he said, running his fingers down her ribs. His nimble fingers unbuttoned her blouse. Molly shrugged out of it, letting it drop to the floor.

Max traced the line of her collarbone. "I'm not ticklish here," he murmured. His hand drifted down the swell of her breasts. "Or here." He ran the knuckle of his forefinger across the curve of her stomach. "Or here."

Molly swallowed, trying to bring some moisture back into her dry mouth. "That's good to know." She practically panted out the words. "But I can't just take your word for it. I'm going to need to test that out for myself."

Max nodded, his expression serious. "Trust but verify. I get it." He winked at her, then took a half step back and pulled his sweatshirt over his head.

Molly sighed with appreciation as she surveyed his body. The firelight cast flickering shadows on his upper torso, a terrain her fingers itched to explore.

She stepped closer, placing her palms flat on his chest. He was warm and solid against her hands, the red-gold smattering of hair surprisingly soft.

He remained still while she ran her fingers over him, indulging her curiosity as she wandered the planes of his torso. She felt the thump of his heart against his breastbone, noticed the change in rhythm when she dipped her head forward and flicked one nipple with the tip of her tongue.

Max sucked in his breath with a hiss as she moved her

hands down, following the vertical line of hair that bisected his stomach to disappear behind the waistband of his pants. She reached for the button of his jeans, but stopped when he grabbed her hands.

"It's my turn," he rasped, lifting her hands and placing them on his shoulders.

Molly nodded. "Fair enough."

He traced the edges of her bra with his fingertip, then dipped his head and navigated the same path with his tongue. His breath was hot on her skin, a second caress that made her knees wobble.

He reached for the front clasp of her bra, fumbling a bit as he tried to unhook it. Molly reached down, intending to help him. But he shook his head. "I've got it," he said, gently lifting her hands to his shoulders once more.

A second later, her bra loosened, releasing her breasts into his hands. Max hummed appreciatively as he rubbed the pads of his thumbs over her nipples. Molly's knees turned to jelly, forcing her to tighten her grip on his shoulders so she didn't fall to the ground.

Max kissed her, slowly lowering her to the floor as he did. Molly was all too happy to follow his lead—her brain was overwhelmed by the fog of arousal, making thought difficult.

The comforter was a soft cushion under her back, though he could have stretched her out on a bed of nails and she wouldn't have noticed. The fire chased the chill from the room, but it was nothing compared to the heat of Max's body on top of hers. He was like a living furnace, warming her from the inside out with his touch.

She shifted, reaching for the button on his pants once more. He pushed himself up, meeting her eyes. "Are you certain?"

Molly nodded, afraid to speak lest she shout, "God, yes!"

Max rolled to the side and shucked his pants. Molly followed suit by lifting her hips to shove her trousers and panties down her legs. When they were both free, they rolled to face each other again.

Molly skimmed her hand across his chest and down his stomach, until she reached her goal. She traced the length of him, enjoying the tension in his muscles as he sucked in a breath.

"Two can play that game," he murmured wickedly. His fingers started at her knee and stroked up the inside of her thigh. Then his hand cupped her center, where the sensitive tissues responded to the smallest of movements.

Max played her body like a musical instrument. Their connection was unlike anything Molly had experienced before. He seemed to know exactly where to touch her, how to stroke and nip and lick and kiss. There were times she felt he must be reading her mind—how else could she explain the intensity of this experience?

She let go of any pretense of control, surrendering to her body's responses. For the first time in her life, Molly silenced the voice of self-consciousness in her head and got out of the way of her own pleasure. She didn't think about what she looked like, or worry that she was too curvy or too plain or too *anything* for Max. She simply jettisoned the self-doubt and let herself *feel*.

From somewhere in the distance, she heard the crinkle of a wrapper. "Oh, good," she murmured. "You have protection."

"I do," he confirmed. "It's taken care of."

He kissed her again. Molly reached for him, pulling him on top of her. She drew her legs up, letting her knees fall apart. Max entered her carefully, giving her time to adjust as he pushed forward. She bit her lip, moaning softly. It

felt incredible to be connected to him, for their bodies to be joined completely in this primal way.

Her release came quickly, waves of pleasure washing over her with an intensity that made her see stars. Max found his completion soon after, his muscles flexing under her hands. He relaxed, slowly settling his weight on top of her. Molly idly ran her hand up and down his back, enjoying the feel of being surrounded by him.

She wasn't sure how long they lay there like that—her brain was pleasantly empty of all thoughts, a slate wiped clean. At some point, Max rolled onto his back. Without saying a word, he gathered her close. Molly snuggled up next to him, resting her head on his shoulder. She threw her arm across his chest, feeling the thump of his heart as the rhythm returned to normal.

Max's hand traced imaginary patterns on her upper arm, a lazy caress that lulled Molly into a stupor. "That was amazing," he said softly, his voice a low rumble that she felt as much as heard.

"Yeah," she murmured. There was more she wanted to say, but her brain was still flying high from pleasure, which made it difficult to think. She stared at the fire, transfixed by the dance of the dying flames.

Max grabbed the edge of the comforter and pulled the thick material across their legs to ward off the cold. "Can you stay the night?" he asked.

His question made her heart want to sing. "Yes," she said.

"Good." He gave her a squeeze, then relaxed again. "We can get into bed eventually. I just don't think I can move now."

Molly chuckled. Once again, they were on the same page. "This is nice," she said on a sigh. "I'm in no rush."

The fire crackled a few feet away, the occasional spark

popping in a bright flare that reminded her of a shooting star. Max's breath was even and regular in her ear, his skin warm against her cheek. Sleep reached for her with welcoming arms, and she surrendered to its embrace with a sigh.

Chapter Six

Present day

Max knew the instant Molly woke, even though he couldn't see her face. She stiffened in his arms, and a slight hitch interrupted her deep, regular breathing.

She didn't speak, but he could practically feel her confusion as she lifted her head off his chest, peering into the dark gondola carriage as she no doubt tried to get her bearings.

"It's okay," he said softly. "We're still in the gondola."

She shivered, pushing up and out of his arms. He let her go, his body instantly registering the cold as she left his embrace.

"How long have we been here?"

"Almost six hours," he said. "The team said they're getting close. Shouldn't be too much longer now." Hopefully that was the truth. He knew the rescuers were working hard to reach them. But there were a lot of factors outside their control, limiting the speed with which they could operate. Fortunately, the gondola carriage seemed to be stable, if cold. As long as things stayed that way, they could wait a while longer.

Molly rubbed her eyes. "How long was I out?"

"Almost two hours."

"Oh, man." She sighed, shook her head. "I'm sorry. I didn't mean to fall asleep. And certainly not on you."

"No need to apologize." He didn't tell her it had been the best two hours he'd spent in a long time.

Holding Molly had kept him from going out of his mind with boredom. Despite the swell of her belly, she'd fit against him perfectly. As soon as she'd nodded off, he'd gathered her into his arms, their bodies coming together in a pose they'd adopted a hundred times before. How many times had they slept like this, wrapped in each other's arms?

Molly was the only woman he'd really held before. Beth hadn't liked to be touched while she slept, so every night they'd retreated to separate sides of the bed, leaving a gulf of space between them. Max had figured he wouldn't be able to sleep any other way, but from the very start he'd always felt more contented with Molly in his arms. Just the weight of her against him brought him peace.

He'd been amazed to find that was still the case. Her earlier burst of anger at his lack of communication had made her seem like a bit of a stranger, and pregnancy had changed her body in ways he didn't recognize. He'd spent most of the time trying to wrap his brain around the fact that as he held her, their baby was cradled between them.

But in spite of all those changes, one thing remained constant: Molly still smelled the same. He'd taken one whiff of her hair and the months of separation had melted away, making him feel as though he'd seen her only yesterday.

Things were different between them, that much was sure. But holding Molly had made him think everything might turn out all right after all.

Provided they got out of here in one piece.

He reached for his phone, wincing a bit as the movement pulled his shoulder.

"Still hurts?" Molly asked.

"It's fine," he said.

She eyed him doubtfully. "I think you're going to need a little more than ice and ibuprofen."

He didn't want to talk about his shoulder, didn't want her to worry about him. "How's your head?" In the gray light of the carriage, he could see that a dark bruise had formed at the edge of her hair. Even though she hadn't hit her belly in the earlier commotion, he'd feel better once she'd been seen by a doctor.

"I've been better," she admitted. "I just want to go home and take a hot bath."

"I'm going to call the fire department again." Impatience bubbled in Max's chest. "We need to get you out of here."

As he thumbed through the call history on his phone, a low hum filled the air. It grew steadily louder, resolving into the characteristic *thwop-thwop-thwop* of a helicopter blade.

Max reflexively glanced up, though he couldn't see through the ceiling of the gondola. "That might be our ride," he murmured.

Sure enough, the sound kept growing louder until it reached a crescendo over their heads. Molly looked nervous. "I probably should have asked this before," she said loudly. "But how exactly are they going to get us down?"

"It depends," Max replied. There were a couple of possibilities—they could rappel down to the ground, or be pulled into the body of the helicopter and ride to safety. Given Molly's inexperience with rope lines and the state of his shoulder, Max sincerely hoped the rescuers opted for the latter option.

Loud thumps sounded on the roof of the carriage. Metal groaned as the rescuers on the roof pried open the hatch of the carriage. A blast of cold air entered the space, and Max drew Molly close to try to keep her warm. A metal ladder descended from the hatch. Max helped guide it to the floor, then stepped back to make room for the rescuers.

The first man descended the ladder quickly. Once inside the carriage, he pushed his ski goggles onto his forehead and glanced around. His eyes landed on Molly, and he smiled broadly.

"Hello, ma'am. My name is John, and I'll be your rescue worker today."

He was a big man, at least five inches taller than Max. Long legs, broad shoulders, muscled arms and a dark beard completed the picture. *Like a lumberjack straight out of central casting*, Max thought sourly. All that was missing were the flannel shirt and ax.

John's size made Max feel a bit inadequate, and it didn't help that Molly was staring up at him like he was some kind of superhero.

Stop it, he told himself. The only thing that mattered right now was getting her to safety. The fact that her rescuer had a pretty face shouldn't bother him. John was just going to get her out of the gondola—nothing more.

John nodded at him. "My partner will take care of you, sir," he said. He glanced up. "Hey, Chris. Plenty of room in here for you to join us."

A second man climbed down the ladder. He was closer to Max's height and build, and had the look of a ski bum. "Howdy," he said.

"Hello," Max replied. "So how are we going to do this? Up or down?"

"Up," said John. "The wind is starting to pick up again,

and we don't want you folks sliding down ropes in case it turns nasty."

Max nodded in agreement. It would be a lot easier for Molly to ride in the helicopter, and they wouldn't have to worry about getting off the side of the mountain after making it to the ground.

"What does that mean?" Molly asked, her worry plain.

Max opened his mouth to explain, but John beat him to it. "I'm going to put this harness on you, ma'am," he said, lifting the gear with one hand. "Then we're going to climb to the roof of the gondola, and the crew in the helicopter will winch us up."

Molly's cheeks went pale. "Okay."

"Don't worry," John said with a smile. "I'll be holding you the whole way."

Max fought the urge to roll his eyes. This guy was really laying it on thick. But Molly seemed to appreciate it.

"All right," she said, nodding. Her eyes widened as John stepped closer, harness in hand.

"Ready?" he asked.

"Sure," she said, her voice a little shaky.

Max clenched his jaw as he watched John's big hands move over Molly's body, tightening straps, securing buckles. *He* should be the one helping her, not this burly stranger.

"What about you?" Chris asked him.

Max reached for the harness and began to strap himself in, his eyes on Molly and John the whole time.

"I take it you've done this before?" Chris asked.

"Yeah. I'm former military," Max said, not really paying attention to Chris.

"Right on, brother," Chris said.

Max didn't reply. He was too busy staring holes into John's back as the man knelt to arrange the straps between

Molly's legs. He reached up to secure a belt around her stomach, but paused when Molly clutched her belly protectively.

John spoke softly, but Max was so focused on the pair of them that he heard him clearly. "Are you—?"

Molly nodded.

John patted her hip, causing Max to see red. "Don't worry," he said quietly. "I'll get you both out of here safely."

"Am I just going to be dangling from a rope?" Molly asked nervously.

"Not exactly," John said. He stood, towering over her. "I'm going to bend my knees, like I'm sitting." He walked over to the ladder, leaning against it as he demonstrated the pose he was going to assume. "You'll sit on my lap, facing me. Lock your ankles around my waist, and I'll keep my arms around you. I'll hold us steady as we go up."

Max thought his head might explode, but by some miracle, he managed to keep his emotions in check.

"First things first, though," John said. He shrugged out of his coat, revealing—*of course*, Max thought—a flannel shirt.

John draped his coat around Molly's shoulders, making Max feel like a giant ass. He wanted to protest, to let everyone know he'd offered her his sweater, but it hadn't fit.

"It's cold outside, and that wind is no joke," John said. "Don't want you turning into a Popsicle on the way up."

"Thanks," Molly said, smiling up at him. "I appreciate it."

"I don't think my coat will fit you," Chris said as he finished checking the fit of Max's harness. "But we have blankets in the chopper."

"No worries. I'll be fine," Max managed to grit out.

"Ladies first," John said, gesturing for Molly to start up the stairs.

She grabbed the first rung, but before she began to climb she glanced at Max. "Are you going to be okay with your shoulder?"

Both John and Chris turned to look at him. "Are you hurt, sir?" Chris asked, his gaze sharpening as he gave Max a once-over.

Max shrugged, wishing Molly hadn't said anything. He didn't want to look weak in front of these men. It was a ridiculous reaction, but he had his pride...

"We got tossed around a bit earlier," he said. "I wrenched my shoulder, but it's fine. I'll be okay for the ride up."

"All right," Chris said. "I know you're a pro, but I'll stand at your back and hold you steady. Will that work for you?"

Max nodded, knowing he couldn't really refuse. These men had safety protocols to follow, and the last thing he wanted was to make their job more difficult.

He watched as first Molly and then John ascended the ladder. Max scrambled up after John, his head popping through the hatch just in time to see Molly climb onto John's lap. She wrapped her legs around his waist and threw her arms around his neck, clinging to his large frame like a barnacle.

A wave of jealousy washed over Max, the emotion so strong he nearly lost his grip on the ladder. It should be *him* holding Molly like that, *him* rescuing her from the gondola. Instead, he had to watch while some stranger lifted his woman and unborn baby to safety.

Except...was she still his woman? Their relationship had been episodic at best, moments of stolen time he'd carved out of his schedule. They'd never made their association public, never let Blaine or anyone else know they were together. They only saw each other when he stayed at The Lodge during his quarterly visits. When Max consid-

ered things from a different perspective, their connection seemed like less of a relationship and more of an ongoing booty call.

The thought left a bad taste in his mouth. He'd never thought of their relationship in such cheap terms before. But as he watched Molly and John rise into the air, he had to wonder if perhaps his actions had made Molly feel that he took her for granted.

He certainly hadn't meant for her to feel…disposable. The problem was, he couldn't offer her anything permanent. After the demise of his first marriage, Max knew he wasn't a forever kind of guy.

But Molly was carrying his child. It didn't get more serious than that.

He relaxed a bit as she and John disappeared into the body of the helicopter. Chris stepped behind him. "Our turn," he said loudly. Max nodded, ignoring the cold gusts of wind buffeting the gondola carriage.

Max felt a tug and then they were airborne, slowly moving away from the roof of the carriage. He knew he should look around, take advantage of the uninterrupted view. This was likely the last time he'd fly through the air without being encased by glass. But he couldn't take his eyes off the door of the helicopter.

Molly was up there, waiting for him. When they'd been stranded in the gondola, it had been easy to feel like life had hit the pause button. In some ways, he wished they'd had more time together, so they could have come to an understanding about how things stood between them. But now they were returning to reality, and they were no closer to knowing what to do next.

"Don't give up on me yet," he murmured. Max knew he didn't deserve a second chance after the way he had treated her, but maybe Molly would listen to him for the

sake of their baby if nothing else. He didn't think they could ever go back to the way things had been between them, but there had to be something he could do to help them move forward, some plan he could devise to make things right again.

He had a goal. Now he just had to figure out how to reach it.

Chapter Seven

"Do you know how much longer this will take?"

Molly tugged the thin sheet over her legs, shifting a bit as she searched for a comfortable position. The hospital mattress was thin, and though both the head and foot of the bed were adjustable, she had yet to find an angle that didn't make her back hurt.

"I believe you're next on the list," said the nurse. "I'm sorry about the wait. It's been a little crazy around here."

Her words triggered a rush of guilt. "No, I'm sorry," Molly said. "I don't mean to complain. I know you guys are doing the best you can after the avalanche."

The woman gave her a grateful smile. "Let me bring you another blanket," she offered. "I know it's chilly in here, and you must still be cold after your ordeal."

"Thank you," she murmured as the nurse left.

Alone again, Molly rested her hand on her belly. The baby had been reassuringly active throughout the afternoon and into the evening. Even though she'd missed her ob-gyn appointment, the ER doctor had mentioned doing an ultrasound to make sure everything was okay. Maybe she'd get to find out the sex of the baby today after all…

Max's face flashed through her mind. Would he be here for the scan? More importantly, did she want him to be?

The helicopter ride down the mountain hadn't taken

too long. John had sat beside her the whole time, a steady presence amid the rush of activity. Max had sat across from her, watching her quietly. Molly could tell there were things he wanted to say, but the noise inside the helicopter kept him from speaking. Then they'd landed, and each of them had been ushered into the back of separate waiting ambulances. She had no idea where he was now. Maybe he was still waiting to see a doctor, too. Or perhaps he'd already been treated and released.

If that was the case, would he wait for her? Or would he leave her here while he made his way back to The Lodge, where Furbert was undoubtedly waiting for him?

At the moment, Molly wasn't sure which option she preferred. Given his reaction in the gondola, it was clear he wasn't happy about the baby. She knew he was still adjusting to the news, but if he was going to ultimately decide to leave, she'd rather he did it now. If he stuck around to try out the role of father and supportive partner, it would hurt all the more if and when he decided the job just wasn't for him. Besides, her baby deserved more than a part-time dad.

But could Max really offer more? He was totally devoted to his charity, a fact that had seemed admirable before. Now it made her wonder if there was room in his life for anything else. He had a track record of prioritizing his work over his personal life. She recalled him telling her about his marriage, the way his commitment to the team had placed a lot of strain on the relationship and ultimately contributed to his divorce. He'd since thrown himself into K-9 Cadets, pushing everything else in his life to the fringes.

Including her.

Molly couldn't find it in her to be bitter, though. She'd known the score when she'd first gotten involved with him. And while she'd accepted the fact that Max didn't think

their relationship could move beyond their quarterly visits, she wasn't willing to consign her child to the same fate. Their baby deserved to have center stage in Max's life.

But would he agree?

She didn't know what kind of history Max had with his own father—he'd never talked about his parents with her before. Now she wondered what kind of childhood he'd had, and what kind of upbringing he wanted for his own kids.

It was one of many conversations they needed to have in the coming days. If Max held true to pattern, however, he would only be in town for the week. They were going to have to pack a lot of decisions into that short period of time, which meant Molly needed to try to keep an open mind. After Max's radio silence in response to her messages, she'd just about accepted the idea of being a single mother; now she had to allow for the possibility that Max would want to coparent their baby.

A soft rap sounded on the door; probably the nurse returning with the extra blanket. Molly called out, "Come in," just as the door was pushed open a crack.

Max peered into the room. "Hi."

"Hi." Relief was a warm rush in her chest, though she quickly quashed the emotion. He was here now, sure. But she couldn't read too much into that. There was still plenty of time for him to walk away.

"May I come in?" He sounded hesitant, which was a departure from his usual confidence.

"Sure."

He slipped inside, revealing a sling on his left arm.

"Are you okay?" she asked as he settled into the chair by her bed.

"What, this?" He lifted his arm slightly. "Yeah, it's okay. Just a little strain."

"Let me guess," she said drily. "They told you to ice it and take ibuprofen?"

He grinned, "Right you are. I tried to save them the trouble, but they insisted on the sling."

Molly rolled her eyes. "You're not a Green Beret anymore. It's okay to be human."

"Never," he deadpanned, leaning back in the chair. "What about you? How's your head?"

"Fine. Just a bump." The doctor who had initially examined her had cleaned a little blood off the spot, but had declared she didn't need stitches. Molly had passed some kind of concussion screen, and the woman had told her to rest and take over-the-counter medication for any pain she might develop.

"What about the baby?"

"I think everything is okay there, too, but I'm waiting for an ultrasound."

Max nodded, absorbing this information. "Um…do you mind if I stay for that?" He looked simultaneously guarded and hopeful, as if he wanted to stay but was prepared to accept no for an answer.

"Yes, you can stay," Molly said. She was glad he actually wanted to be there for the scan, though perhaps he needed to see the baby to truly believe this was happening.

They sat in silence for a moment. "I'm surprised you're still here," she commented. "I figured you'd leave after being seen to get back to Furbert."

"I'm sure he's fine," Max said. "I managed to get ahold of Blaine, who said none of the cabins were affected by the avalanche. I left out food and water, so he should be good for a while."

Molly was glad to hear it. Furbert really was a sweet dog, and she'd hate for anything to happen to him.

There was another rap on the door, and this time a doctor entered, pulling a rolling cart after him. "Hi there,"

he said, his tone friendly. "I'm Dr. Fitzpatrick, the OB on call tonight. Just going to do a quick scan to make sure the baby is all right."

"Sounds good," Molly said.

Dr. Fitzpatrick eyed Max as he set up the ultrasound. "Are you the baby's father?"

Max's eyes widened slightly. "Yes," he replied. Molly thought she heard a hint of surprise in his voice, as if he didn't quite believe he was really here.

"Great, great," Dr. Fitzpatrick said as he pushed buttons and twisted knobs. He turned to Molly. "Ready for the goo?"

Molly smiled wryly. "I suppose."

"It's warm," the doctor assured her. "I wouldn't give you cold stuff."

"Thanks." She tugged up the gown, and Dr. Fitzpatrick tucked a sheet across her hips. Then he applied a healthy dollop of gel to her abdomen; true to his word, it was pleasantly warm on her skin.

"Here we go," he said. He applied the wand to her belly. After a few seconds, a steady *thump-thump-thump* filled the air.

"Is that—?" Max leaned forward, his expression rapt as he stared at the grainy images on the screen.

"The heartbeat, yes," Dr. Fitzpatrick said. "Nice and strong." He made a few notations on the screen, and a number popped up. "One hundred fifty beats per minute—that's perfect."

Molly smiled, the last of the tension draining from her body. She'd been fairly certain the baby was okay, but it felt good to have it confirmed for sure.

"You've got a wiggle worm in here," Dr. Fitzpatrick commented, moving the wand over her belly. "Lots of movement."

"Is that okay?" Max's voice was closer now. Molly

glanced over to find him standing by the bed now, his seat abandoned.

"Oh, yes. We like to see that," the doctor replied.

"Is there any way you can tell if it's a boy or a girl?" Molly asked. "I was supposed to find out today."

"I can try," the doctor answered. "Let's see if this little one will cooperate." He moved the wand around, showing them arms, legs, hands and feet. "That's the heart," he said. "Here's the stomach."

Molly felt Max grab her hand, but she was too fascinated by the images on the screen to look at him. "Here are the baby's kidneys, and this little dark spot is the amniotic fluid in the stomach."

"The fluid is inside the baby?" Max sounded confused and a little worried.

Dr. Fitzpatrick nodded. "At this stage, babies are practicing their swallowing skills. They swallow the amniotic fluid, which helps their gut to develop."

"My God," Max murmured, clearly amazed.

"Here's the brain—all the bits are there," the doctor continued. "And now let me try…yep, there we go." He clicked something, freezing the picture on the screen. "There's your answer."

"Okay," Max said slowly. "Can you help me out a little here? What are we looking at?"

"It's more a matter of what you're *not* looking at," the doctor explained.

"It's a girl," Molly said softly. She glanced at Dr. Fitzpatrick for confirmation. "Right?"

He nodded, seeming pleased she had figured it out. "Yes, indeed. You're having a baby girl."

A surge of emotion surged through Molly, making her eyes well up with tears. She hadn't thought it was possible to feel more love for the baby in her womb, but in that

moment, her heart seemed to grow even larger. "A girl," she whispered, barely able to speak past her happiness.

She glanced up at Max, hoping to share some of the joy of this moment with him. He was as pale as a ghost, his wide eyes fixed on the screen. "A girl," he said a little hoarsely.

Dr. Fitzpatrick smiled. "Congratulations," he murmured. "I have two daughters myself. I can confirm girls are a lot of fun."

Max nodded mechanically, but Molly could tell he wasn't really hearing the doctor. "A girl," he repeated to himself.

The doctor eyed Max, then turned to Molly with an amused look. "It seems the news comes as a bit of a shock."

"In more ways than one." Molly sniffed, dabbing at her eyes with the sheet. "But he'll adjust." And if he didn't? She'd have no problem showing him the door.

She leaned back against the pillow, a dreamy smile on her face as the doctor wiped the gel off her belly.

"Everything looks good to me," Dr. Fitzpatrick said. "Follow up with your regular doctor in a couple of days, but I see nothing to worry about. Congratulations to you both."

"Thank you," Molly said, unable to contain her grin.

"Thanks," Max echoed woodenly.

Dr. Fitzpatrick wheeled the ultrasound machine out of the room. As soon as the door closed behind him, Max sank back into the chair. He looked positively shell-shocked, staring off into space though clearly seeing nothing.

Molly studied him a moment, trying to give him a little time to process the news. "What do you think?"

"Hmm?" he said absently.

"I asked you what you think," she repeated, not bother-

ing to keep the edge from her tone. "You don't seem happy about the news the baby is a girl."

Max shook his head. "No, it's not that. It's just..." He trailed off, still staring into space. "I haven't thought about kids in a long time—not since the early days of my marriage. And even then, when I did think about them, it never occurred to me I might have a girl."

It seemed her earlier fears had been correct. Max wasn't interested in children. And now that they knew the sex of the baby, he could use that as another excuse to walk away.

"I'm sorry to disappoint you," she choked out. Tears filled her eyes again, but in sorrow this time.

"I didn't say I was disappointed," he said quietly. "Just surprised." He rose and began to pace. "Can't you give me a little time to process this? You've known about the baby for five months—I only found out hours ago."

Anger bubbled up in Molly's chest. "And whose fault is that?" she snapped. "I called several times, trying to find out when you'd be back so I could tell you in person."

"I know," he said weakly.

"I get that you're shocked, but don't act like I tried to keep this a secret from you."

"I know," he repeated. His shoulders rose and fell as he let out a long sigh. "And I'm sorry I didn't respond—I truly am. But are you ever going to forgive me for that? Or are you going to stay mad forever?"

His question took some of the wind out of her sails. She was forced to admit he had a point, though that didn't mean she was ready to let go of her hurt and anger quite yet. Still, if they were going to move forward, they would have to find a way to forgive each other for these misunderstandings.

It was the least their daughter deserved.

"I'm not going to continue to punish you," she said fi-

nally. "But I spent the last five months feeling used and disposable. It's going to take me a little time to get over that."

Max nodded. "I'm sorry I made you feel that way." He walked back over to the side of her bed. "If I had known..." He shook his head. "Well, we can't change the past. So I'll make a deal with you—I'll be patient with you if you can be patient with me."

That sounded reasonable. "I can do that." It would be hard not to think the worst whenever Max didn't appear excited or interested in baby stuff, but she'd just have to remind herself he was still adjusting to the thought of fatherhood. He'd probably never imagined having a child like this. She couldn't really blame him for his reaction—she wasn't exactly thrilled about having a baby with a man who didn't even live in the same town, but like Max had said, she couldn't change the past.

His light green eyes warmed as he stared down at her. "Thanks," he said simply.

"It's only fair," she replied.

He was quiet a moment. "So," he began, "how are you feeling? Are you getting morning sickness or anything?"

Molly shook her head. "Not anymore. It was a bit rough at first, but I started feeling better a few weeks ago."

"That's good," he said. He glanced at her belly, clearly trying to think of something to say. "Can you feel it—uh, her," he corrected immediately, his cheeks turning pink. "Can you feel her move yet?"

Molly nodded, smiling as the baby shifted inside her. "She's actually moving now. Do you want to try to feel her?"

"Really?" A note of hope was plain in his tone.

"Really." Molly took his hand and placed it on her lower belly. "Push in a little," she instructed. Max did as she

said, and a few seconds later the baby kicked. "Did you feel that?"

She realized as soon as she saw his face the question had been unnecessary. Max looked both awed and surprised, his eyes shining with wonder.

"That was really strong!" He sounded delighted. His obvious excitement helped smooth the edges of Molly's hurt emotions, and she felt herself softening toward him.

"Is it always like that?" he asked.

Molly shook her head. "Not yet. It mostly feels like flutters when she moves. But my doctor told me as she gets bigger and starts to run out of room, I'll feel her movements a lot more."

"That's amazing," he said. "Does it seem strange, or are you used to it by now?"

He seemed genuinely curious, which was another point in his favor. Molly let her guard drop another inch...

"At first it was kind of weird," she confessed, smiling a bit at the memory. "I wasn't used to sharing my body like that, you know?"

He nodded, then laughed. "Actually, I don't know. But I can imagine."

"I've gotten used to it. But there are still days when I feel like she's taking over."

"When is she due?"

"September 25," she replied. "At least, that's the hope. My OB told me first babies don't always cooperate."

"Let's hope this one will."

"This one will what?"

The new voice in the room made Molly jump. Both she and Max looked at the door to find Blaine standing just inside the room. "Sorry," he said, a bit sheepishly. "I did knock."

His gaze zeroed in on Max's hand, still on her belly. Blaine's eyes narrowed as he looked at Max, then at her.

Max jerked his hand away. He was clearly flustered, but he covered it by walking over to Blaine. "Good to see you, man."

"You, too." The pair engaged in the standard male one-armed embrace/chest bump ritual. "You okay?" Blaine said, nodding at Max's sling.

"Just a little strain," he answered. "No big deal. What about you?" Max jerked his chin at the bruise darkening the side of Blaine's face.

"Yeah, I'm okay. Got tossed around a bit in the avalanche, but all's well that ends well."

Blaine turned to Molly. "What about you?" He walked over to the bed, peering at her head. "Looks like you've got a nasty bruise there."

Molly reached up to gingerly touch her forehead. In truth, she'd forgotten about the bump in the wake of the ultrasound. "I think it looks worse than it is," she said, though in truth, it would probably hurt more tomorrow.

"I'm glad you're both okay," Blaine said. "I was worried."

"So were we," Max said drily. "But the rescuers were absolute pros."

"Was anyone else hurt?" Molly asked. Since they'd been brought straight to the hospital, she hadn't gotten an up-close view of the aftermath of the avalanche. Even though it hadn't looked like there had been much property damage, it was possible skiers and snowboarders had been caught up in the wall of snow and ice.

"From what I've heard, the injuries aren't too serious," Blaine said. "Josh and Tilda are okay. Josh and I actually got caught up in it—we had quite a ride down the mountain."

"My God," Molly gasped. "That sounds terrifying."

"Oh, yeah," Blaine confirmed. "Fortunately, Josh had a transponder on his jacket, so the rescuers knew right where to find us. We're both a little bruised, but nothing bad." He clenched and unclenched his hand, wincing a bit. "Somehow I managed to keep hold of him the whole way down."

Molly smiled. "Sounds like those paternal instincts took over."

"And a good thing, too," Blaine said. "I just got him. I'm not about to lose him now."

"Is there a lot of property damage?" Max asked.

Blaine shook his head. "I don't think so. Overall, we got really lucky with this one."

"That's good," Molly said. "Is the road to The Lodge clear? Or are guests stranded up there?"

"They're stuck for now," Blaine replied. "But the crews estimate they'll have the roads clear again by tomorrow morning."

Molly nodded. "I'll call my staff and ask them to do an extra check on the guests. Do you know if there's enough food on site to accommodate everyone?"

Blaine and Max exchanged a look. "I don't know," Blaine replied. "And I don't think you need to worry about it right now."

"I have to do my job," she protested.

Max piped up. "Or maybe you could let the people who weren't trapped on a gondola for the last six hours take care of things while you focus on resting."

"That sounds like a good idea to me," Blaine said, nodding emphatically.

Molly glanced from one man to the other. "You don't have to gang up on me," she muttered.

"Mols, everyone at work knows you were stuck on that

gondola," Blaine said. "No one is expecting to hear from you right now. In fact, the world won't stop turning if you take a couple of days off."

"I don't know," she said doubtfully.

"It'll be good for you," Blaine pressed. "You might feel fine now, but a scare like the one you had can come back to bite you later. I know I'm going to take a little time off to keep an eye on Josh."

"He's right," Max confirmed.

"Besides, I'm sure the rest of the family would appreciate it if you stayed at sea level for a little bit. Where is Mason, anyway?" he asked. "I figured your brother would be here to check on you."

"He, ah, doesn't know I'm here," Molly said. "I didn't tell my family I was trapped in the gondola."

Blaine raised one eyebrow. "Why not?"

"I didn't want to worry them." It had seemed like a good idea earlier, but in the face of Blaine's scrutiny, Molly wondered if she'd made the right decision.

"I see." Blaine shrugged. "Well, the cat's out of the bag now. The media was all over the rescue effort, and it's only a matter of time until your names are released to the press. You might want to give your brother a heads-up before he hears it on the television."

"I will," Molly said. But just the thought of talking to Mason right now was exhausting. She knew her family deserved to know the details of her ordeal, but she simply wasn't up to dealing with their reactions. Maybe she could send out a reassuring text and call them in the morning, after she'd had some sleep…

"You look tired," Blaine said, not unkindly. "I'm going to step out and make a few phone calls, get this guy a place

to stay. Then I'll come back, and after you're released, I'll take you home."

"I can get a cab," she protested, but Blaine shook his head.

"This isn't a debate," he said. "I'm not going to let my cousin take a cab home from the hospital."

"But I don't know when I'll be getting released," she protested. "You can't stay here all night—Joshua and Tilda need you," she said, referring to her cousin's son and girl-friend. Blaine had recently reconnected with Tilda, his high school sweetheart and the mother of the son he hadn't known he had. Molly knew they were all trying to make up for lost time, and she hated to be the reason Blaine wasn't with his family tonight.

"It's fine," he said. "They'll both understand. Who do you think sent me here after we learned you'd been in the gondola all afternoon? Tilda wants me to make sure you're okay. No more arguments," he said, just as she opened her mouth again.

Molly finally nodded, recognizing she wasn't going to win this one. "Thank you," she said quietly.

"Of course," Blaine replied. He looked at Max. "Let's get you squared away."

Some unspoken communication passed between the two men. Max nodded his head, a hint of wariness in his eyes. "Sounds good," he said. He turned to Molly. "I hope you get some rest tonight."

"Thank you." Disappointment welled up inside her chest, but she quickly quashed it. Of course Max couldn't acknowledge the nature of their connection in front of Blaine—no one knew they had been seeing each other. "Maybe I'll see you at The Lodge before your stay is over."

"I hope so," he said. She could tell by the look in his

eyes he wanted to say more, but Max settled for a nod before turning and following Blaine out of the room.

Molly leaned back against the thin hospital pillow with a sigh. A few moments ago she'd been hopeful about the future. But if Max couldn't bring himself to share their relationship in front of Blaine—a fellow veteran and friend—would he ever be able to go public with the news?

She rested her hand on her belly. "We've got a long road ahead of us, little one," she whispered. "But no matter what, I will always be here for you."

MAX BRACED HIMSELF, certain Blaine would fire at him with both barrels once they were away from Molly. But his friend merely led him down the hall to a cluster of chairs, a makeshift waiting room of sorts.

Blaine took one seat, pulling his phone from his pocket as he did. Max took a seat nearby, feeling a bit on edge.

"We need to find you a hotel, buddy," Blaine said. He tapped on his phone screen as he spoke, apparently gathering information. "There's a B and B not far from here, or you can stay at the discount motel chain for the night."

"There's really no way up the mountain tonight?"

Blaine shook his head. "I'm afraid not. Don't worry— The Lodge will comp your stay. It's the least we can do, given what happened today."

A spike of worry needled Max. "I don't mean to be a diva, but I can't stay in town. I need to get back up the mountain sooner rather than later."

"Furbert came with you?" Blaine asked, correctly guessing the reason for Max's sense of urgency.

"Yes." And although Max had been sure to leave out food and water, the dog would need to be let out before morning.

"Does he do okay with strangers? Because I can have one of our people check on him."

"That should work," Max said. He rattled off a few of the commands Furbert was used to hearing, to make it easier on the staffer who checked on him.

Blaine nodded. "No problem." His fingers flew across the screen as he typed out a message. "It's done," he said, glancing up a minute later.

"Thanks," Max said. Knowing Furbert was going to be taken care of helped ease his mind.

"Anytime," Blaine said. "So…how long have you and Molly been together?"

The question came without warning, as if it were just another topic of regular conversation between them.

Max shifted. "I don't know that we're really together," he hedged.

"I see," Blaine replied. "So how long have the two of you been hooking up?"

Max frowned. "Hooking up" was too crass a description for what they were doing. "It's more than that," he protested. What they had went beyond mere sex—Max felt intensely connected to Molly on an emotional and spiritual level, as well.

He just didn't know what to do about it.

"All right," Blaine said with exaggerated patience. "It's complicated, I get it. But you still haven't answered my question."

"Two years," Max said.

Blaine's eyes widened. "Isn't that how long you've been coming here to relax?"

Max nodded. There was something freeing about telling his buddy this secret. He knew discretion was important to Molly, but he was talking to Blaine now as a friend, not an employee of The Lodge. And given the personal nature of Blaine's question, Max felt certain he was trying to determine if his cousin was okay, not if a fellow employee was engaging in ill-advised behavior with a guest.

"Wow," Blaine said softly. "I had no idea."

"That was by design," Max replied.

The other man processed this for a few seconds. Then he said, "And now she's pregnant."

It wasn't a question. Max knew Blaine had put two and two together when he'd stepped into the hospital room. Still, Max stiffened defensively. He'd only known about the baby for a few hours—he hadn't had time to process the news properly. Talking about Molly's pregnancy wasn't something he wanted to do right now. But he couldn't ignore his friend.

"Yeah," he said with a sigh.

"I take it from your reaction this is a shock?"

Max nodded.

"How far along is she?" Blaine asked.

"About five months," Max replied.

"Whoa. That's half the pregnancy." Blaine frowned slightly. "That doesn't sound like Molly," he said, almost to himself. "I can't believe she kept something like this a secret from you for so long."

"She didn't," Max said quickly. It was important Blaine knew she had contacted him; he didn't want Molly's cousin thinking the worst of her.

Max leaned forward in his chair, glancing around to make sure they were alone. There was a man sitting on a small sofa a few feet away, but he appeared to be asleep. "She reached out to me several times over the past few months. But I was so wrapped up in a major fund-raising push I didn't get back to her."

"But now you know."

"Yeah." He leaned back with a sigh. "She blurted it out when the avalanche hit. Things were pretty dicey there for a few minutes. I think she was afraid we were going to die, so she wanted me to know."

"Man." Blaine shook his head. "That's a memorable way to find out you're going to be a father."

Max actually laughed. "Tell me about it."

"What are you going to do?"

"I'm not sure," Max admitted. "We weren't exactly planning this, you know?"

"Yes, I'm familiar with that feeling," Blaine drawled. Tilda, Blaine's high school sweetheart, had gotten pregnant on their prom night. She thought she had miscarried their baby, but when she'd realized the truth, Blaine had already left for basic training. Blaine had missed a lot of time with his son, and Max knew his friend was thrilled to have the boy in his life now.

"Two years is a long time to be together, though," Blaine continued.

Max shook his head. "It was never anything formal," he said. "More of an understanding. And I'm not quite sure what Molly expects of me now. She's not exactly demanding a ring."

"She won't," Blaine cut in. "That's not her style, and you should know that by now."

The subtle rebuke stung, but it was the truth. Molly wasn't the type of woman to beg, especially not for something as important as a serious commitment.

"Obviously, I'm going to make sure Molly and the baby are taken care of," Max said. "I'm just not sure about the rest."

Blaine studied him for a moment, his expression unreadable. "What's holding you back?"

Max shifted, his friend's scrutiny making him uncomfortable. "You know I tried the marriage thing before. It didn't work."

"Molly isn't Beth," Blaine pointed out.

It was true, but that didn't make the thought of mar-

riage any more appealing. "I think I'm just not cut out for marriage."

"Hmm." Blaine sounded unimpressed.

"What?" Max sounded defensive, but he didn't care. It was clear the other man had something more to say. Might as well let him get it out of his system.

Blaine narrowed his eyes. "You're scared, dude. I get it. But if you think being a part-time dad is going to be a viable long-term strategy, you've got another think coming."

"I never said—" Max began, but Blaine cut him off.

"You're thinking you and Molly can carry on as before. You come for a visit once every three months, and in the meantime, you cut her some checks to make sure the kid has everything they need. I'm telling you right now, that's not going to work. Molly deserves more than that, and so does your child."

Max clenched his jaw, anger building in his chest. No one had talked to him like this before, at least not since his time in basic training. The fact that Blaine was his friend was the only thing keeping Max from unleashing his temper and giving the man a verbal beatdown.

"You done?" he said, his voice tight.

Blaine actually smiled, as if he was enjoying Max's reaction. "For now," he said. He stood, then reached down and grabbed Max's arm to pull him out of the chair. "Come on, let's get you to that B and B. More and more press are descending on the town to cover the avalanche. The motel will be crawling with them." He slapped Max's good shoulder. "You've got a lot to think about. A good night's sleep will help."

"I hope you're right," Max muttered, his anger draining away as fatigue took center stage. He *was* tired. Even though being trapped in the gondola hadn't been physically strenuous, the cold and stress of the ordeal had taken

their toll on his body. Once upon a time, he'd endured far worse conditions for far longer and come out the other side fine. But his tolerance had waned since retiring from the military. Normally, he didn't notice the difference. Now, though? He felt weak and far older than his thirty-seven years.

Blaine glanced over and slowed his pace. "It's going to be okay, buddy," he said. "You don't have to figure everything out tonight. You and Molly have time to decide what to do next."

"Yeah," Max said, only half-convinced. They'd already lost so much time—he didn't want to waste any more being indecisive.

"Cut yourself some slack," Blaine advised. "You've had a hell of a day. Tomorrow will be better."

"I thought the only easy day was yesterday," Max joked.

Blaine shook his head and made a face. "What, are you a SEAL now? Get out of here with that crap."

"Just trying to embrace the suck," Max said, smiling at his friend's reaction.

"That's not a bad strategy," Blaine replied. "But a word of advice? Don't say that in front of Molly. I can tell you from experience, women generally don't appreciate the poetic nature of military expressions."

They pushed open a set of double doors and walked into the parking lot. A cold wind gusted, sending small piles of snow swirling along the asphalt. Max shivered a bit, but was immediately distracted by the sight of several news trucks parked close to the hospital.

"My God," he said softly, slowing his pace to take in the line of reporters standing in the cold, huddled and shivering as they clutched microphones and spoke into cameras. "You weren't kidding. It's a zoo out here."

"Keep moving," Blaine muttered. "And don't make eye contact."

They walked faster, heads down. But they made it only a few feet before a voice shouted out, "Hey, it's the man from the gondola!"

Max swore under his breath.

"Green truck, straight ahead," Blaine directed. They jogged for it, ignoring the commotion behind them as half a dozen reporters and their attendant camera crews thundered across the parking lot in pursuit.

"Buckle up, buddy," Blaine advised as they slammed the truck doors shut. "This is gonna be fun."

Blaine gunned it. Max was slammed back in the seat as the truck shot forward, pulling out of the parking spot before the reporters had a chance to pen them in. Max glanced in the side mirror as they put the hospital behind them. The media folks had already begun to trudge back toward their original spots, close to the ER entrance.

He was glad they'd escaped the scrum, but worry washed over him as he thought about Molly. "You can't drag Molly through that," he said. Part of him wanted Blaine to turn around so Max could stay with Molly and guard her from any overly nosy reporters who might try to get into her room. But he knew their return would only heighten the media furor...

"I won't," Blaine replied, sliding him a glance before returning his focus to the road.

"Promise me," Max demanded. "She shouldn't have to run through a cold parking lot after everything she's been through today."

"I'm a highly trained operative, with loads of experience in both covert operations and hostage extractions," Blaine drawled. "I think I can sneak my cousin out of the hospital without the press getting wind of it."

"Maybe I should help," Max mused. "I could create a distraction, draw their attention."

"Or you could stay in and get some rest," the other man said. He pulled into the driveway of a large Victorian-style house. Light shone through the windows, casting golden squares on the floorboards of the wraparound porch. The place looked friendly and welcoming, but Max couldn't get his mind off Molly, alone in the hospital room.

Well, not exactly alone, he thought. The baby was with her.

The thought should have brought him comfort, but instead only heightened his worry. He was so wrapped up in his thoughts he didn't notice that Blaine had climbed out of the truck. Suddenly, the passenger door swung open.

"Let's go," Blaine said.

"I think I should stay and help you," Max replied. "Make sure Molly gets home okay."

"Nope." Blaine grabbed his arm and tugged him out of the truck. "You're going to head inside. They're expecting you." He reached past Max and locked the door before slamming it shut.

"Wait!" Max protested, as Blaine circled around the hood and climbed into the driver's seat once more.

Blaine rolled the window down a crack. "I'll be back in the morning," he called. "Sleep well, princess!"

Max stood in the driveway, amusement and frustration swirling in his chest as he watched Blaine drive away. Deep down, he knew his friend would take care of Molly.

"Maybe it's for the best," he told himself as he turned and headed up the stairs to the house. Molly was probably happy to have a break from him, given the fact that they'd been trapped together all day. A little time apart might help them both. After all, they were going to be seeing each other a lot over the next few days.

But as Max stepped inside the warmth of the house, a small voice in his head wondered if he would ever get tired of being around her.

Chapter Eight

Someone was pounding on her door.

Molly groaned and rolled over in bed, squinting at the clock on her nightstand. Eight seventeen in the morning. Who could possibly be visiting now?

Normally, she was already up and about and on her way to work by this time. But she hadn't been released from the hospital until around ten thirty last night. True to his word, Blaine had returned to give her a ride home. He'd draped a jacket over her shoulders, placed a ball cap on her head and led her out a side door. "You don't want to get caught by the press," he'd said.

Molly hadn't argued. At that point, she'd been so tired she would have agreed to almost anything if it had meant getting closer to her bed. Blaine had dropped her off around eleven, but before she could go to sleep, she'd wanted to take a hot bath and wash the day off her skin.

She'd finally crawled between the sheets a little after midnight, feeling warm for the first time in hours.

Sleep had claimed her quickly, but her dreams had not been peaceful. She frowned as images flitted through her mind: Max, standing cold and unmoving as she tried to hand him their baby. Then his face twisting in cruel smile as he grabbed the baby from her arms, walking away as

she lay chained to a hospital bed, unable to follow. It didn't take a psychiatrist to interpret those nightmares.

She shook her head to dismiss the disturbing thoughts. She stared at the ceiling for a few seconds, trying to muster the motivation to get up and answer the door. But her bed was so comfortable, and her head ached…

The knocking stopped. *Oh, good*, she thought, closing her eyes once more. Whoever was at her door had given up; she could go back to sleep in peace.

An electronic jingle started up from the direction of her nightstand. Molly muttered a curse as she reached out, fumbling blindly for the phone. She opened her eyes a slit, pressed the green button on the screen and closed her eyes again.

"Hello?"

"Open the damn door, Molly," her brother demanded.

She sighed heavily. "Good morning to you, too, Mason."

"I'm serious, Mols. Let us in."

"Us?" She really wasn't in the mood for company. Mason was one thing—she could handle him. But she didn't want a large audience this morning.

"Elaine is with me," he said, referring to his wife.

He wasn't going to leave her alone until she relented—she knew from experience that her brother was nothing if not stubborn. "Give me a minute," she told him, ending the call before he could reply.

She pushed herself up, swinging her legs over the side of the bed. The change in position triggered a wave of dizziness, but it passed quickly. Moving slowly, she shoved her feet into slippers and grabbed her robe.

She opened her front door to find Mason standing on the welcome mat, fist raised to start pounding again. Molly lifted one eyebrow. "Really? I told you I was coming."

"You took your time about it."

She shook her head as she turned around and trudged into the kitchen. Footsteps sounded behind her as Mason and Elaine followed.

"To what do I owe this early-morning pleasure?" she said, making a beeline for the coffee maker.

"Why didn't you tell us you were trapped on the gondola yesterday?" Mason demanded.

"I didn't want you to worry," she replied. The heavenly smell of coffee rose into the air as she scooped fresh grounds into the filter. She added water to the reservoir, then pressed the start button. *Soon*, she thought longingly.

Mason touched her shoulder. She turned to really look at her brother for the first time since his arrival. His normally styled hair was mussed, as if he'd been running his hands through it. Instead of his usual suit and tie, he was wearing torn jeans and a college sweatshirt that had seen better days. "Of course I worried," he said, pulling her in for a hug.

"We had to find out about it through the news," Elaine chided, her voice dripping with disapproval. Her long blond hair was pulled back in a messy bun and she wore only a hint of lip gloss on her otherwise bare face. Yet she still managed to look like a cover model, even in her yoga pants and slim-fitting fleece jacket.

Molly felt a niggle of insecurity about her own appearance. She hadn't bothered to comb her hair or brush her teeth before answering the door, and her comfortable pajamas and fuzzy robe left much to be desired in terms of fashion. But she wasn't planning on going out today, so really, what did it matter how she looked?

"I'm sorry," Molly said as her brother released her. "I didn't think it was going to take so long to get out of there, and I didn't want to scare anyone."

"That's what family is for," Mason pointed out. "If I had known you were up there, I could have—"

"What?" she cut in. "What exactly could you have done?" Her brother looked as if she'd slapped him, so she softened her tone. "I appreciate the thought, but we were in contact with the rescue team the whole time. There wasn't much to do but wait. I knew if I told you I was in the gondola, you would have been climbing the walls, or worse, getting in the way as you tried to 'help' the rescuers do their job. Besides, I figured you had your own job to worry about."

Mason was the director of sales for the Colton Empire, the family nickname for the all-encompassing company that included The Lodge, The Chateau and several other properties in Roaring Springs. As a popular, smooth-talking businessman, Mason had likely spent much of yesterday afternoon reassuring investors and potential clients in the wake of the avalanche.

"That still doesn't mean I had to find out from a reporter!"

"You're right, and I apologize. I didn't know it was going to be such a news spectacle. But I'm fine, so let's move on."

He eyed her forehead. "You don't look fine."

Molly touched the bump on her head with gentle fingers. "The swelling has actually gone down."

"It looks terrible," Elaine said snidely.

Instead of replying, Molly sighed and poured herself a cup of coffee. She gestured to the pot. "Help yourself."

Mason looked horrified as she raised the cup to her lips and took that first fortifying sip. "What?" she asked, frowning at him.

"Are you sure you should be drinking that in your condition?"

A chill shot through her limbs at his words. "What do

you mean, my condition?" Did he know about the baby? How was that possible? She hadn't told anyone but Max and John, the man who'd lifted her to safety yesterday. She couldn't imagine either one of them had been in contact with Mason...

"There's an article in today's paper that says you're pregnant." He studied her face as he dropped this little bombshell.

"What?" Molly felt the color drain from her face. She leaned back against the counter, gripping the edge with her free hand. "Let me see."

Mason pulled out his phone, typed on the screen for a few seconds. Molly felt Elaine's eyes on her, but she couldn't meet her sister-in-law's gaze.

She wasn't ready for people to know about the baby. She'd barely told Max, and he was the father! A sense of panic gripped her, squeezing her ribs until it was hard to breathe. She'd hoped for privacy while she and Max figured out what to do next. The situation was difficult enough without adding public scrutiny to the mix.

"Here it is," Mason said. He handed his phone over, and she stared at the screen, blinking to focus on the text.

The article was a rundown of yesterday's events, detailing the rescue with a sort of breathless tone that was perhaps better suited to a tabloid than a serious newspaper. She bristled at the description of her "clinging desperately to the mountain man of a rescuer, gratitude and attraction shining in her eyes." But the real kicker was the last paragraph:

But perhaps more than two lives were saved today? This reporter overheard a conversation between Maxwell Hollick, charity mogul, and an unidentified man. It sounds like Ms. Gilford is in the family way. What's more? Max Hollick might be the father! What does all this mean for

Mr. Hollick's charity organization, K-9 Cadets? Will a little human soon be joining the dog pack? Time will tell!

Molly turned to face the counter, setting down her coffee and the phone before she dropped either.

"So it's true?" Mason asked quietly.

She nodded.

Behind her, she heard Elaine suck in a breath.

"Is Maxwell Hollick the father?" Mason asked.

"It doesn't matter," she muttered.

"Of course it does!" her brother exclaimed. "I read up on this guy, Mols. He's ex-Special Forces and apparently quite well-known for his charity work. How on earth did you meet him?" His tone was skeptical, as if he couldn't quite believe a man like Max would ever be interested in a woman like her.

Anger bubbled in her chest. "Like I said, it doesn't matter."

Mason ignored her warning tone. "Why don't you want to talk about him? Are you ashamed?"

Molly turned to face her brother again. "No," she said, her voice lethally quiet.

"I don't understand why you didn't tell us about this earlier." He flung out his arms and began to pace the length of her kitchen. "We're your family, Molly. We could have helped you."

"I didn't want any help," she replied.

Mason's reaction was a perfect example of why she hadn't told her family about the baby. Her brother meant well, but since her parents had retired to spend their golden years traversing the country in their state-of-the-art luxury RV, he had appointed himself "head of the family." It was a nice thought, but Molly didn't need her younger brother lecturing her about her life choices. Their sister, Sabrina, felt the same way. She'd recently graduated from college,

but rather than return to Roaring Springs to settle down in a job, she'd elected to stay in Denver and live with some friends. Molly was happy for her younger sister, but according to some texts she'd received from Sabrina, Mason wanted her to come home.

"Molly—" he began, but she cut him off before he could start up again.

"Enough," she said, making a slashing gesture with her hand. "I'm not going to discuss this with you."

Mason snapped his mouth shut, a hurt look entering his blue eyes. He stared at her for a moment, as if expecting her to say or do something. But Molly simply returned his gaze, refusing to engage with him on this issue.

Sighing softly, he reached behind her to retrieve his phone from the counter. "May I use your bathroom before we go?" He sounded subdued, almost disappointed.

"Of course."

He walked away, leaving her alone with Elaine.

Molly turned to face her sister-in-law. Elaine was no stranger to the little tensions that flared up between the Gilford siblings. Still, Molly hated to argue in front of her.

"I'm sorry about that," she said, the words trailing off as she saw the look on Elaine's face.

The other woman was staring at her belly with a look of such naked yearning it broke Molly's heart. *Oh, no*, she thought, guilt washing over her like a tidal wave.

It was no secret Mason and Elaine had been trying for a baby. A few months ago, Mason had mentioned they were having trouble in that department, but he'd waved away Molly's expressions of sympathy.

"It'll happen eventually," he'd said confidently.

But given Elaine's current expression, it seemed things were still not working out the way they wanted.

Molly reached for the other woman, intent on comfort-

ing her. Elaine jerked away, her eyes flickering up to Molly's face. "Don't touch me!" she snapped.

"Elaine, I'm so sorry," Molly began.

She laughed, but there was no humor in the sound. "Is that right? Well, I guess that just makes everything better now, doesn't it?"

Not knowing what to say, Molly pivoted to pick up her coffee cup. When she glanced back, Elaine's look had turned to one of disgust.

"I don't understand," she said, shaking her head for emphasis. "Mason and I have wanted a baby for so long. I know he told you. But did you know how long we've been trying? Two years. Two years of disappointment after disappointment, with nothing to show for our efforts. Do you know how many times I've been poked and prodded? How many painful procedures I've gone through, all in an attempt to figure out why my body doesn't work the way it should?"

Molly said nothing, knowing there were no words that could offer the other woman any comfort.

"And then," Elaine continued, her voice rising in pitch and volume, "you get yourself knocked up on what amounts to little more than a glorified one-night stand! Tell me how that's fair?"

Molly inwardly cringed at her sister-in-law's description of events, but didn't respond.

"You don't even want this baby, do you?" Elaine threw the question out like a gauntlet, a challenge of sorts that Molly knew she couldn't win.

"That's not true." But even as she uttered the words, a memory flashed in her mind. Seeing those two lines pop up on the pregnancy test had filled her with doubt and worry, and for a time, Molly had vacillated between her options. Shock and stress had kept her from feeling like

a mother, made her question if she even wanted to be one at this time in her life.

Things had changed during her first OB appointment. They'd performed an ultrasound to make sure everything looked okay so far, and Molly had seen the baby for the first time. She hadn't been much to look at then—she'd had the appearance of a small gray gummy bear. But the instant Molly had seen the image, a fierce love had filled her, smothering all her doubts and worries.

Now? She couldn't wait to meet her daughter, to hold her for the first time and kiss her petal-soft cheeks. Just the thought of it warmed her from the inside and made her want to smile.

Elaine ignored her protest. "Oh, please." She grabbed a paper towel from the roll on the counter and dabbed her eyes. Molly ached to hug her, but knew the other woman wouldn't welcome the gesture.

"And the worst part?" Her sister-in-law wrapped her arms around herself, shaking a little as she did. "Mason would make such a wonderful father. Your baby daddy probably can't even be bothered to return your calls."

That barb hit a little too close to home. Tears pricked Molly's eyes. "I didn't do this to hurt you," she said. "I love you and Mason too much to ever deliberately cause you pain."

Elaine met her gaze, her green eyes wide and red-rimmed. "That should have been my baby," she sniffed. "Not yours."

Frustration welled in Molly's chest, testing the limits of her sympathy. "My pregnancy has no bearing on your ability to have a baby. It's not like there are only a finite amount of babies to go around—you and Mason can still get pregnant."

"No, we can't," she said flatly. "We've exhausted all of

our options. The fertility treatments didn't work, and we can't afford to keep trying."

The revelation shocked Molly into silence for a few seconds. "I'm so sorry," she said finally. "I had no idea."

Elaine didn't say anything—she simply stared into space. Molly wasn't certain the other woman had even heard her.

The silence in the kitchen was broken by Mason's return. He half stumbled into the room, clutching his phone in one hand. His expression was a combination of shock and disbelief, and his face was so pale Molly instinctively reached for him, fearing he might fall down.

"What is it?" she asked. Her heart started to pound— something was clearly wrong with her brother.

He shook his head, as if trying to fling off a net. "The avalanche," he said. "It's uncovered the bodies of several women."

"Oh, no," Molly cried. "That's terrible." She frowned, confused. "But I thought the rescuers said yesterday there weren't any fatalities?"

"These are...old bodies," Mason said, grimacing. "Victims."

Molly shook her head. It was unsettling news to be sure, but why was Mason so distraught?

"There's more, isn't there?" A stone of worry formed in her stomach as apprehension sent a chill down her spine.

Mason nodded, his eyes shiny with unshed tears. "Sabrina," he whispered.

Their sister's name sent a jolt through Molly. Denial welled up even as the logical part of her brain acknowledged the truth. "No." She shook her head, taking a step back. "No, no, no."

Mason rubbed his eyes with one hand, his voice muted when he spoke again.

"One of the bodies is hers. She's dead."

FURBERT BOUNDED DOWN the trail looking like his joints were made of springs as he darted from one tree to another, stopping here to sniff, there to mark his territory. Max ambled along behind him, happy to let the dog burn off the excess energy he'd acquired from being cooped up inside yesterday afternoon and last night.

The B and B had been a nice place to stay, all things considered. Max had taken a hot shower and climbed into the too-soft bed, falling asleep almost as soon as his head had hit the pillow. It was a skill he'd retained from his soldiering days—even though his mind was occupied with a million different thoughts and worries, his body was trained to sleep whenever it got the opportunity.

He'd woken a few hours ago, his brain immediately starting up the soundtrack of questions and what-ifs that had plagued him since yesterday's revelations. But before he could indulge in some heavy-duty thinking, he'd first needed to make sure Furbert was okay.

Fortunately, Blaine's predictions had been correct. The road up the mountain had been clear, and the cab hadn't had any trouble taking him to The Lodge. Furbert had been excited to see him, practically dancing in place as Max had entered the cabin. Max had been pleased to find that fresh water and food had been set out for the dog, and furthermore, Furbert hadn't had any accidents on the carpet. Not wanting to tempt fate, Max had taken the dog for a walk before even bothering to change his clothes.

Now, as he breathed in the fresh, cool air and felt the pleasant burn of exercise in his legs, Max's head began to clear.

He was going to be a father.

A weight settled over him once again as he recalled the image on the sonogram screen: a tiny baby, arms and legs and hands and feet all immediately recognizable. The

curve of chin and nose, the slope of the belly and roundness of the head; all parts there. All perfectly formed.

Real.

And part of him.

He knew that, too, without a doubt. Even if Molly had been with other men in the times they'd been apart, it didn't make sense for her to try to pin this pregnancy on him if he wasn't the real father. He was wealthy, yes, but he knew she had a trust fund so money wasn't an issue for her. Given their geographic separation, she'd be better off claiming a local man as the father rather than him. As much as he was stunned by the existence of this baby, he couldn't deny it was his.

So what should his next move be? And moreover, what did Molly expect of him?

Marriage was off the table. After his relationship with Beth had fallen apart, Max had come to the realization that he wasn't cut out for being a husband. It wasn't in his nature to be fully committed to more than one thing at once. He was so wrapped up in his work with K-9 Cadets, he simply didn't have the time or the energy to expend on a full-blown relationship.

But…he couldn't leave Molly to raise their daughter alone. He wanted to be a part of the baby's life, wanted to know her and have her know him in return. He wasn't going to be one of those deadbeat dads who only saw their kid once or twice a year, if at all. He'd had a good relationship with his own father, and wanted the same for his child, as well.

So how was he going to reconcile the demands of his work with the responsibilities of being a dad? Moreover, where did he and Molly go from here? Did they have a future together as a couple, or were they destined to remain connected only by virtue of their child? It was the

million-dollar question, the one he had to find an answer for before this visit was over.

A rabbit streaked across the path, flushed from the undergrowth by Furbert's inquisitive explorations. The dog let out a happy yip and shot after the small creature, plunging headlong into the bushes.

"Furbert!" The last thing Max needed was to lose sight of his dog on the mountain. He wasn't familiar enough with the terrain to feel comfortable letting Furbert run loose, even if the dog was having the time of his life.

A niggle of worry tickled the base of Max's spine as the seconds ticked by with no sign of the canine. Then he heard the bushes shake and let out a sigh of relief. The months of obedience training had been worth it—Furbert trotted back onto the trail, his demeanor nonchalant despite the fact that he was coated in mud from his belly down.

"Really, buddy?" Max asked with a sigh. Time to head back to the cabin so they could both get cleaned up.

Furbert put up a token protest at the sight of the bathtub, but Max was able to coax him in with a little effort. After his own shower, Max flipped on the television, wanting some background noise as he dressed.

An attractive woman was on the screen, talking about the avalanche. "—gruesome discovery," she was saying. "So far, several bodies have been recovered, and authorities say there could be more."

Max stopped in front of the television, his attention captured. What was she talking about? Blaine had said there were no fatalities from yesterday's scare. Had he been misinformed?

"How long have the bodies been hidden?" asked a news anchor from off-screen.

The woman frowned into the camera. "That's just it, Clark. Authorities are telling me some of the bodies look

like they've been buried for years, while others seem to have been placed more recently." She held her hand up to her ear, listening for a few seconds. "Clark, I can now confirm that the identity of one of the bodies is that of Sabrina Gilford, a young local woman who recently graduated from college."

"Was she ever reported missing?" asked the anchor.

"No," replied the woman. "Our sources say she was not listed as a missing person."

The news anchor and reporter continued their back-and-forth, but Max couldn't hear them over the rush of blood in his ears.

Sabrina Gilford. Molly's sister.

Did she already know her sister's body had been found? God, he hoped so. The thought that she had learned about her sister's death from a news report made him simultaneously heartsick and angry.

He threw on some clothes, a sense of urgency pushing him forward. He had to get to Molly, had to know if she was okay. She must be devastated—he couldn't let her suffer alone.

"Let's go," he called to Furbert as he shoved his feet into shoes. After yesterday's accident, he wasn't leaving the dog alone in the cabin any longer than necessary. But beyond that, he wasn't certain if Molly would allow him to comfort her. If she wanted nothing to do with him, she might at least respond to Furbert…

He clipped the leash onto the dog's collar, then set off quickly down the path for the main lodge. Keeping one eye on the ground, he thumbed through the contacts on his phone until he pulled up Blaine's number.

"Yeah?" Max could tell by the tone of his friend's voice he had heard the news.

"Can you take me to Molly?"

"I spoke to her earlier this morning. She doesn't want company."

"Please," Max said, dodging a low-hanging branch. "I won't bother her. I just want to bring Furbert for her."

Blaine sighed heavily. "Okay. But promise me you won't try to argue if she wants you to leave."

"Of course I won't," Max said. "I'll be in the main lobby in a few minutes."

"Roger that."

Max shoved the phone into his pocket and picked up the pace. *Hang on, Molly*, he thought. *I'm coming.*

Chapter Nine

Someone was at her door again.

Molly sat on the couch, feeling numb as she heard the knocks. It wasn't Mason, that much she knew. He and Elaine had left shortly after hearing the news of Sabrina's death. Molly would have liked for him to stay so they could comfort each other, but she didn't feel right around Elaine at the moment. It was going to take time for the memories of her sister-in-law's tirade to fade and for her hurt feelings to recover.

Normally, Molly would talk to Mason about what his wife had said, but she wasn't about to pile more on him at the moment. She'd seen them to the door, then settled on the sofa and tried to process what was happening between fielding phone calls from concerned and shocked relatives.

As the knocking persisted, Molly considered going back to bed and drawing the covers over her head. Maybe if she went back to sleep, she'd wake later to find this was all a nightmare conjured by stress. Surely her sister wasn't really dead! Molly had heard from her not that long ago— Sabrina had been headed out to a bar with friends. Her sister had seemed normal, with no indication that there was anything bothering her. How, then, had she ended up buried in the snow in Roaring Springs?

It's a mistake, Molly decided. That had to be it. The

body recovered probably looked like Sabrina, but it wasn't really her.

She got to her feet. Might as well answer the door, tell whoever was on the other side that her sister was fine. Then she'd call Mason—he'd be so happy to know it was all just a misunderstanding.

Max and Furbert stood on the porch, both sporting worried expressions.

Molly blinked in surprise. "Uh, how did you get here?"

"Blaine brought us," Max said. He turned and waved.

Looking past his shoulder, she saw Blaine in his truck. He rolled down the window. "I know you didn't want to be bothered, but I thought you might like to see the dog," her cousin yelled.

Molly glanced down at Furbert, who was staring up at her with kind eyes. The muscles of her throat tightened, making it hard for her to speak. So she nodded instead.

"Call me when you want me to take 'em back," Blaine continued. He stared at her with such open concern that she nearly started crying on the spot. But that was silly, when she knew everything was okay.

"Thanks," she managed to choke out. "I will."

She stepped back to allow Max and Furbert inside her home. Max stopped in the hallway, waiting for her to shut the door. When she turned back, she found him watching her with his brow furrowed.

"Where's your sling?" She gestured to his arm, no longer held in place against his chest.

"What? Oh, I took it off. I'm fine," he said dismissively.

Molly shrugged, accepting his assessment.

"How are you?" he asked quietly. He grimaced. "I know that's a ridiculous question, under the circumstances, but I don't know what else to say."

"I'm okay," she replied. Surprise flickered across his

face. "No, really, I am." She began to walk toward the den, dog and man following her.

She reached for her phone and sat on the couch. "It's a mistake, you see," she said, pulling up her list of contacts. "I was just getting ready to call Sabrina when you knocked on the door."

Max stood in front of her, his green eyes full of sympathy as she dialed. The phone rang and rang, until finally, her sister's voice mail picked up.

Hmm. That was strange. Normally Sabrina answered when she called her.

"It's me," Molly said. "Call me when you get this, please."

She hung up, shot Max a glance. "She's probably busy."

"Molly," he murmured softly. He knelt in front of her, reached for her hands.

"I know," she said, lifting them up so he couldn't touch her. "I'll text her. Maybe she's in a movie or something and can't answer her phone." She typed out a quick message, then leaned back and waited for her sister's response.

Max said nothing. Furbert jumped onto the sofa and curled up next to her, his body a warm weight against her side and the outside of her thigh.

As the minutes ticked by with no response, Molly began to worry.

"Maybe her battery died," she said, a sick feeling spreading over her. "Or maybe her phone was stolen. Or she left it at home."

Max reached up and brushed a strand of hair behind her ear.

"She's not dead." She tried to sound forceful, but her voice shook. "She can't be."

"What did the police say?"

"I don't know. I didn't talk to them—Mason is the one

who got the call." And he hadn't told her exactly what they'd said, just that Sabrina's body had been found. Molly had been so shocked at the news, she hadn't thought to question him, to find out why the police thought the body they'd found belonged to their sister.

"I'm sure he got it wrong," she insisted, tapping on her phone again. She'd simply call the police and ask for an explanation. That was probably the fastest way to get this all cleared up.

Molly was patched through to Deputy Sheriff Daria Bloom. "Ms. Gilford... I'm so sorry for your loss. How may I help you?"

"That's just it, Deputy Sheriff Bloom. I'm calling because I think there's been a mistake. My sister is in Denver—there's no way you uncovered her body today."

The line was silent for a moment. When the other woman spoke again, it was with the careful tone one used when talking to a scared child. "Ms. Gilford, I know the news must have come as a shock. But I can assure you—"

"How do you know it was Sabrina?" Molly interrupted, tired of this game.

"Several physical characteristics matched those of your sister."

"Sabrina isn't the only woman with long curly hair," Molly replied.

"Yes, ma'am," Deputy Sheriff Bloom said. Her tone was kind—she seemed like a nice woman, but Molly wasn't in the mood for placations. "However, there were other identifying marks we used to make the identification."

"I want to see the body," Molly declared. It was clear she wasn't getting her point across over the phone. She simply needed to talk to Deputy Sheriff Bloom in person and show her why she was wrong.

Max sucked in a breath. "Molly, no," he whispered.

"I'm not sure that's a good idea," Deputy Sheriff Bloom began, but Molly cut her off again.

"I'm going to the hospital," Molly told her. "The news said the bodies had been taken there for an initial examination. Please meet me?"

The other woman sighed. "All right, Ms. Gilford. In my experience, it's best if you don't do this alone. Is there someone who can come with you? A friend who can meet you there, perhaps?"

Molly glanced at Max. "Yes," she said, hoping he'd agree to accompany her.

"Very well," said the Deputy Sheriff. "I'll see you in an hour."

"Thank you," Molly said sincerely. In sixty minutes, this would all be cleared up.

She hung up and met Max's worried gaze. "She's going to meet me at the hospital morgue. Will you come with me?"

"You know I will," he said quietly. "But do you really think this is the best idea? Once you see her body…" He trailed off, considering his words. "There are some things you can't unsee, Molly. I don't want you to remember your sister lying on a slab in the morgue."

"I have to know," she said. "I can't accept that she's gone, not without seeing for myself."

He studied her for a moment, his green eyes so intense she felt like he was trying to see into her soul. *Let him look*, she decided. She had nothing to hide.

Finally, he nodded. "All right. I can understand that."

"Do you think…" She stopped talking as she realized the question was probably too silly to bother asking.

"Do I think what?" Max prompted in a low, gentle tone.

She took a deep breath, accepting the fact that she was about to look ridiculous. "Do you think we can bring Furb-

ert, too?" Seeing a dead body wasn't going to be pleasant. It would be nice to have the dog around to help take her mind off things when it was all over.

"He probably can't come into the hospital with us, but he won't mind waiting in the car."

Molly nodded. "Let's bring him, then. I'll go get my keys."

This is a bad idea.

Max walked next to Molly through the hospital parking lot, toward the main entrance of the building. Furbert was happy to stay in the car, and he'd made sure the windows were cracked so the air didn't get too stuffy. It was still cold enough that the car wouldn't overheat—in fact, Molly had thrown a few blankets into the back seat so the dog could burrow in if he got too cold.

Confident that his dog was cared for, Max was free to totally focus on Molly. Her reaction to her sister's death bothered him. Denial was a common response to traumatic news, but she seemed to be taking it a bit far. The problem was, he didn't know what to do about it. If he tried to force her to acknowledge the truth it would only hurt her. But he couldn't stand by and watch her completely detach from reality.

Max hated for her to view her sister's body—he'd seen his share of corpses while serving overseas, and it was a sight he'd never forgotten. He didn't want Molly to have that image in her head for the rest of her life. But if that was what it was going to take for her to accept the fact that her sister was gone... Well, all he could do was support her as much as she would let him. Hopefully that would be enough.

Molly had been silent during the drive, and he hadn't pressed her to speak. There was a fragility about her, a

sense that she was holding herself together through sheer force of will. He admired her strength, but at the same time, he wanted to take her in his arms and pull her close. He didn't know the right words for this situation, but he could show her with his body that she wasn't alone.

But that would have to wait. They walked through the sliding glass doors into the hospital. An information desk was situated straight ahead. By unspoken agreement, they both headed for it. Just as they reached the counter, a woman walked up. She was carrying a folder close to her chest, but behind the file Max saw a gleam from the badge she wore on a chain around her neck.

"Ms. Gilford?"

At Molly's nod, the woman held out her hand. "Deputy Sheriff Bloom."

Molly shook her hand, then Max introduced himself. "Thank you for meeting me," Molly said.

"Of course." Deputy Sheriff Bloom gestured for them to walk with her. "Before we go to the morgue, do you mind if we talk for a few minutes? There's a small office just down this hall we can use."

"Okay." Molly bit her lip. Max could tell she wasn't crazy about the delay. One of the things he admired most about Molly was her determination—if she made up her mind to do something, she was going to see it through. That was why he'd agreed to accompany her here—he'd known she was going to come, one way or another. Better for her to have a friendly face present than to do this alone.

Just as she'd said, Deputy Sheriff Bloom led them into a small room. It held a round table with a few chairs scattered around it, but not much else.

Deputy Sheriff Bloom took a seat, and Max and Molly did the same. She placed the folder on the table in front of her.

"I understand you have some questions about the process we used to identify the body of your sister." Her tone was no-nonsense, bordering on brusque. "I wanted to show you the evidence we have before you go downstairs."

Molly swallowed hard, nodding. A candle of hope flickered to life in Max's chest. If the deputy sheriff was doing what he thought she was, they might be able to convince Molly the police had gotten it right without ever visiting the morgue.

Deputy Sheriff Bloom opened the folder. "The first thing to note is that the body matches the overall physical characteristics of your sister. Her height, weight, approximate age. Her hair." She slid a photograph across the table, and Max spied a tangle of brown curls, stretched out on a metal table alongside a ruler.

"The next thing we look for are scars or other identifying markers." She slid another photo toward Molly, this one a picture of a tattoo. "We know from her social media accounts that your sister got a tattoo about six months ago." Another photo joined the first; Sabrina grinning as she pointed to an identical tattoo on her arm.

Molly's face turned pale. Max felt his heart crack for her. "How did you know to look at her social media?" she whispered. "What made you think to do that in the first place?"

Deputy Sheriff Bloom's golden-brown eyes were kind as she looked at Molly. "We found her driver's license in her pocket." Another photo was slid across the table, proving the veracity of her words.

Molly let out a small moan at the sight. She reached out blindly, gripping Max's arm. He scooted closer, leaning against her so she could feel his reassuring presence.

"But we got the final confirmation this morning," Deputy Sheriff Bloom continued. "Just before we called your

brother, the lab informed us the fingerprints of the body we found match those of your sister."

Molly's hand tightened around arm. "I see." She exhaled with a shudder, her body seeming to deflate into the chair.

Deputy Sheriff Bloom was quiet for a moment. When she spoke again, her voice was quiet, as if she were trying not to disturb Molly. "Would you still like to go to the morgue?"

"No." She shook her head. "No, that won't be necessary."

Molly leaned against him, her head down as she stared at her hands. Max looked at Deputy Sheriff Bloom, who was watching Molly with sympathy in her eyes.

Thank you, he mouthed. He draped his arm around Molly's shoulders, drawing her as close as their two chairs would allow.

Deputy Sheriff Bloom nodded in understanding. "Do you feel up to answering a few questions, Ms. Gilford? We're trying to piece together your sister's movements over the last few weeks, in the hopes of discovering when she met her killer."

It was on the tip of Max's tongue to ask if this could wait, but Molly straightened up and nodded. "I'm not sure how much help I'll be, but I'll try my best."

"Thank you." Deputy Sheriff Bloom gathered up the photographs and placed them back into her folder.

"How long…" Molly trailed off, then cleared her throat. "When did Sabrina die?"

"We're not certain yet. Once we do a cursory exam of all the victims, we're going to send them to the state facility in Denver for further testing. Based on our initial findings, though, we estimate she was killed about three weeks ago."

Molly absorbed this information with a small nod. She closed her eyes and took a deep breath. "Did she suffer?"

Max stiffened and shot a quick look at the deputy sheriff. No matter how her sister had died, there was only one answer Molly needed to hear right now.

"We think it was over quickly."

Molly let out a sigh, her shoulders relaxing a bit. She shook herself. "I'm sorry. You said you had questions for me, but I'm the one who's been doing all the asking."

"Don't apologize. You've had a terrible shock. It's only natural you want to know more about what happened."

Molly dabbed at her eyes, nodding. "I'll help you in any way I can."

"I appreciate it." Deputy Sheriff Bloom folded her hands on the table, leaning forward slightly. "Can you tell me about the last time you heard from your sister?"

"It was about a month ago," Molly said slowly. "She texted me. Said she was going out with friends."

"Did she seem normal?"

"As far as I could tell." She reached for her bag, dug out her phone. "Here are her messages." She tapped the screen, then slid the device across the table.

Max studied Molly's face as Deputy Sheriff Bloom scrolled through the messages. The color was coming back to her skin, though her eyes had a haunted look about them that he thought might linger for a while. She was clearly trying to put on a brave face, even though this had to be the worst day of her life. Her courage reminded him of the men and women he'd served with, and a surge of emotions welled in his chest; pride in her strength, sympathy for her loss, worry for how she would cope in the long term. More than all that, though, was the desire to stand by her side as she moved forward.

His thoughts were interrupted by Deputy Sheriff Bloom

passing the phone back to Molly. "Thank you for that," she said. "Do you know if your sister had any enemies, anyone who might wish her harm?"

Molly frowned. "That sounds sinister."

"I don't mean to sound like she was living in a James Bond movie," Deputy Sheriff Bloom said. "But maybe she had a nasty breakup? Or a coworker she butted heads with?"

Molly shook her head. "Not that I know of...she never mentioned anything like that."

Deputy Sheriff Bloom nodded, as if she'd expected that answer. "If you remember anything she said, even in passing, please don't hesitate to reach out." She withdrew a card from her pocket and handed it to Molly. Then she stood, indicating she was done with her questions.

Max helped Molly to her feet. She stayed close to him, so he put his arm around her again. "Thanks for meeting with me," Molly said. Twin spots of color appeared on her cheeks and she ducked her head. "I know I was being unreasonable earlier. Thank you for being so kind to me."

The other woman stepped close and took one of Molly's hands between her own. "Like I said before, you don't need to apologize. I'll keep you up to date on the investigation."

"Thank you," Molly said.

The deputy sheriff nodded and walked out of the room, leaving Molly and Max alone.

"How are you doing?" he asked quietly.

She sighed, her shoulders sagging under his arm. "I'm not sure."

Taking a chance, Max kept his arm around her and pivoted to bring them face-to-face. He brought his other arm up and slowly drew her forward, giving her time to reject his embrace.

She dropped her head against his chest, sinking into the

hug. Max buried his nose in her hair. "I'm so sorry, sweetheart," he said, moving one hand up and down the valley of her spine. "I wish I could make this better for you."

His heart broke as she began to cry. Quiet sniffs at first, but soon she was sobbing, her body heaving as she fought to draw in choked breaths.

Max held her close, his body absorbing her shudders as his shirt soaked up her tears. He wasn't sure how long they stood there, but gradually her breathing began to even out and the sniffles subsided.

"What can I do for you?" He wanted to help her, to charge into the fray for her, to do whatever it took to make her smile again.

"Just take me home." Her voice was dull, like a black-and-white sketch of her normal full-color self.

"All right." He took her arm and led her out of the hospital. When they neared the car, she dug into her purse and handed him the keys. "Do you remember how to get to my house?"

Max nodded, taking the keys from her hand. Without saying another word, she crawled into the back seat and reached for Furbert.

Max settled behind the wheel, eyeing the pair of them in the rearview mirror. Furbert half sat, half stood in her lap, his head leaning into her shoulder as Molly wrapped her arms around him.

"Good boy," Max murmured. He started the car and began the drive back to Molly's, one eye on the road and the other on the duo he cared for more than anything else in the world.

Chapter Ten

Molly moved on autopilot, walking from the car into her house with no true awareness of her actions. She sat on the sofa, feeling numb from the neck down. Everything was muted—the brightly colored throw pillows next to her looked pale, and sounds seemed distorted, as if she were hearing them underwater. She felt a warmth at her side; *Furbert*, she realized dimly. *I should pet him*, she thought. But she couldn't seem to muster the energy to do so.

Suddenly, Max was in front of her. He took her hands, cupped them around something warm. *Tea.*

She stared at the mug for a moment, trying to remember what to do with it. The world seemed foreign, as if she'd been dropped in a parallel universe where everything was just a bit *wrong*, a knockoff that upon closer inspection revealed itself to be a cheap imitation of the real thing.

"Molly."

The sound of her name brushed aside some of her mental fog. Max was sitting on her other side, one arm draped across the back of the sofa, his free hand helping steady the mug in her lap.

"Are you hungry?"

She blinked at the question. What did that even mean?

"She's gone."

Max's features softened. "I know."

"Why did this happen?"

He took the cup from her hands, set it on the low table in front of them. Molly missed its warmth, but she didn't bother to protest.

"I don't know."

She stared at the table until it grew blurry. "What am I supposed to do now?"

Max pulled her against his side. He was solid. Warm. Strong.

"You live," he said simply. "You remember her, try to honor her memory. You carry on."

His words made a strange kind of sense. But even though he hadn't said much, his advice seemed like an impossible task.

"I—I don't know if I can do that."

He stroked his hand up and down her arm. She focused on the sensation of his touch, an anchor in these unfamiliar waters.

"You can," he said. His voice was low and deep, his chest rumbling against her side. "Right now, the grief is so strong you don't think you'll ever be able to function again. But little by little, you'll find a way to keep going. Your sadness won't ever leave. But you will get better at dealing with it."

She wanted to believe him, she truly did. But it sounded too good to be true. "How do you know?"

"I've lost people, too," he confided. "The circumstances were different, but they're gone all the same."

"I'm sorry," she said. Her pain was so great, she wouldn't wish this on her worst enemy.

His hand stilled on her arm. Then he chuckled softly. "You are amazing," he said.

"What do you mean?" That seemed like an odd thing to say, under the circumstances.

He pressed a kiss to the top of her head, then rested his cheek there. "You're in the middle of processing the shock of your life. And yet you're still worried about my experiences from years ago."

"If what you said is true, then the loss still hurts."

"It does," he confirmed. "But the rest of what I said is true, too. The pain isn't so acute now—it's more like a dull ache. A sore spot in my heart that I've gotten used to living with."

Maybe he was right. Maybe someday the pain would fade. But in this moment, Molly couldn't imagine a day when she wouldn't feel like her heart was being torn in two.

"She was so beautiful," she choked out. Memories of Sabrina filled her head, a movie reel of growing up together.

"Tell me about her," Max said softly. "If it doesn't hurt too much to talk about her."

"No... I think I'd like that." If she shared her memories of Sabrina, someone else would know about her. Part of her sister would still live on, in some small way.

She started talking, haltingly at first, then picking up speed as the words flowed out of her. Despite their seven-year age difference, she and Sabrina had often ganged up to pick on Mason when they were all kids. Max laughed as she recounted some of their antics, such as the time they'd woken up early one Christmas morning and hidden all of Mason's presents, convincing him that Santa had skipped him that year. Or when they'd switched the labels on some of his toiletries, so he'd reached for his mousse and wound up using shaving cream in his hair instead.

"Poor guy," Max said, his chest vibrating with laughter. "He didn't stand a chance against you two."

"Don't feel too sorry for him," Molly retorted. "He paid us back, I can assure you."

"It sounds like you were all close, despite the pranks. I'm sure your parents were happy about that."

"They were." Molly smiled, enjoying the moment of reverie. Then a black wave washed over her, stealing her breath. "Oh, my God," she said, fresh tears forming. "My parents. I have to tell them she's gone."

Furbert pressed himself against her side, apparently sensing her renewed distress. She ran one hand through his fur, grateful for the small tactile distraction. "How am I going to do this?" As bad as her pain was, she knew her parents' grief would be even more palpable. Molly hadn't even met her daughter yet, but already the thought of losing her was enough to take her breath away. How would her poor mother handle this news?

"The police may have already contacted them," Max pointed out. "If they haven't, why don't you let the deputy sheriff handle it?"

"No." Molly shook her head. As hard as it was going to be to tell them Sabrina was gone, her parents deserved to hear it from a family member. "I don't want a stranger to tell them she's dead."

"Fair enough," Max said. "But why don't you and Mason tell them together? That way, you don't have to do this alone."

She nodded. The idea of Mason helping her brought a small measure of relief. If they spoke to her parents together, her mom and dad might take comfort in knowing their two remaining children were fine, under the circumstances.

She glanced around. Where was her phone? Might as well get this over with—the news would not improve with keeping.

"Stay here," Max said. "I'll get your bag."

He rose from the couch. She felt his loss immediately, an unmooring sensation that made her stomach churn. Her hand tightened in Furbert's coat; in response, the dog shifted so that his front legs were stretched out in her lap. He pressed his head to her chest, hugging her as best as he was able.

Max returned a few seconds later. "Good boy," he said softly, placing her bag on the cushion he'd just left.

"He is," Molly concurred. "You know, I don't even like dogs. I don't dislike them, but I've never considered myself a dog person."

"That's okay," Max said. "Furbert won't hold it against you."

She smiled, then pulled her phone free. Keeping one hand on Furbert, she called her brother.

"Yes?" Mason sounded exhausted, as though it had taken all his energy to answer her call.

"How are you?" It was such a prosaic question, but she didn't know what else to say.

"How do you think?"

Molly immediately understood his reply. "I know," she said softly.

"It just doesn't make sense," he said, a bit of emotion seeping into his voice. "I keep going over and over it in my head, but I can't understand why she's gone."

"I know." She let him rage, listened as he said what she'd been thinking all day.

"I don't know what to do," he said finally.

"I don't, either," Molly admitted. "But I do know we need to call Mom and Dad."

Mason sighed heavily. "I… I don't think I can do that, Mols."

Molly closed her eyes, feeling a weight descend on her

shoulders. "I won't make you," she said. "But it would mean a lot if you helped me do this."

"I can't." There were tears in his voice now. "I can't hurt Mom like that."

And you think I want to? A flush of anger rushed through her, making her want to scream. Instead, she took a deep breath. "Please, Mason. I want them to hear both our voices."

"I'm sorry, Molly. I just don't have it in me right now."

She bit her tongue, choked back the words she wanted desperately to say. Deep down inside, she recognized that adding to Mason's pain wouldn't lessen her own. "All right," she said finally. "I'll check in with you later."

"I love you." There was relief and regret in his voice, as if he knew he'd let her down but was incapable of doing anything about it.

"I love you, too." Molly ended the call and dropped her forehead to rest on Furbert.

"Come on," Max said gently. "Why don't you lie down for a bit? Collect yourself before you call them."

It was a tempting suggestion, but she knew if she didn't tell her parents now, she'd lose her nerve.

"Not yet," she replied. "I have to tell them now. It's been too long already."

"Okay."

Molly stared at Max, feeling as though she were truly seeing him for the first time that day. He'd been unquestioningly supportive, a rock she'd clung to as her emotions had raged and grief had battered her from all sides.

She'd known he was a good man—had known it from the start. But his actions today had shown her he cared about her, more than any words ever could.

Molly didn't know what their future might hold. Truly, she couldn't worry about it now, not with her sister's death

still so fresh. But the mountain of anxiety she'd been carrying around ever since learning she was pregnant began to lighten.

He didn't think of her as just a fling—someone to have fun with and leave when things got too heavy. If it were that simple, he'd have left after learning about the baby. But he was here, standing beside her while she dealt with the aftermath of Sabrina's murder.

Maybe things would work out between them after all. Maybe she didn't need to be so worried about how they were going to handle adding a baby to their lives. She clung to the small hope, the only bright light in this otherwise dark time.

"Molly?"

She shook her head, dispelling the distracting thoughts. It felt wrong to even think about planning her future when Sabrina no longer had one.

"Are you sure you want to do this right now?"

No.

She nodded. "Yes," she said, swiping tears from her eyes. "Will you...will you stay with me?"

Max's green eyes warmed with an emotion she couldn't name. He moved her bag, then sat next to her once more.

"You know I will."

It was his stomach that woke him.

Max opened his eyes, peering into the dimly lit room. *Where am I?*

He took a deep breath. As Molly's scent filled his nose, it all clicked into place.

Molly's house. Her bedroom. Sabrina's murder.

He turned his head to the side. Sure enough, Molly was curled against him, her body warm and soft. She slept peacefully now, though she hadn't started out that way.

The call to her parents had been tough. Max had heard her mother's cries, even though Molly had kept the phone pressed to her ear. She'd sat silently, absorbing their reaction. When their screams had stopped, she'd tried to offer words of comfort through her own tears.

The whole thing had been heartbreaking. Max had felt powerless, unable to do anything but bear silent witness to Molly's agonizing pain.

When it was over, Molly had crumpled, sagging into herself like a deflating balloon. Max had scooped her up into his arms and carried her to bed. He'd intended to leave her, to let her rest while he took care of a few things he'd noticed around the house, like the trash that needed to be taken out and the dry dishes that needed to be put away. But as he'd tried to draw back, Molly gripped his wrist.

"You said you'd stay," she'd whimpered.

"If that's what you want."

At her nod, he'd slid into bed beside her. She'd immediately embraced him, resting her head on his shoulder. Furbert had jumped onto the mattress as well, arranging himself at Molly's feet. The two of them had done their best to comfort her as she'd cried herself to sleep.

At some point, he'd fallen asleep, as well. But now he was hungry, and he was willing to bet Furbert was, too.

He glanced at his watch—just after 6:00 p.m. Time to get up and see about fixing dinner. Molly might not be interested in food, but it was important she ate something. She needed to keep up her strength for the baby.

Moving carefully, Max climbed out of bed. He took his pillow and placed it next to Molly, hoping she wouldn't miss him right away.

Furbert lifted his head in inquiry. "Stay," Max commanded softly. He didn't want Molly to be alone when she woke.

After a quick stop in the bathroom, he made it to the kitchen. A check of the freezer revealed a frozen lasagna—that would work for the two of them, but he had to find something for Furbert, as well.

He had more luck with the fridge. There was a package of ground turkey, and he found a box of rice in her pantry. "Looks like we all get to eat tonight," he muttered to himself as he began heating the oven, boiling a pot of water and cooking the meat.

Molly shambled in about twenty minutes later, Furbert at her side. She took one look at him standing by the stove and nodded. "It wasn't a dream." Her tone was matter-of-fact, with no hint of emotion.

Max shook his head. "I'm afraid not."

She didn't reply. Instead, she walked over to a cabinet, retrieved a bowl and filled it with water. She set it on the floor in the corner, then moved to the small table by the window and sat.

It was a small gesture, one that hadn't taken much effort. But the fact that she'd done something kind for Furbert in the midst of her own grief heightened his regard for her even more.

Max stirred the turkey, unsure of what to say. She'd been so emotional earlier in the day, he didn't know what to make of her preternaturally calm demeanor now.

"What are you making?"

"Lasagna for us. Turkey and rice for Furbert."

"Oh."

"Is that okay? I'll make sure to replace the groceries I use for him." He didn't want her to think he and his dog were going to eat her out of house and home.

"It's not a problem," she said, waving away his concern. "I just didn't realize he could eat people food."

"Yeah." Max relaxed, relieved he hadn't upset her.

"There are some foods that are good for him, and a lot that isn't. But meat and rice is a nice treat for him."

Molly watched him quietly. He couldn't read her expression, but she seemed almost...normal. If he hadn't known about the events of the day, he'd have thought she was simply in a contemplative mood.

She said something, though she spoke so quietly he couldn't hear. "What's that?" he asked as he dumped the turkey and the rice in a large bowl and began stirring.

Molly gave him a small smile. "I was just saying you look good in the kitchen. A real natural."

Max laughed, though her words worried him a bit. He still wasn't sure how they were going to work things out between them. The news of Sabrina's murder had cast a pall over everything, dulling the earlier sense of urgency they'd both felt to come up with a plan.

He wasn't going to leave Molly and the baby in the lurch—that much he knew. But he also still knew he wasn't cut out for marriage. It would be better for both of them if Molly didn't get any ideas about domestic bliss, since that was one thing he couldn't give her.

The oven timer dinged, saving him from having to reply. He set Furbert's food next to the water bowl, then retrieved the lasagna. Molly grabbed some plates and silverware, setting the table as he put the lasagna on the table and fetched them drinks. They moved well together in this kitchen ballet, which Max found surprising. He'd never achieved this kind of synchronicity with Beth, not even in the early days of their marriage when they'd still been madly in love. Joint ventures in the kitchen had always resulted in them bumping into each other, and not in a deliberate, flirtatious way.

Maybe that should have been my first clue, he mused as he sat across from Molly.

"Thanks for cooking," she said.

"It's the least I could do." He picked up his fork and dug in. The sounds from across the room told him Furbert was enjoying his meal, as well. Molly didn't really eat, though—she pushed the food around on her plate but didn't seem to take a bite.

"Not hungry?" he asked.

She lifted one shoulder in a shrug. "Not especially."

"What about Little Bit?"

The corners of her lips lifted. "Is that what you're calling her?"

Max ducked his head, feeling his cheeks heat. In truth, the name had just popped out. He hadn't meant to assign a nickname to the baby, but it felt right. "I guess so."

"I like it. It's sweet."

He looked up to find her smiling at him. He smiled back, pleased to see her take a real bite of food.

They ate in companionable silence. It felt nice to just sit with her, to be in her presence and not feel like he needed to talk. He was used to schmoozing potential donors or eating with his team of administrators, meals that involved constant conversation with very little quiet time for reflection or thought. The need to be "on" all the time was exhausting, but it was a sacrifice he had to make for the good of K-9 Cadets. This simple dinner with Molly reminded him again of why he'd been drawn to her in the first place—there was a stillness about her that allowed him to relax. He never felt like he had to put on a show for her; the way she looked at him made him feel like he was enough, just the way he was.

Did he do the same for her? Did he bring her peace, allow her space and room to breathe? Hopefully so; surely she wouldn't have asked him to stay today if she were uncomfortable around him. She'd always been happy to see

him before. At every visit, he'd loved to see her pretty blue eyes light up when she'd first catch sight of him. Her obvious pleasure had made him feel ten feet tall, and he'd done his best to show her how happy he was to see her, as well.

There was no denying they were good together. But now that they'd added a baby to the equation, how would that alter their chemistry?

Babies changed relationships. Several of his friends from the service had come home to a wife and new baby, only to find their marriage irrevocably different, and not always for the better. He knew three men alone who had gotten divorced in the first few years after adding a baby to the family. Their reasoning? "She's not the same person I married. Everything I do is wrong, and I'm tired of getting treated like a second child." These were men who had dedicated their adult lives to serving their country; they didn't make commitments lightly. For them to walk away like that meant things had to have been really bad.

As Max stole glimpses of Molly across the table, worry began to nibble in earnest at the edges of his thoughts. She seemed the same to him now, her sister's death notwithstanding. But how would motherhood change her? How would fatherhood change him, for that matter? What if they turned into people who no longer recognized each other?

They couldn't put a child in the middle of that kind of uncertainty. It wasn't right. So where did that leave them?

"What's wrong?"

He looked up to find Molly studying him, her brow furrowed. "I was just thinking," he said.

"About the baby?"

Was she a mind reader? Or were his thoughts evident on his face? "That. And other things," he confessed.

"We have a lot to talk about," she replied.

He pushed his empty plate forward and leaned his elbows on the table. "Yes, we do." He felt his muscles tense as he braced himself to start this conversation.

"But not today." Her voice wavered slightly, betraying cracks in her composure.

"All right." Waiting wasn't going to make things any easier, but there was no need to address the elephant in the room now. Molly had dealt with enough today—he didn't need to add to her stress. "Whenever you're ready."

She traced her fork through the sauce on her plate. Max noticed she hadn't eaten much, but at least she'd taken a few bites.

"I don't know why I'm so tired," she said with a sigh. "I napped the afternoon away."

"Maybe it's for the best," he told her. "If you're asleep, you don't have to think." It was a strategy he'd used before, after the dissolution of his marriage. It had worked, too—for a little while.

Molly nodded. She pushed to her feet, reached for her plate.

Max jumped up. "Let me do that." He took the plate from her and gathered his own. "Why don't you go lie down?" She made a face at that suggestion, so he tried another one. "Maybe there's something mindless on television?"

"Maybe." She didn't sound excited by the prospect. "On second thought, I think I'll just go to bed." She stopped next to him, looking up hesitantly.

He could tell she wanted to say something, but wasn't sure how to go about it. "What is it?" He brushed a strand of hair away from her face, his fingertips caressing the shell of her ear. The contact sent sparks shooting up his arm, a potent reminder of their undeniable chemistry.

"I don't want to be alone tonight." The words spilled out of her, bouncing between them.

His heart kicked at the immediate implication of her confession, but he quickly quashed his baser impulses. She bit her lip and closed her eyes, clearly embarrassed.

"I'm sorry," she said. "I don't mean—"

"It's fine," he soothed, running his hand down her arm. "I know what you're asking. And the answer is yes. I'll stay with you."

"Thank you." She offered him a grateful smile, her eyes shiny with tears.

"Don't mention it. Now go on. I'll get this cleaned up and join you in a few minutes."

Max watched her walk away, conflicting emotions swirling in his chest. He wanted to be there for her, to be the man she needed him to be. But past experiences had taught him he wasn't any good at relationships.

What, then, could he offer her?

And would it be enough?

MAX MOVED CAREFULLY as he slid into bed a little later that evening. Molly appreciated his consideration, but he needn't have worried about disturbing her. She was awake, and likely would be for some time yet.

She was lying on her back, staring at the ceiling. A night-light in the hall just outside her bedroom provided a small glimmer of illumination in the dark, enough for her to see the blades of the ceiling fan spinning overhead.

Wanting a different view, she turned her head to look at Max, hoping to catch him with his eyes closed so she could study his face. She'd done that a lot when they'd first started seeing each other; some of her favorite moments with him had occurred while he was sleeping. She'd loved to watch him dream, see the play of unguarded expressions

that crossed his face while he slumbered. He was so composed and controlled while awake, which made seeing him like this even more special. Max had shared his body with her, but by sleeping next to her, he'd also shared his soul.

She felt a little jolt as her eyes met his—she hadn't expected him to be watching her.

"Hi," he whispered.

"Hi," she whispered back.

He was lying on his side, his body several inches away from hers.

A sudden chill swept over her, making her shudder.

"Cold?"

"Yes," she said. The temperature of the room hadn't changed, but out of nowhere, her brain conjured up one of the pictures Deputy Sheriff Bloom had shown her earlier: the image of her sister's hair spread out on the steel table of the morgue.

Molly bit her lip, trying hard not to cry as she imagined the feel of the cold metal against her back. Even though the objective part of her brain knew Sabrina was dead and could no longer feel anything, it hurt to think of her sister lying alone on that unforgiving surface.

"Let me help." Max's voice was soft and soothing. His hands gently guided her onto her side, facing away from him. Then he slipped his arm around her waist and pulled her close, until her back was snug against his chest.

Molly immediately felt warmer, though the image of Sabrina took longer to fade from her mind's eye. She focused on the feel of Max against her body, of the rise and fall of his chest as he breathed, the warm weight of his palm splayed across her baby bump.

His scent surrounded her, bringing her comfort with every breath she took. God, how she'd missed him these past few months! He was more than just her lover—some-

where along the way he'd become her best friend, and she'd missed the simple joy of talking to him. Her anger over his absence and lack of communication had drawn battle lines between them, but it didn't always have to be that way.

Molly was still trying to process Sabrina's death, but the loss of her sister was already making her think twice about Max and the baby. Life was too short; should she really spend it feeling hurt about what couldn't be, rather than grateful for what could?

Her hip was starting to ache; she shifted a bit to ease the pressure on the joint. The discomfort was a reminder of all the small ways pregnancy had made her feel like a stranger in her own body.

She moved again, bringing one knee up, then sliding her leg back down when that failed to provide relief. Maybe if she put a pillow between her knees…

"Molly?"

"Hmm?" she said absently.

"Can you, ah, stop wriggling?"

There was an odd note in Max's voice that made her pause. It was then that she felt a new sensation against her lower back.

"Oh," she said, understanding dawning at once.

"Sorry." He sounded sheepish. "I didn't mean to… well, it's just that you started moving, and I can't exactly control…" He released her and rolled onto his back. "Please don't take it the wrong way. I'm not trying to put the moves on you or anything."

The loss of his touch left her feeling bereft. Without stopping to think, Molly rolled over until she was facing him again. She placed her hand flat on his chest, her palm resting over his heart.

"It's okay," she said softly. "I don't mind."

She felt his heartbeat speed up. "What are you saying?"

"I'm saying that I'm tired of thinking. I just want to get out of my head right now. With everything that's happened recently, I can't stand to be in my own thoughts anymore."

She began to move her hand down his chest, feeling his muscles twitch in response to her touch. "I miss you," she whispered. "If I've learned anything over the past couple of days, it's that life is too short. I don't want to have any regrets."

Max placed his hand over hers, flattening it against the hard planes of his stomach. "I don't want you to have any regrets, either," he said, his voice husky. "Are you sure this is what you want? We still have so many unresolved issues between us. Won't this only complicate things even more?"

"Only if we let it," she said. "I'm not asking you for any promises. Can't we just have this moment out of time?" Molly struggled to find the words to explain her desperate need for a connection. The abyss of her grief yawned wide; if Max didn't pull her back from the edge, she feared she would topple over.

Max studied her face, his eyes dark shadows only a few inches from her own. "All right," he said softly. His breath ghosted across her lips, a prelude of what was to come. "Tell me what you want."

"You," she said, her voice cracking on the word. "I just want you."

It was all she'd wanted for the last year and a half, when she'd first felt herself start the downward slide into love. But she couldn't tell him that. This moment was an escape for both of them. They could talk about emotions later, when they returned to the real world. For now, she simply wanted to lose herself with Max, to shut off her brain and let her body take control.

Max traced his fingertip along the curve of her cheek,

sending a shiver down Molly's spine. "All right," he said again. "You have me. I'm all yours."

If only that were true. She pushed the thought aside as Max drew her close, his hands on her skin awakening nerves that had gone dormant due to lack of use.

Soon, Molly was awash in sensation, clinging to Max and the promise of respite from her mind he provided. She didn't know what tomorrow would bring, or how things would change between them. All she had was this stolen moment with him, a chance to recapture their magic in the midst of terrible circumstances.

It would have to be enough.

Chapter Eleven

"Everything looks good," Dr. Allen told Molly at her morning appointment, giving her a reassuring pat on the knee. "Your baby's right in the middle of the growth curve and shows no signs of being affected by your ordeal in the gondola."

Molly sighed, feeling a flash of relief. It was the first good news she'd heard since word of Sabrina's murder. And while she'd believed the OB from the hospital when he'd said the baby was fine, it was nice to have her regular doctor confirm it.

"I'm so glad," she said. "How big is she?"

Dr. Allen glanced at her tablet, which displayed the results from Molly's earlier ultrasound. "Looks like about fourteen ounces, give or take a few. She's about as long as a banana right now."

"That doesn't seem very big." It was the first time Max had spoken, aside from introducing himself to Dr. Allen.

"Don't worry—she won't stay little for long. She's going to keep putting on weight, and toward the end of the pregnancy, she'll grow by about half a pound a week."

"I'm okay with small," Molly said quickly.

Dr. Allen laughed. "That's what all my patients say." She stood, offered her hand to Molly and then Max. "I'll

see you next month. Call my office if you need anything before then." She turned to Max. "It was nice to meet you."

"Same here," he said. "Thanks, Doctor."

"My pleasure."

The door *snicked* shut behind her, leaving Molly and Max alone once more. She glanced over at him—he was studying the clutch of ultrasound pictures they'd been given after the scan, a slight frown on his face.

"What's wrong?"

"I hate to say it, but I think she might have my nose." He flipped a photo around, tapping the profile image that showed the curves of the baby's face.

Molly laughed. "It's a little early to tell, but you might be right."

"Poor girl," he muttered, shaking his head.

"There are worse things in life than having your nose." In fact, Molly thought his nose was rather cute, but she didn't think he'd be happy to hear it.

He helped her slide off the table, and they walked through the office, headed for the parking lot.

It was a sunny day, the sky a pale, perfect blue. Molly glanced at the mountain as they walked toward her car. The avalanche had left a gash in the snowpack on the mountain, a scar that would eventually disappear when winter brought fresh powder to the area. The poles that supported the gondola lines looked like dark toothpicks from this distance, and she saw a few tiny brightly clad dots moving around—the workers who continued to assess the system, making repairs to get it operational again.

She shuddered, remembering all too well the terror of hanging precariously in the air, fearing that with each gust of wind they would plummet to the ground.

"Doing okay?" Max eyed her curiously over the roof of the car.

"Fine," she said. "Just having a flashback to the other day."

"That was pretty scary," he agreed. "Even for me. And I've voluntarily jumped out of perfectly good airplanes before."

Molly slid into the passenger seat as Max got behind the wheel. "I had no idea you were scared," she said. "You seemed so calm the whole time, like it was an inconvenience to your day, but nothing to be afraid of."

"I was putting on a brave face for you," he admitted. His cheeks turned pink as he ducked his head. "I knew you were scared, and I didn't want to make it worse. I figured if I acted like everything was okay, it would help you feel better."

His confession gave her a warm fuzzy feeling inside. "It did," she told him. She wanted to reach over and take his hand, but wasn't sure how he'd respond.

HER MIND FLASHED back to last night, and Max's tenderness as they'd made love. He'd seemed to understand her need for touch, her desire for reassurance they were still alive. She'd told him she didn't want anything from him, and that had been the truth. But against her best intentions, she'd given him another piece of her heart.

She was glad he'd come to her doctor's appointment, as well. His interest in the baby made her feel good, and she took it as a positive sign for their future. In fact, if the time they'd spent together lately was any indication, they wouldn't have too much trouble adjusting to living together if things worked out between them.

"When are your parents getting into town?"

The question cast a pall over her thoughts. "They should be here by Friday," she said. They'd been in eastern Canada when she'd called, so it was going to take several days for them to make the drive home. In the meantime, Mason had

actually volunteered to make the funeral arrangements, a task Molly appreciated him claiming.

"It's the least I can do," he'd said yesterday. "Since I made you break the news to Mom and Dad alone."

Molly hadn't pointed out the fact that Max had actually been with her during the call. She'd simply said thanks and offered to help if he needed it.

"I know I said I'd give you time, but we do need to start talking about what comes next." Max kept his gaze on the road as he drove them through town.

Molly's shoulders tensed, though there was nothing negative about his tone. "All right," she said. "What are your thoughts?"

His grip on the wheel tightened, the knuckles of his fingers going white before he relaxed again. "I want you to know that I will absolutely support the baby, no matter what happens between us."

Molly nodded. "Thank you," she said quietly. It was an outcome she hadn't taken for granted, and it took some of the weight off her mind to know that Max would financially contribute to the expenses of raising a child.

"Of course." He fell silent, and after a few seconds, Molly realized he wasn't going to say more.

"How do you think this is going to work?" she prodded. "How often do you think you'll see the baby?"

"I'm not sure," he admitted. "A lot of it depends on K-9 Cadets, and how frequently I'll be able to break away for a visit."

Molly's heart sank at his words. Without necessarily meaning to, Max had dashed any hopes she'd had that they might stay together as a family. She closed her eyes, trying to prevent tears from welling up.

"So there's no way you can run the charity from here?"

He sighed. "I suppose it's possible, but..."

"But what?"

"I don't think that's such a good idea."

"Why?" Before he could answer, Molly felt a dam break free inside her, and her words spewed out in a torrent. "Why can't you stay here? Why can't we try to be a family? We're good together, you and I. We've always had a connection, don't you think?"

"Yes, but—"

"But what?" Frustration bubbled up inside her, finding a release as she raised the volume of her voice. "I've never felt so comfortable with anyone before, Max. And these past few days showed me that the magic between us isn't confined to the fun of your visits—it's there in the everyday tasks, the mundane. Even the bad," she said, her thoughts on Sabrina. She shook her head, focusing on the here and now. "Why can't we just try to be together for real?"

"I tried that before, Molly," he said, his voice tight. "It didn't work."

"She cheated on you!" Molly couldn't believe he was going to punish her for the actions of his ex-wife. "Do you honestly think I would ever do that to you?"

"No. But that's not the point."

"Oh? Well, enlighten me, please." Anger was burning away her frustration, loosening her tongue. "If you don't think the worst of me, then why aren't you willing to give us a shot?"

"Because I don't have it in me!" Max pulled into her garage and jerked the car into Park. He turned to face her, his green eyes blazing. "Beth didn't cheat on me because she was a bad person, but because I left her alone in our marriage. Apparently, I'm only good for one thing at a time, and right now that's K-9 Cadets."

Molly stared at him, unable to believe what she was

hearing. "That is the biggest load of crap I've ever heard in my life."

Max looked away. "It's the truth."

"No, it's not. Your ex-wife told you that to justify her actions. And for some reason, you believed her. Probably because you felt guilty about being gone so much. But believe me, Beth's actions were her own. No one made her cheat on you, least of all you."

"You don't understand." His voice was low, barely audible in the stillness of the car.

Molly shook her head, a sense of finality washing over her. "You're right... I don't." She climbed out of the car and headed for the door. After a few seconds, she heard the car door slam and knew Max was following her.

She stepped aside to let him unlock the door, then took the keys from his hand. Pushing inside the house, she walked past Furbert and dropped her purse on the kitchen table. When she looked back, Max was standing in the doorway, Furbert at his feet.

"You do what you think is best, Max," she said, reaching for a glass. "I'm not going to beg you to be with me." She filled the glass with water, took a sip to ease the ache in her throat. "But know this—things have changed now. I'm not going to let you pop in and out of my life whenever you feel like it. That was fun for a time, but I deserve more. And so does our daughter."

"I know that."

"Good."

He was quiet a moment, then asked, "What happens now?"

She made a shooing gesture with her hand. "Go home, back to your work. Just don't expect me to take you back when you decide in a few years that you're missing out on

the most important parts of life." Her hand came to rest on her belly, her tone defiant.

Max studied her for a moment. "It doesn't have to be all or nothing," he said tersely.

"It does for me," Molly said. "I need more than a part-time partner."

He looked down, clenching his teeth. "Fair enough."

"Besides, do you honestly think you can be a drop-in dad to this baby?"

"You make it sound so terrible." Max looked up, took a step closer. "Why can't I have it both ways? Why can't I run my charity and visit my daughter on a regular basis? I could fly out here once a month, stay for a week at a time. What's wrong with that?"

She nearly laughed at his suggestion. "I'm sure it would start out that way," she replied. "But how long would it take before you got so busy you missed a trip? Just one at first. But as your organization expanded, or you needed to raise more funds, it would get easier and easier for you to push those visits aside. Then, you'll turn around and it will have been six months since you've seen her, or a year. Finally, you'll decide you may as well not come at all, since it's already been so long."

Max didn't reply. But she could tell by the expression on his face he'd heard her.

"That's not fair to this baby," she said quietly.

"So what are you saying?" His voice was flat, emotionless. "That you want me to walk away? That if I'm not willing to give you everything you want, I may as well stay out of your lives completely? I never thought you were one for issuing ultimatums." He crossed his arms, glaring at her.

"I'm not," Molly replied evenly. "I will never keep you from seeing your daughter. But I won't let you disappoint her, either."

"She's my baby, too," he said, a warning glint in his eyes.

"Then I guess you'd better do right by her," Molly said. "Hopefully you won't let your hang-ups about commitment ruin your relationship with her the way they did ours."

Max shook his head, dropped his arms. "This is getting us nowhere."

"On the contrary," she shot back. "I think it's been quite illuminating." Her heart was breaking in two, but at least now she knew where she stood with Max.

Or didn't, as the case was.

He drew in a deep breath, his chest expanding with the effort. "I'm going to go for now. But I'm not leaving town yet. As far as I'm concerned, we still have a lot to iron out."

"Really? Because it seems to me we've already covered all of the important stuff. The rest is just details. I'm sure your secretary is more than capable of handling those. I know how hard it is for you to do the little things, like returning emails or phone calls."

Max flinched, and Molly immediately felt guilty for the dig. She had promised not to punish him forever for that mistake. But her intentions were no match for her roiling emotions at the moment.

Max nodded. "I suppose I deserved that." He took a step back, glanced down. "Come on, boy," he said to Furbert. "Time for us to go."

Furbert got to his feet, looking as worried as possible for a dog. He glanced between Max and Molly, as if hoping one of them would explain what was happening.

Molly followed Max and the dog down the hall, intending to lock up after them. But just as she stepped forward to shut the front door, Max whirled on his heel, bringing them face-to-face.

"I wasn't lying earlier, Molly," he said. His breath was

warm on her cheek, his eyes flashing green fire. "I will be back. We aren't finished here."

"You'll forgive me if I don't hold my breath." She shut the door before he could reply, realizing only after she did so that he had no way to get back to The Lodge. For a split second, she considered letting him back in and calling for a cab, but decided against it. He could walk into town, or call Blaine for a ride if he was feeling lazy. Either way, she wasn't going to worry about it.

Emotions rattled inside her, bouncing around like bees in a bottle. Molly forced herself to walk into the den, sit on the sofa. It felt strange to be alone after being around Max and Furbert all weekend. The house seemed so much bigger without the two of them there.

The adrenaline from the argument faded, leaving her feeling hollowed out and heartsick. Unable to think of anything else to do, Molly lay down on the couch. Staring up at the ceiling, she surrendered to her tears.

"WHY, DEPUTY SHERIFF BLOOM, how nice it is to see you."

The booming voice stopped Daria in her tracks. She'd stopped in the diner for a quick bite to eat, and had seen the mayor and Russ Colton walk in together. She'd quickly finished her lunch and started for the door, hoping to avoid talking to them. But it seemed she wasn't going to make a clean getaway after all.

She turned and offered a smile to both men. "Nice to see you, Mayor. Mr. Colton."

"You, as well." Mayor Dylan smiled up at her. "Do you have a minute? I'd love to bend your ear."

It wasn't really a question, and they both knew it. She nodded, pulling out one of the free chairs at their table.

Russ Colton sat across from her, a glass of tea in his hand. "Hell of a thing, that avalanche," he said, turning

to glance out the windows of the diner. "We were lucky no one was hurt."

"Yes, sir," Daria replied. She studied his face as he took a sip from his glass, searching for her adoptive father's features in his own. Joe Colton, former president of the United States, had adopted her when she was very young. He and his wife had been loving parents, and Daria had wanted for nothing while growing up. But Daria needed to make a name for herself based on her own merits, not because of her connection to her father. So she'd changed her last name back to Bloom and set off in search of her biological family in the hopes of learning more about them and her past. The trail had led her to Colorado, and Daria had fallen in love with the area. She'd settled in Roaring Springs, learning only after the fact that the Colton family's reach extended here, as well.

No one had discovered her secret...yet. And she intended to keep it that way. Most of the Coltons in town were nice—she certainly had nothing bad to say about Trey Colton, the sheriff and her boss—but Daria was quite happy to remain on the fringes of their lives, apart from the drama inherent in such a large family.

Mayor Dylan leaned forward. "I'll get right to the point, Deputy Sheriff. What's going on with those bodies?"

"We're still investigating," she began, but he interrupted.

"Yes, yes, of course. But I was hoping you had some new information to share. Have you been able to identify anyone yet?"

She glanced meaningfully at Russ Colton, hesitating. Mayor Dylan waved away her silent inquiry.

"You can speak freely in front of Russ."

Daria wasn't so sure about that, but she couldn't very

well contradict the mayor in front of the most powerful businessman in town.

"We have positive confirmation that one of the bodies is that of Sabrina Gilford." She was confident one of the other bodies belonged to April Thomas, a young woman who had been missing for over a year, and whose mother had come to town a few months ago searching for her. But Daria was keeping her thoughts to herself on that one until the forensic results were in.

A shadow crossed Russ's face; Sabrina was his niece. Daria didn't think Russ had been an especially doting uncle, but the news had likely come as a shock.

"I had heard that," the mayor said. "But what about the others?"

"We're still in the process of trying to make identifications. We've sent the remains to the state lab in Denver. Some of the bodies are in advanced stages of decomposition, making the process more difficult."

Mayor Dylan nodded, running his hand down his face. "I see."

"I'm happy to keep your office updated on the progress of my investigation," she offered, hoping to put an end to this conversation.

"I'd appreciate that," the mayor said. "Do you think this is the work of a serial killer?"

"I do, yes." Both the mayor and Russ Colton gaped at her, as if they'd been expecting a different answer. "Six bodies buried in the same location is not a coincidence."

"No, I suppose it's not." Dylan frowned. "Do you think he's still here?"

"If it is indeed a he, I imagine he's still around, yes. Ms. Gilford hasn't been dead for very long. That suggests whoever killed these women is still active in the area."

"My God." The mayor leaned back in his chair, shaking his head in disbelief. "Here in Roaring Springs."

"I'm afraid so," she confirmed. Daria glanced at her watch; she really needed to get back to the station. Hopefully the mayor would let her go soon.

"What are you going to tell the public?"

Ah, she thought. *That's why he wanted to talk to me.* "I'm going to tell them what we know so far. We're obviously not going to release all the information we have, but the fact that we discovered six bodies here is national news."

Mayor Dylan frowned again, clearly unhappy that word of the gruesome find had spread beyond Roaring Springs. "Be that as it may, I think you should downplay the serial killer angle."

Daria lifted one brow. "Mr. Mayor, with all due respect, I don't have to say the words *serial killer*. The press is only too happy to speculate about that without any input from me."

"But you can help shape their reports," he insisted. "The way you react to their questions will determine how sensationalistic their angle becomes. If you make it seem like you agree with the idea there's a serial killer using Roaring Springs as his hunting ground, that will turn into the story."

"It seems to me that *is* the story," she replied.

"But you can't be sure the victims are all connected until the medical examiner has finished his work."

Daria conceded his point with a nod.

Dylan leaned forward, planting his elbows on his knees. "Listen, I know you have a job to do. And I'm not in any way trying to stifle your investigation. But the film festival is scheduled to begin soon. You know how much money that puts in the town's coffers."

And your friend's as well, Daria thought to herself. Russ was the CEO of the Colton Empire, the name his father had given to the corporation that encompassed The Lodge and The Chateau, two locations that were always sold out during the annual film festival. Daria knew several of Russ's children, as well as some of his nieces and nephews, also had local businesses in town or nearby. The Colton family was so entwined with Roaring Springs that anything that was good for the area was good for their bottom line, too.

"If the media get fixated on the idea of a serial killer here," the mayor continued, "people will start to worry. They might decide the film festival isn't worth the risk of staying here. If the festival goes under, that'll be the end of it. The town won't be able to recoup that lost income, and the festival itself will likely never be successful again. We can't let that happen."

Daria sighed quietly. She understood the point the man was making, and his concerns for the town. But she had to balance his worries about money with the very real possibility that greater publicity about this case would generate more leads for her to follow as people contacted the department with tips. These five unidentified women, whoever they were, hadn't been invisible. People around town had seen them, talked to them. Someone out there likely had information that could help Daria catch the killer. But if the mayor insisted she keep things quiet, she might never get to hear it.

"A certain amount of publicity is a good thing," she began, hoping to explain her reasoning and draw the mayor to her side.

Dylan was having none of it. "I'm asking you this as a favor," he said, though his tone made it clear that was far from the truth. "Roaring Springs cannot afford this scan-

dal right now. By all means, continue your investigation. But do it quietly."

Daria took a deep breath, then nodded. Agreeing with the mayor was the only way she was going to get out of this conversation. Besides, his request made a certain kind of sense.

"All right. I won't emphasize the possibility we have a serial killer in the area."

He smiled broadly, pleased to have won.

"But," she continued, causing his smile to freeze, "I won't ignore those questions, either. I understand your concerns about the film festival and the financial future of this town. But I have a responsibility to protect the residents of Roaring Springs. At some point, they will need to know if there is a predator in their midst."

"Of course, of course," Dylan said, his tone syrupy sweet. He stood, clasping his hands together as he leaned forward. "And believe me, I will do everything in my power to help you keep this town safe. I just think it's best you not draw any premature conclusions before all the forensic data is available."

"Fair enough, Mayor." Daria managed to keep the edge out of her voice. She didn't need him telling her how to do her job, but it was easier to play nice. "I'll be in touch."

She rose and shook hands with both men. "I look forward to hearing from you soon," Dylan said. "Be sure to let me know if my office can assist your investigation in any way."

Daria nodded. "Thank you, sir," she said, knowing the diners at nearby tables were openly watching them. The last thing Daria wanted was for rumors to start swirling that there was bad blood between the mayor and the sheriff's department.

She headed to the parking lot, pulling out her cell phone

as she walked. The lab guys probably didn't have any new results to report, but it wouldn't hurt to check. The mayor wasn't known for his patience—it was only a matter of time before he called her, wanting updates on the case. It would make her life easier if she had something to tell him.

Chapter Twelve

Molly applied the last strip of painter's tape to the frame around the door on Wednesday morning and took a step back, eyeing her handiwork. She'd never painted a whole room before, but the guy at the hardware store had walked her through the basics and she'd followed his instructions. Now that the trim in the room was protected by blue strips of tape, she could start on the walls.

Transforming the guest bedroom into a nursery was going to be a big job. Molly was ready to throw herself into the project; hopefully, it would serve as a good distraction from the rest of the world.

She walked over to the paint can and tray in the middle of the floor and knelt, reaching for the opener. But just as she fit the metal tool under the lid, someone knocked on her front door.

Her first instinct was to ignore the sound. She wasn't in the mood for company, especially not Max. He might think there was more that needed to be said, but as far as Molly was concerned, she'd heard enough yesterday.

Max had made it very clear that they didn't have a future together. And while he might think he could swoop in and spend time with the baby whenever his schedule allowed, Molly knew that arrangement wasn't going to last long. He'd already blown her off, and that was for a trip

he took only four times a year. If he thought he was going to fly out here once a month, he was either delusional or lying to himself.

Molly felt like the biggest fool. She'd gotten involved with Max knowing he was only good for a fling. But somewhere along the way, she'd made the mistake of falling for him. Then she'd compounded her mistake by thinking he felt the same way about her. She'd convinced herself they could be a family, that the two of them could find happiness together as they raised their child.

She certainly knew better now.

The knocking persisted. Molly got to her feet with a sigh. She wasn't going to be able to paint the nursery in peace with that racket going on in the background. Might as well open the door and tell Max to leave; otherwise, he was liable to stand there all day.

She flung open the door, ready to send him on his way. But it wasn't Max who stood on her welcome mat.

It was Elaine.

"Oh," Molly said dumbly. "It's you."

Elaine smiled, though it didn't reach her eyes. "Hello," she said. "I was hoping to talk to you."

"Now's not really a good time," Molly hedged. She couldn't handle another verbal attack right now, not while she was still trying to process Sabrina's death and Max's rejection. Her poor heart simply couldn't take any more.

"Please? I'll only stay a moment." There was something subdued, almost broken about her that softened Molly's resolve. *She's suffering, too.*

"All right." Molly nodded and stepped back, holding open the door for Elaine.

She led her into the living room and sat on the sofa, gesturing to the chair. "Can I get you something to drink?" she offered automatically.

Elaine sank onto the chair, clutching her purse to her chest as though she feared someone was going to jump out from around the corner to snatch it.

"No, I'm fine."

"How's Mason?" Molly hadn't spoken to him since yesterday afternoon. Apparently, the police weren't going to release Sabrina's body anytime soon, so he'd put the funeral planning on hold. He'd still sounded tired, and Molly worried he wasn't getting enough rest.

"He's stressed," Elaine confirmed. "He's working so hard to help organize the film festival, but he hasn't been sleeping. He says every time he closes his eyes, he sees Sabrina's face."

"Oh, God," Molly said, understanding the problem far too well. Her thoughts were dominated by her sister and Max; neither subject brought much comfort right now. "He can't go on like this. Maybe his doctor can give him something to help him sleep?"

"I'm going to call his office and ask," Elaine replied. "But that's not actually why I stopped by."

"Oh? What's on your mind?"

Elaine scooted forward until she sat perched on the edge of her seat. "I've been doing a lot of thinking, and I've figured out a solution for your issue." She nodded meaningfully at Molly's belly.

She felt her hackles rise. "I didn't realize I had an 'issue.'"

Elaine continued as if she hadn't heard her. "The way I see it, this baby is coming at a bad time for you. You clearly weren't planning on it, and I don't think you're ready to be a mother. But I am."

Molly stared at Elaine, too stunned to speak. Was she actually proposing Molly hand over her daughter?

Apparently mistaking her silence for interest, Elaine

carried on, the words flowing faster as her excitement ratcheted up. "Mason and I can't have children. But we want so desperately to be parents. Why don't you let us adopt your baby? That way, your life can carry on as normal, and we can complete our family."

Her plea tugged at Molly's heartstrings. Not because she was interested in giving up her child, but because it was clear Elaine was emotionally invested in this idea.

"Elaine, I—" she began, but the other woman cut her off.

"It really is the perfect solution. Mason would have a child he's biologically connected to, and we would love the baby like it was our own."

"What does Mason think of this idea?" Molly needed to know if her brother was on board with this preposterous plan, or if it was something Elaine had come up with on her own.

Her sister-in-law looked away. "He doesn't know about it. I was hoping to surprise him with the good news."

That made Molly feel a little bit better. At least her brother didn't seem to have designs on her baby.

"Elaine," she said, feeling her way into a response. It was clear the other woman was in a fragile mental state. Molly didn't want her rejection to make things worse, but she had to make it clear she had no intention of giving up her baby. "I appreciate the offer. It's clear you've put a lot of thought into this, and I know you're coming from a place of love."

Elaine nodded, her smile bordering on manic.

"So that's a yes?"

Molly shook her head. "No, it's not. I know your heart is in the right place, but I'm not interested in putting my baby up for adoption."

"But..." Elaine's smile slipped. "But you can't possibly

mean that! It would be the best thing for everyone! You don't want to be a single mother, and Mason and I can give the baby everything!"

"I know it will be hard doing things on my own, but I'm prepared to make sacrifices." Molly got to her feet. She was done talking to Elaine about her baby. It was clear the other woman was struggling with her own demons, and while Molly felt for her, she didn't have the emotional energy to help her.

"No." Elaine shook her head, as if she could change Molly's mind through sheer force of will. "No, you just need to give it more thought."

Recognizing the futility of trying to argue with her, Molly instead focused on getting the other woman out of her house. "Elaine, as I said before, I'm really busy. I need you to leave now, please." *And I need to call Mason.* She knew her brother was already overwhelmed, but he needed to know his wife was becoming unhinged.

Elaine got to her feet, one hand digging in her bag. Molly assumed she was fumbling for her car keys, but when she withdrew her hand, she wasn't gripping a key chain.

She was holding a gun.

Molly took a step back, her heart jumping into her throat. "Elaine..."

"I didn't want to have to do this," her sister-in-law said. "But you leave me no choice."

"Please, put the gun down," Molly cajoled, her voice shaking. "This isn't necessary."

"Apparently, it is. Now come on." She gestured to the hall, clearly expecting Molly to accompany her somewhere.

"No." If she went with Elaine, she was as good as dead.

In response, Elaine cocked the gun. The sound turned Molly's guts to water. "Move."

Molly's legs wobbled as she took a step. "What are you going to do? If you kill me, the baby dies, too."

"I know that." Elaine urged her toward the door. "I'm not going to kill you. Not yet, anyway."

"Then what—" Molly stopped before the door, trying to stall. Elaine dug the muzzle of the gun into her lower back, pressing so hard against her that Molly cried out.

"Don't get any ideas," she warned. "I want you alive, but I can still make you hurt if you don't do what I say." She reached past Molly and threw open the door, then shoved Molly forward.

"My car," she directed.

Gun at her back, Molly had no choice but to do as she was told.

"You don't have to do this," she said, glancing around as she walked down the porch steps. Her home was set back a bit from the street, in a small grove of trees. Normally, Molly enjoyed the privacy. Now she wished her neighbors could see what was happening.

"I tried to do things the easy way," Elaine reminded her. "You didn't want to cooperate."

The car beeped softly as she unlocked it. She herded Molly into the passenger seat, then trotted around the hood and climbed behind the wheel. She placed the gun in her lap. Molly breathed a little easier now that it was no longer pointed at her, but she wasn't out of the woods yet. Maybe she could distract Elaine and grab the gun? She thought about simply lunging for it, but Elaine wasn't going to give it up without a fight. Molly couldn't risk the baby getting shot in the struggle.

Elaine caught her eye. "Don't even think about it," she warned.

Molly decided to try a different tack. "Think about what you're doing here. It's not too late to let me go back inside. We can forget this ever happened."

Elaine stuck the key in the ignition and turned. "We're past that now," she said.

It was horrifyingly clear to Molly that her sister-in-law was planning on stealing her baby. "What are you going to tell Mason?" she asked. "You can't just show up with a baby and expect him to accept it with no questions."

A shadow crossed Elaine's face, and Molly realized she hadn't thought that far ahead. "Put away the gun and let's just talk. I'm happy for you and Mason to be involved in the baby's life—parties, sleepovers, you name it." It would be a cold day in hell before Molly let Elaine anywhere near her child, but the other woman didn't need to know that right now. "We can all be one big happy family."

"Sunday dinners and walks in the park?" Elaine sounded wistful.

Molly nodded. "Absolutely. All of it."

Elaine looked at her, a glint of sadness in her green eyes. Then Molly's head snapped back, her nose exploding in burst of pain that had her seeing stars.

"Do you think I'm stupid?"

Molly grabbed her nose, squinting through tears as Elaine screamed, "I know you're only trying to get me to let you go. It's not going to work. Now shut up before I do something you'll really regret."

Molly slouched against the window, too dazed to react. The scenery passed by in a blur as Elaine stepped on the gas. Molly's hands felt warm; she pulled them away from her nose, noting with a sense of detachment that her palms were slick with blood.

"Don't touch anything!" Elaine snapped.

Molly didn't respond. She tried to pay attention to where

they were going, but Elaine turned onto an old logging road that took them into the forest.

"Put this over your head." Something soft landed in Molly's lap. A pillowcase.

She hesitated, only to hear the gun cock again. "Don't make me ask you again."

Molly tugged the fabric over her face, her view of the outside world disappearing. If she'd thought things were bad before, the loss of visual cues made it worse. Every breath she took remained trapped in the folds of the fabric, making her feel light-headed. Her nose throbbed with every beat of her heart, and a trickle of blood ran over her lips and down her chin to drip onto her shirt.

Claustrophobia reared its ugly head; Molly pushed down the panic, knowing if she started to cry she wouldn't be able to breathe. Better to conserve her strength for later. She wanted to protect her baby, but that didn't mean she was going to let Elaine treat her like a lamb being led to slaughter. She'd cooperate for now, but Elaine had to leave her alone sometime. That was when she'd make her escape.

Her life—and that of her baby—depended on it.

"AM I CRAZY?"

Furbert cocked one ear in Max's direction, but otherwise didn't move. Max sighed, feeling disgusted with himself.

"Of course I am. Who the hell asks a dog that kind of question?"

Furbert let out a soft woof of agreement, then closed his eyes again with a sigh. Max shook his head. If only he could rest as peacefully as his dog.

He hadn't slept much last night. Every time he closed his eyes, he saw Molly's face, her expression a mixture of

hurt and betrayal. *I did that to her*, he thought. *I caused that pain.*

It made him feel like the lowest of the low, knowing he'd let her down. And truly, if there were any other way, he would have embraced it with open arms. But he just couldn't be all that she needed him to be. The recognition of that fact filled him with shame, and he'd spent most of the night and all of the morning wrestling with his short-comings.

The heart of the issue was that he *wanted* to be the one for her—her partner, her lover, her friend. If he was being honest with himself, he'd even go so far as to say he wanted to be her husband. But he felt like a little kid with empty pockets, nose pressed up against the glass of the toy store, gazing longingly at what he wanted but couldn't have.

"She thinks she wants me." He shoved off the sofa and began to pace, the movement helping him think. Little did Molly know that if he committed to her, she'd soon grow tired of him and his divided loyalties. Beth had hated K-9 Cadets from the start; it only stood to reason Molly would soon grow to hate it, too, since it consumed so much of his time.

So no, Molly didn't actually want him. She wanted the *idea* of him. During his visits, it had been easy to shut out the world and pretend they were the only two people on the planet. The seclusion had made life seem better than it really was—after all, they'd deliberately ignored the problems and stresses of daily life, focusing instead on each other. It was a nice way to live, but it couldn't last.

And while he agreed with Molly that they were great together, he worried that the strength of their connection would fade when tested against the slings and arrows of everyday living. Would she still think he was funny when

he forgot to put gas in the car? Would he still find her irresistible when she didn't pick up her shoes?

They'd had a great run together, there was no denying it. And though there was a small part of him that wanted to take the leap and see how they fared going forward, a larger part of him thought they might be better off leaving their relationship in the past. They would always be connected, thanks to the baby. But that didn't mean he had to continue to indulge in his feelings for Molly.

"It's for her own good," he told himself. He marched into the kitchen, poured another cup of coffee. Molly didn't realize it now, but he was doing her a favor.

It was for his own good, as well. Now that he'd told her there was no future for them together, he could start getting a grip on his emotions. They were going to have to see each other a lot for the sake of their daughter—he needed to have his feelings under control so he didn't wind up pining over Molly for the rest of his life. Better to close that door and move forward with his life; if he continued to look back, he was liable to go mad.

"Right," he said to the empty kitchen. "That's sorted, then."

So why did he still feel at a loss?

No matter. He just had to keep moving. Draining his coffee, he set the mug in the sink. "Come on," he called to Furbert. "We're going out."

What better way to test his newfound resolve than by visiting Molly? She wasn't going to be happy to see him again, but he only had a few days left in town and he wanted to iron out the details of his visitation plan before he headed home. And yes, okay, he wanted to check on her. But his interest was strictly platonic; he simply wanted to make sure the woman carrying his child was feeling better.

Even though his heart still ached over leaving her so upset yesterday.

He walked into the living room to find Furbert still snoozing on the couch. "Seriously, dog, I mean it. We're going out now." Molly loved Furbert, Max knew that much. He wasn't about to show up at her house without him.

The dog yawned widely, then grudgingly hopped down. Max clipped a leash to his collar and grabbed his jacket. As they set off down the path to the main building of The Lodge, he pulled out his phone and called for a cab. Blaine wouldn't mind giving him a ride, but Max didn't want to involve his friend in his personal troubles, especially since Molly was the man's cousin. He'd just have the taxi drop him at Molly's house and call the guy back when he needed to leave.

Now if he could just figure out what to say...

Chapter Thirteen

The car jerked to a stop, causing the back of Molly's head to crash against the seat. She jumped as Elaine grabbed her hands.

"Hold still," Elaine snapped.

Something cold touched Molly's wrists—*handcuffs*, she realized, just as the metal rings snapped into place. She felt the car move as Elaine got out, and a few seconds later, a chilly gust of air blew across her when her door was opened.

"Let's go." The other woman grabbed her arm, half pulling, half dragging her from the car. Molly started walking, stumbling a bit over the uneven ground. Based on the crunch of their footsteps and the feel of the ground beneath her feet, Molly guessed they were in a gravel parking lot.

The fact did nothing to help her narrow down their location. There were a lot of places in Roaring Springs and the surrounding area that were unpaved. She couldn't use their travel time as a marker, either; even though she hadn't been able to see where they were going, Molly had registered the many turns Elaine had taken. Unless she missed her guess, they hadn't left Roaring Springs at all.

She felt a flicker of hope at the possibility she wasn't

far from home. That meant help was nearby. All she had to do was escape.

They stopped; Molly heard the jingle of keys, followed by the squeak of door hinges. Elaine pushed her forward, her tight grip on Molly's arm the only thing keeping her upright as she stumbled over the threshold.

Their footsteps echoed as they walked, giving Molly the impression they were in a large, empty space. The air was still and cold; she couldn't smell anything but blood right now, but she was willing to bet the place had a musty scent to it.

After what seemed like an eternity, Elaine pushed her down. Molly felt an instant of panic as she fell, only to land on a thin mattress. While she caught her breath, Elaine fumbled at her ankles, snapping restraints into place. Suddenly, the pillowcase was yanked off her head.

Molly squinted as light flooded her eyes. After a few blinks, her vision cleared enough for her to register her surroundings.

She was in a warehouse office, a small room in an otherwise cavernous space. A pane of glass looked out on the warehouse proper, presumably so the boss could keep an eye on things from the comfort of his chair. There was a rusty metal desk shoved against the wall opposite her, and a matching file cabinet to her left. She sat on a metal bed, the kind that were used in hospitals back in the day. The thin mattress was a poor cushion for the springs that held the bed frame together—Molly's butt already hurt from sitting there.

She glanced down to find that Elaine had hooked her ankle to one ring of a set of handcuffs. The other ring was attached to a chain that was anchored to the floor. There was a bucket next to the desk, but no other furnishings.

"Home sweet home," Elaine trilled.

"You can't be serious," Molly rasped. "You can't possibly mean to keep me here."

Elaine looked around. "Why not? You're inside, out of the elements."

"I'll freeze!" It was already decidedly chilly inside the office; the temperature would plummet once the sun set.

Elaine stepped to the file cabinet and tugged on a drawer. It opened with a metallic squeal of protest. She reached inside, then threw a blanket on the mattress. "Here you go."

Molly eyed the dingy fabric with alarm. "That won't be enough to keep me warm!"

"You'll be fine," Elaine said dismissively. "It'll be summer soon; you won't even need it then."

Panic began to claw up Molly's throat. "What about food? Water? Or do you mean to starve me to death?"

Elaine tapped the other drawers. "There are provisions in here. Water bottles, some rations. Prenatal vitamins." She laughed. "We need to make sure the baby gets everything it needs."

"Please," Molly said, her eyes welling with tears. "Please don't do this."

"I'll visit you, of course." Elaine carried on as if she hadn't heard a word of Molly's plea. "I'll restock your food and water every couple of days. And I have a handheld Doppler, so we can listen to the baby's heartbeat together."

She sounded excited, as if it was going to be a bonding activity for the two of them.

"You can't leave me here." Molly sniffed, the action sending a fresh jolt of pain through her nose. "What if something happens to you and you can't get back to me? I'll die, and so will the baby!" She knew Elaine didn't give a damn about her, but maybe she would reconsider this crazy plan for the sake of the baby?

Elaine's smile slipped, and for a second, Molly thought she might have actually gotten through to her. Then she shook her head slightly and took a step toward the office door. "I'll leave you to settle in now. Try to get some rest— I'll be back soon to check on you."

She stepped out of the office, her boot heels making a clipped sound on the cement floor of the warehouse. Molly stood and tried to follow, but drew up short as the handcuff bit into her ankle. "Elaine!" she called. "Please, don't leave me here!"

When her sister-in-law didn't answer, Molly screamed her name. But the other woman kept walking, her form growing smaller as she got closer to the door. Through her tears, Molly saw a blurry rectangle of bright light flash at the end of the warehouse. Then the door slammed shut, casting the space in dim grays once more.

She sank back onto the thin mattress, her chest heaving as she sobbed. "I'm so sorry, baby." She whispered the words over and over again as she held her belly between her hands. "I *will* get us out of here."

But…how?

SHE WASN'T HOME.

Max frowned and knocked on the door one last time. But just like his previous knocks, this one went unanswered.

He pulled his phone from his pocket and dialed Molly's number. Maybe she was out running errands? If that was the case, he'd happily sit on the porch steps until she got back home.

The phone rang and rang, but Molly didn't answer.

Hmm. It wasn't like her to ignore his calls. Then again, she'd never been so angry with him before.

Worry tickled the base of his spine. He dialed Blaine.

"Have you heard from Molly today?"

"I don't even rate a proper greeting anymore?" Blaine joked.

Max tamped down his impatience. "Sorry. Hello. Have you heard from Molly recently?"

"No. Why?"

"I'm at her house, and she's not answering her door."

"Maybe she's not home."

Max rolled his eyes. "Yes, thank you, Sherlock. But she's not answering her phone, either. Can you call her?"

"Why do you need me to call her? If she's not picking up, she's not picking up."

Max sighed. Why couldn't Blaine just do what he asked without making a federal case about it? "We had a fight yesterday. I don't know if she's not answering the phone because it's me calling, or if she's not answering it at all."

"Ah." There was a world of knowing in Blaine's tone. "Gotcha. Stand by a minute… I'll give her a ring from my office phone."

Max heard his friend punching buttons. Then he spoke again. "So…what'd you fight about?"

"*Star Wars* versus *Star Trek*," Max drawled.

"Really?" Blaine sounded genuinely surprised.

"No," Max growled. "Of course not. What do you think we argued about?"

"I can guess," Blaine said. He was quiet for a second, then said, "Nope, she's not picking up. It went to voice mail."

His stomach flip-flopped as his concern for her grew. "Listen, I know you probably think I'm overreacting, but do you have a spare key for her house, or know someone who does?"

"You think something's wrong?" Blaine's tone was serious now, and he knew his friend was paying attention.

"I'm not sure," Max said. "I just have a gut feeling that things aren't right. What if she's sick and can't reach the phone? What if that bump on her head is more serious than the doctor thought?" Visions of Molly lying unconscious on the floor danced through his head, feeding his worry for her. "I guess I'm being extra paranoid now that I know about the baby, but I want to make sure they're both okay."

"I can understand that. Tell you what—if anyone has an extra key to her place, it's her brother Mason. I'll give him a call, tell him to head your way. You mind waiting there for him?"

"Nope. I'll park it on the porch steps until he gets here."

"All right. I'll call him now and text you his ETA."

"Thanks, man." Max felt a small measure of relief knowing Blaine was taking his concerns seriously. "I appreciate it."

"Don't mention it," the other man said. "Sit tight. We'll get to the bottom of this little mystery soon."

It was a good twenty minutes before Mason arrived at Molly's house. Max had long since given up sitting quietly on the porch steps and was pacing back and forth, wearing a rut in the floorboards in front of Molly's door. Furbert sat on the welcome mat, watching him patiently.

Molly's brother climbed down from the cab of his pickup truck and glared at him. The man looked like hell—his hair was disheveled, there were dark circles under his eyes, and it was clear he hadn't shaved in days. As he approached, Max noted the lines of strain around Mason's eyes and lips. When was the last time the man had slept?

"Thanks for meeting me here," he said.

Mason stopped a few feet away from Max. "So you're the one who got my sister pregnant." It wasn't a question.

Mason's gaze traveled from the top of Max's head down to his shoes, clearly taking his measure.

"Ah, yes, that's me." This wasn't exactly how Max had envisioned meeting Molly's family. The disappointment in Mason's voice was evident; he didn't imagine her parents would be any more excited. Furbert moved to sit at his feet, a show of solidarity that Max appreciated under the circumstances.

"What are your intentions regarding my sister?"

"That's actually what I came to discuss with her," Max said, hoping to steer her brother to the issue at hand. "But Molly isn't answering her phone or the door."

"I know. Blaine told me." Mason's lips tightened. "That's not like her." He walked over to the door, rapped hard on the wood. When she didn't respond, he took his keys from his pocket.

"I'm only doing this because I want to make sure she's okay," he said, tossing the words over his shoulder as he fit the key into the lock. "I'm not here to do you any favors."

"I understand," Max assured him. All he cared about was making sure Molly and the baby were fine. He and Mason could work on their differences later.

Mason pushed the door open. "Molly?" he called out loudly. There was no response, so the two men and dog entered the house.

Max knew right away she wasn't there. The space had an empty feel to it, and the air was still. Mason called her name a few more times, but it was clear she wasn't going to respond.

They checked all the rooms, just to be sure. Max lingered a moment in the doorway of the guest bedroom, which had been taped in preparation for painting. There was a can of paint, a tray and a roller in the center of the room. He saw a pink smudge on the label of the can and

realized with a jolt that Molly was starting work on the baby's nursery.

She shouldn't be painting in her condition. He wasn't an expert, but surely inhaling paint fumes while pregnant was a bad idea. *This should be my job.*

Out of nowhere, a sense of longing struck him. He wanted to be the one to help Molly put the nursery together, to assemble the crib, to hang the curtains. He wanted to pick out blankets and stuffed animals and clothes, to compare playpens and swings and car seats and help her shop for all the million things babies seemed to need.

Mason came to stand next to him, peering into the room. "I guess this is going to be the nursery." He spied the supplies on the floor. "She probably went to the hardware store for something."

"Maybe," Max said. But he wasn't convinced. Something about the house felt wrong, though he couldn't put his finger on what.

"Come on," Mason said, walking away. "I'm sure she'll be back soon, and she won't be happy to discover we've let ourselves in."

Max reluctantly began to follow Molly's brother. "Don't you find it strange she isn't answering her phone?"

Mason shrugged. "Maybe she just doesn't feel like talking to anyone right now."

It was a reasonable explanation, especially given the events of the past few days. Molly had been through the emotional wringer—it was possible she wanted to unplug from the world for a while and recharge her batteries.

Max wanted to believe that, but his gut kept insisting something was wrong. So instead of joining Mason at the front door, he veered off through the kitchen.

"What are you doing?" Mason called, clearly exasperated.

"Just checking one last thing," Max replied. He reached the door that led to the garage and swung it open.

"Are you done yet? I don't want to be here when she gets home."

Max's stomach churned as he looked into the garage. "I don't think that's going to be a problem."

"How can you be sure?" Mason's voice was getting closer; he was apparently coming to check on Max.

Max stepped to the side so Molly's brother could see what he was looking at.

"Because her car is still here."

Chapter Fourteen

Molly shivered on the thin mattress, her body curled into a ball in a bid to conserve heat.

Her earlier assessment was correct—the threadbare blanket Elaine had left her did little to keep her warm. She'd searched the other drawers of the file cabinet, hoping to find another blanket or even a towel, but had come up empty-handed.

It was shadowy in the office, though a dim gray light shone through the dusty glass panels set high into the walls of the warehouse proper. Molly wasn't wearing a watch, but if the light was anything to go by, the day was fading away into evening. She was already freezing—how was she going to survive the night, when the temperature dropped even further?

I have to keep moving. The thought propelled her off the bed. She wrapped the blanket around herself like a cloak and began to pace the confines of the office, as much as her tether would allow. She'd already tested the strength of the chain, finding it frustratingly solid. She'd scoured every inch of the dirty floor for a discarded paper clip or stray staple, anything she could use to try to pick the lock of the handcuffs around her ankle. But she'd found nothing.

Now, as she walked, she tried not to let her mind wander. She'd learned earlier in the day that if she didn't con-

trol her thoughts she'd wind up thinking about Max, and that would make her cry. Her still-swollen nose couldn't handle any more tears, so Molly focused on her current situation, trying to come up with a way to break free from her prison cell.

Four steps forward, turn, four steps back. Over and over again. It wasn't much of a route, but the movement did make her feel a bit warmer.

Darkness fell as she walked. There had to be something she could use to get out of here, some tool she had overlooked in her initial panicked search. The desk was empty, but perhaps if she ripped one of the drawers free from its tracks she'd find a screw or a nail or something equally useful...

Something scuttered along the floor nearby. Molly's heart jumped into her throat, and she scrambled onto the bed. A soft squeak came from the corner of the office.

Rats, she realized. Probably here for the crumbs she'd dropped earlier when eating a granola bar.

Bile rose up the back of her throat. Molly swallowed hard, determined not to throw up. It was bad enough she'd already had to pee in the bucket by the desk. She wasn't going to make the situation even worse by vomiting all over herself.

She hugged her knees and began to rock, hoping the movement would help keep her warm. The bedsprings dug painfully into her flesh, making it hard to find a comfortable position. She shifted on the mattress, then gasped as inspiration struck.

The bedsprings! Maybe she could pry one free and use the end to pick the lock of the handcuffs!

A surge of adrenaline pushed her to her feet. She knelt by the bed, heedless of any rodents nearby. Feeling blindly in the dark, she shoved her hands under the mattress and

encountered a wire mesh secured to the metal bed frame by several tight coils. If she could take it apart, she might be able to make a lock pick!

Something brushed her leg. She screamed, eliciting a startled squeak from her furry companions. Forgetting her mission, she jumped back onto the mattress. It wasn't comfortable, but it was a damn sight better than the floor.

It took a few minutes for her heart rate to return to normal. "Okay," she told herself. Somehow, the sound of her own voice made her feel less alone. "We obviously can't do this now. We'll just wait for the sun to come up, and then we can try again."

Her daughter shifted inside her, as if communicating her agreement with the plan.

"We've got this." Molly put her hand on her belly, patting softly. There were a million different reasons why this plan wouldn't work, but she refused to consider them now. Here in the cold darkness, she needed to focus on hope. It was the only way she would make it through the night.

MAX AND MASON stood on Molly's front porch, staring down the driveway in the fading light of the afternoon.

"I'm not sure we needed to call the police just yet," Mason said. "For one thing, we're not even certain she's missing."

Max didn't bother to look at the man. "She's not here. She's not answering her phone. Her car is still in the garage, and her purse is sitting on top of the washer. Where, pray tell, do you think she is?"

"Maybe she went for a walk?" Mason suggested weakly.

"No."

After finding Molly's car in the garage, Max had wasted no time calling the police. The dispatcher had told him help

was on the way, but since it wasn't an emergency call, they weren't a high priority.

"Don't you have any family connections in law enforcement?" Max had asked after hanging up.

"Well, my cousin Trey is the sheriff..." Mason had said hesitantly.

"Call him."

"I'd hate to waste his time."

"Call. Him."

So Mason had made the call. Trey had promised to come. There was nothing to do now but wait.

And Max hated it.

His imagination ran wild, coming up with increasingly disturbing scenarios. What if Molly had taken a walk as Mason suggested, but been mauled by a bear or a mountain lion? What if she was lying in a ditch, bleeding and in pain? How would they ever find her?

His thoughts were interrupted by the appearance of a car. The vehicle turned into Molly's driveway, then stopped abruptly as the driver caught sight of Mason's truck and the two of them on the porch.

Max squinted in the gloom. "Is that the sheriff?"

"No." Mason leaned forward. "I think that's Elaine's car."

"Who's Elaine?"

"My wife." Mason waved at the driver. The car started forward again, pulling in behind Mason's truck. After a moment, the engine turned off and the driver's door opened.

Mason headed down the porch steps. "Hey, baby," he said to the blonde woman who emerged from the car. "What's going on?"

"Ah, nothing. What are you doing here?"

"We're looking for Molly." Mason and Elaine walked

to the porch. She noticed Max, gave him a nod. He nodded back, studying her.

She seemed nervous, shifting her weight from foot to foot as she stood in place. Her eyes darted around, landing on him, then Furbert, then Mason, then the front door.

"Where is Molly?" she asked.

"We don't know," Max said before Mason had a chance to speak. "Have you seen or heard from her today?"

"Me?" She huffed out a laugh that sounded forced. "No. I'm the last person she'd want to talk to."

"Oh? Why's that?"

Elaine ducked her head. "We got into an argument the other day."

"You did?" Mason stared at his wife in surprise.

She nodded. "I said some unkind things to her after finding out about the baby."

Understanding flashed across Mason's face, and he pulled her close for a hug. "She knows you didn't mean them," he said.

Elaine closed her eyes. "That's why I'm here," she explained once Mason had released her. "I wanted to apologize."

Max tilted his head to the side as he watched her. There was something about this woman that didn't add up, though Mason didn't seem to think anything was wrong. But who showed up unannounced at dusk to apologize?

Another car turned onto the driveway. This driver pulled confidently forward, and in under a minute, a tall, broad-shouldered man walked toward them. "Mason. Elaine." He nodded at each one in turn. Then he looked at Max. "Trey Colton," he said, extending his hand.

Max shook it. "Max Hollick."

Recognition flashed across Trey's face. "I know you by reputation," he said. "Your charity does good work."

"Thank you," Max replied reflexively. "I appreciate you coming out this evening."

"No problem. Now who wants to tell me what's going on? Mason, you said you're worried about your sister?"

Mason opened his mouth, but Max jumped in first. "I'm the reason he called." He explained his connection to Molly, then listed his concerns, including the fact that her car was still in the garage and her purse in the house. "She's pregnant," he finished. "I just want to know that she and the baby are fine."

Trey nodded, taking it all in with a quiet competence that made Max feel a little better. "Let's walk through her house," Trey suggested.

At his suggestion, they all traipsed inside. Max, Mason and Elaine stood in the living room while Trey explored the home, quietly moving from room to room.

Elaine continued to fidget as Trey searched. Even Mason noticed; he put his hand on her arm. "Everything okay?" he asked.

She nodded. "I'm just worried about Molly. I can't imagine where she'd go."

Max said nothing. He didn't trust himself to speak around Molly's brother and sister-in-law. It seemed that Mason was in denial about Molly's absence. Perhaps that was how the man coped with stress. That was fine for him, but Max wasn't about to sit around and twiddle his thumbs while he hoped for Molly's safe return.

After a few minutes, Trey joined them in the living room. "I see no signs of foul play," he said, confirming what Max had already observed.

"She didn't just disappear," Max insisted.

"Probably not," Trey said. "But I'm afraid it's too early to file a missing persons report."

"What can we do in the meantime?" Max wasn't about

to passively wait out the clock. He'd organize a search party himself if it came to that.

"I'll alert my team, tell everyone to be on the lookout for Molly. Maybe someone will find her walking through town or headed home. I'm afraid that's all I can do for now."

Max bit his tongue. "I see," he said shortly.

Trey looked at each one of them. "I know you're all worried. This is out of character for Molly. But given the shocking news we've all had recently…" He trailed off, shook his head. "I'm hoping she just wanted some time to think and clear her mind."

"I'm sure that's it," Mason said, looking relieved at his cousin's suggestion.

"Yes," Elaine echoed weakly. "That must be it."

Max narrowed his eyes at the two of them, but didn't respond. "All right," he said, knowing it was futile to argue. "I suppose we'll just have to wait."

Trey nodded. "I'll check in first thing tomorrow morning. In the meantime, let me know if any of you hear from her."

"We will," Mason promised.

Trey headed for the door. "Mason, can I trust you to lock up here?"

"Yes," Mason replied. "Sorry to have bothered you."

"It's not a bother," Trey repeated. "Hopefully Molly will turn up soon, wondering what all the fuss is about." With a nod at Max, Trey walked out of Molly's house.

Max waited until he heard the man's car start. Then he turned to Elaine. "Can you give me a ride back to The Lodge?"

She flinched. "Um, surely it would be better if Mason—"

"I can't," Mason replied. "I've got to head back to the

office, close up some things before going home. It won't take you long, sweetie."

"All right." She swallowed, pasted on a false smile. "I suppose it's not a problem."

"Thanks," Max said flatly. He followed her out to the car, Furbert trotting after him.

"Oh," she said, drawing up short. "Your dog."

"Don't worry," Max replied matter-of-factly. "He won't mess up your seats." He moved past Elaine and opened the back door of her sedan. Furbert hopped inside, arranging himself on the seat. Then Max opened the passenger door, pausing for a second as he caught sight of a small dark spot on the upholstery.

Is that blood?

He couldn't go in for a closer look, not without arousing suspicion. So he climbed into the car, shutting the door after him. When Elaine opened her door, the courtesy lights inside the car flashed on again. Max took advantage of the momentary illumination to examine the headrest of his seat as he turned and grabbed the seat belt. There, clinging to the fabric, was a single golden strand of hair.

A chill went through him at the sight. Elaine had blond hair, but Max knew in his bones this strand belonged to Molly.

He forced himself to buckle the seat belt as if nothing was wrong. But inside, his mind was churning.

Elaine had taken Molly—he knew that much, even though his conclusion would never stand up in a court of law. But why would Mason's wife do that? She'd mentioned having an argument with Molly earlier. What had they fought about?

What had driven this woman to kidnap Molly? More importantly, what had she done with her?

Was Molly already dead? Had Elaine come back to her

house to get rid of any evidence she'd left behind? Maybe so, but neither he nor Mason nor Trey had noticed anything unusual. If Elaine had killed Molly, she would have had to do it elsewhere.

Why go back to the house at all, then? She'd clearly been coming for something. But whatever the reason, she'd had to change her plans upon catching sight of Max and Mason.

He didn't for one minute believe her line about coming to apologize to Molly. And while her hesitation upon first seeing her husband and Max could be read as surprise, he knew in his gut it was shock that had made her pause. She'd had to come up with a lie on the spot to explain her presence, and while she may have fooled Mason, Max wasn't so easily convinced.

What should he do now? He wanted to grab the woman by the shoulders and shake the truth out of her. His fingertips itched with the urge to do violence, to extract a confession from her by any means necessary. If this woman had killed Molly... He released the thought, knowing that if he followed it to its conclusion, he'd lose the tenuous grip he had on his self-control.

She's not dead, he told himself. She couldn't be. He wouldn't allow it, and that was that.

He slid a glance at Elaine as she drove. Should he prod her a bit, see if she revealed anything? Or would she panic if he got too close to the truth? Only one way to find out...

"Where do you think Molly is?"

Elaine jumped at the sound of his voice, though he'd spoken quietly. "Oh! Ah, I'm sure she's just taking a little time for herself." A trill of a laugh escaped her, the sound more suited to a garden party than a serious conversation.

"I hope you're right," he said sincerely.

"Honestly, you shouldn't worry," Elaine said. "Besides,

I hear through the grapevine you're leaving soon? Maybe Molly is simply lying low until you're gone."

"Or maybe she's avoiding you," he suggested. "After all, you're the one who fought with her the other day."

Elaine didn't respond, but he thought he saw a flash of emotion cross her face.

"What did you argue about, anyway?"

"You wouldn't understand." But Max could tell by the set of her mouth she wanted to say more. So he remained silent, hoping she'd continue to talk.

She didn't disappoint. "You're the baby's father, right?"

He nodded.

"Well, you should know Molly isn't taking proper care of herself."

"How's that?"

"She's drinking coffee. You're not supposed to have caffeine during pregnancy. And when I was there the other day, I saw beer in her fridge."

Max had noticed that the other night, too, but he wasn't worried. The evidence Elaine found so damning was nothing more than a treat Molly had bought for him during his last visit almost six months ago.

"You think she's drinking alcohol?"

Elaine shrugged. "All I know is that if that was my baby—" She broke off, pursing her lips.

Her words made the hair on the back of Max's neck stand at attention. Was Elaine jealous of the pregnancy? Had she taken Molly as part of some kind of bizarre "intervention" she'd deluded herself into thinking was necessary?

Before he could think of another question, she pulled into the round drive in front of The Lodge. "Here you are," she announced, relief evident in her voice.

Max climbed out of the car and opened the door for

Furbert. "Thanks for the ride," he said evenly. He held the passenger door open so she couldn't take off. "I hope you and Mason will let me know if you hear from Molly."

"Naturally. But as I said before, I wouldn't worry. I'm sure she's fine."

Max closed the door and watched as Elaine sped away like her hair was on fire. Her nervous demeanor, her words regarding Molly's behavior, the possible blood spot on her car's seat and the blond hair clinging to the passenger headrest—it all pointed to Elaine's involvement in Molly's disappearance.

"Three strikes," he muttered to himself. In the service, he'd had a simple philosophy—there's no such thing as a coincidence. So the fact that Molly's sister-in-law just happened to have a suspicious-looking spot and blond hair in her car on the same day Molly went missing? It was as good as a confession to him.

So what now? The sheriff wasn't likely to act on the basis of Max's suspicions. He seemed like a good man, but one who followed the rules. Max didn't have time for "by the book," not when Molly's life and that of his unborn daughter were at stake. Maybe it was time to dust off some of his old covert skills…

Max walked into the lobby of The Lodge and marched up to the concierge desk, Furbert on his heels.

"I need to rent a car."

Chapter Fifteen

Molly came awake with a jolt, her eyes flying open and her heart thumping hard against her ribs.

She glanced around the room. Rusted desk, dilapidated file cabinet, thin blanket—yep, all still there.

She wasn't aware of having fallen asleep—hadn't meant to, in fact. But sometime during the night, fatigue had gotten the best of her.

Her body ached, a combination of the chilly air and her uncomfortable quarters. Her muscles were so stiff she felt as though she were sporting a full-body cast. God, would she even be able to move—?

Only one way to find out. Slowly, carefully, she pushed herself into a sitting position. After a few steadying breaths, she placed her feet on the floor and stood up. A moan escaped her as her legs protested her weight. The sound echoed in the empty, cavernous warehouse, startling a nesting bird in the rafters. It took off with an indignant chirp, feathers rustling as it flew. Molly watched the bird escape through one of the broken windows set high in the wall, wishing she could scale those heights herself.

She squinted at the window, trying to gauge the time. The light was thin and watery, a pale illumination that did little more than allow Molly to see her hand in front of her face. But it was better than the total darkness of last night.

Her stomach growled and her throat cried out for water. Molly shuffled over to the file cabinet, the chain at her ankle clanging as she moved. She grabbed a granola bar and a bottle of water and returned to the bed, lowering herself onto the mattress with a grunt.

She chewed without tasting, eating only to keep up her strength. When she was done, she put the trash in one of the empty desk drawers. After availing herself of the bucket, she stood in front of the bed, eyeing it with a frown.

The light was stronger now, which made things easier. Molly lifted the mattress, getting her first good look at the wire mesh underneath. Thin metal wire was laid out in a grid pattern, with each strip anchored to the bed frame by a tightly coiled metal spring. If she could pry one of the springs free, she could expose the end of one of the wires. It looked small enough to fit in the lock of the handcuffs at her ankle, and since she had nothing but time on her hands, she should eventually be able to release the lock.

Molly knelt next to the bed, ignoring the ache in her thighs and knees. She grabbed the closest spring and gave it an experimental tug. Rust flaked off into her hand and rained onto the floor with a soft patter. The metal of the spring was rough, and it scratched her hands as she pulled and shoved and pried, trying to move it from its spot. Her fingers and palms began to sting as rust and grime came into contact with the lacerations. Hissing through her teeth, Molly continued her efforts until her hands were slick with blood.

She wiped them across the front of her shirt and attacked the spring again. Now that her skin was dry she was able to get a better grip on the metal. Her arms began to ache as she continued to pull, but gradually the spring began to move, rewarding her for her efforts.

Excitement thrummed through her as she worked one

end of the spring free from the tiny hole in the bed frame. "Come on," she muttered. Her fingers slipped, losing purchase. The spring slid out of her grasp, falling back into place. Molly cursed a blue streak, but dried her hands on her shirt and started again. Now that she knew she could move it, she was determined to keep at it until the spring was free.

After several minutes of effort, the spring slid out of its berth with a metallic scratch. Molly let out a triumphant yell and rocked back on her heels. She'd done it!

Now that the spring was no longer under tension, it was easy work to unhook it from the metal wire that made up the grid. Molly soon held the free end of the wire in her hand, ready to use.

She tried to bring her ankle close, but the angle was too awkward. Thinking fast, Molly put the mattress back onto the bed and climbed on top. From that angle, she was able to tug one side of the mattress up so she had access to the wire. She sat with her legs folded crisscross style, putting the handcuff around her ankle in close proximity to the wire. The wire wasn't very long, so she still had to contort herself a bit, but she was able to insert the thin metal end into the lock of the cuffs.

She grinned, feeling a flicker of hope for the first time since Elaine had abducted her.

"We're on our way, baby," she said, pushing her hair out of her face so she could focus on the task at hand. "I'm going to get us out of here."

MAX SHIFTED IN the front seat of his rental car, trying to find a more comfortable position. It was chilly in the car, but he and Furbert had huddled together under a blanket most of the night, so he was actually pretty comfortable.

Certainly warmer than he'd been during many nights on patrol in the desert.

Could Molly say the same? Was she inside somewhere, out of the elements? Or had Elaine staked her to a tree in the woods without a backward glance? And just what was driving this woman anyway? Why target Molly, who was one of the kindest people he'd ever met? Was she really that upset over Molly's perceived pregnancy infractions?

Please let her be safe.

It was the concern that had dominated his thoughts all night. After Elaine's shady actions, Max had decided he couldn't risk letting her out of his sight for long. She was connected to Molly's disappearance, and it was only a matter of time before she slipped up and gave herself away.

Hopefully sooner rather than later.

The concierge had pulled a few strings to get the rental car, and Max had wasted no time driving to Mason and Elaine's house, stopping only for a few provisions. He'd parked down the street and settled in to watch, knowing in his gut that Elaine was up to something.

There was a desperation about her, a brittleness that made him think she was about to snap. Mason didn't seem to recognize his wife's facade; Max had the impression Mason spent more time at work than he did with Elaine. So either he wasn't around enough to see his wife was troubled, or he threw himself into his job so he didn't have to deal with the problem. Regardless, Mason clearly wasn't going to be any help.

That was fine. Max was more than capable of operating alone.

He'd briefly considered calling Blaine, but didn't want to bother his friend. Furthermore, he didn't want to put Blaine in the position of having to act against one of his

cousins. Better for Max to tackle this solo. He could always call for help if it came to that.

So he'd sat in the car, watching and waiting through the night for Elaine to make her move. She was spooked. Unless Max missed his guess, Elaine hadn't thought anyone would notice Molly's absence so soon. She was likely panicking, rethinking what she'd done.

Hopefully it wasn't anything permanent.

In the small hours of the night, Max had forced himself to once again consider the possibility Molly was dead. It had made him physically ill to even think about a world without Molly in it, but he wanted to be emotionally prepared in case the worst had happened.

His reaction had forced him to rethink his position on things. Once upon a time, he'd known how precious life was. How precarious it could be, and that he couldn't count on tomorrow. The service had taught him that things weren't always in his control, and he shouldn't take anything for granted. But somewhere along the way, he'd forgotten that lesson. He'd been too afraid to take the leap with Molly because he'd let his fears dictate his thinking. And the worst part? He'd lost sight of the truly important things in life—family, friends, love.

Max knew better now.

He would always be proud of K-9 Cadets. But it would no longer be his life's focus. Now that he was faced with the possibility of losing Molly forever, his earlier worries about commitment faded into nothingness. There were definitely things he needed to work on, and the path they walked together wouldn't always be smooth. But an imperfect life with Molly was far better than a perfect life without her.

If she'd still have him.

The only thing that worried him as much as Molly's

uncertain fate was the thought that he'd irreparably damaged his chances with her. She'd opened her heart to him the other day, laying bare her hopes for their baby and their future. And he'd shut her down, making it clear he didn't think they had what it took to go the distance. He'd give anything to be able to go back in time and swallow those words, to stop himself from causing her so much pain.

He marveled at her response as he replayed the memories of their conversation. Even after breaking her heart, Molly had said she was still amenable to letting him see their baby. Her willingness to continue to be around him for the sake of their child was yet another sign of her selflessness and kindness. She was far better than he deserved, and he was going to spend the rest of his life trying to make her see that he knew how special she was.

Furbert nudged Max's leg, interrupting his thoughts. "Need a bathroom break, buddy?" The dog gazed up at him with knowing brown eyes, and Max reached out to scratch behind one of his ears. "Good idea. Let's stretch our legs a bit."

He climbed out of the car and led the dog to the end of the street, away from Mason and Elaine's house. It was growing lighter by the minute, and their neighbors were already starting to leave for work. If anyone noticed them, Max wanted it to look like he and his dog were out for a walk, nothing more.

While Furbert did his business, Max kept an eye on the house. He heard the rumble of a truck's engine from somewhere nearby. A few seconds later, Mason's truck backed out of the driveway and headed down the street.

Max glanced at Furbert, who was now sniffing at another patch of grass. "Come on," he said, giving the leash a gentle tug to get the dog's attention. He felt bad that he hadn't been able to give his friend a longer break outside

the car, but now that Mason had left for work, Max was willing to bet Elaine would make her move soon.

Sure enough, his instincts were proven correct when she pulled out of the driveway a few minutes later.

"Bingo," he whispered. He felt the adrenaline hit his system as he turned the key in the ignition. Thanks to his years of experience, the hormone surge didn't make him jittery. Rather, a sense of calm descended over him, his senses hyper-focused and attuned to his environment.

He waited about a minute after Elaine had left before pulling into the road behind her. It was possible she was simply going to the grocery store or headed to the gym. If that was the case, he and Furbert were in for a long, boring day.

But Max didn't care. He'd follow her around forever, because he knew in his bones that at some point, she'd lead him to the woman he loved.

Chapter Sixteen

Molly swore as the wire slipped out of the lock once more, skittering across the smooth surface of the cuffs. Picking the lock was proving to be more difficult than she'd anticipated. She was able to fit the wire into the lock opening, but it seemed no matter how she rotated or jiggled or pushed it, she couldn't find the right angle to release the catch.

Her frustration was at its peak, but she refused to give up. There was no telling when—or even if—Elaine would be coming back. Molly wasn't going to sit around waiting for fate to catch up with her. She owed it to herself and her baby to keep trying.

Her fingers were still stiff, though now it was due to clutching the wire rather than the cold. It was growing steadily brighter inside the warehouse; morning was well under way by now. Molly wasn't sure how long she'd been working, but it didn't matter. She was determined to continue until she was either free or dead.

Obviously, she was hoping for the former outcome.

She released her grip on the wire, bending and straightening her fingers to release some of the tension. A short break wouldn't hurt, and might even help if it restored some of her manual dexterity.

Max's face flashed through her mind. With his Special

Forces training, he'd know just how to get out of these handcuffs. Of course, he probably wouldn't have let himself be taken in the first place, gun notwithstanding.

She closed her eyes, imagining he was with her now. *Don't give up*, he'd say. *You're doing great.*

He'd been so calm during their time in the gondola. Had it really only been a few days since the avalanche? With everything that had happened, it felt like a lifetime ago.

Her mind drifted, remembering the solid feel of his body against hers as she'd leaned on him. The way it had felt to wake up in his arms, pretending for a few seconds that nothing had changed between them. She'd love to be able to go back to that afternoon, when she was still ignorant of her sister's murder and Max hadn't definitively broken her heart yet. Sure, she'd been hanging precariously in a glass carriage, risking death with each gust of wind. But compared to her current situation, that seemed like a cakewalk.

All because of Max's presence.

It was amazing how his company made her feel better. From swinging in the gondola to her sister's murder, having Max by her side made her feel grounded, like she could handle anything.

But he wasn't here now. And he'd made it clear he didn't want to be her rock, didn't want to walk through life by her side. So she was going to have to figure out a way to take care of things on her own.

The thought galvanized her into action once more. She examined the end of the wire, used her thumbnail to bend it just a smidge. Then she inserted it into the lock, feeling blindly for the latch that would set her free.

A little to the left… No, up a bit… A hair to the right…

The wire suddenly sank in a bit. Molly's heart jumped

into her throat and she took a deep breath, trying to hold her hands steady so they didn't jerk the wire free.

Working carefully, she prodded here, poked there. One little twist, and then...

The cuff around her ankle slid open, releasing her. Molly jerked her leg away with a sob, and the cuffs and chain slid off the mattress to clatter on the floor.

Molly got to her feet, tears blurring her vision. Relief made her feel light-headed, so she sat on the bed once more to collect herself.

Her chest heaved as she gulped air, trying to organize her thoughts. She'd get out of here, follow the road until she found someone, anyone to help her. As soon as she made it back to Roaring Springs, she was headed straight for the sheriff's office.

A noise at the far end of the warehouse caught her attention. The door opened, and in walked Elaine, carrying a paper bag.

Molly's mind raced as she considered her options. She could run now, try to make her escape while Elaine had her hands full. Or she could pretend to still be restrained and wait for the other woman to leave. That was the safer choice, especially if Elaine had brought her gun again.

But if Molly could overpower her sister-in-law, she could grab her keys and use her car to escape. After the long, cold night Molly wasn't in the best shape to attempt a walk back into town. The only abandoned warehouses Molly knew about sat a few miles outside Roaring Springs, a bit off the main road. If that was indeed where she was, having the car would definitely make life easier.

Elaine was getting closer; she had to make a decision.

Molly bent forward and snagged the open end of the handcuffs. She bent her leg at the knee, tucking her ankle under her opposite thigh. Then she stuck the chain under

her ankle, to make it look like she was still attached. She leaned back against the wall, forcing herself to sit still while Elaine approached.

"Good morning!" Elaine sounded chipper. "I brought you a few more supplies." She set the paper bag on the desk and began unpacking it.

"How was your night?"

"Cold," Molly said shortly. How was she going to do this? Positionally, she was at a disadvantage. It would take a few seconds for her to stand up, plenty of time for Elaine to go on the defensive. Maybe she could use the chain as a whip, lashing out at Elaine before she could react? She stroked the cold links with her fingertip, considering the possibility.

"This should help," Elaine said. She pulled out a metal thermos and handed it to Molly. "Hot tea."

Molly smiled, unable to believe her luck. "Thank you," she said.

"Of course," Elaine replied. "As I told you before, I want you to stay healthy." She turned back to the bag, reaching in for more items.

Molly hefted the thermos in her hands. It was a nice, heavy weight, and with a handle on the side to boot. Exactly what she needed.

Elaine continued to chatter as she pulled items from the bag and placed them on the desk surface. While she talked, Molly slowly rose from the bed and moved to stand behind the other woman.

"I brought you another blanket…" Elaine trailed off as she turned and realized Molly was no longer sitting on the bed. She looked to the side, just in time to meet Molly's eyes as Molly brought the thermos crashing down onto her head.

Elaine collapsed in a heap on the floor. Molly dropped

the thermos and ran, not bothering to check if the other woman was still alive. She rushed through the empty warehouse, fearing that at any second Elaine would rise up and shoot her in the back.

The shot never came. Molly burst through the door, throwing up her arm to shield her eyes from the bright sunlight.

She was free.

MAX TRAILED BEHIND Elaine's car, keeping his distance so as not to draw her attention. She drove through town, headed for the outskirts. He had to back off a bit as traffic thinned out, but it was easy enough to keep her in sight.

A few miles outside Roaring Springs she turned on a side road. Max slowed down, then did the same, hanging back to let her get ahead. He needn't have worried. Elaine sped forward, oblivious to her surroundings. She pulled into the parking lot of what looked like an abandoned warehouse. Max stopped his car about a hundred yards away, partially shielded by a clump of bushes. As he watched, Elaine pulled a paper bag from the passenger seat of her car and entered the warehouse.

Supplies? he wondered. Food, perhaps? Maybe toiletries? Whatever it was, Elaine clearly hadn't come to set up a garden party.

Max waited, imagining her progress through the warehouse. He didn't want to spook her too soon, or she might hurt Molly.

Convinced she was too far into the building to hear the engine of his car, he pulled in beside her, putting the passenger door of his rental only inches from her driver's door. If she tried to escape, she wouldn't be able to get behind the wheel easily. Hopefully it was a precaution he

didn't need to take, but Max knew from experience that in an operation, every second counted.

He climbed out of his car, leaving the door open so she wouldn't hear it shut. Then he approached the building carefully, his gaze assessing as he studied the structure. The door Elaine had used appeared to be the only entrance on this side. What about the back of the building? Was there another entry point he could use to take her by surprise?

Max started for the nearest corner, intending to scout the perimeter. His emotions urged him to run inside, to chase down Elaine before she could do anything to Molly. But his training wouldn't allow him to rush into a scene without more information. If Molly was in there, his best chance of helping her depended upon him keeping his cool.

He'd made it only a few steps when the door Elaine had just used burst open with a sound like a shot. A figure stumbled out, blond hair flying as she ran.

Molly!

She threw up her arm to shield her eyes from the sun. Max took a step toward her. "Molly!" he cried.

She flinched at the sound of his voice. Without looking at him, she pivoted away from him and tried to run.

Max caught up to her easily, wrapping his arms around her to keep her from falling on the uneven ground.

Molly fought like a wild thing, bucking and twisting and scratching at his hands and arms. "Let me go!" she yelled.

"Molly, it's me! It's Max!" He tightened his grip, applying just enough pressure to keep hold of her without hurting her. "It's Max!"

She stilled in his arms. "Max?" Her voice sounded small, but oh so hopeful.

"Yes," he said, trembling a bit as emotions threatened to overwhelm him. "I'm here, Molly. I'm here."

She turned around, blinking as she stared up at his face. When she met his eyes, she burst into tears.

He held her close as she sobbed against his chest, keeping one eye on the door in case Elaine should emerge.

"What happened?" He pulled back enough to get a good look at her. Her hair was a tangled mess, her face pale and tear-streaked. But it was the sight of her shirt that made his heart skip a beat.

Dried blood smeared the front of her belly, horrifyingly dark against the white fabric.

"Where are you hurt?" He fumbled with the hem of her shirt, trying to pull it over her belly. "Is the baby okay?"

"I'm okay," she said. "It's from my hands."

She held them up so he could see her palms. Her skin was crisscrossed with dozens of shallow scratches, most crusted over with scabs but some still oozing blood.

Relief flooded Max, and he pulled her against him once more. She was fine. The baby was fine.

He could have stayed like that forever, holding her close, reveling in the fact that she was whole and alive and *here*. But he couldn't fully relax until he knew there was no longer a threat to Molly.

"Where's Elaine?"

Molly shuddered. "Inside the office. I hit her on the head with a thermos and ran after she collapsed. I'm not even sure if she's alive."

"I'll find out."

"No!" She tightened her grip on him. "Please don't leave me."

"I have to check," he said softly. "But you won't be alone."

He led her over to his car and opened the door to the back seat. Furbert let out a happy yip at the sight of Molly.

She climbed inside the car and threw her arms around the dog.

Max withdrew his cell phone and handed it to her. "Do you know where we are?"

She nodded. "Good. Call the sheriff and tell him. Have them send an ambulance—no, make that two ambulances." No way was he going to ask Molly to share a rig with Elaine.

She nodded again, her blue eyes impossibly wide. "Please be careful," she whispered. "She might have a gun. That's how she forced me to go with her. I couldn't risk her hurting the baby..." Molly trailed off, tears filling her eyes.

Max knelt and cupped her cheek with one hand. "You don't ever have to explain your actions to me. I know you did what was best for you and the baby."

"I tried to," she said, sniffling with a wince.

"You did," he replied firmly. "Don't ever doubt it."

He gave her hand a squeeze, then released it. As he walked away from Molly, he tamped down his emotions and tried to get his head back in the game. Until he knew what had happened to Elaine, he couldn't fully relax.

He yanked open the door of the warehouse but didn't enter yet, waiting a second to see if Elaine was going to fire on him.

Nothing.

Cautiously, Max knelt and peeked around the corner, scanning the space before leaning out again.

From what he could see, the warehouse was abandoned. There were a few wire shelves set up along the far wall, but nothing that would provide cover. The office was situated at the opposite end of the building, a plate-glass window separating the space from the warehouse proper. Presumably, Elaine was in there.

Max made a quick trip back to the rental car.

"Is she dead?" Molly asked tearfully.

"I don't know yet," Max said. "I can't see her from here." He popped the trunk, grabbed the tire iron inside. It was a poor defense against a gun, but he felt better having a weapon to hand.

After another quick look to make sure the coast was clear, he entered the warehouse. Moving fast and staying low, he crept along the wall toward the office.

He crouched below the window, inching toward the door. Pressing his back to the wall, he listened hard, straining to hear any sounds from within.

Elaine was still inside—he could hear her breathing. *Not dead, then.* He felt a small spurt of satisfaction at the realization; after what she had done to Molly, Max wanted the woman to enjoy a long stint in prison.

He risked a glance into the room. She was sprawled on the floor, apparently unconscious. Max knew better than to assume, though. He hadn't come this far to get shot by a woman playing possum.

She didn't move when he entered the office. He knelt next to her, spying a large, bloody gash on her forehead and a dented green thermos on the floor nearby. *Way to go*, he thought, feeling a burst of pride at the evidence of Molly's handiwork.

A quick pat down turned up a small pistol in Elaine's front jacket pocket. A chill went down Max's spine as he imagined a different outcome for this fight, one in which Elaine had managed to grab her gun before Molly had clocked her across the head. A few seconds of hesitation, and he might be standing over Molly's lifeless body instead of Elaine's unconscious form.

Max glanced around the room, his anger building as he took in the surroundings: a rusted-out metal desk and file

cabinet, a hospital bed that looked straight out of a horror flick, and a thick metal chain anchored to the middle of the floor.

But it was the plastic bucket by the desk that nearly pushed him over the edge.

"Damn you," he muttered.

Elaine began to stir, moaning softly. Not trusting himself to remain civilized, Max grabbed the handcuffs dangling from the end of the metal chain. He snapped the open end around Elaine's wrist, tightening the bracelet until it was flush against her skin so that she had no chance of sliding free.

"Let's see how you like it," he growled.

Sirens wailed in the distance, the high-pitched sound music to his ears. Hopefully the sheriff and ambulances would arrive soon. Molly looked superficially fine, but he wouldn't rest easy until she and the baby had been checked by a doctor.

Max stood and walked out of the office, leaving Elaine alone on the filthy floor. He paused just outside the warehouse, bending at the waist to set her gun on the ground in plain sight. Then he headed for the rental car, back to his woman and his baby and his dog.

His future.

Chapter Seventeen

"Back so soon?" Dr. Fitzpatrick tutted as he walked into Molly's room. "Don't take this the wrong way, but I had hoped not to see you again."

Molly smiled, appreciating the man's lighthearted tone. "I feel the same way. The last few days have been…challenging."

His lips pressed together as he nodded. "So I heard. I'm so sorry you went through that." He gave her foot a soft pat. "I'm glad you're okay."

"Me, too." She blinked, determined not to cry. She'd shed enough tears recently to last a lifetime.

"I peeked at your chart before coming in," Dr. Fitzpatrick said as he began flipping switches and turning dials on the ultrasound machine. "From what I saw, you're doing fine. A little dehydrated, but that's why they have you hooked up to this." He gestured to the IV line running saline into her arm. "We'll take a quick peek at the baby to confirm she's okay, too, and then send you on your way."

"That sounds nice," Molly replied. She wanted nothing more than to go home, crawl into her comfortable bed and sleep until the baby was due.

"I saw your husband in the waiting area, talking to the sheriff. Would you like me to wait for him to finish before I start the scan?"

Molly didn't bother to correct the doctor's misapprehension. "Ah, no. That's all right. I'm not sure how long he'll be tied up." It was the truth, but she still felt a twinge of guilt for proceeding in Max's absence. He probably would have liked to see the baby again.

"Fair enough," Dr. Fitzpatrick said. "Here comes the goo."

Less than a minute later, her daughter was on the screen. Molly watched as the baby kicked and rolled, seemingly unaware of the troubles going on in the wider world.

"Just as I thought," the doctor said as he moved the wand over her belly. "She's looking good."

He finished up and handed Molly a small towel with a smile. "Nothing to worry about here, mama. Your baby is doing just fine."

"That's good to know." A sense of relief washed over her, carrying away her last lingering worries. Now that she knew her baby was all right, she could truly relax.

Dr. Fitzpatrick pushed the cart toward the door. "Get some rest," he advised. "You've been through a lot. You need time to heal, and not just physically."

Molly nodded, a lump in her throat. "Thank you," she croaked.

He gave her a parting smile and left, unaware of how right he was.

Molly's body was fine. Sure, she had a few bumps and bruises, but nothing a hot bath and a good night's sleep couldn't help. No, the part of her that was truly broken was her heart.

First Sabrina. Then Max. The hits had come fast and hard, with no time for her to recover before suffering the next blow. What she needed more than anything was to retreat from the world so she could work on stitching her

heart back together. Her baby deserved a happy, healthy mother, not a broken shell of the person she'd once been.

A soft knock sounded on the door. Max poked his head into the room. "Mind if I come in?"

Speak of the devil, she thought. She nodded her permission. He walked over to the side of the bed and looked down at her, his green eyes warm.

"Everything okay?" he asked. "I thought I saw the OB leave."

"You did," she confirmed. "He did a quick scan to make sure the baby is okay. He said everything looks good."

"I'm glad to hear it." He let out a sigh.

"How did your interview with Trey go?"

Max nodded. "I think it went well. I just told him what I knew, what I'd done." Something about the set of Max's mouth made Molly think that wasn't all they'd discussed, but she didn't press the issue.

"And what did you know? You never told me how you found me." Now that the immediate shock of her ordeal was over, she was curious to know exactly how Max had been in the right place at the right time.

"It's kind of a long story," he said. He pulled a chair closer and sat down. "It all started yesterday afternoon..."

Molly listened in amazement as he told her his side of things, from going to her house to following Elaine's car out to the warehouse. "Wow," she said, truly impressed. "I'm so glad you figured out something was off with Elaine. I wouldn't have known what to do after calling the sheriff's office. Thank you for not giving up."

He shrugged, blushing a little. "It gave me an excuse to dust off my skills," he said, deflecting her gratitude.

"I'm just glad you were there to play the hero."

"Oh, please," he said. "You didn't need me. You came tearing out of there before I had a chance to save you."

He reached for her hand, holding it between his own. The corners of his mouth turned up. "It was a real blow to my ego, let me tell you."

Molly laughed, rolling her eyes. "You look like you survived."

"Just barely." His expression turned serious now. "After hearing Elaine's plan to take the baby and kill you…" He trailed off, shaking his head. "I don't ever want to come close to losing you again."

Molly didn't know what to say to that. She studied his face, noticing the dark circles under his eyes and his wrinkled clothes. He looked like a man who'd been through hell. In another time, she would have taken him into her arms and held him while he slept. But he didn't want that from her anymore.

"There's something I want to say to you, but I know this might not be the best time."

She frowned. "What's on your mind?"

He took a deep breath. "I made a mistake, Molly. Earlier, when we talked about our future. I told you I didn't think I could give you what you need, that we wouldn't work. But I realize now I was wrong."

It was exactly what she'd hoped to hear from him. Two days ago. Now? She wasn't so sure…

"And what caused this revelation?" It was a complete reversal of what he'd said earlier. Hard to believe he'd so thoroughly changed his mind in such a short period of time.

Max leaned forward, lifting her hand to brush his lips across the back of her knuckles. "When I thought you were…dead," he said, grimacing over the word, "it made me reevaluate my life. I know now that I was wrong to put my work before you, before us. You and the baby are the

most important things in my life, and I want to be here for the two of you, to give you everything you need."

It sounded so beautiful, the realization of all her hopes and dreams. So why couldn't she accept that what he was saying was true?

Max's eyes searched her face. "You don't look happy."

"I don't think I am," she replied.

He frowned. "But… I thought this was what you wanted."

Molly lifted one eyebrow. "It was. But when you put it like that, I have to wonder if you really mean it, or if you're just saying it because you think that's what I want to hear."

"Why would I do that?"

"That's the part I can't figure out," Molly said. She sighed. "I want to trust you, Max, I do. But I can't think straight right now. You broke my heart the other day." Tears welled in her eyes, and he looked away, guilt flashing across his face. "How do I know you're not going to do it again?"

"Molly, I won't—"

"You say that now," she interrupted. "But have your feelings really changed? Or is this just a knee-jerk reaction in the wake of Elaine's actions?"

"It's not," he said firmly. "It's more than that."

She shook her head. "Max, you said you couldn't commit to me because you're already so involved with your charity. That hasn't changed. So why do you suddenly think you can multitask, when before, you'd made up your mind that wasn't possible?"

"Don't you see? When we spoke before, I'd lost sight of what's most important to me. You and the baby."

"So you're ready to be a full-time dad now? No more monthly visitations?" Molly didn't bother to keep the edge from her tone.

Max winced. "Not my best idea, it's true. But to answer your question, yes. I do want to be here for the baby, from the beginning."

Molly absorbed his words, wishing she could let go of her hurt and doubts and trust everything he was saying. She could tell from the look in Max's eyes that he genuinely believed he was telling her the truth. But she wasn't ready to take the chance that he wouldn't change his mind once the shock of this experience wore off and real life set in again.

Max gave her a sad smile and got to his feet. "I can see you don't believe me. And that's my fault. But I'm serious—I want us to be together, to raise our daughter together as a family."

Molly said nothing. She held his gaze, wishing she could give him the answer he so clearly wanted.

"I'll leave you now. Blaine is here…he said he'd take you home. Again," he added with a soft laugh. He leaned in, pressed his lips to hers in an impossibly sweet kiss. "But we're not finished yet. I'm going to prove to you I meant every word I said here tonight."

"Max…" She shook her head, unable to see how he could do that.

"Don't worry," he said. "I know what I need to do. You just rest. Take care of our little one." He placed his hand on her belly, a large, warm weight against her skin. As if sensing her father's touch, the baby shifted and kicked.

Max's eyes widened. "Was that—?"

Molly couldn't help but smile. "Yes. That's her."

A delighted grin spread across his face. He leaned over, putting his mouth close to her belly. "Hello, Little Bit. I'm your daddy. I have to go now, but I'll be back soon." He paused a second, then added, "I love you."

Molly blinked away tears, touched by his heartfelt sen-

timent. He was normally so serious and reserved; it was nice to see him soften toward their daughter.

He straightened and met her gaze. "Call me when you're ready to see me again."

"Aren't you going back home on Friday?" They would have to figure out some kind of visitation schedule before he left. Molly knew if she waited until he was back at work, she'd be talking to his secretary instead of him.

"No." Max shook his head. "I've canceled my flight reservation."

His answer surprised her. "How long will you be staying in town?"

His green eyes sparkled with an emotion she couldn't name.

"Indefinitely."

"ARE YOU SURE you don't need anything, dear? The girls and I would be happy to cook for you, run errands or do laundry. Anything you need."

Molly held the phone to her ear and smiled on Friday morning. "I appreciate the offer, Aunt Mara. But I know you and Phoebe and Skye already have your hands full planning the film festival." Her cousins had both dropped by yesterday to check on her. She'd enjoyed seeing the twins, but could tell they were stressed to the max already. Phoebe was coordinating the awards ceremony for the festival, while Skye was focused on making all the arrangements for the movie stars who would be attending.

"But that's not all," Skye had said, practically vibrating with excitement. "I've been asked to cover the festival for an online magazine." She'd rattled off the name of the site, and Molly had pretended to recognize it. "They want me to do live interviews with the stars from several of the events! I can't wait!"

Molly had smiled, happy for her cousins. Their joy was a bright spot in her otherwise gray mood.

"We'll always make time for family," Aunt Mara said, pulling Molly back to the present conversation. "I know your parents are due to arrive today. Please call me when they get in. I want to see them."

"I will," Molly replied. She ended the call, then dialed Mason. He hadn't responded to her calls or texts yesterday, and she was worried about him.

"Hello?"

Relief filled her at the sound of her brother's voice, even though she could tell he was in a bad way. "Mason! I've been trying to reach you."

"I know."

"Are you okay?"

He sighed. "No. I'm not." He was silent, and for a second, Molly thought she heard him crying.

"Mason, please come over. Or let me come to you."

He sniffed. "I can't, Mols. Not right now."

"You know I don't blame you, right?" In the aftermath of her rescue, it had become abundantly clear that Elaine had acted alone. Mason hadn't had any idea of his wife's awful plan or of her actions. He'd been horrified to discover what she'd done, and he'd called Molly just as she was leaving the hospital, apologizing profusely for what had happened.

"I know," he replied. "But that doesn't mean I don't blame myself."

"Please don't," Molly said. "You're not responsible for what other people do."

"That's sweet of you to say…"

Molly heard a voice in the background that sounded like an intercom. "Where are you?"

"I'm at the airport," Mason said. "I need to get away for a while. Sort some things out."

She tightened her grip on the phone, alarmed at his words. She'd already lost her sister; was she going to lose her brother, as well? "Where are you headed?"

"Away," he said shortly.

"But…" She cast about for something to say, something to convince him to stay in town. He needed to be around family right now, to know that they all still loved and supported him. "What about your work on the film festival? You can't just leave Phoebe and Skye and Aunt Mara in the lurch!"

"I'm not. Seth is going to take over for me. I already told Phoebe."

Molly recognized the name—Seth was one of the managers at The Lodge. He seemed nice enough, but his inclusion at the last minute must have heightened Aunt Mara's stress level.

"What about Elaine? You're just going to leave her?"

"I'm not abandoning her," he said, an edge to his voice. "She's at the state psychiatric hospital, for crying out loud. They'll take care of her while I'm gone."

"I wish you wouldn't do this," Molly said. "Mom and Dad will be here today. Don't you want to see them?"

"I have to get away," Mason said softly. "My life is in shambles right now. I need to figure out how to put it back together."

"Okay," she said simply. "Just know that I love you, and I'll be here to help you when you're ready to come home."

"Thanks. I needed to hear that." He sighed. "I've got to go. They're boarding my flight."

"Have a safe trip."

"Thanks. Take care of yourself, Mols. And the baby, too."

He hung up before she could respond. Molly set the

phone on the coffee table and remained on the couch, processing this latest development.

She closed her eyes, seeing Max's face. It would be nice to talk to him about Mason, tell him what was going on. He'd know just what to say to make her feel better, and Furbert would press himself against her side until she was so busy paying attention to him she'd forget to be worried.

Her hand hovered over the phone, but she pulled it back. She couldn't call up Max every time she was upset. She needed to find new ways of dealing with her feelings, so that when he went back to his old life she wasn't left out in the cold.

Searching for a distraction, she picked up the remote and turned on the television. Maybe there was something mindless on. She flipped through the channels, pausing when she saw Max's face.

He's on the news, she realized, leaning forward. But why?

A reporter was asking him questions about her abduction and his role in her rescue. "How do you know the victim, Molly Gilford?"

"Molly and I have been seeing each other for a little over two years now," Max said easily.

Molly blinked, surprised to hear him publicly acknowledge their relationship.

"And is it true you're expecting your first child together?"

"Yes, that's correct. I'm very excited about it."

Molly placed her hand on her belly, recalling the tender look on his face as he'd told their daughter he loved her.

The woman smiled. "I can imagine. You said earlier you're planning to move to Roaring Springs. Will you be able to manage your charity, K-9 Cadets, from here?"

"I'm not too worried about that," Max replied. "You

see, I'm stepping down as managing director of K-9 Cadets. I want to focus on Molly and our family, and while I love my work, it simply takes up too much time. I'll be staying on as a consultant, but the actual day-to-day job of running the organization will fall to my replacement."

The reporter made another remark, but Molly didn't hear what the woman said. She was too stunned by Max's announcement to pay attention to anything else.

He was resigning from K-9 Cadets? And moving here?

She shook her head, hardly daring to believe it. But he'd just confessed, on television, that he wanted to focus on their family.

It was a hell of a statement.

Suddenly, his voice echoed in her head. *I'm going to prove to you I meant every word I said here tonight.*

And so he had.

Max had rearranged his life to make sure he'd have time for her and the baby. He'd turned his world upside down, then done the equivalent of shouting the news from the rooftops. It was a big, bold, unmistakable gesture on his part. Not something he could easily reverse or undo. No, these changes were the kind that would stick.

Molly grabbed the phone, needing to hear his voice. To know this was real, not just some strange hallucination on her part.

He answered on the first ring. "Molly?"

"You said for me to call you when I was ready to see you again. I'm ready now."

She heard the gust of his breath over the line. "That's good," he said, chuckling softly. "Because I'm in your driveway."

"You are?" She walked to the front door and stepped onto the porch. Sure enough, Max's rental car was sitting in front of her house. "Are you going to come in?"

He climbed out of the car, followed by Furbert. He walked up to the porch steps, phone still at his ear. "I wasn't going to bother you. I was just coming to see the baby." He gave her a wink, then reached out, touching her belly gently with his free hand.

"She'll be happy to hear your voice again."

Max began to climb the stairs, stopping when they were at eye level. "I missed you," he whispered, shoving his phone into his pocket.

"I missed you, too," she admitted.

He leaned in to kiss her, but she held up her hand. "Is it true?"

"Is what true?"

"I just saw you on the news. You're really stepping down as managing director?"

He nodded. "I am. The search is on for my replacement."

She examined his face, looking for any hint of regret. But his soft green eyes held only warmth as he stared back at her.

"And you're moving here, too?"

Another nod. "That's the plan."

"Where are you going to live?"

He tilted his head to the side. "See, that's the thing. I was kind of hoping you could help me with that." A boyish grin spread across his face.

Molly couldn't help but smile in return. "I think I can do that. But I have some conditions."

"Oh? Name them." He leaned in, pressing his mouth to hers.

She indulged in the kiss for a moment, then pulled back. "Rule number one—always use a coaster."

Max kissed her again. "Okay," he said against her lips.

"Rule number two—put the toilet seat down when you're done."

He pulled her close, lifting his hand to trace the curve of her cheek. "I can do that."

Molly shivered as sparks of sensation raced down her limbs to settle low in her belly. "And rule number three—don't ever leave."

Max smiled as he wrapped his arms around her. "That won't be a problem, I promise you. I love you, Molly. I'm never letting you go again."

His words triggered a flood of joy in her chest. "I love you, too, Max." She pressed her forehead against his, sharing his breath. "I think in some way I always have."

"I do look my best when I'm fresh from the shower," he drawled.

Molly threw back her head and laughed. "Let's test that theory, shall we?" She took his hand and led him across the porch.

"I'll go wherever you want," Max said. "As long as you go with me."

Molly paused on the threshold. "You've got yourself a deal."

Max dipped his head and kissed her soundly. Then he took her hand and they stepped inside the house.

Together.

* * * * *

COMING SOON!

We really hope you enjoyed reading this book. If you're looking for more romance, be sure to head to the shops when new books are available on

Thursday 13th June

To see which titles are coming soon, please visit

millsandboon.co.uk/nextmonth

Also by Tyler Anne Snell

Also by Lara Lacombe

Discover more at millsandboon.co.uk

Tyler Anne Snell genuinely loves all genres of the written word. However, she's realized she loves books filled with a little more than the a little more than the se of both. Tyler live med husband and their ding or writing, she's ng on her blog, *Almost T* her snenanigans, visit tylerannesnell.com

Lara Lacombe earned a PhD in microbiology and immunology and worked in several labs across the country before moving into the classroom. Her day job as a college science professor gives her time to pursue her other love—writing fast-paced romantic suspense with smart, nerdy heroines and dangerously attractive heroes. She loves to hear from readers! Find her on the web or contact her at laralacombewriter@gmail.com